HOFFA™

TWENTIETH CENTURY FOX PRESENTS

IN ASSOCIATION WITH JERSEY FILMS AN EDWARD R. PRESSMAN PRODUCTION A DANNY DeVITO FILM

JACK NICHOLSON   DANNY DeVITO   HOFFA   ARMAND ASSANTE   J.T. WALSH   ROBERT PROSKY

MUSIC BY DAVID NEWMAN   EDITED BY LYNZEE KLINGMAN, A.C.E. AND RONALD ROOSE   PRODUCTION DESIGNER IDA RANDOM

DIRECTOR OF PHOTOGRAPHY STEPHEN H. BURUM   CO-PRODUCER HAROLD SCHNEIDER   WRITTEN BY DAVID MAMET

PRODUCED BY EDWARD R. PRESSMAN, DANNY DeVITO AND CALDECOT CHUBB   DIRECTED BY DANNY DeVITO

©1992 TWENTIETH CENTURY FOX

These credits are tentative and subject to change.

HOFFA™

A novelization by Ken Englade

Based on the screenplay by David Mamet

HarperPaperbacks
A Division of HarperCollinsPublishers

This is a work of fiction. The characters, incidents, and dialogues are products of the author's imagination and are not to be construed as real. Any resemblance to actual events or persons, living or dead, is entirely coincidental.

HarperPaperbacks   *A Division of* HarperCollins*Publishers*
10 East 53rd Street, New York, N.Y. 10022

First printing: December 1992

Printed in the United States of America

HarperPaperbacks and colophon are trademarks of HarperCollins*Publishers*

❖ 10 9 8 7 6 5 4 3

For Tiny and Brenda,
old, dear friends and loyal supporters

•••

Acknowledgments

My thanks to the present and former staff at Wayne State University in Detroit, especially Mary Mahr, Joann Condino, Leslie Hough, and everyone at the Walter P. Reuther Library. Special gratitude also is due Ed Mahr of Albuquerque, who helped pave the way. Special thanks, too, to Pam Olguin.

1

1 9 7 5

Sometimes Jimmy Hoffa spoke so softly that Bobby Ciaro had trouble hearing him. This was one of those times.

"You think he really wants to settle this?" Hoffa whispered, barely moving his lips in a style he developed while serving time in a federal prison in Pennsylvania.

Ciaro turned down the radio. "What was that?"

Hoffa repeated himself and Ciaro nodded. "Oh, yeah," he replied. "I think he realizes that none of us got anything to gain as long as this keeps up."

Hoffa grunted, then leaned back in the passenger seat and closed his eyes.

Ciaro turned the radio back up and concentrated on the traffic, competently guiding the new, green Pontiac Grand Ville south on Interstate 75 at a steady fifty-nine miles per hour, slightly over the speed limit but not enough to make it worth a cop's while to pull them over. The first thing you learned as a professional driver, he thought, was to watch the goddamned road. He could jabber away all day long from

1

behind the wheel and never let his eyes drift from the highway. Particularly *this* stretch of highway. As far as he was concerned, it was a death trap, jammed as it was with beat-up old trucks driven by farmers on their monthly trip to the city and vans crowded to overflowing with screaming kids and frazzled parents. Man don't watch what he's doing here, he told himself, *kaboom*, he's dead, sideswiped by a horny teenager trying to impress his girlfriend, or unable to stop in time for a young mother slamming on the brakes while turning to swat one of her loudmouthed brats. On the radio, Gordon Lightfoot was singing about how every time he thought he was winning he was losing again.

Ciaro chuckled to himself. Maybe that ought to be our theme song, he thought. It's been the story of our lives, mine and Jimmy's, for almost twenty years, even before Kennedy and McClellan, those pricks, began their vendetta against the boss. But that's history now, he reminded himself with no little amount of satisfaction. At least one of those bastards won't be giving nobody no trouble no more. And the other is so old it don't make no difference. Could be that's our problem, he thought. We're all getting old.

Gordon Lightfoot faded, his voice replaced by that of another male, younger, more energetic. "This is WDDM, in downtown Detroit, Michigan," the deejay burbled. "At the tone, the time will be one-thirty P.M.," he said, pausing for the dull gonglike noise. "After this message, the headlines and the weather."

Hoffa, who had appeared to be dozing, shifted uncomfortably. "You want to hear this?" Ciaro asked, his hand moving toward the control knob.

"Nah," Hoffa replied. Then, after a pause: "The only news I want to hear is we got this business finished and we can get back to doing what we do best."

Ciaro flicked a quick glance at his friend and

employer, then shifted his attention back to the road. The years, five of them in that shitheel prison, hadn't been that bad on the boss, he reflected. He still looked like he could more than hold his own in a brawl. His brown hair was streaked with gray and he had added a few pounds, but he kept that in check by his obsession with physical fitness, his rigorous weightlifting program, and his daily walks. His hands, knobby, callused, and hard as rocks, still looked powerful enough to squeeze the core out of a golf ball.

Hoffa was wearing a pair of tan slacks and oxblood loafers, with his customary white socks peeping out between shoe and cuff. Those fucking white socks, Ciaro thought. Ever since I've known the boss, more than forty years now, he's never worn anything but white socks. Says colored ones make his feet sweat. Big deal. Who cares if his feet sweat?

Hoffa stretched, drawing his arms back behind his head and flexing. When he did, his biceps strained the armbands on his burgundy polo shirt, and the miniature penguin on his chest did a little jig.

"You hungry?" Ciaro asked.

"No," Hoffa said. "Jo fixed me a sandwich just before you came. You?"

"I had a late breakfast," Ciaro replied. "Ain't that the shits," he added lightly. "Here we're going to a restaurant and neither of us wants to eat."

"The purpose is not to eat," Hoffa reminded him sternly. "We're going to see if we can get this problem settled."

"I know, I know," Ciaro grunted. "I was just trying to cheer you up a bit. You know, make you laugh a little."

Hoffa gazed at Ciaro fondly; he loved the man more than he loved his own brother. "We've been through some shit, Bobby, over the years, and we'll get through this, too," he said kindly. "Besides"—he grinned, revealing a wide expanse of strong, white teeth, one of his most distinguishing features and one the cartoonists loved to caricature—"you couldn't pay me enough to eat with that asshole anyway. He might drop rat poison in my salad."

"Not a chance." Ciaro grinned, too. "He don't have the balls to do it himself. If he decided to get rid of you, he'd hire some schmuck to do it for him while he stayed somewhere safe and made sure his ass was protected."

Hoffa nodded grimly in agreement but said nothing.

For ten minutes they rode in silence, each lost in his own thoughts. When Ciaro saw the sign for the Machus Red Fox, he wheeled the Pontiac into the parking lot and slowly cruised down the rows of vehicles.

"You see him?" Hoffa asked.

"Not yet," Ciaro replied, searching for a late-model Cadillac, predictably one with windows tinted so dark that nobody could see inside.

"Wait a minute," he said, spotting a two-tone Caddy in a corner of the lot. But as he drew closer he saw it was empty and that it had out-of-state license plates to boot. "Delaware," he said, disappointedly as he drove slowly by. "Just some fucking tourist stopping to feed his face."

The lot was jammed with semis, big eighteen-wheelers that continually crossed and recrossed the country, carrying everything from toilet paper and dog food to industrial waste. When truckers passed through this part of Michigan, the Red Fox was one of their favorite stops. It was one of those kinds of places, Ciaro reflected, where your spoon stood up in a cup of coffee, where the hamburgers were so sloppy you almost had to take a shower after lunch, and so greasy you could use the residue in your crankcase. It was the kind of place where you could joke and shoot the crap with other truckers. Not like those places with snaky plants hanging in the windows and stuff on the menu called "tofu" or some shit like that. Those places with the tight-ass, skinny little waitresses who hoped they could attract a rich and preferably old vascular surgeon looking for a new, young wife. Or maybe, as a second choice, a good-looking, rising executive from General Motors.

Approaching one of the semis, one with a New Jersey plate, he gave it a professional examination. It was a shipshape rig, he noted, running over the vehicle with his practiced eye. Clean and well maintained, with big black mudflaps, the ones that featured a shapely broad in chrome silhouette. On the right rear was a bumper sticker, red lettering on a white background. *Old truckers never die,* it said, *they just get their Peterbilt.* On the other side, keeping the art work in symmetry, was another. Dark lettering on a light blue background. *When in Doubt, Whup It Out,* it read.

"Whatcha think?" he asked Hoffa, pulling into an empty space near the rear of the lot, not far from the tractor-trailer. Since it was still lunchtime and the Red Fox was a popular restaurant, the parking spots closer in were all filled. "Park or leave?"

Hoffa looked at his watch. "It's one-forty-seven. Where the fuck is he?"

"You want to wait?" Ciaro asked.

"Fucking A," Hoffa snapped. "I agreed to come. We made a long trip. We might as well give him a few minutes. I don't want him to be able to say that Hoffa didn't try."

"Maybe he got stuck in traffic," Ciaro said.

"Yeah"—Hoffa sneered—"and maybe I'm the Queen of England."

Swiveling to look at Hoffa directly, Ciaro noticed the sheen of sweat covering the man's smooth forehead, the way beads of perspiration combined to make small rivulets that ran down the side of his face, dripping off his strong jaw.

"You comfortable, boss?" he asked solicitously. Reaching for the fan switch, he clicked it forward a notch, sending an increased flow of refrigerated air in Hoffa's direction. "You want me to kick this thing up to max?"

"Nah, Bobby, that's fine," Hoffa said. "It's just the heat. I never remember July being this hot in the old days."

Ciaro smiled. "There's a lot of things now that ain't what they were like in the old days," he noted philosophically. "Some are better. Some are worse."

"Ain't that the truth," Hoffa replied, jiggling his right leg impatiently.

"So he's late," Ciaro said. "What else is new? You ever know a guinea who cares anything about the time? They run on their own clocks."

"No!" Hoffa said sharply. "This is *my* time he's playing with. He may not care about *his* time, but he goddamn ought to be more considerate of mine. I promised Jo I'd be back by four so I could get the grill started so we could have steaks on the patio tonight. But if he don't get here pretty quick, we ain't going to make it."

"He'll be here," Ciaro said soothingly.

"He'd better," Hoffa said angrily. "I don't like being forced to play that son-of-a-bitch's games."

Ciaro said nothing, sweeping the parking lot with his eyes one more time. "You want me to go call him up?" he said after a few minutes.

Hoffa shook his head.

They sat in silence for another ten minutes. As they waited Hoffa grew increasingly agitated, obviously not a man who suffered another's disregard for punctuality.

"You okay?" Ciaro asked quietly.

Hoffa nodded. That motherfucker, he thought.

Why can't he be on time? Then he remembered what Jo would say. "Be calm, Jim," she would tell him. "Learn some patience." Not much fucking chance of that, he thought, laughing to himself. I'm sixty-two, and if I haven't learned any patience by now, I'm probably not going to. Sixty-two! he repeated to himself. Jesus, where has the time gone? I don't *feel* like sixty-two. I feel like thirty-two. I know that I *still* have a lot to do and not enough time to do it.

He glanced at Ciaro, who was anxiously watching the entrance for the first sign of Dally D'Allesandro's Caddy. The years, Hoffa thought, are beginning to show on Bobby. Unlike himself, Ciaro wasn't obsessed with physical fitness. His stomach, once as hard and flat as an asphalt highway, now bulged over his belt. His jowls sagged like a basset hound's, and his hair had receded considerably in the front, his onetime widow's peak a forgotten memory. But his mind was still as quick as Joe Louis's right had ever been, Hoffa conceded, and he was mentally every bit as tough as the former heavyweight champ, the guy who grew up, as he and Ciaro had, on the streets of Detroit.

Drumming his fingers nervously against the dash, Hoffa tried to soothe himself by concentrating on the sounds of the traffic: the hum of tires on smooth pavement, the roar of suddenly revved engines, the squeal of brakes, and the occasional bleat of a horn. It was like music to his ears, he thought, as good as any concert he had ever been to or wanted to go to. As he struggled to divert his thoughts from the impending meeting, he thought about Ciaro. His memory flew back to when they first met. It was in the fall, he recalled vividly. And it was dark. And the highway wasn't nearly as crowded as that same road was today.

2
. . . .
1938

Jimmy Hoffa was barreling down the two-lane blacktop behind the wheel of a Ford three-window coupe, speeding as usual and pushing the little car as fast as it would go. By the time he drew abreast of the Chevrolet truck parked on the shoulder, it was too late to stop, so he drove down the road for almost a quarter of a mile before applying the brakes and executing a neat U-turn.

More slowly than he had been traveling the first time, Hoffa retraced his path, passing the truck going the opposite way. Twenty yards on the other side of the vehicle, Hoffa did another U-turn and pulled in behind it. On his second pass, he spotted the top of the driver's head, which was barely visible through the side window. He's getting a few minutes of sleep, Hoffa thought. He must really be tired.

Opening his car door, Hoffa stepped out onto the gravel shoulder. "If I'm not back in ten minutes," he told his companion, a slim blonde, "go on back without me."

Fastening the top button on his shirt, he slid the

8

knot of his tie into place, straightened his fedora, and strode resolutely forward. He ain't going to be very happy to see me, Hoffa thought as he approached the truck. Unconsciously he wiggled his shoulders and clenched his fists a few times to get the blood flowing through his upper body, just in case he had to swing into action and defend himself. In the few months since he had signed on as an organizer with the International Brotherhood of Teamsters, he had learned enough to be careful about approaching a driver who appeared to be asleep in his vehicle on the side of the road. It had become popular of late for men bent on assault and robbery to sneak up on snoozing drivers, incapacitate them before they fully woke up, steal their money and often their truck—along with the cargo—and leave the unfortunate driver along the side of the road, either beaten unconscious or dead. To be safe, most drivers locked themselves inside their cabs and slept with a weapon at hand, usually a club or a length of pipe, but sometimes a pistol. It also was possible, Hoffa knew, that the apparently sleeping driver might be a management decoy; that the person behind the wheel was not really a driver but a company-hired goon setting a trap for union organizers like himself. It was a tactic some companies had adopted recently to counter the Teamsters' stepped-up membership drive. In either case, Hoffa knew, the man in the cab could, likely as not, come out swinging. Or worse.

Playing by his own rules for self-preservation, Hoffa approached the truck as noisily as he could; the last thing he wanted was to give the driver the impression that he was trying sneak up on him.

The driver, who had heard him coming, unobtrusively tightened his grip on a tire iron he kept on the seat next to him for just such emergencies. Bobby Ciaro wasn't born yesterday, you dumb fuck, he muttered to himself, half opening his eyes so he could see the stranger when he poked his head into the cab.

Hoffa, not a total novice at this sort of thing either, did not walk directly to the cab. Instead he stopped about five feet away, far enough to be out of the driver's swinging range but close enough to see inside. It was too dark to make out all the details, but the moon was bright enough for him to distinguish the form of a man slouched across the seat, his head resting against the driver's-side window with his legs extended across the seat toward the passenger door.

"I'm going to bet that you're awake in there," Hoffa called out.

When he got no response, he tried again, only louder. "Are you?" he yelled.

At that, Ciaro bolted upright. "Whaddaya want?" he demanded in a far-from-friendly tone.

"I figured I'd like to talk to you?" Hoffa said as companionably as he could.

"About what?" the driver responded.

Deducing that he was in no immediate danger of having to square off against a physical attack, Hoffa moved closer to the truck. Raising himself on his toes since his five-foot-six-inch frame was too short to let him see inside without some kind of help, he peered inside, looking first at the driver's hands. He noted with satisfaction the scars between the fingers, the sign of an experienced over-the-road trucker. Since they often had to make long trips where time was important, they fought sleep as long as possible. One way of doing that was to keep a lighted cigarette between the fingers with the lit end close to the flesh. If they started to doze off, the cigarette would burn down and jolt them awake. Hoffa was inwardly delighted to see the scars. At least he ain't a company thug, he told himself.

Satisfied that he had found a veteran driver, Hoffa examined him from head to toe. He was a brawny, dark-haired man in his midtwenties. About the same age as me, Hoffa thought. The driver wore his flannel shirt with the sleeves rolled up, revealing a pair of hairy, well-muscled arms, conditioned by years of loading and unloading heavy freight. His eyes were set deep between heavy, dark brows that met in the middle over a nose that obviously had been flattened more than once. His lips were thick and curled back, almost in a sneer. Hoffa could not see his teeth clearly, but he knew that several of them would be chipped and one or more would be missing—the results of unremembered fights in forgotten alleys. The man needed a shave, but that was to be expected if he had been on the road for several days. Since the passenger's window was open, Hoffa sniffed. He could smell cigarettes, but no booze. Good, he thought, he ain't a drunk either.

"What the fuck do you care, man?" Hoffa said, finally answering Ciaro's question. "You ain't making money sitting here by the side of the road. Get up. Start driving. Put me in the cab and I'll keep you up."

"You with the Teamsters?" the driver asked, betraying more belligerence than curiosity.

"Fucking A."

"I can't take you, fella," the driver said, his tone unyielding. "They find out you rode in my cab, I'm out of a job."

Figuring he had solved that problem, Ciaro started the truck and began to slip it into gear.

Hoffa, displaying amazing agility for a short, stockily built man, leaped in front of the truck and shouted at Ciaro.

"Well, I'm coming with you whether you like it or not. So you'd best get used to it."

Ciaro, unaccustomed to being shouted at by strangers, yelled back, "The fuck you are."

"The fuck I'm *not*," Hoffa bellowed, quickly slipping out of his jacket. As Ciaro pulled onto the highway Hoffa leaped onto the gas tank, grabbing the door and tossing his jacket through the open window onto the seat. As the truck accelerated he opened the door and climbed inside.

Ciaro whirled on him, raising the tire iron menacingly. "I said get the fuck out of my cab," he said.

Hoffa, trying to appear casual, reached into his shirt pocket and extracted a pack of Camels, which he tossed onto the dash in front of Ciaro. "Have a cigarette," he said with a grin.

"I said get the fuck out of this cab," Ciaro replied, refusing to be mollified. "They find you in here, it's my job."

"You want to live your life that way?" Hoffa asked. "What kind of fucking pussy are you? Some guy in Duluth going to tell you who goes in the cab?"

Ciaro half turned toward Hoffa and started to speak. "I said—"

"Fuck what you said," the union organizer snapped. "Who's driving this truck?"

"I said—"

"And *I* said, 'Who's driving this motherfucking truck?'" Hoffa screamed. "What's your name?"

"Ciaro. Bobby Ciaro."

"Hey, Bobby Ciaro. Hey . . . hey, Mr. Bobby fucking Ciaro. Look slanty at me all you want to, dago. You want to pull the rig over and fight it out, fine, we'll do that."

When Ciaro's right foot failed to move toward the brake, Hoffa knew he had won that round. "You ain't going to do that, are you? So instead you drive and listen to me."

Ciaro opened his mouth, but Hoffa quickly cut him off. "Yeah, yeah, yeah, yeah. Don't talk, Bobby. Listen. Listen to what I'm fucking telling you. *Listen* to me."

Ciaro stared at Hoffa, then abruptly jerked the steering wheel to the left and pulled, bouncing, onto the shoulder.

"*Listen* to me," Hoffa implored. Grabbing Ciaro's left hand he raised it until the scars were clearly visible. "I *know* what those are, baby. I got 'em, too. I know what it is to be out there. That's why I want you to listen to me."

"I just did," Ciaro replied, snatching his hand out of Hoffa's grasp. "Now get the fuck off my cab."

"All right," Hoffa said calmly. "Or what? What are you going to do?"

"I'm going to beat the fuck out of you."

Hoffa smiled. "No, you're not," he said, "and I'm going to tell you why. Because if you were going to, you already would have. You see? And that's the thing about a fucking negotiation. You got a point. I got a point. You want to kill me, but we're both sitting here talking. We're both sitting here talking," he repeated, "just like the Kroger Company is going to sit and talk to you. Just like the management is going to talk to you when you walk in there. They're going to bitch and call out the cops and blow all sorts of fucking hot and cold, and threaten you with every fucking thing in the world, and if you *sit* there, you see, just like I'm sitting here, talking to you, eventually you're going to strike a bargain."

He paused to let what he had said sink in.

Ciaro stared at him, and then, as if nothing Hoffa said had penetrated, repeated, only a little more calmly, "Get out of my cab."

Hoffa shook his head. "Baby," he said, "you got balls. And if you get lucky, you can kill me. Barring that, however, you're going to hear my speech about the Teamsters. So why don't you just drive the truck."

Shrugging, Ciaro pulled back onto the highway.

For the next hour, as they traveled through the night down the length of Michigan, Hoffa explained to Ciaro how the Teamsters began as the Team

Drivers International Union in 1899 when nine Midwestern locals were given a charter from the American Federation of Labor. They were, of course, all operators of horse-drawn vehicles.

Three years later some of the members broke away and started a new organization, which was called the Teamsters National Union. Its main goal was to raise the base pay of drivers, who at that time were being paid about twelve dollars for an eighty-hour week. But despite a spurt in membership to almost fourteen thousand men, the TNU began falling apart, mainly as a result of corruption within the ranks.

"They had some fuckers in there who thought they could do anything," Hoffa explained. "Even join up with the goddamn owners in return for kickbacks. There's nothing worse," he spat, "than guys who would sell out their own brothers for a few lousy bucks."

In an attempt to save the union, Hoffa explained, "long before you and me was born," AFL President Samuel Gompers in 1903 engineered a merger of the original group, the Team Drivers, and the splinter group, the TNU. The result was the creation of a third group called the International Brotherhood of Teamsters, Chauffeurs, Warehousemen and Helpers of America.

"That's why they call us the Teamsters." Hoffa grinned, relishing the fact that he had a captive audience, that the next truck stop was still miles down the road and there was no place Ciaro could dump him except on the shoulder. And he had already shown his unwillingness to do that.

"What I'm trying to say," Hoffa said, groping for the right words, "is that we got to stick together. Our strength is that there are more of us than there are of them. Right now we've got a half million—*a half million!*—members around the country. We believe that if we join together, like brothers, we can beat their butts."

He laughed. "Speaking of butts . . ." He reached for the cigarette package that he had tossed on the dash. Discovering there was only one cigarette left, Hoffa fingered it gently and looked at Ciaro. Breaking it in half, he put both segments between his lips and lit them. "This is what brotherhood is," he said, extending one segment to Ciaro.

"The thing of it is . . ." he said, pausing to take a deep drag, "the thing of it is: what is too much? They had their way, what would it be? You'd be working slave labor, be driving the roads for nothing. Loading, unloading the trucks. Just like you are. If you had *your* way, they'd be driving the trucks and you'd be sitting up in their offices fucking their cute secretaries. What does everyone want? Just all there is. It's as simple as that. All that I'm saying is that for our side—*our* side, that's yours and mine—there's a lot more there for us. That's right. That's just what's due us and that's possible."

"Like what?" Ciaro broke in.

"Like downtime pay," Hoffa replied quickly. "There's pay for deadheading. There's mileage. There's a whole lot of shit, all the things I've been saying. It's right there, Bobby. Not only is it possible, *it's right there.*"

"No . . ." Ciaro began.

"Yes!" Hoffa yelled. "Yes. It's right there. When they have to negotiate . . . when they say to you, 'Ride with the Teamsters and you lose your job—'"

"They treat us like dirt," Ciaro conceded.

"I know that," Hoffa agreed.

"Every couple of weeks some son-of-a-bitch falls asleep because he's been driving for eighteen hours—"

"I know that."

"If we're stuck ten, twelve hours because a rig is broke down, we don't get no pay."

"I know that," Hoffa repeated. "Why do you think we're trying to strike the company? You see—"

"I can't go out on strike."

"You can't afford *not* to go," Hoffa argued. "You see—"

"What's that?" Ciaro broke in.

Hoffa squinted through the windshield. Ahead of them a truck stop loomed into view.

"I'll get out here," Hoffa said, rolling down his sleeves and groping on the dash for his cuff links.

"How are you going to get back?"

Hoffa shrugged. "Another driver. A guy like you." Reaching into his wallet, he extracted a business card. Turning it over, he took a pen from his pocket and wrote something on the card, then offered it to Ciaro. "Now listen to me, baby. I want you to stop by—"

"I can't sign up with you," Ciaro protested.

Hoffa watched as Ciaro reluctantly slipped the card into his pocket. "You will sign up," he predicted confidently, "but I didn't *say* sign up. I said 'stop by.' I want you to stop by, and—"

He stopped in mid-sentence. "Uh-oh," he said, peering into the darkness.

Following his gaze, Ciaro could make out the forms of four men huddled around a late-model sedan.

"Drop me here," Hoffa commanded. "You don't want to be seen with me."

Ciaro did not argue. Slowing the truck, he angled toward a far corner of the parking lot, away from the men. When the truck was between them, Hoffa opened the door and jumped lightly to the ground, disappearing quickly into the darkness.

"Don't forget," he said just before he leaped. "Come by and see me."

Ciaro, intent on the men, did not reply.

3

1 9 3 8

"**W**here you going?" Georgie Ventura asked a few days later.

"Kreger's," Hoffa replied, pulling on his jacket.

"Back to the scene of the crime, huh?" Ventura grinned. "Just can't stay away. Like you was in love with the place or something."

"Fuck you," Hoffa replied good-naturedly. "Wasn't any crime. Them was the good old days."

The two of them smiled conspiratorially. Seven years previously, when both of them were only eighteen, they had been the ringleaders behind an impromptu strike at the Kreger Grocery & Baking Company on Green Avenue, not far from the West End neighborhood where Hoffa, his recently widowed mother, brother, and two sisters had lived since moving to Detroit in 1923. Born in the tiny town of Brazil, Indiana, the second son and third child of an Irish Protestant mother and a Dutch father, Hoffa had been seven when they arrived in the city. But by the time he took a job at Kreger's ten years later, making

17

thirty-two cents an hour, he felt like a Detroit native.

Hoffa and Ventura were disturbed, among other things, by the bullying tactics of a supervisor named Dave McKusic. One night after McKusic arbitrarily fired two members of their crew to create job openings for his cousins, Hoffa and Ventura convinced the other unloaders to join them in a stop-work action. They would wait until a shipment of highly perishable material arrived; then the company would have to agree to their demands or face losing several thousand dollars. The opportunity came soon when a freight car loaded with Florida strawberries was switched to their unloading dock. Knowing that the berries would spoil in less than two hours if they were not placed under refrigeration, the men refused to work until management agreed to talk to them about their demands.

With a promise to negotiate, the men went back to work. The next morning the leaders, including Hoffa and Ventura, met with a management representative to discuss the situation. In the end, management capitulated, agreeing to get rid of McKusic, give them a thirteen-cent-an-hour pay raise, along with a guarantee of at least six paid hours of work every day, and create a modest life-insurance plan. More important was Kreger's concession to recognize the newly formed workers' group as a bargaining unit, a rare occurrence during those times when unions were hated by almost everyone, including a large percentage of the general public, which looked upon them as communist-front organizations.

The victory was so unusual that it drew the attention of Andrew O'Leary, the labor reporter for the pro-union *Detroit Tribune*. O'Leary mentioned the event in his weekly column and christened the leaders behind the successful strike the "Strawberry Boys," a sobriquet that would stick to them the rest of their lives.

A little more than a year after the strike, Hoffa and

Ventura quit Kreger's to go to work as full-time organizers for the Teamsters. There were two Teamsters locals in the city at the time and both were in serious financial trouble. Combined, the two locals had fewer than five hundred members and their bank accounts were bare. As organizers for the financially destitute organizations, neither Ventura nor Hoffa was paid a salary, but they scraped by on commissions for new members they signed up.

When it became evident that both locals could not survive the Depression, the two groups were merged. Local 299, which was in marginally better shape than its sister unit, became the dominant group. After the Depression, when union membership began to rise, Hoffa was promoted to business agent for Local 299. On the books, his pay was to be twenty-five dollars a week, but the local remained so poor that the full amount was hardly ever paid. Usually Hoffa took ten dollars a week. Sometimes he took only five. As membership continued to grow, a new unit was created, Local 1077, and Ventura was named a business agent as well.

Despite the wedge Hoffa and Ventura had created at Kreger's in 1931 by introducing the first union into the company, progress had not continued. By 1938, the workers' situation at the facility had deteriorated to the point that Hoffa felt it was imperative to make a move to bring the union into a position of power once again. Management refused to discuss the issues: "We will never negotiate," was the proclamation from the top. The only alternative left, Hoffa knew, was a strike.

"You going to go back and stir 'em up all over again, huh?" Ventura asked.

"I'm going to try," Hoffa said, pulling on his fedora. "You want to come with me?"

"Can't," Ventura answered succinctly. "I've got something going over at Delacorte and Sons. Wish I could, though. Sometimes I miss the old place."

"Yeah." Hoffa laughed. "Like you'd miss a case of the clap. If you get free later, come on over. I got a feeling there's going to be enough action to go around for everybody."

"Luck," Ventura told Hoffa as he opened the door. "Give 'em hell."

Organizers of the strike had planned the action for the week before Thanksgiving, when the holiday vegetables would be flooding into the fruit and vegetable warehouse, a time when the company would be extremely vulnerable. Hoffa had arranged to be at the job site to help organize the work stoppage and provide moral support to the demonstrators.

The Kreger warehouse, a low-slung, unattractive building, was between Green and West End, just south of Fort. To get to the building, Hoffa parked his coupe on Vanderbilt, well away from the warehouse, and walked the three blocks to the site. Heading up West End along the eastern boundary of Fisher Body's Fleetwood plant, he was making the turn onto Bacon to get to the unloading area when he had to leap out of the way to avoid being hit by a Kreger-bound Chevrolet truck.

"You dumb fucking asshole," Hoffa screamed, extending the middle finger of his right hand as he scrambled out of the truck's path. The driver, oblivious, barreled down the short street and threatened to run down a group of picketers, who had formed a line at the entrance. As the truck sped past him Hoffa glanced at the man behind the wheel. "I'll be damned," he said in surprise. "That's Mr. Bobby fucking Ciaro."

Stopping to talk to the picketers, Hoffa made some suggestions regarding the dispersal of forces, then strode resolutely toward the unloading dock. Standing on the platform was a burly, middle-aged man in work pants and a heavy jacket. He had a dark wool stocking cap pulled down over his ears and a cigar clamped tightly in his teeth. That could be McKusic's younger brother, Hoffa thought to himself as he approached the foreman, he looks and acts exactly like him, right down to his beady fucking eyes and three-day growth of beard.

"*Back* it up, *back* it up. *Drive* it . . . *back* it up . . . are you looking at me?" The foreman, named Burns, was screaming at Ciaro, who was maneuvering his vehicle into position at the dock.

"I hear you," Ciaro growled, unhappy with being talked to like a rookie driver. "I'm coming in and you'd better get your ass out of the way if you don't want to be in Fido's plate tonight."

"What did you say, Ciaro?" the foreman demanded pugnaciously. "I don't think you were talking to me."

"I just said I'm coming in, Burns. I know what I'm doing. I know how to drive a fucking truck."

Hoffa stood silently on the side, watching as Ciaro backed expertly up to the dock, and Burns scribbled on his clipboard. Neither Burns nor Ciaro noticed him amid the bustle.

"Okay, Ciaro," Burns ordered, having finished his paperwork. "Get on the line. Let's get this mother-fucker unloaded."

Ciaro nodded, stripping off his windbreaker. Tossing it onto a stack of empty boxes, Ciaro stepped briskly across the platform to where men already were unloading the crates of produce. He picked up a crate and joined them.

Falling into place among the antlike bearers, Ciaro went down a short flight of steps and was carrying his box toward a storage area when Hoffa stepped forward, blocking his path.

"You dumb fuck," Hoffa barked. "You almost ran me down a minute ago. Don't you have a brain in that dumb fucking dago head . . . ?"

"What the shit," Ciaro said, recognizing Hoffa but still as surprised at seeing him as Hoffa had initially been at seeing Ciaro. "What are you doing here? Get the fuck out of my way."

In the background, Burns was screaming. "Keep it moving, keep it moving. Don't pay any attention to these asshole union guys. You want to keep working, keep the line moving."

"I'll get out of your way," Hoffa said sarcastically, bunching his fists. "I'll get out of your way because I'm going to put knots on your head, you dumb fucking wop."

The worker behind Ciaro had put down his crate and was advancing on Hoffa.

"What the fuck you want?" Hoffa said, turning toward the approaching worker. "You want some of my ass? I'll give you some," he said, punching the man hard in the stomach. As he doubled over, Hoffa hit him on the side of the head. Then, as the would-be attacker staggered drunkenly, Hoffa kicked him hard on the side of his knee. Howling in pain, the man collapsed.

Ciaro, thinking the other worker was taking care of Hoffa, had continued walking with his crate, obeying Burns, who was screaming, "Keep it moving, keep it moving, you cocksuckers."

"I ain't through with you yet," Hoffa yelled at Ciaro's back, ignoring the man writhing on the ground. Turning to another worker approaching with a crate, he urged him to join the Teamsters pickets.

"If you put it down, they can't move it," Hoffa argued. "Put it down, pal. Put it down. You're saying, 'I know, but I need my job.' I'm saying the Teamsters will *guarantee* your job, we'll *guarantee* your wage. The Teamsters want you to join up. We want you to come out on strike. We want you to organize, to stop the unfair exploitation."

"Get the fuck out of my men's way," Burns hollered at Hoffa, "or I'm going to have to come down there and kick your ass."

"Then come on down," Hoffa screamed back. "I ain't afraid of you."

Turning to another man passing by with a crate, Hoffa added, "I ain't afraid of any of you cocksuckers. What are you afraid of? If you ain't scared, how come you don't put down that crate and join your brothers on the line? You're afraid you'll lose your job, that's why. You're working for *peanuts* and they can fire your ass anytime they want."

Hoffa walked backward, keeping pace with the crate-carrying worker. "Put it down," he urged. "Let that shit spoil, pal. Let it sit there and rot until they decide to negotiate."

The man hesitated, which spurred Hoffa on. "You ever pray you could be strong enough to make something of yourself?" he asked the man in a conversational tone. "Well, today is the day when your prayers can come true. Put the crate down and come over with your brothers."

The man stopped and stared at Hoffa. "You know," he said softly. "You're right. I've had enough of these assholes. They treat me like I'm shit and I'm fucking tired of it."

"Goddamn right you're tired of it," Hoffa agreed. "You *ought* to be fucking tired of it. Come over and join us and we'll treat you better. We'll make sure *they* treat you better."

Grinning, the man tossed the crate to the ground, ignoring the ears of corn that went skittering across the littered wooden floor. "You got yourself a new member," he said.

Hoffa smiled. "Smart man!" Turning to the other workers, he bellowed, "Did you see that, you men? He put the crate down. Now *you* put them down. Let the fucking vegetables spoil. Let them move the fucking things themselves, and then see how long they'll 'never negotiate.' Put the fucking crates down, cross the line, and join the Teamsters!

"Good! Good!" Hoffa shouted as several more workers put down their crates and walked off. "Put them down and don't pick them up until the terms are *right* for you. You got a right to negotiate. You got a *right* to speak up for yourselves. You got a *right* to demand a fair wage."

He stopped when he sensed movement behind him and turned to see Ciaro bearing down on him, his fists clenched, his eyes blazing.

"*You!*" Hoffa screamed at him. "You son-of-a-bitch. You smoked my cigarettes. You listened to my jokes. For eighty-five miles we got along like brothers. That's what *I* did for *you*. Now what are you going to do for—"

"That fucking Burns," Ciaro interjected. "He thought we were friends. He just fucking fired me and it's your fault. You cost me my job, you little heinie!"

"I ain't German," Hoffa replied. "I'm Dutch. It's just like a fucking wop not to know the difference."

"I don't give a fuck if you're Ethiopian," said Ciaro. "I'm going to get your ass. You'd better watch every step you take because one day I'm going to be waiting for you."

"Blow it out your ass." Hoffa sneered. "You ain't man enough to take me now or anytime. You're just a big fucking bag of wind."

Ciaro shook his fist menacingly. "Remember what I told you," he shouted, stalking off.

Hoffa shrugged. "Listen to that asshole," he said, turning back to the workers. "You see what happened to him? That dickhead Burns fired him because he *thought* he was a friend of the Teamsters. That just goes to show you how you stand with these guys, these pricks who can fire you just for looking cross-eyed. Don't put up with that shit anymore. Drop those crates and join the Teamsters!"

Three days later Hoffa and Billy Flynn, an organizer for Local 299, paid an evening visit to the Idle Hour Laundry at Vernor and Lansing to try to talk the owner, Harold Burleson, into recognizing a group of his drivers and negotiating with them on wages and working conditions.

"I ain't going to do it," Burleson told the pair, as he leaned on the yellowing Formica table. "This is my business and I'll run it like I want. Those guys work for *me*, and if they don't like the way I run things, they can go work somewhere else."

"That ain't the point," Hoffa argued. "They *like* working for you. They *like* their jobs. They don't *want* to go anywhere else. All they want is a little more money. A little more to take home and give to their wives so they can hold up their heads as wage earners. All they want is a little more money and a little more time off. Sixty hours a week is too much to expect of your men. They want a little time off so they can see their kids once in a while, take them to the zoo, take their boys fishing, get to know their kids before they grow up and move out."

"It ain't going to work, Mr. Hoffa," Burleson responded steadfastly. "I pay my drivers the same as every other businessman in this part of town—"

"No, you don't," Hoffa interrupted. "You pay them ten cents an hour less."

"Well, almost the same," Burleson conceded. "But if I give them another ten cents an hour, like you want, they'll start taking advantage of me. If I do what you want and give them a deal where they work only fifty-five hours a week, the next thing you know they'll only want to work fifty. Before long, they'll be demanding forty-five or forty—"

"No, Mr. Burleson," Hoffa broke in, "you ain't listening. *I'm* not saying to give 'em a ten-cent-an-hour raise, *I'm* not saying give 'em a fifty-five-hour week. All I'm saying is *talk* to these people. Sit down and *negotiate* a settlement with your drivers. That's what unionism is all about, negotiation. Me and Billy ain't here to tell you how to run your business. We don't even represent your drivers. They ain't Teamsters. Not yet anyway. We—that's me and Billy—want you to *talk* to them, negotiate with them. And then if they feel happy with the results, then they'll come join the Teamsters because me and Billy helped them. *Then*, when the Teamsters represent them, I'll come back and talk to you. Me and you will negotiate some. That's *all* I'm saying, Mr. Burleson."

"That's what I'm afraid of," Burleson replied, staring at Flynn, who loomed over him.

"*Afraid?*" Hoffa asked in mock surprise. "You're afraid of Billy? And *me?* Aw, come on, Mr. Burleson, we're reasonable people."

Burleson looked again at Flynn, a six-foot-four giant with a five-inch-long knife scar along the left side of this throat and a cauliflower left ear, a souvenir of an early and unhappy attempt to be a professional fighter, and he shuddered. "About as reasonable as my wife when she wants money for a new dress," he stammered. "Now how about getting out of here so I can close up? If I don't get home, my wife is going to make me eat a cold dinner."

Hoffa sighed. "Okay, Mr. Burleson, okay. We're going. But we ain't quitting. Me and Billy will be back in a week or so."

"Don't waste your time, Mr. Hoffa. I already told you. I ain't talking to a group of *employees*. If they don't like the way I run my business, let 'em go work for somebody else. There're drivers out there begging for jobs."

Hoffa felt his temper rise. "Okay," he hollered. "Be that way. Don't say I didn't give you a chance. I tried to talk sense to you, but you wouldn't listen. I'm finished with you." Throwing up his hands, he stalked out of the building. He stopped at the curb, his hands jammed into his overcoat pockets, waiting for Flynn to catch up.

"That's one hardheaded motherfucker," Hoffa said when Flynn joined him.

"Don't worry," Flynn replied icily, "he'll come around."

"He sure as shit will," Hoffa agreed, pulling a notebook out of the pocket of his overcoat and flipping it open. Pausing to write himself a reminder to revisit Burleson, he did not immediately see the figure that materialized out of the shadows and stopped at his side.

"Hello again," the newcomer growled. "I told you I'd be seeing you."

"Ciaro!" Hoffa exclaimed. "Goddamn, you're persistent."

Ciaro removed his hand from his pocket. Clutched in his fist was a knife with a six-inch blade.

"Let's walk down this way a little bit," Ciaro said, nudging Hoffa with the blade and gesturing to the gaping entry to an alleyway that ran alongside the Idle Hour, providing access to the laundry.

"What do you want?" Hoffa asked angrily, yielding reluctantly to Ciaro's prodding. "You think you're going to stick me with that? You think because you got a knife you can take me?"

"You cost me my job," Ciaro mumbled between gritted teeth.

Hoffa managed to sound nonchalant. "So what? You should have joined the brothers and we would have *guaranteed* your job."

"Shut up!" Ciaro growled. "You talk too fucking much. But I'm going to fix that. I'm going to cut your throat."

"You're obviously a man with a profound sense of justice," Hoffa said mockingly, unintimidated.

Flynn caught up with them.

"What's the problem, boss?" he asked Hoffa.

Ciaro turned to him. "Back off," he ordered. "I got no quarrel with you."

Flynn studied the man with a professional eye. "Well, yes, you do, lad. You got a beef with my partner, you got a beef with me." Taking a step forward, he reached out a hand, as if to take Ciaro's arm.

When Ciaro jerked away, Flynn saw the knife for the first time.

"You'd pull a knife on a guy who was unprotected?"

"Get fucking back," Ciaro warned.

"No," Flynn said, speaking reasonably. "I couldn't have that on my conscience." Reaching inside his coat, he removed a black revolver from the waistband of his trousers.

"You see." Hoffa smiled. "As I was just telling Mr. Burleson in there, life is a negotiation. It's all give-and-take. Negotiation don't mean I win and you lose. It means what is the middle ground in which we both, since we got to live together, can be content." Unexpectedly his grin faded. "I'm sorry about your job," he said. "I really am. I didn't mean to get you fired."

Ciaro stared at Flynn's pistol. Nodding, he slowly raised his left hand and closed the blade on the knife. "You make a good argument," he said, turning to Hoffa and grinning himself. "I can see your point."

Hoffa smiled. "I like you Bobby 'Tough Guy' Ciaro. You're practical man and you don't scare easy. Besides, you got a sense of humor. What say we go get a cup of coffee?"

4
· · · · · · · · · · · ·
1 9 3 8

Sitting in a back booth at Black's Café on Vernor at Grand, Hoffa asked Ciaro how he had found him.

"Shit, that was easy," Ciaro replied. "I just waited outside the local until you left and I followed you. Thought I was going to freeze my balls off waiting for you to come out of that goddamn laundry. What took you so long?"

"That's a story in itself," Hoffa began.

"Well, tell it," urged Ciaro. "I got nowhere to go. Not like I had a job or nothing."

"I really am sorry about that," Hoffa said. "You got to eat and I got to eat. I got no desire to hurt you."

"What he done, he done for the workingman," interjected Flynn. "I'm a workingman, too, and I got a right to eat just like the two of you. Everybody's got a right to eat."

"That's right," Hoffa nodded.

"But you take these fuckers," Flynn said, gesturing toward Hoffa's notebook, which was resting on the tabletop. "If a guy's an honest laundryman and he signs with the Teamsters, no problem. But then some cocksucker—"

"Did you see that guy?" Hoffa asked Ciaro. "That guy back at the Idle Hour?"

"I seen him," Ciaro agreed. "So what?"

"That cocksucker don't believe in collective bargaining," said Flynn. "Collective bargaining protects the workingman. But a cocksucker like Burleson, he won't organize, he won't join the brotherhood, he won't go along. He's willing to let his brothers pay the price."

"He don't want to negotiate wages or nothing for his drivers," said Hoffa.

"Every laundry in my district, the owners have let the drivers sign up. But this cocksucker Burleson, is *he* signed? He is *not* signed, I tell you. And he's willing to cut his prices . . . cut his wages . . . do anything he can to attract business from honest men." Flynn slapped a meaty hand on the table.

"He's a stubborn old fart who feels if his men don't like the way he treats 'em, they can leave," Hoffa added.

Ciaro nodded. "I heard that before."

"The problem is," added Flynn, "we can't leave it like that. If we let Burleson screw us around, Oppenheimer over in Ventura's district will be trying the same thing. Then it'll be Swartz over on Grand—"

"You get the picture?" Hoffa interrupted.

"Sure, I get the picture," said Ciaro. "But what are you going to *do* about it?"

Hoffa and Flynn exchanged glances.

"You say you ain't got no prospects of working?" Hoffa asked.

"That's what I said."

"You want a little work? One night anyway?"

"One night's better than nothing."

"Okay," Flynn said. "Meet us here tonight, about nine."

Ciaro started to say something, but Hoffa held up his hand. "Don't ask no questions," he said. "If you want a night's work, be here. If you don't, forget we ever had this conversation."

"In the meantime," Flynn said amiably, extending a huge, scarred fist, "why don't you give me that knife? Only chinks and niggers go around with knives. You want to go like a white man, get a gun."

Ciaro hesitated long enough where Hoffa thought he was going to have to take the blade away. Then, smiling slightly, Ciaro dug in his pocket, palmed the knife, and handed it to Flynn. "See you tonight," he said.

The three men sat squeezed into the cab of the Dodge truck that Flynn had provided, Ciaro behind the wheel, Flynn in the middle, and Hoffa in the passenger spot.

"How come I'm driving?" Ciaro had asked when they met outside Black's.

"Because that's what you're being paid to do," Hoffa had replied.

"Where do I drive to?"

"Wherever I tell you. Right now we're going back to the Idle Hour Laundry. You remember where it is?"

"Sure," Ciaro said.

"Then let's go."

As the three of them watched, a uniformed patrolman strolled down the street, twisting the doorknob on each of the small businesses he passed.

Flynn sighed and reached into his overcoat. "Five minutes he'll be gone," he said. Fishing a pint-sized whiskey flask out of his overcoat, he unscrewed the top, inverted it, and poured whiskey into it, filling it to the brim. "To Detroit's finest," he said sarcastically, downing the shot. Making a face, he blew out and shook his head violently from side to side, like a horse winded after a sprint. "Come on," he whispered to the cop, "hurry up. I got places to go and people to see."

When the officer was four doors past the Idle Hour, Hoffa nudged Flynn sharply in the ribs. "Let's go," he said tightly.

The three men walked briskly to the back of the truck. Flynn jumped nimbly into the cargo area and returned almost immediately, a metal can in each large hand. Ciaro smelled gasoline.

"What the fuck—" he started to say.

"Get back in the cab," Hoffa told him softly but with authority. "Turn the engine on and wait. Keep it in gear in case we have to get out of here in a hurry."

Ciaro, biting off whatever comment he was about to make, nodded silently and returned to the cab.

"Okay, Billy," Hoffa whispered to Flynn. "I guess we're up."

They walked across the sidewalk to the front door of the laundry, lugging the cans. Furtively Flynn studied the street in both directions, then nonchalantly reached out and, with a rock he produced from his pocket, smashed a pane near the knob. Sticking his fist through the opening, he unlocked the door and disappeared inside. Hoffa was right behind him.

Ciaro, from behind the wheel, watched them go into the laundry and noticed that they left the door ajar. A few minutes later, bored and slightly nervous, he was reaching into his pocket for a Camel when an explosion rocked the vehicle and shattered windows along the street.

"Holy shit!" he exclaimed, looking over his shoulder in alarm.

Before he could form another coherent thought, he saw Hoffa on the sidewalk, smoke wisping off his heavy coat. Flames leaped out the laundry's blast-shattered windows. Hoffa was in a crouch, bent over at the waist and moving backward. By the light of the flames, Ciaro could see that he was dragging something across the cement.

"Flynn!" he said aloud.

He was about to get out to help when Hoffa looked up, caught his eye, and waved him back. Within seconds, it seemed, a fire truck, a police car, and an ambulance were crowding the street.

"You're the guy who found him?" a gray-haired, tired-looking policeman asked Hoffa in a tone reflecting only mild concern.

"That's right, Officer. Me and my buddy were driving by when we heard an explosion and I saw that guy staggering out the door of the shop. What is it, a laundry?"

The officer nodded, his face expressionless.

"So we stopped and I ran over to see if I could help. Just when I got there, the guy collapsed at my feet. Jesus, he didn't look too good. His clothes was all burned and his face looked like he'd been hanging over a barbecue grill."

"And that's all that happened?" the cop asked, looking suspiciously at the scorch marks on Hoffa's coat. "How'd you get your coat burned?"

Hoffa looked down, seemingly seeing the marks for the first time. "Aw, shit!" he exclaimed. "I guess I got burned while I was helping that guy. His clothes was still on fire."

"Oh, yeah," the cop said. "You didn't say that the first time."

Hoffa looked puzzled. "Didn't I? Well, I guess I just forgot, seeing as how it was such a terrible experience and all. But, yeah, his clothes was burning and I kind of swatted out the flames."

The cop looked dubiously at Hoffa, his glance traveling to his hands, which were red and starting to blister. "Yeah, I guess you did," he said wearily. It was not the first incident of its kind he had seen.

"Where'd you take him?" Hoffa asked, feigning nonchalance.

The cop looked at him again. "What's the difference? You didn't know him, did you?"

"Nah," Hoffa replied smoothly, "but I kind of feel responsible for him since I found him and all. Just thought I'd check and see how he's doing."

"Right," the cop said, locking eyes with Hoffa. "St. Mary's," he added after a long pause. "Over on Grand."

"Yeah," Hoffa said, staring back at the cop. "I know where it is."

Turning to Ciaro, he said, "Why don't we stop by there? Just see how he is and then we'll be on our way."

"Okay," Ciaro replied, taking his cue from Hoffa.

At the hospital, Ciaro and Hoffa ran into another police roadblock. A captain, who looked just as world-weary as the cop on the beat, asked Hoffa to go through his story yet again.

". . . and when I saw his clothes was on fire, I tried to beat the flames out with my hands. I guess I done okay because pretty soon they wasn't flaming no more—"

"Okay, okay," the cop broke in. "I get the picture. Maybe I ought to put you in for a medal or something?"

"Nah, you don't have to do that," Hoffa said disingenuously. "We was just trying to be good citizens."

"So you done your duty."

"Just like anybody would have."

"And now you just want to make sure you saved his life."

"Just thought I might sleep better."

"The hero visits the dying."

Hoffa paused. "Dying? Did you say dying?"

"Well, shit," the cop replied. "'Course he's dying. Burns like that, you don't slap a little butter on 'em and get up and go home."

"Jesus, I didn't know he was dying."

"You still want to see him?"

Hoffa looked rattled. "Well, yeah," he said, recovering. "I mean, it's the least we could do, right? Help this poor bastard and then can't just abandon him. Leave him to die all alone."

"He ain't all alone," the cop said. "There's a priest with him."

"A priest?" Hoffa said, surprised. "Where'd the priest come from?"

"The rectory across the street," the cop said. "Always a priest on call. This ain't the first guy who's ever been brought in about to croak."

"Oh," Hoffa said. "Yeah. Sure. I guess you're right. Must happen all the time."

"But the *citizens* who help aren't always as solicitous as you are, Mr. Hoffa," the cop said pointedly. "Usually they can't wait to get away. Afraid they'll have to go to court or something. Sometimes maybe even scared we'll think they was involved."

"Well, I can see how they might sometimes think that," Hoffa answered smoothly. "I mean, being on the scene right there and all."

"Yeah, sometimes we get silly ideas like that."

"Well, can we see him or not?"

The cop shrugged. "Why not? He don't have long anyway."

• • •

Knowing the patient was terminal, the emergency-room doctor had ordered him admitted to a special section of the hospital designed to afford dying patients a modicum of privacy in their last hours. It consisted of a small section of tiny rooms, each equipped with an iron-railed bed, two straight-backed chairs, and a metal night table.

When Hoffa and Ciaro slipped into the cubicle, Flynn was stretched out on the narrow cotlike bed, covered from neck to toe with a white sheet. His face was bandaged from his chin to the crown of his head, with openings left for his mouth, his nostrils, and his eyes. An IV tube was attached to his left arm, which was resting on top of the sheet. The room was dimly lit, its only illumination coming from a wall fixture over the bed. Flynn's laborious breathing filled the room, a deep wheeze followed by a liquidy gurgle.

As Ciaro leaned closer he could see that Flynn's eyes were open and he was staring fixedly at the ceiling. His eyelashes had been burned off, making his eyes look exaggeratedly round. The pupils had opened so wide that his normally blue eyes looked black. When the two entered, Flynn swiveled his glance in their direction, then quickly looked away, showing no sign of recognition.

Leaning over Flynn, on the side of the table opposite Hoffa and Ciaro, was a portly priest who appeared to be in his late fifties, a purple cloth draped around his neck. A short, Irish-looking man with a thick mop of snow-white hair, he was quietly explaining the situation to the burned man. He barely looked up when Hoffa and Ciaro entered.

"Too much damage," the priest was saying softly. "There's nothing they can do."

Flynn continued to stare at the ceiling.

"Are you Catholic?" the priest asked.

Flynn did not respond.

"If you are," the priest continued, "now is a good time to be thinking about getting right with God."

No response.

"No matter what you've done in your life, no matter what horrible sins you may have committed, God is willing to forgive you."

Flynn remained impassive.

"Confession is a wonderful thing, my son. It frees the soul and makes it clean, so when you see your Maker, you're as innocent as you were on the day you were born."

Flynn gave no indication that he understood.

"And as much as I hate to have to be the one to keep telling you this, my boy, you *are* going to meet your Maker. And pretty soon, too."

Flynn's eyes were unblinking, expressionless.

"You don't have to tell me everything," the priest continued. "Just indicate to me, even by a nod or a wink, that you're sorry for your sins, so I can give you the last sacrament and you'll be ready to go to God. Do you want that? Do you want to be free from sin?"

For the first time since they had entered the room, Ciaro noticed a slight response from Flynn. His eyes fluttered briefly and his lips moved the tiniest bit.

Noticing the effort, the priest leaned forward. "I see, my son, that you understood what I've been saying. I take it that you would like to confess and I can give you absolution."

Flynn's lips moved again. "Fff . . . fff . . . fff . . ." he stuttered.

"What's that, my boy?" the priest said, leaning closer. "I can't quite make it out. *'Father?'* Is that what you're trying to say?"

Ciaro, fascinated by the drama being played out before him, leaned close on Flynn's other side, as if he, too, were anxious to absolve the man of his transgressions. Watching carefully, he saw Flynn's eyes narrow with the effort of concentration. The dying man took a deep breath, as if he were about to submerge himself in a pool and swim to the bottom.

"Try," the priest whispered encouragingly. "See if you can say the words, 'I'm sorry.'"

"Fff . . . fff . . . fff . . ."

"What's that? I can't make it out. *Father?*' Father, what?"

Flynn summoned all his remaining strength. His lips peeled back and, loudly and clearly, he spoke his last words.

5
....
1 9 7 5

Even with the air conditioner going full blast, it was still like a steambath inside the Pontiac.

Sweat was running down Ciaro's face so copiously it looked as though he had just emerged from the shower. "I *know* it was never this fucking hot in the old days," he moaned, pulling at his pale blue polo shirt, which was as wet as if it had been pulled from a washer in the middle of the rinse cycle. "I don't care what those goddamn weathermen say. The government's just trying to fuck us around like they always do. They just don't want to tell us that the atom bombs changed all the world's weather patterns."

Hoffa grinned weakly. The sweat patches under his arms had extended outward until they met precisely over his breastbone. He looked like he had a three-inch-thick band around his torso. "It's hot, all right," he conceded, "but I don't think it's because of the atom bombs. It's just summer in Detroit. The city always has been a bitch in July and August. That's one of the reasons me and Jo got the place at

Lake Orion, to escape the heat of the city."

"I wish I'd done that," Ciaro said, nodding. "Now anything on a lake anywhere within a two-hour drive is too goddamn expensive. You got yourself a real place there."

"Don't I know it. I'll bet it's fifteen degrees cooler. Goddamn, I wish I was there right now, sitting on the deck, drinking a nice cold glass of iced tea. Waiting for the charcoal to get red so I could put the steaks on."

"Holy shit," Ciaro broke in, "you really know how to break a guy's balls."

Hoffa shook his head, like a fighter who has just taken a hard right to the ear.

"Jesus," he said, "I really must be getting old. Things like the weather never used to bother me. I was always too busy to be concerned with creature comforts. Goddamn, Bobby, you realize I been working for more than fifty years. *Fifty-plus years!* That's longer than a lot of people live. Even if you deduct the time we was up at Lewisburg. And I always tried to keep busy there, best I could. Goddamn, that was terrible. Pulling old cotton out of mattresses and putting new cotton in. Day after day. Week after week. Worse than a goddamned assembly line."

"No sense thinking about that, Jimmy. That's all over and done with," Ciaro broke in, not wanting Hoffa to get started on another antiprison tirade. Not that he didn't have reason to feel that way, Christ knows, Ciaro told himself, but I just ain't in the mood to put up with that shit today.

"You remember your *first* job, boss?" Ciaro prodded, trying to change the subject.

Hoffa smiled to himself. That fucking wop can read me like a book, he thought affectionately. "Sure, I remember. I remember a little wagon my daddy made for me and Billy and how we first used it to play in. But then when Daddy died and Mama had to take in laundry, I used that fucking wagon to haul other people's dirty clothes to the house—"

"No," Ciaro interrupted. "I mean a *real* job."

"Oh," Hoffa said. "You mean one where I worked regular hours and got a regular paycheck?"

"Yeah, that kind of job. The kind of job a white man would have."

"Well, shit," Hoffa said, "I guess that would be when I quit school and went to work at Frank & Seder's."

"The big department store? I never knew you worked there."

"Started when I was fourteen," Hoffa said proudly. "After I decided that if I hadn't learned everything teachers could teach me after the seventh grade, that I wasn't going to learn it. I was a stockboy. Worked sixty hours a week and made twelve dollars. Thought that was good money and I was damn glad to get it. Took it all home to Mama."

"Jesus, can you believe that? You remember how we actually worked our asses off, ten hours a day, six days a week, for fucking *nothing*! I mean it costs that much to go to a fucking movie now."

"I probably would've stayed there, too, if it hadn't been for the Depression. Frank & Seder's had a management trainee program and I was all hot to be a manager."

"Fuck me! I just can't see you as a manager."

"Me neither." Hoffa laughed. "Not now. Not as a manager in a department store anyways. Maybe that was the only good thing the Depression done for me. It got me out of the department store and into Kreger's."

"That's where you met Georgie, right?"

"Yeah. Me and Georgie was real tight. We pulled a fucking strike at Kreger's when we was only eighteen.

Refused to unload strawberries. The *Tribune* called us the Strawberry Boys. I ever tell you about that?"

"Only about a million fucking times."

"Oh," Hoffa said, abashed. "Well, that's what you get for starting me talking about the old days. Anyways, it was because of Georgie and the job at Kreger's that I got involved in the union in the first place."

"One thing just sort of led to another, huh?"

"Yeah. Before I knew it I was an organizer, a young punk trying to sign up every warm body I could find. In those days the unions needed people. Any kind of people. All kinds of people."

"Shit, I'd forgotten about stuff like that." Ciaro laughed. "You remember the time, when we was desperate for members, you told Georgie that the Teamsters would take anybody whose job had anything to do with wheels?"

Hoffa beamed. "Told him that watches had wheels and that made it okay to sign up anybody wearing a watch."

"And that fucker came back with applications from accountants and waiters and nurses and grocery clerks and bag boys and—"

"Don't forget the embalmers." Hoffa chortled. "That was my favorite. The embalmers."

"Oh, yeah." Ciaro laughed. "Georgie claimed they qualified because they had those little carts that they carry stiffs on. Said those carts had wheels and they drove 'em, so that qualified them to be Teamsters."

"Well," Hoffa said, "don't make fun of it. The movement's been our life. If it hadn't been for the Teamsters, no telling what we would've been. I never would've met a lot of great people."

"Like Billy Flynn?" Ciaro said, inexplicably overwhelmed with memories of the Irishman lying in the hospital bed at St. Mary's after the explosion at the Idle Hour Laundry.

"Flynn was one." Hoffa nodded. "Dan Tobin was another. And you."

"Oh, yeah," Ciaro snorted. "Me! Shit, you remember how you met me? Remember that night on old Twenty-four?"

"I remember . . ."

"How you all but hijacked me and my rig."

"I remember."

"And then at Kreger's—" Ciaro paused, his voice taking on a keener edge. "Shit, Jim, you cost me my job. Remember that? My fucking *job!*"

Hoffa stared at him. "You ain't never going to forgive me for that, are you?"

"Oh, I forgive you," Ciaro said more softly. "Working for you has been a hell of a lot better than driving a fucking truck. I just like to remind you of it every now and then."

"Don't blame me," Hoffa said. "It was your fault, you dumb fucking dago. You never should've let a stranger in your cab."

"Uh-huh."

"Don't know why you had so much trouble learning that. It's fucking basic. Don't *never* let *nobody* in your cab," Hoffa lectured. "Not in your *cab*, not in your *house*, not in your *heart*, Not *nowhere*. Not nobody nowhere unless he's a friend to labor."

"Ain't that the truth," Ciaro agreed, regretting that he had steered the conversation in this direction.

"But if he *is* that friend to labor—"

Ciaro dragged his index finger across his brow, flicking the sweat off onto the floor of the Pontiac like a wiper clearing the windshield after a downpour.

"Jesus, it's hot," he broke in, hoping to change the subject again. "I got to have some liquid. You want a cup of coffee?"

Hoffa disliked being interrupted. Even by Bobby Ciaro. And especially on an afternoon when the temperature was probably going to set a record, an unbearably hot afternoon when he was trapped in a closed-up car in a treeless parking lot waiting for a meeting that he didn't want to be a part of. Fuck the meeting, he thought. Fuck Fitz. And fuck Dally, too. But he articulated none of this. Instead he clamped his jaws shut to stop himself from saying something he might regret later, even to Bobby. Lifting his arm, feeling a new river of sweat run down his side as he did so, he looked at his watch. "Shit!" he cursed. "Where *is* that cocksucker?"

"I didn't hear you on the coffee?" Ciaro said, ignoring the outburst. "You want some?"

Hoffa shook his head. By making an effort, he picked up his earlier train of thought. And he repeated, "But if he *is* that friend to labor . . ."

6
· · · · · · · · · · · ·
1 9 4 1

All things considered, Hoffa told himself as he sat in his Ford in the dark, waiting for the right time to make an entrance, I'm getting pretty fucking sick of Kreger's.

From where he sat, he could easily see the pickets a half block away, marching resolutely outside the company's main gate. Back and forth . . . back and forth . . . half in the shadows of the flickering torches they had attached to poles and stuck in the ground in front of the wire fence. The men themselves were mainly silent, marching soundlessly while a man standing on top of a nearby truck urged them on.

". . . but if he *is* a friend to labor," the speaker was saying through a megaphone, "*he is the only friend you got,* and you best listen to that man. If he's got the scars on his knuckles . . . if he's got the muscles in his arms . . . if he's been out on the road like you and me . . ."

Hoffa sighed. Time to go to work, he thought. Tapping a dozing Bobby Ciaro on the shoulder, he motioned him to rouse himself and follow him.

Without speaking, they climbed out of the car and began walking toward the group of picketers. Their route took them down a line of trucks that were queued up waiting to get through the gate.

Hoffa could still hear the speaker, but not as clearly now that the trucks were between them. The man was still extolling his version of the benefits of the labor movement.

"Yeah, yeah, yeah," Hoffa mumbled as he listened, "so much bullshit. He knows the words, but he don't know the music."

"What's that?" Ciaro asked.

"Nothing, Bobby. I was just talking to myself."

Stopping abruptly, Hoffa leaped onto the running board of the closest truck and stuck his face six inches from that of the driver.

"Why don't you pull it over, pally," he said affably. "Why don't you team up with some people who are going to stand with you. Because to these Kreger people, you're a part of the truck."

"That's right, pal," added Ciaro, who had joined Hoffa. "You're just part of the truck. You're the nut behind the wheel."

"They find some way to replace you cheaper," Hoffa began, "and you—"

Hoffa halted. The driver had produced a pistol from under the seat and was now pointing the weapon directly between his eyes.

"Get the fuck down off my cab," the driver said coldly.

Without a word, Hoffa and Ciaro jumped down and resumed their trek toward the head of the line. As they got closer to the gate Hoffa could hear the speaker more clearly.

". . . that the race of labor, as the race of Israel of old, is saddened, and our women mourn, we . . ."

Hoffa quit listening to study the approach of

Frank Fitzsimmons, a new organizer for Local 299. A pudgy, soft-looking man a couple of years older than himself, Fitzsimmons had come into the organization on the recommendation of Dan Tobin. Hoffa wasn't sure yet about Fitzsimmons, but he knew better than to ignore a suggestion from the Teamsters' international president. Politics was politics.

"They ought to shoot that motherfucker," Hoffa said to Ciaro and Fitzsimmons, referring to the man with the megaphone. "Let him organize the dead."

Fitzsimmons grinned nervously, not sure how to react.

As Hoffa spoke the line of trucks started to inch forward, passing through the picket line and into the Kreger compound. Looking closely, Hoffa could see that a path had been opened by a large group of men armed with pistols, rifles, and shotguns.

"Where the fuck did *they* come from?" Fitzsimmons asked.

Ciaro shrugged. "Hired by Kreger's," he said. "It ain't a big fucking deal. They do it all the time."

"You mean they have their own fucking *army?*"

"Don't you read the fucking papers?" Hoffa asked him sarcastically. "Don't you know all the companies do it? Don't you remember the UAW strike in Flint, where company goons beat the shit out of the pickets, sending fourteen of them to the hospital?"

"Or how about what happened in south Chicago?" Ciaro chimed in. "The steel-company owners equipped their goons with thirty-caliber machine guns, which they proceeded to use against unarmed demonstrators. They killed eighteen people that time, including a crippled World War One veteran who was attacked by strikebreakers because he was selling tickets to a union fund-raising dance."

"No shit!" exclaimed Fitzsimmons. "I had no idea."

Hoffa rolled his eyes. But instead of pursuing the

issue with his new organizer, he shouted at a small contingent of armed men who were riding on the running board of a passing truck.

"Get down off that truck, you fucking stooges. You scabs!" Putting as much disgust in his voice as he could muster, he asked rhetorically, "What is lower than a scab?"

The men stared at him impassively. It was nothing personal; they were there to do a job, and if Hoffa tried to interfere, he would be required to pay the price. Hoffa knew the rules. He did not make a move. But that did not mean he could not operate his mouth.

"Nothing!" Hoffa screamed at the men. "There's *nothing* that's lower than a fucking scab. Where is your self-respect?"

"They don't have any self-respect," Ciaro joined in, enjoying the game. "You got to be human to have self-respect. And these fucking goons ain't human. They're just fucking slime."

He grinned. They did not grin back.

Stepping boldly in front of a truck whose driver was shifting gears, Hoffa held up his hand like a policeman and defied the driver to run him down. The man slammed on his brakes, stopping just inches short of Hoffa, who, the best that Ciaro could tell, was trying to imitate a fire hydrant.

"They're going to screw you, pal," Hoffa yelled at the driver. "You think they're going to be loyal to you because you crossed this line? You know what you are to them? The same as you are to us. You're nothing but a fucking scab. A scab and a traitor."

The driver put his truck back into gear, gunned the engine, and released the clutch, sending the vehicle forward.

Ciaro, shocked to see that Hoffa gave no indication he was going to move, reached out a thick arm and dragged him out of the truck's path just in time.

"That cocksucker would've run you down," Ciaro screamed. "You got to watch these guys. They ain't got nothing to lose except their jobs."

"Fuck them," Hoffa shouted back. "They're fucking scabs."

Ciaro and Hoffa were so caught up in the action that they failed to see two men approach silently to their rear. The men, dressed somberly in dark suits, white shirts, and ties, were clearly neither picketers nor part of the Kreger goon squad. Saying nothing, they slipped into the shadows, their backs to a parked truck. Folding their arms across their chests, they watched.

"We're blowing this fucking strike," Hoffa said to Ciaro. "I got to make some converts or my family don't eat this week. Where's the justice in this?"

As he spoke several police cars, sirens wailing, screeched to a halt at the head of the line. As if their arrival were a signal, the tailgates of several of the waiting trucks dropped open and men carrying base-ball bats, pieces of lumber, and sections of pipe jumped to the ground.

"Oh, hell," Hoffa exclaimed to Ciaro. "Now we're going to get into another fucking brawl. If we could keep you son-of-a-bitching dagos off our backs, we might be able to get somewhere."

Pointing at the man with the megaphone, who was still on his truck-top perch and still screaming, Hoffa said, "That son-of-a-bitch is running this strike all wrong. If it was up to me—"

"Holy shit," interjected Fitzsimmons, who had paled noticeably at the sight of the men pouring out of the trucks. "This could get fucking serious."

Ciaro glanced at Fitzsimmons. He looks like he's going to vomit, he thought. Either that or shit his pants.

"See you guys later," Fitzsimmons said, moving quickly away from the line of approaching goons. "Keep your heads down."

Ignoring Fitzsimmons, Ciaro turned his attention toward the man with the megaphone.

". . . but in our sadness," he was saying, "there is one thing. There is a seed and it is the seed of unity."

Hoffa, repelled by the man's oratory, shook his head in loathing. "Why don't he fucking learn how to handle a situation like this?" he asked Ciaro plaintively.

Ciaro shrugged. "Just some bureaucrat who don't know shit from shinola," he said.

"That just makes it harder for us," Hoffa said, striding toward one of the trucks. "Let's see if we can't rescue this fucking disaster."

When he moved, the two men who had been watching from the shadows moved with him, inching closer, but still staying in the background.

Catching the movement out of the corner of his eye, Hoffa noticed the pair for the first time. Inspecting them quickly, he judged that they were no immediate threat and whatever they wanted could wait. What was of greater concern was the imminent collapse of the demonstration. In an effort to prevent that, he jumped on the running board of the closest truck.

"We're with the Teamsters, friend. We're with you."

The driver quickly rolled up his window and goosed his truck forward, shaking Hoffa off his perch.

As the vehicle pulled forward Hoffa opened the toolbox and extracted a long piece of metal, a crowbar that was part of a trucker's standard equipment. Weighing the bar for balance, he nodded in satisfaction. Unobtrusively he slipped it under his arm, close to his body. Then he turned to meet the two men who had been watching him.

The men advanced slowly on Hoffa, who backed carefully away, stepping into the mouth of a nearby alley. So far, not a word had been spoken.

Hoffa raised the crowbar.

The two men paused and reached into their pockets. They drew pistols, which they leveled at Hoffa.

It took Ciaro, who had not seen the confrontation, several minutes to realize that Hoffa was no longer at his side.

"Jimmy!" he called. "Where you at?"

"Over here," Hoffa answered softly, keeping the crowbar over his head and his eyes on the two men. "But watch yourself. We got company."

Ciaro, following the sound of Hoffa's voice, hurried to the alley. When he saw the two men, he pulled up short.

"What the fuck!" he exclaimed, spotting the pistols.

The men glanced quickly at Ciaro, then turned their attention back to Hoffa, keeping their weapons pointed at his chest.

Ciaro, realizing an attack was not impending, barked at them. "Who are you? he demanded. "What do you want?"

The men did not answer.

"I think they want me, Bobby," Hoffa said calmly. "But I haven't the faintest fucking idea why."

"What is this?" Ciaro asked, walking slowly toward the two men.

One of them swiveled and pointed his pistol at Ciaro. In Italian, he told him to stop and come no closer.

Ciaro's jaw dropped open in surprise. "Oh," he said softly, "so that's what this is all about."

"La sua presnza e richiesta," said the man who had his pistol pointed at Ciaro.

"He says," Ciaro translated, turning toward Hoffa, "that some people want to see you."

Hoffa relaxed and lowered the crowbar. He studied the men for several seconds, then turned toward Ciaro.

"Well, what the fuck are we waiting for?" he asked, tossing the crowbar on the ground. It made a hollow ringing noise that was drowned out in the clamor at the Kreger gate.

"Follow us," one of the men commanded.

As directed, Hoffa and Ciaro climbed into the Ford and followed the two men, who had retrieved their black Cadillac from a nearby side street. Slowly, in order not to attract police attention, the two-car caravan wound its way deep into Detroit's Little Italy. The Caddy pulled to the curb across the street from a restaurant called Trattoria Antonio. Hoffa swung in behind it.

When the men made no effort to leave their car, Hoffa and Ciaro climbed out of the Ford and walked in their direction.

"Is that where we're going?" Hoffa asked, nodding to the restaurant, which was empty except for two young couples sitting at widely separated tables.

"I don't know," Ciaro replied. "But I think we're going to find out."

After a short exchange in rapid Italian, Ciaro pointed to the building next door to the restaurant. "That's where he says to go," he said, gesturing toward a plain-looking storefront distinguished only by a large glass window across the narrow front. Gold lettering on the window read THE PALERMO CLUB and, underneath, in smaller letters, MEMBERS ONLY. From the street they could see through the window that the main room was dark and empty.

"No one's home," Hoffa muttered.

"They're there," Ciaro assured him. "Otherwise we wouldn't have been brought here. There must be a private room in the back." He turned to the man behind the wheel of the Caddy. Without speaking, the man waved at the building and nodded, indicating they should go inside.

"Just remember one thing," Ciaro whispered to Hoffa as they crossed the street, "don't lose your temper. No matter what they say, keep calm. Don't let 'em get under your skin. Okay?"

"Get under my skin about what?" Hoffa asked, perplexed.

"I ain't sure," Ciaro said, keeping his suspicions to himself. "But we're going to find out soon enough."

Hoffa was surprised that the door to the club was unlocked, and even more surprised to find that the room they entered was so sparsely decorated. It contained three card tables, each with four chairs, and a battered couch that leaned tiredly against one wall. Except for an ashtray on a stand sitting next to the couch, there was no other furniture.

Ciaro glanced around, then motioned for Hoffa to follow him across the room and down a short hallway dimly lit by a weak bulb in an overhead fixture. At the end of the passageway was a partly open door. Through the crack they could see a bright light. Ciaro strode briskly down the hallway, his heels clicking sharply on the bare plank flooring. Hoffa, determined not to be intimidated, followed at his own quick pace, practically stepping on Ciaro's heels. Neither man felt the need to speak.

When they got to the end of the hall, Ciaro rapped twice on the door, pushed it open, and stepped inside. Hoffa was a half step behind him.

Blinking in the light, Hoffa saw that there was a dining table in the center of the room, covered with a starched white cloth. There was no evidence of food, however, only coffee. Three men were seated around the table, each with a small espresso cup in front of him. The men looked up when Ciaro and Hoffa entered, but made no effort to rise. By way of greeting, they simply stared.

At the head of the table was a frail-looking man in his late fifties. His hair and skin were so dark that Hoffa at first thought he was a black man, but then he noticed that his features were European rather than negroid. Looking closer, he could see that the man's mustache and hair were streaked with gray and there were deep wrinkles at the corners of his eyes, which, in the overhead light, looked black. On his right was another man, somewhat younger but still middle-aged. He was not as dark as the man sitting at the head of the table and his hair had less gray. On the old man's left was a much younger man, someone close to Hoffa's age, who was as fair as the old man was dark. The younger man sported a small, neatly trimmed mustache and was dressed stylishly, if somewhat ostentatiously, in a dark brown pin-striped suit and a maroon tie with a small pattern that Hoffa could not make out. All three were smoking Lucky Strikes from a pack sitting on the table. Two husky men and a frail youth dressed as a waiter hovered in the background.

"Signore Scialla," Ciaro said, recognizing the man immediately. "I'm Bobby Ciaro and this is Jimmy Hoffa."

The old man, nodded slightly, but made no attempt to shake hands.

"Jimmy," Ciaro continued, quickly recognizing the others, "this is Signore Antonio Balluchio," nodding at the man on Scialla's right, and "Signore Carol D'Allesandro."

The man on Hoffa's left, D'Allesandro, the one

closer to Hoffa's age, smiled brightly, the only one to signal a welcome. Instead of offering his hand, he nodded slightly. "Hi," he said easily in unaccented English, "glad you could make it. I've heard about you."

Hoffa nodded, quickly assessing the situation. He knew from what he had heard on the street that Scialla ran a manpower rental service, hiring out lower-level members of his organization to large companies, particularly automobile manufacturers, as strikebreakers. He did a lot of business with Ford, Hoffa had heard. And he had undoubtedly supplied the men who were in the trucks at that evening's demonstration at Kreger's.

Smiling to himself, Hoffa noted the irony of a dedicated union man like himself, a man who had led more strikes than he could count, being summoned—commanded was probably a better word—for a meeting with a man who rented out strikebreakers.

"Sit!" Ciaro told Hoffa, pointing to the empty seat at the other end of the table. "Mr. Scialla wants to talk to you."

Hoffa plopped into the straight-backed chair and leaned forward, placing his hands palm down on the table in front of him.

"So?" he said, drumming his fingers on the tabletop. "You brought me here. What do you want?"

Scialla focused on Hoffa's nervous fingers. *"Di che ha paura?"* he asked.

Ciaro glanced quickly at Hoffa. "He wants to know what you're afraid of," Ciaro translated. "Why you're so nervous."

Hoffa's eyes widened and his fingers stilled. "Tell him it's none of his fucking business," he responded, speaking slowly and carefully. Ciaro gave him a sharp look. "Tell him!" Hoffa insisted. "Tell him what I just said."

Ciaro, shrugging, turned to Scialla. "*Ha detto di dire,*" he said, "*non sono cazzi suoi.*"

Scialla waved his hand angrily. He understood.

"He's not real happy about dealing with you—" Ciaro began before being interrupted by Scialla.

"*Voglio fargli sapere il sequente: che lui sta costando i soldi ai miei aici, che gli sta costando il lavoro, che lui sta fottendo tutta la mia operazione!*"

"He says," Ciaro said evenly, "that you are costing his friends money, that you are costing them jobs—that you cost me my job—that you are pissing on his fucking operation."

Hoffa opened his mouth to reply when Scialla snapped, "*Zitto!*"

Hoffa did not have to speak Italian to know it meant "shut up." He closed his mouth and waited for Scialla to continue.

Scialla spoke rapidly, running his words together, and Ciaro had to rush to keep up with his translation. "He says," Ciaro said, talking over Scialla, "why should he not take you out in the alley and beat you until you beg for death? That is the question, when you fuck with the livelihood of himself, and of the people under his protection. For that matter, why should he not take you out and kill you?"

Hoffa stared fixedly at the old man and said, more to Ciaro than to Scialla, "What the fuck is it with him? I've never done anything to him."

"That don't matter," Ciaro broke in. "You represent labor and his people represent management. He don't make no fine distinctions about personalities."

"*Zitto!*" Scialla repeated, glaring at Ciaro. "*Non ha paura Lei?*"

"He wants to know why you ain't afraid."

"Tell him if I am . . ." Hoffa said, staring at Scialla, "that if I am, it's none of his fucking business."

"*Se fosse nel psoto mio, che cosa farebbe Lei?*" Scialla

said when he heard the translation. It sounded more conciliatory than belligerent.

"He wants to know," Ciaro translated, "what would *you* do if you were in his place?"

Hoffa paused. That's a reasonable question, he thought, put in a reasonable tone of voice. Sensing that the moment of highest tension had passed, that he wasn't going to be killed or taken into the alley and beaten senseless, that the old man had been bluffing to try to scare him, Hoffa relaxed, slumping slightly in his chair.

"Tell him," he said in a conversational tone, "that if he gives me a cup of coffee, I'll answer his question."

When Ciaro translated, the old man responded with the barest hint of a smile. Turning to the boy dressed like a waiter, Scialla ordered refreshment for his guests.

7
· · · · · · · · · · · ·
1 9 4 1

Walking up to Local 299's new headquarters on Trumbull Avenue, near Tiger Stadium, Hoffa could hear the president, Ron Mahoney, as he struggled to bring order to the chaos that reigned within the building.

". . . and the end of the strike," Mahoney was saying, "and I want to emphasize that the *successful end* of the strike at Kreger's is why we're here celebrating tonight."

His words were met by a cacophony of yells, whistles, catcalls, and foot stomping.

As Hoffa walked through the door Mahoney was waving his arms and trying to be heard over the roar. "Can I have your attention for a minute?" he said, but his words were drowned out. "Please!" he said louder. When that failed to reduce the noise, he screamed, "Goddammit, shut up! I need your attention for a minute. Just one damn minute then you can tap another keg."

Hoffa joined Ciaro and Fitzsimmons, who were leaning against the wall on Mahoney's left.

• • •

"Sounds like he's having a little trouble." Hoffa chuckled.

Both Ciaro and Fitzsimmons had mugs in their hands, filled with beer. "You want a beer?" Ciaro asked, slurring his words slightly.

Hoffa stared at him. "You know I don't drink, Bobby."

"But this is a special—"

"There ain't no special occasions for me as far as drinking goes," Hoffa said tartly. "I ain't a fucking Puritan. I don't care if you drink, as long as you're sober when I need you. I just don't like it. It ain't for me."

In response to Mahoney's repeated pleas for quiet, the noise in the room subsided to the point where Mahoney felt he could at least be heard.

"As I was trying to say," he bellowed, "the end of the strike at Kreger's is due to one thing, and one thing alone: the efforts of one man. A man who went out there . . . went out there in the cold . . . who was out there day and night speaking the word, spreading the word, and the word was *Teamsters,* and the word was *unity.* And it overcame the scabs, it overcame the company, it won the day, and it won us our contract."

Hoffa turned to Ciaro. "Jesus," he said, "how much has *he* been drinking?"

Ciaro smiled. "You really want to know?"

"No."

"And here is the man," Mahoney thundered, "who led us through the fight. Here is the man who beat Kreger, the man who broke them down and took us in. Our new business manager, Red Bennett!"

A man with an ear-to-ear smile and an oversized mug of beer clutched in his fist, climbed unsteadily onto the stage.

Hoffa stared at him. "Holy Jumping Jesus," he breathed. "That's the asshole who was on top of the truck last night. That dick with the megaphone."

Ciaro grinned cynically. "Told you before, Jimmy, there's no end to some people's stupidity."

It was Bennett's turn to try to establish order. As Mahoney had done, he tried waving his arms, but the effort tossed him off balance, and if Mahoney had not been there to grab him, the new business manager would have fallen off the platform. Regaining his footing, he extended both his arms over his head and clasped his hands together, like a heavyweight who has just won the world title.

"My friends," he began.

Hoffa decided he had enough. Buttoning his coat, he started walking toward the door.

"Where you going, Jimmy?" Ciaro asked.

Hoffa shrugged. "Out of here. I need some air. The bullshit is up to my chin and rising."

"I'll go with you," Ciaro said, slipping into his coat.

"Me too," said Fitzsimmons, who, Hoffa could see, was farther gone than Ciaro.

Falling in behind Fitzsimmons was a young man Hoffa had never seen before.

"If you hadn't gotten the wops to back off," Fitzsimmons said to Hoffa once they were outside, "we never would've won the strike."

"That's right," Hoffa said brusquely.

Fitzsimmons motioned to the young man, who had been standing several feet away watching the three of them. "C'mere, Petey," he said, motioning the youth forward.

"Jimmy," Fitzsimmons said, "I want you to meet my nephew, Pete Connelly. Petey, this is the great Jimmy Hoffa."

"Hi," Hoffa said, extending his hand. "Glad to meet you."

Connelly grimaced when Hoffa gave him his killer handshake, honed by his weightlifting program. "Hi, Mr. H-h-offa," he stammered. "This is a real pleasure. I mean a real f-f-fucking pleasure."

"That's okay, kid," Hoffa said, "no need to overdo it."

The youth, a skinny eighteen-year-old decked out in a suit that was ten years too old for him, blushed and stared at the ground.

"I'm s-sorry," he said, "I d-din't mean nothing."

"I know you didn't, kid," Hoffa said. "Don't worry about it."

"Hey, Petey," said Fitzsimmons, trying to recover. "Tell Jimmy you was glad to meet him and go get another beer."

"I was," Connelly said. "I mean, I am. Glad to meet you, that is."

"Come by one day next week," Hoffa said, sorry that he had been abrupt. "We'll go get a cup of coffee or something."

Connelly smiled. "S-s-sure," he said. "I'd like that. See you later, Uncle Frank," he said, turning to Fitzsimmons.

"Yeah, Petey," said Fitzsimmons. "Go have a good time. But don't drink too much. Don't be like your old uncle." Turning to Hoffa, he slapped him on the back, bringing a frown to Hoffa's face. "Jimmy. . ." he began.

"Yeah," Hoffa replied, "I'm terrific, ain't I? Real fucking terrific."

"Jimmy," Fitzsimmons said, slowly shaking his head. "I got a lot to learn from you."

Hoffa smiled. "That's true," he agreed.

Delighted that the tension had passed, Fitzsimmons grinned back. "How'd you do it, Jimmy?"

"You don't want to know," Hoffa said, turning serious.

"Yes, I do," Fitzsimmons replied. "That's why I asked."

Hoffa looked at him. "I see," he said slowly.

"I want to know. I really do."

Hoffa waved his arm in the air, as if he were swatting flies. "Nah," he said. "You're drunk. If I tell you, you'll want to show off. You'll tell your nephew and anybody else who'll listen. Then tomorrow morning I'll be in deep shit."

"No," Fitzsimmons insisted. "I really want to know. I want to put it together. I want to be the guy who—"

"I'm sure that you do, Fitz," Hoffa said, interrupting him, "so I'm going to give you a piece of advice. Don't ask for something that's going to be a burden if you get it. Something like information, like 'what a guy did.'"

He paused, studying Fitzsimmons to see if he was understanding what he was saying or if he was too drunk. Deciding he was getting through, he continued. "You want to know what I did? Okay, I'll tell you. I went to the wops. I told them, 'Don't drive Kreger trucks. Don't provide scab labor. Help the Teamsters.' And the chief wop, a guy named Scialla, said, 'Why should I?' And I said, 'Let the Teamsters drive the Kreger trucks. Half of the trucks we drive, we take them to a warehouse of your choosing and you steal the contents.'" Again he paused.

"What do you think about *that*, Fitz? Does that *shock* you? Or does it *delight* you?"

Fitzsimmons grinned drunkenly and clapped Hoffa on the back. "Jimmy . . ."

"So there it is, Fitz. There's a negotiating tactic you can use next time you get jammed up."

"Jimmy," Fitzsimmons said, as much to himself as to Hoffa, "you're one fucking guy." Louder, he added, "Me. I'm going to go out. Get drunk . . ." He giggled. "Get drunker, that is. And then I'm going to get laid."

"I don't blame you," Hoffa said. "It's a great victory, a famous victory."

"Want to come with me?" Fitzsimmons asked hopefully.

Hoffa smiled. "Nah," he said. "I got some things I got to do. You go get laid. Have a good time."

"Okay, Jimmy. Okay. Maybe next time."

"Maybe next time," Hoffa said, starting down the street.

Ciaro, who had been talking to another Teamster a few feet away, noticed Hoffa leaving and jogged to catch up.

"What did you tell him?" he asked when they were a half block away.

Hoffa thought carefully before he answered. "Here's the thing," he said slowly, picking his words guardedly. "A guy's close to you, you can't slight him. You can't slight that guy because of the position he's in. A real grievance can be resolved. Differences can be resolved. But an imaginary hurt? A slight? You do that and the motherfucker is going to hate you until the day he dies. Should I have told him?" He shrugged elaborately. "Six to five and pick 'em . . ."

Ciaro was not sure how to respond to that, so he said nothing.

A block later they walked by a newsstand. A boy about ten hung over a fire in a trash can, trying to keep warm.

"Want to buy a paper, mister?" he asked expectantly.

"I used to do that," Hoffa said to Ciaro. "I used to stand out on a street corner peddling papers.

Froze my ass off in the winter and baked in the summer. But it was good discipline. Taught me that a man's got to work if he's going to make his way. There ain't nothing wrong with work, just like there ain't nothing wrong with getting paid for your work, too. This kid ought to be home studying. He's probably got school tomorrow. Instead he's standing out here on the cold fucking street trying to make a few pennies."

"Mister, you want a paper or not?" the boy asked.

Hoffa laughed. "Just like I was," he told Ciaro. "A smart-ass kid." Digging in his pocket, he came up with a nickel, which he handed to the boy. "Give me a *Tribune*," he said, "and keep the change."

The boy looked at the nickel. "Last of the big spenders, huh?"

Hoffa laughed again. "Work for it, kid. If you don't work for it, it ain't worth it. When you get old enough to drive, come see me. I'll make you a Teamster."

"I'll probably starve to death before then," the boy replied, "if I don't make more than this."

"Then get another job," Hoffa said. "Go to Kreger's. They need some help to replace some scabs."

Walking away, he unfolded the paper and glanced at the headlines. "Look at this, Bobby," he exclaimed. "We made the fucking papers."

Across the top of the pro-union publication, running the full eight columns, was the headline: KREGER GIVES IN TO TEAMSTERS; STRIKE ENDS IN UNION VICTORY.

Ciaro, glancing over Hoffa's shoulder, tried to grab the paper away. "What's it say, Jimmy? What's it say?" he asked excitedly.

Hoffa slapped his hand away. "Just a fucking minute," he said good-naturedly, "I'll read it. Let's get some light."

Walking hurriedly, the two all but sprinted to a nearby street lamp. Unfolding the paper, Hoffa, with Ciaro peering over his shoulder, looked again at the front page.

By Andrew O'Leary

Determined members of Local 299 of the International Brotherhood of Teamsters, who have been fighting an on-again off-again battle with the Kreger Grocery & Baking Company for most of this year, won a decisive victory yesterday when Kreger's capitulated to the strikers' demands and agreed to negotiate its first contract with the union.

The victory came when a large group of men, who had been hired by Kreger's to keep its supply lines open, unexpectedly evaporated, leaving the company with no choice but to negotiate.

"We don't know who those guys were or where they went," Local President Ronald Mahoney told the *Tribune,* "but we sure as h- - - wasn't sorry to see them leave. Their departure made our victory possible."

Terms of the contract are still to be negotiated, but they are expected to be favorable to the union, which is asking for a substantial raise for its drivers as well as a laundry list of other benefits.

The victory was especially sweet for the Teamsters, who, less than eight years ago, were on the verge of collapse in Detroit.

In the last few years, however, Teamsters membership in the Motor City has risen steadily and the union is now one of the city's largest and strongest after the United Auto Workers.

Mahoney praised the leadership of his men, especially that of Clarence "Red" Bennett, and the tenacity of the strikers. "They are the real heroes of the whole thing," he said.

Not mentioned by Mahoney was the role played by one of his most aggressive organizers, James R. "Jimmy" Hoffa, who has been on the front line of the Teamsters' effort ever since he left Kreger's six years ago to go to work for the IBT.

While he still worked at Kreger's, Hoffa was instrumental in securing a labor contract between the company and the men who manned the loading docks.

"Sure, Mr. Hoffa played a role in this," Mahoney said, "but so did everybody in the local. It was a real group victory." (continued on page 14)

Eagerly Hoffa flipped to the back of the paper. "Ah," he said, reading it quickly, "the rest of the story is just the usual bullshit."

"Well, that's enough," Ciaro commented.

"Yeah," Hoffa sighed. "Ain't that something?"

"You're fucking A," said Ciaro. "You did good."

"What's that up there?" Hoffa said five minutes later. "Looks like somebody's in trouble."

Fifty yards ahead of them a van was pulled over to the curb and the driver was kneeling in front of the vehicle, trying to align a jack with the axle.

"Got a problem, buddy?" Hoffa asked when he and Ciaro reached the vehicle.

The driver, slightly out of breath from working the jack, looked up in mild surprise. "Nah," he said. "Just a fucking flat. Happens all the time."

"How about we give you a hand," Hoffa said, stripping off his overcoat and suit coat and rolling up his sleeves.

"You ain't afraid to get your hands dirty?" the man

asked skeptically.

"No," Hoffa replied, "I ain't afraid to get my hands dirty. I ain't afraid to get them bloody either, baby. I ain't afraid of any motherfucking thing. You know why?"

"No, I don't know why," the driver said. "Tell me."

"Because I'm part of a brotherhood," Hoffa said. "My name is Jimmy Hoffa and I'm with Local 299 of the International Brotherhood of Teamsters."

He looked at the flat and at the jack. "Pal," he said to the driver, "see if you can find me something to chock this wheel with, just to make sure the fucker don't roll or nothing."

"I been thinking, Jimmy," Ciaro said after the driver had wandered off to search for a rock or a piece of lumber.

"That's good," Hoffa puffed, putting pressure on the tire iron to loosen the nuts. "It don't hurt a bit to think."

"I been wondering, Jimmy, what kind of money you make organizing."

Hoffa stopped and looked at him. "Ten bucks each new member," he snapped. "Plus ten percent of the first year's dues."

"That's what you make?" Ciaro said in surprise.

Hoffa grinned at him. "No," he said. "What I make is none of your fucking business. That's what I'm going to pay you if you come to work for me."

The driver returned with a broken brick, a piece large enough to slip under the wheel.

"Thanks," Hoffa said, accepting the brick. "Now I want you to listen to something."

"I'll listen to any man who ain't afraid to get his hands dirty," the truck driver told Hoffa. Turning to Ciaro, he added, "That's the first man I ever seen who was willing to take off a suit jacket to help a trucker change a tire."

"Someday," Ciaro said, beaming proudly at Hoffa, "this man's going to be president of the United States."

Hoffa looked up. "Fuck that," he said. "Someday I'm going to be president, all right, but it's going to be president of the fucking Teamsters."

8
1 9 7 5

"I got to have something to drink, Jimmy," Ciaro said, "My mouth's drier than a whore's pussy."

Hoffa stared out the windshield, drumming his thick fingers against the dash. At first Ciaro worried that Hoffa had not heard him, that the air conditioner had drowned him out.

"Jimmy," he began.

"I heard you, Bobby," Hoffa said, his voice betraying his tension. "I'm just weighing my options here. Where the fuck is Dally?"

Ciaro shrugged. As far as he was concerned, that was one of those stupid questions that had no answer, like the nuns used to ask when he was a kid in school about how many angels could dance on the head of a pin. At eight years old, his answer had been, "How the fuck should I know?" which earned him a backhand across the mouth.

"We been here how long now?" Hoffa asked rhetorically, glancing at his watch. "Forty-five minutes! That cocksucker's kept us sitting in a parked car on the hottest day of the year for forty-five minutes. One of these days he's going to pay for that. I don't know how or when, but he's going to pay, that prick."

Since there seemed to be nothing else to say, they sat in silence.

"Tell you what we're going to do," Hoffa finally said.

Ciaro, who had been sitting draped across the steering wheel, his arms raised so the air conditioner could blow unimpeded across his thick torso, raised his head. "Yo, boss."

"You armed?" Hoffa asked unexpectedly. "You packing?"

The question surprised Ciaro. It was one he thought Hoffa did not have to ask. "Always, Jimmy," he said. "Always."

"Don't lighten up on me now," Hoffa said warningly.

"Oh, no, Jimmy. I ain't—"

"I'm *serious*, Bobby."

"So am I, Jimmy. I ain't kidding you. You know me better than that. You don't think I got to be this old by not taking precautions."

"You got a piece stashed in the diner, too?" Hoffa asked.

Ciaro nodded.

"Can you get to it?"

Ciaro nodded again.

Hoffa pondered that information for what seemed like a long time. Finally he said, "You want to go check it?"

"If that's what you want, I'll go check it. But it's there. Take my word for it. *I know it's there.*"

Hoffa looked at him. "And you don't think *I* got to be this old by not being careful? I want you to go check it."

Ciaro straightened up and reached for the door handle.

"Where the fuck is D'Allesandro?" Hoffa asked.

"I don't know, Jimmy," Ciaro said tiredly, thinking he was getting awful damn sick of being asked that question, considering he couldn't possibly answer it.

"I want you to call him up."

Ciaro, who had been about to open the door, stopped. "If that's what you want, Jimmy, but I can tell you right now he ain't going to be in. At least that's what his gofers are going to tell me."

"Call him up anyways," Hoffa insisted. "He ain't here either, so where the hell is he? What the fuck? I'm sitting here waiting for him for forty-five minutes. It's supposed to be a simple meeting. Instead I'm sitting here sweating more than I would be in a steambath at the Detroit Club and I'm worrying about whether you can get your hands on a fucking pistol."

"Shotgun," Ciaro interjected, correcting him.

"Okay, okay. A fucking shotgun then," Hoffa growled. "All this shit for just a simple meeting, a problem that could be resolved very easily if only that fucker would show up."

"I'm sorry he ain't here," Ciaro said, trying to calm Hoffa, who was getting increasingly upset.

"You fucking wops," Hoffa spat, lashing out at Ciaro in an unconscious attempt to relieve his frustration. "You people!"

Ciaro remained silent, letting Hoffa have his say. When Ciaro did not respond, Hoffa said, almost apologetically, "You cocksucker. Why did you want to be born into a race like that?"

Ciaro smothered a grin. "Just bad judgment, I guess."

Hoffa, calmer, smiled slightly. "You fucking A well told. Tell you what. You go to the diner. Sit lookout. See what's going on in there. In the meantime you call him. If you can get him, tell the motherfucker I'm not going to sit here all day. Tell him he'd better get his ass down here, because if he don't, we're leaving."

Ciaro nodded. "Okay, Jimmy," he said, reaching again for the door handle. "I'll call him."

"Wait a minute," Hoffa said, putting a hand on Ciaro's shoulder.

Ciaro, who had been about to step out of the car, turned to look at him. He raised his eyebrows.

"Let me have your pistol."

Ciaro stopped short. Hoffa had never made a request like that before. He had always disdained weapons, at least as far as he personally was concerned. Not because he was repelled by the thought of possible violence; he just didn't think much of firearms. Hoffa was a street fighter, a man who was proud of his prowess with his fists. He had grown up in an era when disagreements were settled without resorting to pistols and shotguns. And he had not changed with the times.

"Why you want it?" Ciaro asked in surprise. "You don't even know how to use it."

"I'm a quick learner," Hoffa said. "Give me your gun."

Ciaro hesitated. Not only because he didn't think Hoffa could use it, but because a pistol was part of *him*, had been as much a part of his everyday attire as a pair of trousers ever since he had met Billy Flynn. "You want me to go *naked*?" he asked in disbelief.

Hoffa nodded, realizing what he was asking of his old friend. "Leave me the piece," he commanded softly. "You go on in the diner. What you call it? The *lupara*?"

Ciaro nodded.

"You go on in the *lupara* and you check it out. Make sure you can get your hands on that shotgun in a hurry. And you try to call D'Allesandro, tell him to get his fucking ass over here. Right now. Or we're leaving. Okay?"

Ciaro nodded.

Hoffa stared at him again. "What the fuck are you so jumpy about? I ain't asking a lot. Go on," he said brusquely. "Get the fuck out of here. *Do* something for a living."

Ciaro exhaled. He knew better than to try to argue with Hoffa when he was this tense. He didn't often get that way, but when he did, Ciaro had learned that the best way to defuse the situation was to leave him alone; say as little as possible and stay out of range until the storm had passed. Standing outside the car, he bent slightly and stuck his head back inside.

"You want something while I'm there?" he asked Hoffa. "A newspaper? A cup of coffee? Anything?"

Hoffa nodded. "I'll take some coffee," he said. "But what I really want is that fucker d'Alessandro to get here so we can have our meeting and I can go home to my wife like I promised. Jo hasn't been feeling well again and I don't want to leave her for too long."

"Okay," Ciaro said. "I'll be back in 20 minutes. You know where I am."

"Go!" Hoffa ordered, waving him away.

"You try to relax," Ciaro replied. "This ain't the fucking end of the world. It's just a goddamn meeting."

Hoffa didn't reply; his attention was turned to the pistol that Ciaro had given him, an ugly, black revolver of the type he had seen on countless TV dramas. Searching for the catch he knew was there, he pushed it and the cylinder swung open, revealing the cartridges nestled inside. Hoffa examined the shells without removing them from the cylinder, then clicked it back into place. Sighing, he bent over and put the pistol on the floor of the car, half under the seat. Then he straightened and stared out the windshield again, seemingly lost in thought. In the background, he could hear Ciaro walking away, his shoes making faint squishy sounds on the heat-softened blacktop.

Ciaro opened the door and walked inside. It was like stepping into his own living room. How many truck stops have I been in in my life? he thought. How many times have I been in *this* truck stop?

The first thing that hit him was the noise, the familiar din of truckers arguing over their blue-plate specials. He could hear snatches of conversations: ". . . that blonde at the Owl Café . . . the fucking Tigers . . . that son-of-a-bitching Supreme Court . . . asshole Nixon . . . I don't give a shit what you say about . . . did you see Carson? . . . that chickenshit cop was hiding . . . and then the guy says . . ."

He glanced around the room, impressed by the size of the crowd. Although he saw several men he recognized, he did not stop to exchange greetings. Instead he walked deliberately across the room, along the counter, passing several truckers who were hunched over their meals, and went straight to the phone booth in the back. Instead of being empty as he anticipated, the booth was occupied by a young trucker, who was hunched over in earnest conversation, one finger plugged into his ear.

Ciaro cursed under his breath. Glancing at his watch, he waited outside the booth, impatiently tapping his foot.

Through the partially open door, he could hear bits of a one-sided conversation. ". . . it busted the fucking fan belt . . . I know . . . What do you think I'm doing? I'm fucking sitting on my . . . Cleveland, yeah, at four P.M. . . . I *know* I'm not going to fucking make it . . . all I'm saying . . . I *know* that . . ."

Ciaro looked at his watch again. This could take all day, he told himself. Walking closer to the booth, he tapped on the glass. When he did, the driver looked up, revealing an unexpectedly youthful face. The man, who looked to be barely in his twenties, had wide-set eyes with incredibly long lashes. They were, however, as flat and black as a newly paved stretch of highway. He had a long, thin nose that gave evidence of having been broken at least once, high, almost Indian-like cheekbones, and unexpectedly full, red lips. Surprisingly for a trucker on a long haul, he was clean shaven, and his long, pointed chin was split with a deep cleft. He's just a kid, was Ciaro's first thought. Jesus, they're getting younger every day.

Slowly, almost insolently, the youth looked Ciaro up and down. Ciaro could imagine him performing the same examination on a woman, and if he had been a female, he would have blushed. The youth raised his hand with the index finger extended, the universal signal for "I'll be through in just a minute, in the meantime don't bug me."

Swallowing his anger, Ciaro turned and walked a few feet to the counter, plopping onto an empty stool. He had no sooner seated himself than the counterman, Fat Albert, waddled over.

"What's yours?" he asked familiarly.

Ciaro gestured toward a booth in the corner. Following his gesture, Fat Albert looked in that direction. There was a middle-aged trucker sitting alone in the booth, but he had his arm slung over the partition that formed the back of the booth, talking to two other truckers in the adjoining cubicle.

Sighing, Fat Albert walked around the counter and strode over to the lone trucker. "Excuse me," he said gruffly. "Don't mean to disturb you, but can't you read the sign?" he asked, pointing toward a rectangle of cardboard sitting in a wooden holder in the middle of the table. It said RESERVED.

The trucker looked at Fat Albert, picked up the sign, and flapped it. "But there wasn't nobody here—" he began.

Fat Albert cut him off. "Sorry, pal, but that's the way it is. You're going to have to find someplace else to sit."

Grumbling, the trucker joined his friends.

"Sorry," Fat Albert said to Ciaro. "If I don't keep an eye on these assholes all the time . . ."

"Don't worry about it," Ciaro said, slipping into the booth vacated by the trucker.

"You want a menu?" Fat Albert asked.

"Nah," Ciaro said. "Just give me a couple of coffees to go. Jimmy's waiting out in the car."

"Sure thing. Coming right up. Anything else?"

"No, thanks. Except I hope that kid doesn't *camp* on the fucking phone."

Fat Albert turned slightly to see where Ciaro was pointing. The youth was still bent over the instrument, but he had opened the door a bit wider to get more air.

"Well," he said into the phone, his voice clearly audible to Ciaro, "you can get it to me, can't you? You *got* to, otherwise I can't move my fucking rig."

Ciaro glanced at his watch and moaned. Restless, he slipped out of the booth and walked back to the counter. Reclaiming the stool, he sat with his elbows on the counter and watched Fat Albert as he picked up two cardboard cups and walked toward the coffee urn.

Rising, Ciaro leaned over the counter until he could see the ledge that ran underneath, inside the serving area. Directly beneath where he was crouching was a sawed-off shotgun. Trying not to attract attention to himself, he leaned farther over the counter, took the shotgun in his hands, and pressed the release so the barrel could swing upward. Seeing that two shells were firmly in place, he nodded in satisfaction and clicked the barrel back into position. Carefully he replaced the weapon on the shelf and sat on the stool, tuning in to the young trucker's conversation.

"Would I call unless I needed it? Well, when is he going to be back? Ten? Okay, tell him I'll call him back in ten minutes." Sighing, he replaced the receiver on the hook and exited the booth.

"It's all yours," he told Ciaro. "But I need it back in five minutes."

Ciaro gave him a look that would fry bacon. "Go fuck yourself," he told the driver. "I got business to take care of, too." Dismissing the young driver, he inserted a coin into the phone and dialed.

The youth stared at the back of Ciaro's head, seemingly unsure about how to react. Ciaro let his eyes roam over the graffiti penciled onto the wall. *Want a blowjob? Call Sue 637-9092 . . . Kill the Queers . . . Acme Auto Parts 543-2214 . . . Get Out of Vietnam!* Ciaro turned his attention to a long message, that had been laboriously inscribed by not one but several people, since each line was in a different hand. *In Chicago, Go To Jody's,* someone had scrawled. *Best Pussy in Town.* Beneath that, someone else had scribbled, *Half the girls in that place have VD.* Another writer had added, *The other half have TB.* And a final line, written by a fourth trucker, said, *Fuck only the ones that cough.* Ciaro smiled, but the grin disappeared when the ringing phone was answered.

"Yeah, Sal," Ciaro said into the phone, "This is Bobby. Where's Dally? . . . Because I'm asking, that's why. You got to have a fucking explanation for everything?"

He glanced at his watch. "At *what* time?" he asked incredulously. "Well, then where is he? Okay, okay. If he checks in, give him this number: two-seven-three-four-nine-eight-five." He listened again while the man on the other end repeated it. "Yeah, that's right. And tell him we're waiting for him, but we ain't going to wait all fucking *day*. . . . Yeah, okay, so long."

Grunting, he replaced the receiver with a bang and exited the booth. As he left, the young driver started to reenter the cubicle. Ciaro put his hand on his chest.

"You can't use it, kid. Sorry."

The driver stopped, eyeing Ciaro evenly.

As he had done to him earlier, Ciaro sized up the driver, noting that he was clad in almost new Levi's that had been starched and crisp a couple of days ago, but after a few thousand miles sitting in the cab of a semi had lost their crease and were due for a run through the washing machine. Instead of a shirt, he wore an unadorned, dull gray sweatshirt from which the sleeves had been cut, revealing slim but well-muscled arms, a gymnast's arms, not a weightlifter's. A large heart was tattooed on the trucker's right biceps. It was pierced with an arrow and was surrounded by slightly faded red flowers. In the center of the heart were the initials J.L., a plus sign, and the initials M.E. On the left biceps, matching roughly in size the heart on his right arm, was the tattoo of a helicopter, a type Ciaro remembered seeing on countless TV news clips from Vietnam. He thought it was called a Huey. Under the helicopter, was a banner that contained the words AIR CAV.

Tattoos also decorated the young man's forearms. On his right was a four-inch-long multicolored Oriental dragon spitting smoke and flame. And on the left was a skull pierced by a dagger. Underneath was the legend, *U.S. Army*. So this guy was a Vietnam vet, Ciaro thought, repeating to himself that he hardly looked old enough to be out of high school.

The driver stared hostilely at Ciaro. "Who the fuck are you?" he asked softly. It wasn't an outright challenge, not the kind of question or tone of voice that really meant, "Let's go out in the alley and settle this, asshole!" but a more subtle taunt that translated, "I hear what you're saying, but unless you can back it up, you can go piss up a rope."

Cojones! Ciaro thought. He's got a good pair, but I don't have time to fuck with him right now. Pressing against the driver's left shoulder, he pushed him gently aside so he could see out the window, across the parking lot. "Excuse me, will you?" he said. "You're blocking the view."

The driver refused to be ignored. Stepping back so he once again stood between Ciaro and the window, he repeated, "I *said*, 'Who are you?'"

Ciaro's eyes narrowed. "You a union driver?" he asked harshly.

"Sure," the driver said, puzzled.

Ciaro reached into his back pocket, extracted his wallet, flipped it open, and proffered it to the driver. "*That's* who I am."

The driver studied it, shrugged, and said, "So?"

"So that's who the fuck I am," Ciaro said, meaning, "Enough is enough, dickhead. You want trouble, you found it."

9
1 9 4 2

Hoffa sat stiffly in his leather-covered chair, his back ramrod straight. His coat was off, tossed carelessly across an empty chair by the paneled wall to his left. His tie was loosened and the top button of his white shirt was undone, indicating a casualness he did not feel. Slowly, he sipped from the glass of water he clutched in his fist, silently reviewing his position. There was no need, he knew, to confer with his colleagues. They were there mainly for show, to help balance the numerical odds against the management "team" that occupied the other end of the twenty-foot-long conference table. Hoffa and colleagues had met until well after 2:00 A.M., hammering out the points they wanted to make in this, the fourth, negotiating session.

To Hoffa's right, a tall, uniformed policeman stood guarding the door that led to the hallway. Through the door's frosted glass, on which RAILWAY EXPRESS AGENCY was written in heavy gold letters, Hoffa could see shapes moving restlessly back and forth. Those were the reporters, the vultures who hovered around gatherings such as this, begging for scraps of information.

At the other end of the table was a man named Harold Davis, the designated chief negotiator for the REA. Flanking him were several other members of his team, all of whom, Hoffa reflected, looked like lawyers or accountants, all prim and proper in their dark-colored double-breasted suits and shiny shoes. How he'd love to have them working for him for a month, he thought. Just a month! That would be long enough for him to show them what life was really like, what it meant—really *meant*—to be a truck driver stuck by circumstances, education, and training in a dead-end job for a piddling wage and virtually no benefits. He would like to see them have to go home to their wives and undernourished kids with the miserably thin pay envelopes that truckers drew, home to a tiny, ill-furnished, frame house that was too crowded, too drafty, and too expensive. When he tried to explain such circumstances to people like this, their typical response was "too bad."

Well, Hoffa thought, in the long run it is going to be too bad for them because times have changed. This ain't the Depression anymore, he wanted to shout. The days when management could run roughshod over the workers and make them eat all kinds of shit are quickly disappearing. The pendulum is swinging; the labor movement is gaining momentum all over the country and management is finally having to pay for previous excesses, for the days when they pissed all over workers, the days when pricks like Harold Davis there, him and his goddamn snotty toadies, did what they wanted at the expense of the workingman.

Hoffa put his glass down on the green coaster decorated with the letters *REA* in white script, taking care to see that no water splashed on the surface of the highly polished oak table.

"*Mister* Davis," he said slowly and, he hoped, reasonably, "I am a man with a legitimate grievance and a legitimate position. I am here in the legitimate interests of my fellow Teamsters and my fellow drivers, who, under the law, have the right to elect—"

Davis held up his hand, like a school crossing guard signaling traffic to halt. "You say 'legitimate,'" he interjected imperiously. "There is nothing 'legitimate' about tying up the country, about tying up the—"

Hoffa interrupted. "Aren't you exaggerating a little?" he asked. "The Teamsters haven't tied up the *country.*"

"You people," David continued as if Hoffa had not spoken, "you people for the last six weeks—"

"*My* people!" Hoffa exclaimed, feigning incredulity. "*My* people? What about *your* people. You're the one who's being hardheaded. The people I represent, the over-the-road drivers, are entitled to a decent wage. They are entitled to representation, and they are entitled to benefits to help make their lives richer and fuller, just like yours are."

"You're misinterpreting," Davis argued. "President Roosevelt . . ."

"Don't bring the president into it!" Hoffa said hotly. "I'm a Democrat, too, but President Roosevelt don't make the laws."

"The newspapers—" Davis began.

"Don't bring the newspapers into it either," Hoffa insisted. "The newspapers don't make the laws neither. If President Roosevelt and the newspapers are ever elected by the Teamsters to replace me, then I will abide by their opinions."

Angrily he rose and stomped toward the door. His fellow Teamsters, thoroughly enjoying the show, rose like automatons and followed their leader.

"Wait a moment," Davis said, his voice rising. "Wait a moment."

Hoffa ignored him, reaching for the door handle. When he did, the policeman moved forward a step, as if to block his exit. Hoffa stopped and stared at the man. "Get the fuck out of my way," he ordered coolly.

The officer glanced at Davis, who nodded slightly. Then, without a word, he stepped aside, letting Hoffa and the Teamsters pass into the hallway.

Walking into the narrow passage, Hoffa was met by the reporters and photographers who had been lounging in the area waiting for something to happen. When Hoffa and the other Teamsters unexpectedly appeared, the photographers reached hurriedly for their boxy Speed Graphics. A red-haired reporter who had been leaning against the wall near the door stepped up to Hoffa, notebook at the ready.

"Mr. Hoffa," he said hurriedly, "my name is Andrew O'Leary from the *Detroit Tribune*."

Hoffa stared at him. Although he had been reading his stories and columns for years, he had never before met the man. He was taller and younger than he had pictured him, and his eyes were red-rimmed and watery, as if he were suffering a painful hangover. Hoffa stopped and waited for the question, blinking rapidly as flashbulbs popped in his face.

"Mr. Hoffa," O'Leary rushed on, "can you tell us what's happening in there? Have you reached an agreement?"

"Have the Nazis landed in London?" Hoffa replied. "Hell no, we haven't reached an agreement."

"What's the hang-up?" O'Leary wanted to know.

"Money," Hoffa replied.

"Just money?"

"And working hours."

O'Leary scribbled quickly on his pad. "That's it?"

"And downtime," Hoffa continued. "And life insurance. And a pension plan. And—"

O'Leary quit writing and stared at Hoffa. "So you really haven't accomplished much at all?"

"That's one way of putting it," Hoffa said.

Another reporter pushed forward. "Johnson," he said. "From the *Chronicle*. Is the president going to send in troops?"

Hoffa looked at him as if he had just asked him for change for a thousand dollar bill. "How do I know?" he replied. "I ain't a fucking mind reader."

"Are the Teamsters going to back down?" the reporter named Johnson persisted.

"The Teamsters *never* back down," Hoffa barked. "We *negotiate*. We come to a meeting of the minds. We explain our position and they explain theirs. Then we agree on a middle ground. Negotiation ain't surrender, for chrissakes. Not for them. Not for us."

"Jimmy," yelled a slim, dark-haired young reporter who did not identify himself. "What's the REA position?"

Hoffa smiled. "The REA position is not to give us nothing," he said. "Naturally we don't exactly agree with—"

"What wage concessions, if any, are they willing to make?" asked O'Leary.

"Look, men," Hoffa said, raising both his hands above his head, revealing large, wet circles in his armpits, "the situation is this. Drivers for the Railway Express Agency are not members of the Teamsters or any other union. They don't pay their men what we refer to as 'union scale.' Their pay rates are much lower. As a result, REA drivers are making a lot less than drivers who are members of the Teamsters, drivers whose representatives have negotiated contracts setting specific wage and benefit payments. I have made it my goal to bring *all* drivers in the country under the Teamsters. That way every driver in every state will be working from the same basic scale. It's fair. It's equitable. *And it's goddamn going to happen.*"

O'Leary smiled fleetingly. "Well," he said, cutting off another reporter who was trying to scream a question, "what is the philosophy behind this position?"

Hoffa responded quickly. "Philosophy?" he said sarcastically. "There ain't any goddamn *philosophy*. My drivers don't want me to be a philosopher. They don't want to hear that highbrow, ivory-tower crap. They want bread and butter."

Johnson, who had elbowed his way to the front until he was standing less than a foot from Hoffa's nose, took up the questioning. "What if the REA won't pay what you're asking?" he interjected.

"Why shouldn't they?" Hoffa countered. "It ain't as if they can't afford it."

"Are you going to insist on your demands?" Johnson continued. "Even if it means disrupting the whole country?"

Hoffa decided to answer straight out. "Look, men," he said loudly, shouting down several other reporters who were vying for his attention. "Let me make the Teamsters position clear. We feel that if an owner— or the REA in this case—absolutely *can't* pay what we're asking, then we ease off. We don't feel there's anything to gain by forcing someone out of business. That way *everybody* ends up out of work. And we sure as hell don't want that to happen. We feel if an owner—or, again in this case, the REA—is able to pay, then he goddamn well *is* going to pay. Otherwise there's going to be trouble. We feel the REA *can* pay. But they ain't. So they're in trouble."

Harold Davis had followed Hoffa out of the room and had remained in the background, listening to what the union organizer had to tell the reporters.

The more he talked, the more agitated Davis had become. At this point he felt he could not restrain himself any longer.

"I think," he fairly screamed, "that this impromptu news conference should end *right now*. I believe the best place to negotiate this proposed contract is in the confines—"

Hoffa smiled to himself. I finally got through to that fucker, he thought. *Now* he's going to be willing to sit down and talk some serious shit with us.

"I don't give a shit what you believe," Hoffa said, setting the reporters to scribbling feverishly. Fighting to keep satisfaction from his voice, feigning anger instead, he continued: "Like I just told these men, the Teamsters *ain't* going to back down. We've been out six weeks and we're prepared to stay out six fucking hundred weeks if that's what it takes for us to prevail. We *demand* better wages. We *demand* more congenial working hours. We *demand* . . ." He paused, staring hard at Davis. "Am I going too fast for you?"

Davis opened his mouth so speak.

"I've still got the floor," Hoffa said loudly. "We *demand* better living conditions for all workingmen, especially REA drivers. We *demand* representation. We *demand* that you do something about our demands."

"Or what?" Davis asked. "What if we don't? What are you going to do?"

Hoffa smiled. "I can't tell you *all* our strategy," he said. "All you have to think about right now is the strike. But from your perspective, it could be worse. A hell of a lot worse. Now think about that for a while."

Davis's face turned a bright red. "You can't talk to me that way," he said hotly. "You can't come in here and try to boss me around. Who in hell do you think you are?"

"Who do I think I am?" Hoffa asked. "*Who do I*

think I am? I'm something you hoped you'd never see in broad daylight. I'm your worst fucking nightmare. I'm a workingman, *Mister* Davis, and the law of the land says I have a right to collective bargaining. Or maybe you've never heard of the National Labor Relations Act, which President Roosevelt—the man whose name you were so free to use just a few minutes ago—signed into law? In case you need a refresher, it gives workers the right to form unions and to *bargain collectively* with management. All Roosevelt did was sign it. He didn't write it and he didn't vote for it, but he did officially make it the law. And that's the important thing: *it is the law.* You're going to *have* to recognize that, beginning with the idea that you're going to have to negotiate with us, starting with an agreement to get rid of your goons, those *thugs* you've hired as strikebreakers."

Davis, much to Hoffa's unexpressed delight, was so angry he was speechless. Sensing this was not the type of image that the REA wanted to present to the press, one of Davis's lieutenants decided it might be better to clear the hallway of the reporters and photographers.

"All right, you guys," he said brusquely, "it's time to go. The show's over for the day. You can wait outside."

"Just a minute," Hoffa said angrily, unwilling to see his best allies scattered. "Just a goddamn minute."

"No!" the lieutenant said. "*You* wait a minute. You can't just libel anybody you feel like anytime you feel like it. If you don't control yourself, I'll . . ."

"You'll what?" Hoffa asked pugnaciously.

"I'll see to it —"

Hoffa threw his arms up in disgust. "Forget it," he howled. "Save your threats." Anxious to get in the last word, he turned to the reporters. "Despite what these REA *negotiators*," he said, stressing the word sarcastically, "would like you to believe, I have men I am responsible to. They have elected me and sent me here to negotiate on their behalf. And what happens when I get here? I am virtually locked in a room and am told, 'Here are our conditions. This is what you have to agree to. Take it or leave it.' That's all I've heard. And I say 'leave it!' I cannot accept an offer I am not empowered to accept. I tell that to this man, this Mr. Davis, and what does he do? He throws the president in my face. I would like to tell him something."

But Davis was not there to be told. At the words "leave it," he had spun on his heels and returned to the conference room, followed by the members of his team.

When Hoffa turned and saw that the REA men had left, he broke into a huge grin. Turning back to the reporters, he happily asked, "Okay, boys. Any more questions?"

Several hours later the workaholic Hoffa was still at his desk at the Teamsters headquarters on Trumbull Avenue. Seemingly as full of energy as he had been twelve hours earlier, he was trying to dictate a letter to an obviously exhausted Pete Connelly.

"Who are the Secret Service?" he said, speaking slowly enough for Connelly to transcribe his words. "They are the modern-day Pinkertons. They are—"

Connelly interrupted. "A lot of the guys won't know what you mean by Pinkertons."

Hoffa, who hated to be interrupted, turned angrily on Connelly. "Are you fucking writing this? Do you want to write this?"

"Hey, Jimmy," Connelly began in what he hoped was a conciliatory tone. "I didn't mean nothing. I just wanted to point out that a lot of the younger guys might not know that the Pinkertons were part of a so-called detective agency who were hired as strikebreakers. I wouldn't have known that myself except for Uncle Fitz. I just wanted—"

"Get out of here," Hoffa ordered him fiercely. Turning to one of the Teamsters who was always hanging around, he repeated the command. "Get him out of here. I *mean* get him the fuck out of here!"

A woman poked her head through the door. "Jimmy," she said excitedly, unaware of Hoffa's mood, "there's a call for you on line two."

Hoffa glared at her. "I don't want to talk to nobody."

The woman looked puzzled. "This isn't just anybody, Jimmy. It's Dan Tobin."

Hoffa glanced at his watch: 10:26. What the fuck is the president of the Teamsters Union doing calling him at almost ten-thirty at night? he wondered. Well, fuck him, too, he thought. I don't feel like putting up with any more shit today.

"Didn't I say that I don't want to talk to nobody?" he shrieked. "Did I say who I *did* want to talk to?"

Puzzled, the woman persisted. "It's *Dan Tobin,* Jimmy. He says he needs—"

"Get out of here!"

"Jimmy, he says he needs to t-t—"

"Okay! Okay! I'll talk to him." Snatching the phone off the hook, depressing the line button, Hoffa spoke into the instrument.

"Hello, Dan," he said, "I . . ." He paused to listen. "Nooooo," he said finally. "Well, what the fuck am I going to do? I got to hold out ."

Another long pause. "Dan . . . Dan . . . Dan, listen to me. They're giving me nothing. The membersh—" Again he listened.

"Listen to me for a minute, Dan. Just listen. They are going to ca—" Rolling his eyes, he removed the receiver from his ear and held it at arm's length. Turning his face toward the ceiling, he waited until Tobin paused for breath. "Listen to me, Dan," he said hurriedly when Tobin gave him a break. "They're going to cave in, I tell you. They're going to cave. Just give me another week and I—"

As he listened, interrupted again, his face grew darker and his eyes bulged. "You want to run this local?" he bellowed into the phone. "You want to unseat me? *You* tell *me*. If you don't want to do that, barring that . . ."

He paused again, staring at the floor, listening. Without another word, he reached out and lifted the instrument off the desk. "Take this!" he roared. With a healthy tug, he jerked the cord out of the wall. "Take this fucking phone and . . ." Turning to face the window behind his back, he heaved the phone through the glass.

While the others stared in embarrassed silence Hoffa grabbed his coat and strode furiously toward the door. "I got a meeting," he said, tossing the words over his shoulder.

10

1942

Hoffa, still riding an adrenaline wave, agitatedly jiggled his leg up and down, making a soft thud on the thickly carpeted floor of the plush black Cadillac. The driver, a low-level Teamsters gofer, kept his eyes straight ahead, watching the blacktop as it twisted north on Lake Shore Road, along Lake St. Clair. Already they were well beyond the ostentatious Grosse Pointe mansions of Detroit's rich and powerful. It was well after midnight and a bright full moon reflected dazzlingly off the dark water. Hoffa and Frank Fitzsimmons shared the backseat while the driver and Bobby Ciaro rode in front.

"Well, Jimmy," Fitzsimmons began tentatively, "what did Tobin want?"

"He wants me to settle with the REA," Hoffa replied, disgust apparent in his voice. "He wants me to call off tonight's march."

"Don't you have to do it then?" Fitzsimmons asked.

"If he wants to run this local, he can come down

here. If he wants to replace me, let him do it."

"But Tobin's the president of the *International*."

"Yeah, yeah," said Hoffa, "but he ain't president of Local 299. I am."

Leaning over the seat until he was speaking almost in the driver's ear, Hoffa urged him to hurry. "Get me there, Larry," he ordered.

"But, Jimmy . . ." Fitzsimmons persisted.

"There ain't no but's about it, Fitz. If Dan Tobin wants to tell me something, he can come down here and tell me. The thing is, he ain't responsible for running this local, while I am. If he's got a gripe he wants to settle with me, he can come down here and we can sit across the table and talk about it. That's all there is to it. End of fucking discussion."

"You're right, Jimmy," Fitzsimmons agreed meekly. As he spoke the car slowed abruptly.

"Why the fuck are you slowing down?" Hoffa asked the driver in consternation.

"There was a cop back there," Larry said, "sitting on the side of the road. Waiting to catch a speeder."

"Fuck the cop," Hoffa said. "If he comes after you, gun it. We don't have time to screw around."

The driver glanced sideways at Ciaro, as if seeking his approval.

"Do as he says," Ciaro said almost in a whisper. "Pick it up. Fuck the cops."

Larry nodded and depressed the accelerator, taking a sharp curve with a loud screech.

"That's more like it," said Hoffa, leaning back.

"You know," said Fitzsimmons obsequiously, "you're right about Tobin. He may be the IBT president, but the locals got to have some authority. It's like when the president of the United States comes out against the workingman—"

Fitzsimmons did not get to finish his thought. In mid-sentence, a dark sedan jumped out from a side road and swerved in front of Hoffa's car, forcing the driver to slam his foot on the brake and throw the Cadillac into a skid.

"Look out!" Ciaro screamed, too late.

"What the fuck!" Hoffa said as the centrifugal force threw him up to the side, causing him to bang his head with considerable force against the frame.

"Oh, shit!" muttered Fitzsimmons.

"Get down on the floor!" Ciaro ordered, digging into his waistband for his pistol. "Get down on the fucking floor and don't come up until I tell you!"

Hoffa put his hand against his head and was surprised when it came away bloody. "That stupid motherfucker," he said, ignoring Ciaro's command and reaching for the door handle, "I'll show him how to drive."

"Don't, Jimmy!" Ciaro warned. "Stay in the fucking car!"

The second vehicle, which had screeched to a stop just ahead of Hoffa's limousine, was sitting firmly astride the road, blocking a forward escape route.

As Ciaro warned Hoffa, to stay put the passenger door of the sedan opened and a tall figure emerged. When the man stepped into the Cadillac's headlights, Ciaro could see that he wore the dark uniform of the Detroit police.

"Holy shit," Ciaro mumbled, fumbling for the safety on his revolver.

In the backseat, a dazed Hoffa was still wrestling with the door handle, cursing under his breath. Finally he got the door open and climbed unsteadily out of the vehicle.

Ciaro, who by then was also out of the car, barked another warning at Hoffa. "Goddammit, Jimmy. I told you to stay back. Get back in the fucking car," he ordered.

Hoffa continued to ignore him. Staggering forward, weaving like a drunk, he went to meet the man, who had stopped several feet away, careful to remain in the glare of the lights so all his movements could be easily detected.

"You cocksucker," Hoffa said, wincing in pain. "What the hell do you think you're doing?"

The man did not reply. Instead he extended a hand and offered Hoffa a clean, pressed white handkerchief.

Staring at the man suspiciously, Hoffa accepted the cloth and put it to his head, grimacing as he touched it to the wound.

He looked closely at the man. He was tall and thin, with a long angular face and thin, bloodless lips. Hoffa glanced down at his chest. Over his breast pocket was a tag with the name "Bladesdale" stenciled on it.

"I know you," Hoffa said slowly, recognition dawning. "You're the cop from the REA meeting."

Bladesdale moved his lips in what he probably thought was a smile. "That's right."

Ciaro, who had been on the opposite side of the car from which the man approached, bolted around the Cadillac and jogged to Hoffa's side. "Let me handle this," he whispered to Hoffa. "Get your ass back in the car."

"Tell him to go away," Bladesdale said quietly to Hoffa. "I need to talk to you. In private."

Hoffa stared at him. Perceiving that there was no immediate threat to him or any of the others, he turned to Ciaro.

"Wait for me in the car, Bobby," he commanded.

"The fuck I will," Ciaro replied, drawing his shoulders back.

"The fuck you won't," Hoffa said sharply. "I want to hear what this guy has to say. If I need you, I'll yell. I don't think he stopped us just so he could shoot me in front of witnesses."

Ciaro looked steadily at Hoffa. Realizing there was

no sense in trying to argue with him, he turned. With a suspicious glance back at Bladesdale, he returned to the Cadillac, mumbling curses.

"What the fuck's going on?" Fitzsimmons asked in a shaky voice, crouching in the backseat.

"Don't know yet," Ciaro said abruptly. "Just sit back and shut up."

Larry, who had not said a word since the incident began, looked at Ciaro. "What do you want to do?" he asked quietly.

"Just sit tight," Ciaro ordered. "Don't do nothing until I tell you."

"Okay," Larry said, relaxing his hands on the steering wheel.

"What the fuck are you doing?" Hoffa asked Bladesdale. "Why were you trying to kill me?"

"Don't be fucking stupid," Bladesdale said. "If I had been trying to kill you, I would have done a better job."

"Then what is this, a shakedown? You want money? A piece of the action?"

"No," Bladesdale said, shaking his head. "I don't want any fucking money. I want to *give* you something, not take something from you."

Hoffa studied the man carefully. "Okay," he said cautiously, "what is it you want to *give* me?"

"Some advice," Bladesdale said. "A warning. Whatever you want to call it."

"Well, give it to me," Hoffa said, growing impatient. "I got someplace I got to be."

"Be smart," Bladesdale said softly. "Call off the march."

Hoffa laughed. "You sound like a fucking echo."

Bladesdale screwed his face into a puzzled frown. "Huh?"

"Never mind," Hoffa said. "But is that what you

wanted to *give* me. Davis sent you out here to try to scare me off?"

"Davis!" Bladesdale spat. "That asshole. If he knew I was here, he'd have me fired in nothing flat. If he even *suspected* I was doing this, he'd have my ass."

"Okay," Hoffa said, "assuming you're straight, why should I call off the march."

Bladesdale lowered his voice. "Because things have been arranged. If you go ahead with the march, some bad shit is going to happen."

Hoffa pondered what he had heard. "What kind of bad shit?"

"Can't tell you. You just have to trust me when I say it ain't going to be nice."

"Who set this up? Who's the dickhead that wants to get rid of Hoffa?"

"Can't tell you that, either. I just wanted you to be on your guard."

Hoffa was silent for a long time. "Why are you doing this?" he said finally. "What's in it for you?"

"Ain't nothing in it for me," Bladesdale said, "except maybe a little peace and quiet at home. My wife's brother's a truck driver. A Teamster. He thinks you're the best fucking thing that's happened to drivers since the Depression ended. If he knew that something happened to you and I could have done something to prevent it, he'd never forgive me. And neither would my wife. Personally I don't give a shit whether you believe me or not. I done what I had to do by telling you this much. The rest is up to you."

Hoffa considered what he had been told. "Thanks," he said at length.

"Don't thank me," Bladesdale said coldly. "I ain't doing it for you. I'm doing it for me."

"Don't matter," Hoffa replied. "You're doing it. And I appreciate it. If I can help you sometime . . ."

"Ain't fucking likely."

"Well, if I can, let me know. Jimmy Hoffa don't forget. He don't forgive and he don't forget."

Bladesdale nodded. "I understand what you're saying." He glanced at his watch. "I got to go. I don't want nobody to know we ever had this conversation. That okay with you?"

"Fine with me," Hoffa said, looking at his own watch. "I got to go, too."

"Remember," Bladesdale said. "Things are in motion. Don't be stupid. Call off the fucking march."

"I'll think about it," Hoffa said noncommittally.

Bladesdale had started back toward his car when Hoffa called out to him. "One more thing."

"What's that?" Bladesdale said, stopping and turning.

"Next time," Hoffa said lightly, "use the fucking telephone, huh?"

For the first time, Bladesdale smiled a real smile. "Aw, go fuck yourself." He laughed, turning again toward his car.

"What was that all about?" Ciaro asked worriedly as soon as Hoffa had returned to the Cadillac.

"Get back in the car," Hoffa said brusquely. "I'll tell you as we drive. Basically, he wanted to warn me about an ambush."

Ciaro's eyes widened. "An ambush?" he said in surprise. Then the import struck him. "At the march. Has to be at the march, right?"

"Right," Hoffa said, removing the handkerchief from his head and looking at the stain. "Now let's move. We can talk on the way."

"What's happening?" Fitzsimmons asked anxiously as Hoffa opened the door. "Are we being arrested? We going to jail?"

"For chrissakes, Fitz," Ciaro muttered, "why don't

you just shut the fuck up."

The night air was damp, still redolent of that afternoon's rain, and chilly. Pools of water dotted the surface, appearing like irregularly shaped holes amid the light-colored pebbles that had been spread over the warehouse roof. A constant banging and clanking, as well as intermittent hisses of steam and the screech of metal against metal, sounded in the distance. Hoffa, Ciaro, and three other men fastidiously avoided the puddles as they jogged toward the edge.

"There it is," Ciaro said as he poked his head over the parapet, sounding almost surprised to find a bustling railyard virtually at their feet.

Hoffa, panting slightly from the exertion of the quick traverse of the open roof, stood next to Ciaro and looked down.

"Looks peaceful enough, don't it?" he commented. "For now anyway."

From where they stood, they could see a half dozen switch engines huffing and laboring among the tangle of bright steel tracks, some pulling several cars at a time, some just one, and one, totally unencumbered, obviously heading toward a rendezvous with a pair of waiting boxcars.

Directly across from them, perhaps two football-field lengths away, was another large warehouse. Unlike the others that lined the tracks, it was brightly lit and conspicuously animated. Through the open doors of the loading docks, men could be seen bustling about, silhouetted against the interior lights. On the outside, spotlights shone against the yellow-on-green sign in the center of the building that read RAILWAY EXPRESS AGENCY in three-foot-tall letters.

Giving additional life to the scene was a group of men parading in front of the docks, just beyond the

REA property line. The men, wearing coats as protection against the sudden change in the weather, carried four-foot-tall placards. Black letters on a white background pronounced that the International Brotherhood of Teamsters was on strike against the REA.

Ciaro turned toward Hoffa and smiled tightly. "Looks like everything's on schedule," he said with satisfaction. Taking note that the wound Hoffa had suffered in that early morning run-in with Bladesdale was starting to seep again, he nodded at Hoffa's forehead. "You're still bleeding," he said.

Hoffa grunted. Tearing his attention away from the scene in the railyard, he removed from his pocket the bloodstained white handkerchief Bladesdale had given him and touched it lightly to the wound. Looking at the small spots of fresh blood, he cursed softly. "Wish the damn thing would either bleed or not. It's a pain in the ass having to keep wiping it."

Ciaro turned to the men who had accompanied them. "Okay, guys, let's go. As they say in the John Wayne movies, 'Over the side.'"

Like well-trained troops, they swung their legs over the railing and climbed, one by one, down a fire escape. Ciaro followed, and then Hoffa.

Once they were on the ground, they hurried across the tracks, aiming at the picket line. As they approached, one striker detached himself from the group and walked up to Hoffa.

"Hey, Jimmy," he said affably.

Hoffa glanced at the man, running his features through his mental file. He prided himself on knowing as many members of his organization as he could, even though it was difficult in these days of rapid expansion. But this one he recognized. Harris, Hoffa told himself, that's his name. Billy Harris.

"Hey, Billy. How you doing?" Hoffa responded.

"Could be worse," Harris replied, happy that Hoffa knew who he was. Matching his stride to Hoffa's, the two walked side by side for a dozen yards before Harris again turned and asked him, concern in his voice, "We marching on them tonight?"

"Maybe," Hoffa said. "We're working on it."

The man nodded grimly, then noticed for the first time the cut on the side of Hoffa's head. "They beating on you?" he asked in surprise.

Hoffa smiled. Nah," he said. "Just a little accident in the car. I'm fine. Ready to go."

"Me, too," Harris replied, turning to return to his friends. "We're with you."

"Thanks," Hoffa said, waving over his shoulder.

As they got closer to the main body a man raced out to meet them, an organizer named Anderson.

"Jim," Anderson said loudly, relief evident in his voice. "Goddamn, I'm glad to see you. Tobin's been driving me fucking crazy, sending messages every five minutes that he wants you to call him." Digging in his pocket, he produced a wrinkled scrap of paper torn from a grocery bag.

Hoffa squinted at the paper. In pencil, barely legible, was a telephone number.

"Tobin wants you to call him right away," Anderson repeated. "In New York. But just in case you can't find a phone, he left a message. Said to be sure to tell you."

"Tell me what?" Hoffa asked, knowing what the answer was going to be.

Anderson dropped his voice, seemingly unwilling to share the news with the other picketers without first imparting it to Hoffa. "He said—and he repeated it three times to make sure I understood—he said to hold off on the fucking march."

Anderson paused, then added, "Actually he didn't use the word 'fucking.' That was me."

Hoffa smiled again and nodded, hardly surprised.

When Hoffa did not immediately reply, Anderson continued: "He said the mood—"

"Okay," Hoffa said sharply. "I got the message. Thanks."

"Tobin said the mood of the newspapers—" Anderson began again.

Hoffa stopped and stared hard at Anderson. "Hey, am I fucking deaf? I heard you. You gave me the message. You done right. Now get back on the line."

Abashed, Anderson turned and walked off the group of picketers.

As soon as he left, a young woman stepped out of the darkness and approached Hoffa. She was wearing a man's coat, which was at least two sizes two large for her, and a handkerchief was knotted tightly around her head. She was tall and skinny to the point of emaciation. With the man's coat that covered her from shoulder to midcalf, Hoffa was not sure it was a woman until she got two steps closer. In one hand she carried a collection bucket, in the other a small sign reading STRIKE RELIEF FUND.

Hoffa dug in his pocket and came up with two loose bills and a handful of change, all of which he dropped into the bucket.

"How's it going?" he asked.

"It's been better," the woman replied in a tired voice.

Concerned by the tone, Hoffa looked more closely at her. Her eyes were ringed with dark circles and there were deep lines at the corner of her unlipsticked mouth. "You holding out okay?"

She shrugged.

"Your family eating?"

"Eating something," she said tersely. "Ain't steak and green vegetables, but we're eating."

"That's good," Hoffa replied. "Need something to

keep your strength up."

"Ain't saying we haven't been better fed," the woman added.

Hoffa gestured toward the picket line, then turned to the woman. Pulling a pack of Camels from his pocket, he offered her one, then took one himself. "These people out here. They want to hold out? Or they want to go back in?"

She accepted a light from Hoffa and puffed deeply on the cigarette, considering her reply.

"A lot of people," Hoffa said in the ensuing silence, "some of those in the union even, they say take the offer and go back in. They want to go back to work."

As he spoke a boy of about four ambled up and stood next to the woman, clutching her coat and staring at Hoffa with large brown eyes. She reached down, put her arm around the boy's shoulder, and drew him closer.

"I'm Jimmy Hoffa," Hoffa said to the woman.

She nodded. "I know who you are."

"International wants me to call the strike off. Let everybody go back to work. Don't make no more trouble."

"Uh-huh." The woman nodded.

"The cops say there's going to be violence. That a lot of people are going to get hurt unless we fold up our tent."

He paused. "You think I should follow that advice?"

The woman gave him an exhausted smile. "It don't matter what I say, does it, Mr. Hoffa? I mean, you're going to do what you've already decided to do no matter what. Aren't you?"

Hoffa nodded grimly. "Yeah, I am. You're right. I got to do what I think is necessary."

"Ain't that what we pay you for?" the woman

added. "To make the decisions. You're the boss, we're the workers. You make the decisions and we carry 'em out."

Hoffa relaxed, satisfied that he was getting a vote of support from a person in the ranks, someone who was telling him the truth and not just what she thought he wanted to hear. Squatting so he would be on eye level with the boy, who had continued to stare at him wordlessly, he reached out his hand. "What's your name, kid?" he asked kindly. "I got a son, too, but he ain't as big as you."

The boy remained mute, letting Hoffa take his limp hand. He continued to stare.

"Is he bashful?" Hoffa asked, glancing up at the woman. "Or is he trying to keep his name secret from me?"

"Does it make any difference?" the woman said. "What his name is, I mean?"

Rising to his feet, Hoffa felt like there was a thousand-pound weight on his shoulders. The burden of responsibility lay heavy upon him and he was again conscious of the gap that existed between leaders and followers, aware that he could chat on seemingly friendly terms with the woman-in-the-ranks, but there would always be a chasm between them, like the difference between an army officer and the enlisted men in his command.

"No, it don't," Hoffa agreed.

"They're all called *something*, ain't they?" the woman added, smiling tentatively for the first time.

Hoffa grinned. "Indeed they are," he said.

As he looked at his watch, his expression turned resolute. "Time to go to work," he told the woman. "Time to put that decision into play."

Followed by Ciaro and the other three men with whom he had crossed the rooftop, Hoffa started to walk away. He took two steps, turned, and looked back at the woman. "Take care of yourself," he said solemnly. "If everything hits the fan, get out of the way. And watch out for little what's-'is-name there, too."

The woman nodded but didn't smile. The boy lifted the hand he had reluctantly offered to Hoffa and gave a child's wave, slowly clenching and unclenching his fingers. "Bye-bye," he mouthed.

11
1942

Hoffa spent fifteen minutes with the men on the picket line in front of the loading dock, trying to buck up their spirits, preparing them for the ordeal he knew was coming. Telling them to hold the line no matter what, Hoffa, Ciaro, and the three specially picked lieu-tenants walked around the side of the warehouse and approached the REA main gate. The scene in front was roughly identical to the one in the back, except the number of picketers was considerably larger.

Two dozen men formed a picket line that moved slowly and silently back and forth in front of the gate. At least twice as many men huddled on the periph-ery, waiting to take their turns on the line. As they waited they hovered over trash cans in which scrap lumber had been dumped and set afire. Seen from a distance, the group could have been supporters of a college football team holding a pregame pep rally. Except for the hush.

The picketers did not chant and shout slogans, as they might during a daytime demonstration, but marched in almost total silence, either exhausted from long hours on the line or intimidated by the darkness, which seemed to drain their bravado and enthusiasm. As Hoffa and his entourage rounded the corner, one of the marchers spotted him and shouted to the others.

"Here comes Jimmy," he called out, pleased to note Hoffa's presence and proud to be the one to announce his arrival.

All along the line, heads turned and men who had seemed dispirited appeared to be revived and reinvigorated simply by Hoffa's approach.

"Hey, Jimmy . . . Good to see you . . . Welcome aboard . . . Glad you're here . . ." they greeted him as he walked the length of the line. As he passed they waved their signs. MARCH FOR SUPPORT read one, RECOGNIZE THE TEAMSTERS. SUPPORT THE STRIKE AGAINST THE REA read another.

Walking up to a young man with a crew cut and freckles across his nose, Hoffa reached out and took his hand. Both men nodded and silently exchanged a signal. Looking at his watch, the man, whose name was Terry Boyers, winked at Hoffa and motioned with his head that Hoffa should step away from the group.

"We ready?" Boyers asked eagerly when they were alone.

"Hmmm." Hoffa nodded.

"We ready to march?" Boyers said.

"How do you read it?" Hoffa asked him.

Boyers pointed across the yard toward the building. "I don't think they're going to do a goddamn thing." He paused and looked steadily at Hoffa. "Do you?"

When Hoffa did not immediately reply, Boyers added, "I mean, what would they gain by violence?" It was as much an attempt to boost his own confidence as a question.

Hoffa, recognizing this, answered, "Yeah. That's a good question all right. What *would* they gain?"

Feeling that his reply had not been all the confidence boost that Boyers had been hoping for, Hoffa slapped him jovially on the shoulder. "Hey," he said, "let's not worry about what they might do, okay? We got to do what we got to do. Right?"

Boyers's blue eyes flashed. "Right!" he said. "We ain't come this far to back down now. Guess you're ready to go, eh? Ready to start?"

Hoffa sighed, running his fingers through his hair. "Don't be in such a fucking hurry," he cautioned Boyers. "I'll tell you when."

The union leader looked over Boyers's shoulder at the scene in front of him, lost in thought. It's decision time, he told himself. If I'm going to listen to Tobin and Bladesdale and call off the march, now's the time to do it. Calling it off, he knew, would be a major disaster; the Teamsters probably would never be able to regain the momentum that had been building during the battle against the REA. If he elected to tell everybody to go home, as the pressure was on him to do, he might never be able to summon the men to march against the REA again. On the other hand, if he went through with it, he very likely would end up with a lot of blood on his hands. Innocent blood. Bladesdale had as much as told him that the goons were waiting, hoping for an opportunity to unleash their violence against the mainly unarmed picketers. Somebody must have told Tobin the same thing, because the IBT president was doing all he could to force Hoffa to abandon the plan.

Hoffa looked around him. As he had been standing there more men had come up to join the group of picketers. All told, when the last of the stragglers arrived in the next few minutes, Hoffa expected to have some two hundred Teamsters gathered in front of the gate, a small army but one that would, he knew, be miserably outgunned if not actually outnumbered by the strikebreaker force that would be summoned by Davis and his REA bosses.

As he ran over his options another man approached from he darkness. Looking up, Hoffa saw that it was Frank Fitzsimmons.

"What you going to do, Jim?" Fitzsimmons asked, tension and anxiety evident in his voice.

"Walk with me," Hoffa said, taking Fitzsimmons's arm and guiding him away from the knot of men.

"You think you'd better call it off?" Fitzsimmons asked once they were away from the others. "Tobin said to call it off. Don't you think you need to listen to him? Listen to orders from the president? At least consider them?"

Hoffa opened his mouth to reply, but whatever he was going to say was lost in the commotion that erupted. Before he could speak, a gun shot shattered the stillness of the night.

Hoffa spun around to face the group of Teamsters, perhaps to see where the shot came from and what its effect had been. As he turned he saw out of the corner of his eye men dropping to the ground all around him, either falling flat on the street or sprinting for cover behind automobiles or the trash cans that still burned brightly.

Gritting his teeth, Hoffa was formulating a command when Ciaro, who had rushed toward his boss at the sound of the shot, grabbed him around the shoulders and pulled him to the ground. "Don't be fucking stupid," Ciaro grunted. "You ain't fucking bulletproof."

Raising his head, Hoffa could see two policemen wrestling with a man in a dark overcoat. They were close enough to one of the blazing trash barrels that he could see that the man clutched a pistol, which he was trying to bring to bear despite the fact that one of the cops was struggling to wrench the weapon from his hand while the other was beating him across the shoulders with his nightstick. It was an uneven and quickly decided match. The cop clubbed the man solidly across the back of the head. With a loud grunt, the man dropped like a steer in the slaughterhouse. As he fell the pistol tumbled from his grip and was scooped up by the second cop. Shoving the weapon in his tunic, the cop grabbed the man's left arm while his partner grabbed his right. Together they dragged him away to meet a fate that Hoffa was certain would not be pleasant.

Nimbly he scrambled to his feet, followed by Ciaro, Fitzsimmons, and Boyers, who had been standing only a couple of feet away. Around them, others got tentatively to their feet and emerged from their hiding places.

Satisfied that no one had been wounded, Hoffa turned grimly to Ciaro. "Well, fuck me," he said resolutely. "If Tobin and the newspapers and President Roosevelt and every fucking *other* body in the world is against me, I *must* be right."

Without giving Ciaro the opportunity to reply, he walked briskly to a nearby truck and jumped on the bumper so the gathered men could see him clearly. "Hey!" he yelled. "You Teamsters! Listen to me, every swinging dick out there!"

Satisfied that he had their attention, Hoffa continued, only slightly less loudly: "We are going to *march* on REA headquarters," he said slowly and deliberately, anxious that there would be no misinterpretation of his orders. "We are going to *demand* that they recognize the Teamsters. We are going to hold together in good order . . . and we are going to goddamn get what we came for."

Having made clear his intention, Hoffa leaped

down and strode briskly off in the direction of the gate. Turning to Boyers, who was grinning broadly, he said, "Let's lead the fucking way."

With Ciaro and Boyers falling in line with him, Hoffa continued directly toward the gate. Sensing that others were not following him as rapidly as he thought they should, Hoffa stopped and turned toward the men.

"Well," he screamed sarcastically, "I thought we were *marching.*"

As if pulled out of shock, the picketers began moving forward in response to Hoffa's orders. He had progressed only two steps when a man ran to his side. Swiveling, Hoffa saw that it was Andrew O'Leary, the *Tribune* reporter he had talked to the day before outside the REA conference room.

"Mr. Hoffa . . . Mr. Hoffa," O'Leary said, breathing heavily from his run. "Are we going to win this strike?"

Hoffa corrected him. "Mr. O'Leary, we already *have* won this strike. We won it when we decided to march."

O'Leary stopped, his eyes wide in fear and excitement. Hurriedly he began scribbling in his notebook, standing erect as the Teamsters poured around him, following Hoffa in the stampede to the REA warehouse.

Ten yards from the gate, Hoffa stopped and surveyed the situation. Now that his decision had been made, he knew exactly what he was going to do; all anxiety had left him. Even though he knew he was walking into an explosive situation, one that would involve gunfire and clubbings, he was composed and unafraid. Calmly he extracted his pack of Camels from his overcoat pocket, removed one of the cigarettes, and lit it. Those standing nearby noted with satisfaction that the hand holding the match was rock steady.

One Teamster just to Hoffa's left raised an ax handle he had concealed beneath his coat. "Let's go," he mumbled to himself. "Let's go get those motherfuckers."

Boyers, who was standing at Hoffa's right shoulder, turned to Hoffa and said, "The right to organize, eh, Jimmy?"

Hoffa, the Camel dangling from his lips, looked steadily at Boyers. "Fuck the right to organize," he said coldly. "Those cocksuckers shot at me."

To prepare for the action he knew was coming, Hoffa reached inside his coat, unbuckled his belt, and whipped it free of the loops. When he lifted it, Boyers could see that it had a heavy metal buckle. Wrapping the strap around his hand so the buckle could dangle loosely, Hoffa tossed away his cigarette and began striding forward.

Ciaro, fulfilling his role of faithful chief lieutenant, turned to the Teamsters as Hoffa began his advance. "Okay, you fuckers," he screamed. "There goes the Little Guy. He's out there; he ain't scared. Now let's get out there *with* him."

With a subdued roar, the group of Teamsters surged forward. As they moved, Ciaro noted that several others had produced weapons. A few of them also had ax handles. Several had shovels, complete with the metal heads. One or two had baseball bats. And some, following Hoffa's lead, had undone their belts and were wrapping them around their fists. One man held a placard aloft, like a battle flag. It read RAILWAY EXPRESS AGENCY UNFAIR TO ORGANIZED LABOR.

Three feet behind Hoffa, ahead of many of the strikers, was O'Leary, his face flushed with anticipation. He paused to write in his notebook, but as he did so he was jostled and pushed forward by the surge of Teamsters behind him. Fuck it, he said to himself. I can remember *this* without notes.

"You motherfuckers!" Hoffa screamed at a group of REA men who had begun pouring out of the warehouse to meet the oncoming Teamsters. "You cocksuckers! You slimy bastards."

The REA men, some of whom had also produced ax handles, baseball bats, and lengths of lumber, were screaming, too, moving forward at a trot, anxious to join battle. One of them ran directly at Hoffa.

Judging the rapidity of his approach, Hoffa timed his move. "Take that, you dickhead," he roared, swinging his belt so the buckle clipped the REA man precisely as he came into range. The man staggered backward, blood streaming from a gash across his forehead. Without a word, he sank to the ground.

"Yes!" Hoffa screamed in excitement. "Yes! Yes! Yes! Let's go men! Let's take these bastards!"

Turning, he urged his men on. "You with the placards. Raise 'em up. Fly 'em high. Let's get those signs *up.*"

Motioning to Ciaro to follow, Hoffa strode briskly a dozen yards out of the way, clearing the path for the advancing Teamsters, who were meeting the REA troops with swinging clubs and fists and excited shouts.

"Where's Fitzsimmons?" he asked Ciaro.

Ciaro shrugged.

"Fitz!" Hoffa called out loudly. "Fitzsimmons, where the hell are you?" He scanned the line then turned to Ciaro. "Keep 'em moving."

Ciaro nodded. "All right, you guys, let's go. Keep going. Don't let those REA fuckers slow us down. Keep advancing. Let's *take* that fucking building."

As Hoffa looked around, studying the mob of Teamsters for Fitzsimmons, he came jogging up. "After this is over," Hoffa whispered to him, "when we sit down to discuss what we did, you're going to hear a lot of shit. Dan Tobin is going to come in and start talking about how he thinks the meeting should go—"

"No," Fitzsimmons interrupted, "you should run the meeting, Jimmy. Not Tobin. You're the one putting your ass on the line."

Hoffa looked at him incredulously. You poor fuck, he thought. You poor dumb fuck. Don't you have any fucking *idea* about how things work, how politics seeps into *everything*. Rather than articulate this, Hoffa simply nodded.

"You're right, Fitz," he said. "But listen to me . . ."

Before he could finish, O'Leary came running up. "You're going to do it," he said fervently. "You're going to make it. You're going to take the REA."

Hoffa did not respond, saying to himself that it was far too early to declare a victory. O'Leary and the others might not know it yet, he thought, but the REA hasn't even started to fight. They haven't even begun to call out the heavy artillery.

O'Leary broke Hoffa's train of thought. "But what about casualties?" he asked. "What about your wounded? How many men you think have been hurt?"

Hoffa shrugged, unconcerned about the number of wounded so far. The toll, he knew, had not even begun to mount.

"You're going to have casualties in *any* conflict," he told the reporter. "The question should be: are the casualties worth the gain?"

"Well"—O'Leary grinned—"are they?"

Hoffa grinned back. "You're fucking A," he said.

As Hoffa spoke a line of trucks began approaching from the other direction, out of Hoffa's view. They looked like army trucks, the kind that were used to transport troops to the front. The cargo portion was covered with canvas and, inside, like the military trucks they resembled, they carried reinforcements. Armed reinforcements.

When he heard the trucks, Hoffa swiveled. As he did so the first vehicle made a tight turn and appeared at first to be retreating. Instead the driver was simply pointing the back of the vehicle at the line of advancing Teamsters. As soon as the driver braked to a halt, someone inside threw back the canvas flap and Hoffa could see that the vehicle was packed with men. As he watched, someone else lowered the tailgate and the men inside leaped to the ground and surged forward. They were armed with pistols, rifles, and tear-gas guns.

Somewhere in the rear, a woman began screaming. The Teamsters, shocked by the sudden arrival of heavily armed reinforcements, just when they felt they were on the verge of breaking through the REA front and rushing into the warehouse, paused to see what the development portended.

Ciaro, who had been pounding an REA man with a baseball bat he had wrenched from the man's grasp, looked up to see what was happening. Out of the corner of his eye, he saw two REA men leap forward and attack Hoffa, who went down under their combined weight.

With a roar, Ciaro quit hitting the man on the ground and jumped to Hoffa's aid. A volley of gunfire erupted and Teamsters began dropping all around him. Some, as they had done earlier, were instinctively hugging the ground for protection. Others were wounded, dead, or dying.

One man near Ciaro let out a loud scream as his right hand disappeared in a cloud of blood and tissue, the result of being struck by a high-velocity bullet fired from a deer rifle. Another doubled over, a geyser of blood erupting from his back where a metal-tipped bullet exited.

As Ciaro heaved himself on top of Hoffa's attackers, the roar of gunfire and screams drowned out all thought.

Inside the warehouse, out of the line of sight of Hoffa, Ciaro, and Fitzsimmons, who was crouching next to a wounded Teamster, his trousers soggy with urine as a result of an involuntary relaxation of his bladder muscles, Harold Davis stood at a window, solemnly observing the unequal battle that was taking place in front of him. Smiling in grim satisfaction, he watched as the line of Teamsters collapsed and the REA troops, led by the newly arrived reinforcements, swept forward, sending the strikers into a bloody, disorganized retreat.

"That ought to teach that arrogant little fucker," Davis mumbled to himself. "Let's see what he has to tell the reporters now about his *successful* negotiations."

12
1 9 4 2

Three days later there was a memorial service at the Teamsters headquarters on Trumbull Avenue. The yellow brick building in the shadow of downtown was jammed with Teamsters and Teamster sympathizers, there to mourn their dead and wounded. The first thing Hoffa had done, even as he and Ciaro were dragging their gashed and bruised bodies away from the scene of the REA massacre, was to begin planning the service. Even though he had never been in the military—indeed, he was exempt from the draft because of his position with the Teamsters, which was considered an organization vital to the war effort—he instinctively knew the importance of regrouping after a battle, especially a bloody defeat. It was crucial, he felt, to gather the troops, to let them grieve for their casualties, then reunite them in furtherance of a common and re-enunciated goal.

As soon as he could find Fitzsimmons among the milling, disorganized Teamsters, Hoffa gave him explicit instructions on what he wanted done, then ordered him to carry through on the details.

Fitzsimmons, grateful for his overcoat, which he kept buttoned from knee to neck to cover the sight, but not entirely the smell, of his "accident," was only too happy to have something to do to take his thoughts off the night's events.

On the night of the service, Hoffa walked into the large central meeting room of the union headquarters and looked around with satisfaction. Fitzsimmons had done a good job. That little mick, he thought, may pay for his keep after all.

The back of the room was filled with wreaths and potted plants. A set of bleachers had been jury-rigged against the wall so all the flowers could readily be seen by the audience. At the forefront of the floral display, in a place of unchallenged prominence, was one huge wreath of bright red roses. It bore a tag reading, *Daniel J. Tobin and the International express their deepest sympathy to the families and friends of their brother Teamsters, fallen in defense of the union and the principles of brotherhood.*

Between the floral display and the audience was an open space that was occupied by eleven flower-covered caskets. Immediately in front of the caskets were several rows of folding chairs, which were reserved for the families of the dead. The spectators, many of them sporting bandages, splints, dark bruises, and swollen faces, were crowded into the back of the hall.

In chairs reserved for them next to the families of the dead sat Hoffa, his wife Jo, and their two young children, Barbara Ann, still a preschooler, and James, barely old enough to walk.

Hoffa turned to his wife. "You want anything?" he asked solicitously. "A glass of water?"

She shook her head, extracting a handkerchief to wipe away tears, which had begun to stream down her cheeks at the sight of the bare wooden coffins.

"I'll be right back," Hoffa said gently. "I got to go talk to somebody."

Again Jo nodded but did not reply.

Making his way around the edge of the crowd, passing by the foot of the caskets, Hoffa approached a refreshment table that had been set up against one wall. Standing at the end of the table were Fitzsimmons, Pete Connelly, Boyers, and several others. They had plates of food in their hands and glasses of punch—liberally spiked—sat on the table, readily at hand.

"Petey and I—" Fitzsimmons began as Hoffa walked up.

Hoffa, anticipating what he was going to say, broke in. "Thanks, Fitz. I appreciate the sentiments. And you done a good job setting this up." Fitzsimmons nodded in grateful appreciation.

Turning to Connelly, Hoffa greeted him in a subdued voice. "Hi, Pete," he said. "How's it going?"

"I'm sorry, Jimmy," Connelly said. "I really am."

"That's okay, Pete. I know you are. We all are."

For several minutes they stood in embarrassed silence, none of them sure what to say. Boyers and the others had strolled off, feeling that Hoffa wanted to be alone with Fitzsimmons and Connelly, which, in reality, was the *last* thing he wanted. It was the first time since the night of the shooting that he had seen Fitzsimmons and he did not feel under any strong compulsion to be isolated with him now. Once he had given him his instructions, Hoffa did not feel it necessary to make sure they were being carried out. He knew they would be or Fitzsimmons, regardless of his political pull with Tobin, would be on the street.

"This roast beef is good," Fitzsimmons said in an attempt to break the increasingly awkward silence.

Hoffa glanced at his plate, seeing that

Fitzsimmons had taken bread from one end of the table, roast beef from the other, and helpings of several things in between, and put them together into a Dagwood-style sandwich. "Yeah," he said, unsure how to respond.

"What's next, Jimmy?" Fitzsimmons asked tentatively. "Where do we go from here?"

Hoffa, unwilling to commit himself yet, not in the hall where a memorial service was being held, and especially not initially to Fitzsimmons, did not answer directly.

"I got some ideas," he said noncommittally.

Fitzsimmons, sensing that it would be inappropriate and perhaps downright foolish to pursue this discussion, nodded and took a bite of his sandwich.

"Is there anything I can do?" Connelly asked.

Hoffa, remembering his last experience with Connelly, the shouting match that had occurred shortly before he left his office and been stopped by Bladesdale, looked coldly at the young man. "Yeah," he said frostily, "you can get my wife a sandwich."

At the word "sandwich," Ciaro appeared at Hoffa's elbow. Taking in the situation in a glance, he locked eyes with Hoffa.

"Need to talk to you," he whispered.

In the background the ceremonies had begun. A preacher with a very deep voice intoned, ". . . and the women of labor weep. The women of labor weep for the fallen, for their men who fell, and for their children, who must . . ."

"Just what we need," Hoffa confided to Ciaro. "A fucking mick on a podium."

Suppressing a grin, Ciaro edged Hoffa away from the crowd. "Come with me," he said, still in a whisper.

Hoffa raised his eyebrows, but followed Ciaro willingly.

They left the meeting room and strolled down a

short hallway to an office that was used by several of the local business agents. It was a sterile-looking, utilitarian room, furnished only with cheap wooden desks and straight backed chairs. Its purpose, Hoffa felt, was only as a place where his lieutenants could do their basic paperwork. The rest of the time—most of the time—Hoffa expected them to be out of the headquarters working the streets. New members didn't get signed up by people sitting at desks. As a result, the trappings of their office was spartan.

There was only one window in the room and it was heavily curtained, more to keep the people inside from public view as to keep out the sunshine. The curtain was in place and only one lamp was lit inside. Most of the room was in heavy shadow and it were]s empty.

"Why'd you bring me here?" Hoffa asked.

"So we could talk for a minute."

"We couldn't talk out in the hall?"

"Out there, even the walls have ears. I wanted to prepare you."

"Prepare me for what?" Hoffa asked, puzzled.

"Dally's outside," Ciaro said quietly. "He wants to see you."

Hoffa was surprised. He had not seen Dally D'Allesandro since the Kreger strike, the night he made his deal with Scialla.

"What's he want?"

"I don't know," Ciaro said. "He just showed up. Sent one of his men to find me and said he wanted to see you outside."

Hoffa pondered this. "Well," he said a minute later, "let's go see what he wants."

It was a beautiful night in Detroit. The air was crisp and clear and the stars shone brightly overhead. It took Ciaro and Hoffa only two minutes to find

D'Allesandro, who was leaning against a shiny new Packard on the edge of the parking lot, talking to two of his men. When they approached, D'Allesandro flipped away the Lucky Strike he had been smoking and moved forward to greet Hoffa.

"We sent flowers," he said, taking Hoffa's hand and elbow. For a heartbeat, Hoffa was afraid that D'Allesandro was going to embrace him in the old-world fashion.

"I saw them," Hoffa said, gripping D'Allesandro's hand warmly. "Thanks for coming."

"This makes me sad," D'Allesandro said in his well-modulated, unaccented voice. With a little training, Hoffa thought, this man would make a hell of a politican. "Nothing is ever settled by violence."

"Yeah," Hoffa agreed. "I've heard that."

As Ciaro had done just a few minutes earlier, D'Allesandro took Hoffa's elbow and carefully steered him away from the group. They had gone just a little way when the union boss paused, staring in the direction of the headquarters.

Following his gaze, D'Allesandro saw that the crowd was beginning to leave the building, the service apparently concluded. "Always looking to you, aren't they?" he asked.

"What do we do?" Hoffa's question was addressed as much to himself as to D'Allesandro. "What do we do now? What do we do next?"

"Of *course* they're looking to you," D'Allesandro added, seemingly not having heard Hoffa's soul-searching questions.

Hoffa shrugged. "Who wouldn't want to have a leader?" he asked.

"And when they've failed," added D'Allesandro, picking up the thread, "they say, 'I'm sorry, boss.' And if they're punished—or forgiven—it's the same thing." He paused, then added, "Isn't it?"

"Either way they're pardoned," Hoffa replied.

"But no one pardons us," D'Allesandro said. "And if they could, we wouldn't let them." Looking closely at Hoffa, he added, "And they would rather that some people die—through your mistake—than that they lived but lacked a leader."

Hoffa, unsure how to respond, remained silent. Side by side, they continued walking, this time back toward the Packard.

They reached the car without any further conversation. When they got there, D'Allesandro again extended his hand. Hoffa took it and nodded.

D'Allesandro got into his car, signaled to the man behind the wheel, and the large limousine pulled out of the lot and disappeared, heading in the direction of Tiger Stadium, now closed and dark for the winter.

Hoffa and Ciaro watched silently as the car passed through the light traffic, then they turned and started walking back toward the headquarters. Just as he got to the door, Hoffa met a woman exiting the building.

A large woman in early middle age, she was clad all in black and her face, even in the weak light from the bulb over the door, was streaked with tears.

Hoffa stopped and said a few quiet words to her. Then suddenly he started to cry, the tears flowing copiously down his cheeks. Ciaro, standing a few feet away, was amazed. Never before had he seen Hoffa exhibit such emotion.

As Ciaro watched, the woman reached up and threw her arms around Hoffa's neck and drew him to her. Still sobbing, Hoffa submitted willingly to the embrace.

As Ciaro watched, fascinated, he became aware of a noise in the background. Tearing his attention off Hoffa, he realized with mild surprise that it was a telephone. Somewhere in the building, a telephone was ringing insistently and no one was taking the trouble to answer it. He stood there and listened to it ring. And ring. And ring.

13

1 9 7 5

As he listened to the phone ringing on the other end, Ciaro thought about the night of the memorial service so many years ago. It was me and Jimmy and D'Allesandro then, he thought, and it's me and Jimmy and D'Allesandro now. Except things are different now. That night we was all friends. Today I ain't so sure.

Subconsciously, he was counting the rings. Six . . . seven . . . he was just about to hang up when someone answered. Ciaro recognized the voice immediately.

"Hey, Dominic," he said, his voice harsh, mixed with relief and anger, happy that somebody finally picked it up, pissed off because he and Hoffa were still being kept waiting at the Red Fox. "This is Bobby, as if you didn't know . . . Yeah, we're still here, me and the Little Guy, but where the fuck is *he?*"

He listened, his eyes roaming around the diner. "Yeah, well, I'm getting tired of hearing . . . How can you not know where the fuck . . . Well, listen." He looked at his watch. "It's five after three and by my book that's—"

Ciaro held the receiver away from his ear and

rolled his eyes. "That's your fucking problem, Dominic," he managed to sneak in, "mine is—"

Again he listened, his eyes wandering, then lighting on the young driver, the kid who had tried to give him some shit. He was still hanging around, waiting, Ciaro figured, for him to give up the phone. Fat fucking chance of that, he told himself, not as long as that was the boss's tie-line to D'Allesandro.

As Ciaro stared the driver looked at *his* watch, sighed, and lifted himself off the stool. Nervously he paced back and forth along the counter. Reaching into a pocket in his jeans, he pulled out a bent cardboard package of Marlboros and took out one of the two cigarettes that remained in the pack. Staring out the window, he removed a battered Zippo from another pocket and absentmindedly lit his cigarette.

Idly the kid studied the engraving on the lighter, one he picked up at the black market in Da Nang. It read, *Yea, though I walk through the Valley of Death I have no fear because I'm the meanest son of a bitch in the Valley.* That's me, the kid thought, the meanest son-of-a-bitch in the valley. Except this ain't a valley, this is De-fucking-troit.

Ciaro watched in silence, waiting for Dominic to run out of excuses. Finally he could take it no longer. "Listen, asshole," he said angrily. "I don't want any more shit. We had a meet. With D'Allesandro. We're here. He ain't. You say he ain't there. Well, he sure as shit ain't here either. And we're getting fucking tired of waiting . . . You what? . . . You don't know . . . Well, find him, you fuckhead!" he screamed, slamming down the receiver and kicking the door open.

The driver turned on his heels, quick as a cat, Ciaro thought, at the sound of the receiver being slammed into its cradle. Without speaking to him, Ciaro strode to the counter and signaled to Fat Albert.

"Where's them coffees, Fat? How long I got to fucking wait just for a couple of coffees?"

Fat Albert, accustomed to Ciaro's moods and temper, sighed in exasperation. Anyone else, he thought, he'd throw him out on his ass. But him and Ciaro and Hoffa went way back, back to the days when Fat Albert hadn't been fat and had made his living as a hard-fisted driver, one of the early Teamsters. He had been at the REA warehouse the night of the massacre and had a six-inch scar down his back to prove it, a souvenir from one of the REA strikebreakers who thought he could cut Albert up and get away with it. Instead Albert had taken the man's knife away, had him down on the ground, and was about to cut his throat when the shooting started. Because of those ties, he let Ciaro get away with a lot. Hoffa, too, for that matter. No matter how busy he was, Fat Albert always kept a booth open for the Little Guy, just in case he happened to drop in. Even when Hoffa and Ciaro were in prison and there was no chance of them showing up, Fat Albert kept a booth reserved. It was a matter of principle, a way of showing his respect.

"On the way, Bobby," Fat Albert called to Ciaro down the length of the counter. "On the way."

Ciaro, still fuming, drummed his fingers on the counter and pondered the possibilities. When the driver, the man to whom Ciaro had already mentally assigned the name "Kid," spoke, it startled him so much he jumped.

"What's that?" he said angrily.

"I just asked," Kid repeated, "if you was through with the phone. I got to make a call myself."

"Oh, yeah. Sure," Ciaro said. "But don't be long. I'm waiting for an important call." Examining him closely, he asked suspiciously, "How come you still hanging around?"

"Don't think I want to be here," Kid answered lightly. "I just can't fucking go anywhere. Not with a thrown torque rod."

"Oh," Ciaro said sympathetically. "That bad, huh?

No wonder you ain't going nowhere. What you doing about it?"

"Talked to my dispatcher. He said they was going to send somebody to fix it. But that was four hours ago. In the meantime, I'm still fucking sitting here."

Ciaro digested what he had said. "Listen, Kid," he said. "I want you to do me a favor. If the phone rings, you answer it. *Whoever* it is, you say, 'He's going to be right back.' You do that for me while I run quick like out to the car."

"Two coffees," Fat Albert said, leaning across the counter. "Here you go."

Ciaro picked up the coffees. "You do that for me? You answer the phone and deliver my message?"

"This union business?" Kid asked.

"Yeah," Ciaro answered. "That's what it is. First, I got to take these coffees out to the car."

"Who's in the car?"

"Who's in the car is My Guy, and who's here is you watching the phone. You scratch my back, I'll scratch yours. You help me out with the phone, I'll make a call and get somebody who'll get that rod out to you quicker than you can start your rig. And that's no shit."

The kid nodded his agreement. "Sounds fair," he said.

Ciaro turned toward the door and was walking away when Kid spoke to him again.

"Who's Your Guy?" he asked. "Who is Your Guy that you all the time got to be his nigger? Who is it you got to run to him when he wiggles his pinky?"

Ciaro paused. In response, he simply smiled. Turning again, he crossed the room, opened the door, and walked briskly across the parking lot.

The trucker watched Ciaro as he crossed the hot asphalt. Watched him all the way to the Pontiac, and then watched him still as he set the coffees on the roof and opened the door.

14
1 9 5 6

Sitting alone in the station wagon, staring at the enveloping forest and the bright blue water of Lake Orion, listening to the profound North Woods silence, Bobby Ciaro had never felt more out of his element. He jumped when a jay squawked in a nearby pine, and the flat slap of a bass jumping on the lake sent him groping for his ever-present pistol. How does Jimmy fucking stand it out here? he asked himself. "He can have his goddamn 'tranquillity,'" he mumbled, "I'll take the city anytime."

Detroit—De-fucking-troit, as Ciaro affectionately referred to it—was only fifty-three miles away, but that was a considerable distance considering the terrain, two and a half hours by car over gritty dirt roads, around hairpin turns, up steep inclines that turned into toboggan runs when it rained or snowed. And the payoff for making the journey, the pot of gold at the end of the rainbow, was a drafty four-room, wood-shingled cabin equipped with little more than a wood stove, four sets of squeaky and incredibly

uncomfortable bunk beds, and a couch Ciaro immediately classified as a Salvation Army reject.

Ciaro looked at his watch and sighed. Shading his
eyes with his hand, he scanned the skies, searching
for the telltale spot in the distance. All he saw, in
every direction, was empty blue, a blue so brilliant
that if he had not witnessed it for himself, he would
never have believed it existed. In the city, he thought,
nobody ever looks at the sky. Nobody ever looks *up*,
nobody, that is, except the hayseeds just in from the
country who had never seen a building taller than a
silo before.

And he listened, *really* listened, straining his ears
for the sound of the seaplane engine, the indication
that the others were on the way.

When D'Allesandro had sent word to Jimmy a
week ago that they needed to talk, that there was an
item of extreme importance that he wanted to discuss, the question had not been whether but where.
It wasn't like the old days, Ciaro reflected, when the
boss had been plain old Jimmy Hoffa, the guy who
could wander in and out of his Trumbull Avenue
office, seeing whoever he wanted, whenever he wanted, wherever he wanted, because who he saw and
what they discussed was nobody's business but Jimmy
Hoffa's and whoever he was meeting with. But those
days—the era when the Teamsters were struggling to
become a force in the labor movement, when the
membership was counted in the hundreds and the
opening of a new local was considered a major
achievement, the days when Jimmy's grandest title
was president of Detroit Local 299—were gone. Now
that the Teamsters had achieved national prominence and had 1.6 million members on the rolls,
more than a billion dollars in the bank, and contracts
with eight hundred different employers, things were
different. It was, Ciaro reflected with pride, the third

largest individual union in the country, behind only
the United Auto Workers and the Steelworkers. And,
even more important, Hoffa was on the way to being
a *real* national power.

Ciaro remembered the night the local—299, in his
mind, would always be *the* local—celebrated its victory
over management at Kreger's, the night that all the
glory had gone to Red Bennett when Jimmy had really done all the work. Bennett, Ciaro thought ironically, who was now feeding the worms in Woodmere
Cemetery, God rest his soul, because he had only a
club and the Pinkerton prick had a pistol and
Bennett was too stubborn and too stupid to run.
Ciaro remembered leaving the local with Jimmy and
how they stopped to help a truck driver change a flat.
And he recalled how Hoffa had revealed his ambition
to be president of the Teamsters. That was the night,
too, that Hoffa had offered him a job as an organizer,
that he became part of the Teamsters' official family.

Well, I still don't have a big title, he thought, but
Jimmy ain't done bad. Ciaro, probably more than
Hoffa himself, remembered each rung of the ladder,
each step Hoffa had climbed to get where he was. He
had been negotiating chairman for the Teamsters
Car Handling Group. He was negotiating chairman
for the Central States Drivers Council, responsible for
contracts in a dozen Midwestern states. He had been
president of the Midwestern Conference of
Teamsters, and he had been president of the
Teamsters Joint Council in Detroit.

Since he had nothing else to do, no distractions to
occupy his mind, Ciaro struggled to put things in
proper sequence. Counting on his fingers, he reckoned that it had been almost four years ago that
Hoffa had been elected a vice-president of the
International, an office that put him right up there
with Dan Tobin and Dave Beck, that stupid, greedy

son-of-a-bitch from the West Coast. Soon after that, Tobin retired and Beck took over. Then Beck named Hoffa to head the powerful Central Conference of Teamsters, which put him in line for Beck's job, the coveted presidency, when Beck decided to retire or when he went to jail, whichever came first.

No question about it, Ciaro laughed to himself, Beck was in deep shit. Not content with raking off a little for himself, which was what everyone expected a man in power to do, Beck had wanted a lot, much more than could be explained away as a little simple graft. First he had demanded a salary of fifty thousand dollars a year, which was a lot of fucking money in anybody's books. Then he wanted an unlimited expense account to go along with the big paycheck. But even that didn't make him happy. He had to go and get his local to buy his house, his fucking house, Ciaro recalled bitterly, just so he could continue to live there rent free.

But that was only scratching the surface. Beck had been so greedy and so blatant about it that he had attracted attention in Washington, especially when he decided to build the new headquarters, that goddamn Taj Mahal that cost the union five million dollars and had imported marble in the lobby, private baths in the executive offices, a 474-seat auditorium, and a free cafeteria complete with a French chef and table service in the executive dining room. Ciaro spat. Executive dining room, my ass! No wonder the congressmen were riled. I mean, just the building was bad enough, but picking a site on Louisiana Avenue, only a third of a mile away from the Capitol, was too fucking much. Now all those politicians, suddenly aware that the Teamsters represented a national power, were all stirred up, like a nest of goddamn hornets, and they were after Beck's ass.

The really bad thing—not that he or Hoffa gave a

shit about Beck—was that Beck's shit splashed on Jimmy, too. All the congressmen heard was "Teamsters" and it didn't make dick to them whether it was Dave Beck or Jimmy Hoffa. As far as they were concerned, *all* fucking Teamsters were crooked. And that included the boss. Because of that, Hoffa had to be careful about who he met and where he met them. It wasn't any secret that D'Allesandro was connected. Shit, everybody knew that, certainly everybody in Detroit and probably every other big city in the country, too, not excluding Washington. What everybody didn't know was that Hoffa was a very loyal guy, a guy who would stick by you once you became his friend no matter what. And, no question, D'Allesandro had helped him back in the early days, back when they were fighting Kreger and a victory meant a lot.

So when D'Allesandro called and asked for a meeting, Hoffa busted his butt to make it happen. He didn't care about D'Allesandro's ties with what the newspapers and the politicians liked to call "the mob." As far as Ciaro and Hoffa were concerned, D'Allesandro and his buddies were in *business.* Until Hoffa came along, they had made a lot of money selling manpower to management, men the owners used as strikebreakers, men who busted the balls, not to mention the heads, of the workingman. Jimmy convinced them that they were on the wrong side, that the days of complete management domination of industry were over, that labor represented the wave of the future. And he had been right. Look at where unions were today and how far they had come. These days, not the least because of Hoffa, a truck driver could hold his head up with anybody. He drew a respectable paycheck, lived in a nice house in the suburbs, and could afford to send his kids to college so they could become doctors and dentists and lawyers and leave the calluses and the grease under the fingernails behind. Shit, that was progress. That was *justice*.

What Ciaro did not understand was why those ass-holes in Washington were so upset. The Teamsters were just doing what management had been doing for fucking ever. When the owners were hiring hoods to break the bones of strikers nobody on Capitol fucking Hill ever got nervous about it. But now that the unions had learned the system, had goddamn taken it away from management, those stuffed shirts were all acting like a bunch of spoiled kids having a temper tantrum.

If Beck got sticky fingers and he embarrassed everybody, then slap his fucking wrist. Throw his ass in jail. But leave the boss a-fucking-lone. Hoffa didn't give a shit about big houses and fancy cars and la-di-da swishy suits. The boss and his family, for chris-sakes, still lived in that little house Jimmy had built in 1939 for $6,800. He didn't have a big fucking estate in the country. All he had was this chickenshit little cabin out in the middle of no-fucking-where, a place you couldn't even find because of the weeds and the trees until Jimmy bought it fifteen years ago for next to nothing and spent every spare hour he could find putting it into shape, if you could call this "shape."

Jesus, Ciaro thought, looking at his watch for the twentieth time, where the fuck are they? Nervously he reached for a cigarette, surprising himself when his fingers touched the rough wool shirt Hoffa had con-vinced him to don for the trip to the lake. Wool, he thought. If God wanted me to wear wool, he would have made me a fucking sheep. Fishing a pack of Pall Malls from the left breast pocket, Ciaro shook one out, jammed it in his mouth, and reached for his lighter. Bored, he groped behind the seat with the hand that was not holding the cigarette and pulled a can of beer from the six-pack he had thankfully remembered to tote along. Getting out of the car, he stretched, popped the top on the beer, and took a long swallow. Alternating drags on his cigarette with sips of beer, Ciaro unenthusiastically watched two jays fighting over what he had decided was a dead lizard.

He was taking the last sip of beer when he heard it, a faint drone off to the south that he at first feared might be an outboard motor. But as it got louder Ciaro decided it was not fishermen after all, but the plane he had been expecting. Again shielding his eyes, he gazed across the lake and saw the small speck in the sky. Thank God, he thought, looking at his watch again. Absentmindedly he set the empty beer can on top of a post in the split-rail fence Hoffa had laboriously constructed around his property and strolled down to the Hoffa-built dock that jutted into Lake Orion.

Ciaro was mildly surprised to see not the one plane he expected but two lining up for a landing on the lake. They must have decided to come in two vehicles, he thought. As he watched, one of the planes landed and glided gracefully to a stop. The door opened and Hoffa leaped out, clad in a dark blue business suit he had bought off the rack at Frank & Seder's and black loafers from Thom McAn's. When he stepped out of the plane's cabin onto the pontoon, Ciaro noticed with an inner smile the white athletic socks that extended halfway up his calf. Emerging behind him were Frank Fitzsimmons and Pete Connelly, who also wore suits, except theirs came from Brooks Brothers instead of the department store where Hoffa once worked as a stockboy, and their shoes were from Fitzgerald's, an expensive men's store off Woodward.

As the second plane was cruising up to the shore, Ciaro pulled Hoffa aside. "Got news for you, boss," he said softly, almost in a whisper.

"Yeah?" Hoffa replied, raising his eyebrows.

"He said he'd have to go with Test Fleet."

Hoffa looked satisfied. "And he said he'd go for it?"

"As it was laid down, with what we said we would do and what he said he would do. Under those circumstances, he'd do it."

Hoffa smiled. "Then sign them with Test Fleet. Give 'em my thanks and send them a bottle of—what the fuck does the little mick drink?"

"Crown Royal."

"Okay, then send him some Crown Royal. And include a little card that says, 'A good business deal benefits all.'" Hoffa could not repress himself; he burst out laughing. "Nah, forget that 'business deal' stuff. Just say thanks."

As they were talking D'Allesandro approached. He, too, wore business attire, but his suit, a rich-looking cashmere blend, had been crafted at a bespoke shop in London, as had his immaculate white-on-white silk shirt and rich crimson tie, the knot of which had been loosened. His shoes were not really shoes but black leather half-boots that were made at a tiny store on Queens Road in Hong Kong, not far from the cricket pitch. His pilot had already started his engine and was preparing to take off. The plane that had carried Hoffa and the others still bobbed gently at anchor while the pilot unloaded the luggage.

"How's your wife?" D'Allesandro asked, taking Hoffa's hand and gripping it warmly.

"She's good."

"And the kids?"

"They're good, too."

Looking down the road to the spot where he figured the cabin had to be, he added, "And how's your new kitchen?"

Hoffa grinned broadly. "It's costing me an arm and a leg," he said.

"You should do it yourself," D'Allesandro said in mock admonishment.

"I *am* doing it myself," Hoffa said. "That's how come it's so fucking expensive."

They both laughed, then Hoffa turned to Ciaro. "Did you bring it?" he asked.

Ciaro, in response, walked to the station wagon, opened the back, reached in, and extracted a long, slim wooden case. Without a word, he opened the box, revealing a highly polished rifle.

Fitzsimmons and Connelly had joined Hoffa and D'Allesandro, and all were huddled around the back of the vehicle. As they watched, Ciaro lifted the rifle out of the case and held it across his chest, like a soldier on parade.

Hoffa nodded slightly toward D'Allesandro. Ciaro, recognizing his cue, hesitated for less than a heartbeat before handing the weapon to the mobster.

Accepting it as eagerly as a woman would take a proffered infant, D'Allesandro cradled it in his arms for a few seconds, then held it out to look at it. Without a word, he opened the action. Seeing it was empty, he looked at Ciaro, who reached in his pocket and withdrew a handful of bullets, which he passed over.

D'Allesandro fitted them into the weapon, chambered a round, and lifted the rifle to his shoulder, swinging it around, looking for a target. When he spotted the beer can that Ciaro had inadvertently left on the fence post earlier, he took aim.

When he fired and the beer can remained in place, Hoffa could not suppress a laugh. "You piece of shit."

Giving him a dirty look, D'Allesandro lifted the

rifle and fired a second time. Again he missed.

"Give me that fucking thing," Hoffa said, extending his hand for the weapon, which D'Allesandro reluctantly handed over.

Hoffa squinted down the barrel and jerked the trigger, sending his shot singing off into the trees.

At that, D'Allesandro laughed. "That'll teach you to make fun of me, asshole," he said with a smile.

Hoffa's jaw muscles tightened and again he lifted the rifle to his shoulder. This time he aimed more carefully and gently squeezed the trigger. The blue and silver can went spinning off into the forest with a loud twang.

Sighing in relief, Hoffa relaxed and tossed the rifle to Ciaro.

Catching it neatly, Ciaro grinned. "About fucking time," he joked. "Who taught you how to shoot? The fucking North Koreans?"

As Ciaro put the rifle back in its case and shoved it into the rear of the station wagon, the pilot arrived with suitcases and three other rifles in neat leather covers. Loading them into the vehicle, he nodded abruptly to Hoffa, returned to the plane, and cranked the engine. Within seconds he was taxiing across the lake. As the five watched in admiration the small plane lifted off, banked, and headed back to the city.

"Well," Hoffa said enthusiastically, climbing into the vehicle's passenger seat, "let's do it."

Connelly, Fitzsimmons, and D'Allesandro squeezed into the back and Ciaro slid behind the wheel.

"I got one small rule up here," Hoffa said lightly as soon as the vehicle was rolling, "that I insist upon."

"What's that?" Fitzsimmons asked, ever the straight man.

"*Nobody*," Hoffa said gleefully, "says fucking *nothing*

about any fucking thing to do with *business.*"

• • •

Exercising his prerogative as host, elder statesman, land owner, and vice-president of the International Brotherhood of Teamsters, Hoffa announced an addition to the agenda. He declared the edicts; he could break them. Despite his admonition against discussion of business, Hoffa figured the time was right to broach the reasons for the trip.

The five of them were in a clearing with knee-high grass, surrounded by trees brilliant with oranges and reds. All except Ciaro were now dressed in customary hunting clothes: khaki trousers, plaid wool shirts, heavy jackets, and silly billed caps. Hoffa's clothes were well worn and looked comfortable; the others still looked like they had only recently been removed from their boxes. Ciaro, who shuddered at the thought of redonning that scratchy shirt and stiff trousers, was dressed in a pair of $6.95 slacks from Sears, a Tiger's sweatshirt, and a tan Eisenhower jacket.

"Why did you want to talk?" Hoffa casually asked D'Allesandro.

"Huh?"

"Talk," Hoffa said. "The reason you wanted to come up here?"

"Oh, *that?*" D'Allesandro grinned. "I thought we were forbidden to talk about business."

"Unless *I* bring it up." Hoffa grinned back.

"All right," D'Allesandro said, halting and placing his rifle butt on the ground. When he stopped, the others stopped as well. "Let's talk about your pension fund."

"Pension fund?" Hoffa said, surprised.

"Do I hear a fucking echo in here?" D'Allesandro asked good-naturedly. "The fund you're going to build with assessments from your members. What are you going to whack your guys?"

"Shit, I don't know," Hoffa replied. "I ain't thought about it yet. Maybe each guy a hundred bucks a year."

"Okay," D'Allesandro said patiently. "Whatever. However much you're going to assess them, you are now the bank, right?"

Hoffa nodded. "I'm with you."

"You got your notes out?"

Hoffa gestured to Fitzsimmons. "Fitz, you got a pencil?"

"Yeah," Fitzsimmons said, digging into his pocket. "I think so." After a quick search, he produced a stub. "Never go anywhere without your pencil, I always say." He looked around to see if anyone picked up on the double entendre. If they did, they didn't smile.

"Okay," Hoffa said, passing it to D'Allesandro, "go ahead."

"You give *us* control," D'Allesandro said smoothly, "of say—for starters—twenty million dollars. You *loan* it to us."

"Give me a piece of paper," Hoffa commanded, holding out his hand.

Fitzsimmons shrugged, indicating he had provided the pencil, somebody else had to provide the paper. Connelly, realizing the burden was on him, searched frantically and was about to give up when he remembered his hunting license. Unpinning the plastic shield from his jacket, he removed the document and handed it to Hoffa. Hoffa gave it to D'Allesandro, too.

"Okay," D'Allesandro said, scribbling on the back of the license, "you take your twenty mil, we're going to put it out . . . and then we pay you five points." He continued to write. "Which means one mil a year."

"One mil!" Hoffa said soberly.

"A few more points," D'Allesandro continued.

"That makes twenty-five grand."

"On top of the mil?" Hoffa asked.

D'Allesandro looked up. "Perfectly legit," he said. "Call it a service charge."

Hoffa bobbed his head, seeing the direction in which D'Allesandro was going. "Now," he said, "the rate goes up, the loan goes up—"

D'Allesandro interrupted. "The rate goes up, the loan goes up, the *vig* goes up."

"The same points?" Hoffa asked.

"Look here," said D'Allesandro. "We're going to Nevada . . ."

"Nevada!" Hoffa interjected.

"Yeah. The Teamsters got the money. They're making the loan. We're paying the points."

Ciaro rolled his eyes. Points. Vig. Loans. Who gives a shit? It's only money. Shit, we used to do things for fun. For the challenge. For the workingman. Now it's fucking money. Bored, he looked around, into the empty blue sky, over the empty blue lake, into the trees at the edge of the clearing.

"You say 'the points,'" Hoffa was saying. "That includes—"

"Look," D'Allesandro explained carefully. "What I'm talking about basically is three streams of income."

"Okay," Hoffa agreed. "I see that."

"Which," D'Allesandro continued, "are all *legal*, mind you. *Legal*, and with the percentages we're talking about, accepted practice. One," he said, holding up his index finger, "four and a half percent of the total."

"Yearly?" asked Hoffa.

"Yearly!" responded D'Allesandro.

Ciaro caught a slight movement out of the corner of his eye. Focusing on the spot, he could see a large shape. Tuning out the conversation behind him, he concentrated harder. The shape, he saw, was a large buck. A very large buck. The biggest buck he'd ever seen, which was not saying a lot considering he'd never *seen* a buck before.

"That's the two-and-a-half . . . and the service charge—"

"No, no, no," argued D'Allesandro. "Listen, James. Let me finish. This is . . . ."

Ciaro, his eyes riveted on the buck, watched in fascination as it watched him, the heavily antlered head turned precisely in his direction, large, liquid brown eyes staring into his. As he gaped the deer moved a tiny fraction, just enough to reassure Ciaro that he was not seeing things.

"This is in *addition* to the two-and-a-half," Hoffa said.

"That's it," D'Allesandro said, writing furiously and nodding. "All right. You're putting your money out . . ."

Slowly, aware that any sudden movement might queer his chances completely, Ciaro moved his hand inside his jacket. Letting his fingers crawl across his stomach, he found his pistol and gripped the butt. Gradually he eased the weapon out until it was free of his waistband. Then, quickly extracting it from his jacket, he leveled it and fired, all in one swift motion. He fired a second time, then a third, the roar of his .45 reverberating through the clearing and across the nearby lake. The slugs, designed by the army to stop an adrenaline-propelled running enemy in midstride, thudded into the buck's body. Without a sound or moving its head, it dropped on its front knees, then slowly keeled over with its underside facing the men.

"Holy shit!" exploded Connelly.

"What the fuck?" echoed Fitzsimmons.

"I think I just got me a deer," Ciaro said calmly, resisting the impulse to lift the weapon and blow the smoke from the barrel, as he had seen John Wayne do in countless westerns.

Fitzsimmons and Connelly ran to the buck, which had hardly as much as twitched since it collapsed, and stood looking at the dead animal in awe. Ciaro followed them more slowly. Finally Hoffa and D'Allesandro, still talking and gesturing, wandered over.

Hoffa looked down, noting how all three of Ciaro's slugs had impacted within a foot-wide circle at the base of the deer's neck, where it melded into the shoulder. "*Good* fucking shot!" he exclaimed, slapping Ciaro on the shoulder. "Way to fucking go."

"Beautiful," agreed D'Allesandro, less enthusiastically.

Turning back to Hoffa, he picked up the thread of their conversation. "At *four* percent, Jimmy, listen to what I'm telling you. You take that—"

"I plow it back?"

D'Allesandro nodded eagerly. "That's it! Now let's take *forty* mil."

15
1 9 5 7

Hoffa was enjoying himself in spite of the venue. Standing at the doorway of the richly paneled Senate hearing room, he had the guard's undivided attention. Nattily dressed in a dark blue summer-weight pin-striped suit, stiff white shirt, and maroon silk tie with a subdued floral pattern, he was explaining how Bobby Ciaro had bagged his first deer.

"And then this cocksucker," Hoffa said, grinning and jerking his thumb over his shoulder at Ciaro, "this cocksucker goes underneath his coat and comes out with this piece. *Kaboom!*" He gestured, pointing his index finger as if it were the barrel of Ciaro's .45. *"Kaboom!"* he said again, jerking his arm in imitation of the recoil of a discharged weapon. "And there goes the fucking deer."

The uniformed guard, who had been hanging on Hoffa's every word, burst into laughter.

"Kaboom! Kaboom! Kaboom!" Hoffa said, stopping to wipe tears from the corners of his eyes. "The lure of the great outdoors."

Alfred Blanchard, Hoffa's chief lawyer, who had already heard the story a dozen times, leaned over and whispered to him. "Let's go sit down, Jimmy," he said, nodding toward the polished oak table near the front of the room. There were several other men, all lawyers, already sitting at the table, seemingly dwarfed by the stacks of law books piled in front of them. "I want to go over some of your testimony with you."

Hoffa waved him off. "Just a minute," he said, turning back to the guard.

"You mean you shot that deer in cold blood?" the guard asked Ciaro, still laughing.

Ciaro, no slouch as a straight man when the occasion demanded, shrugged elaborately. "He pulled a knife on me," he said, sending the guard into a fresh paroxysm of laughter.

"Now!" said Hoffa, just warming up. "This guinea cocksucker—wait . . . wait . . . wait! This *goombah* has a dead deer on his hands. So what does he do? He doesn't have a knife to skin the fucker. Neither does anybody else. So he starts digging in his pockets and he comes out with a nail file."

Behind the group there was a slight commotion. The guard, alert to such disturbances, swiveled to see what was happening. At the entrance, another guard was blocking the way of a slight young man in a blue and white seersucker suit. As he watched, the young man raised his arms and threw back his head in frustration.

"You've got to let me in," he argued. "I have to get through."

"Why?" the guard wanted to know. "What makes you think you're so important that I let you in? You see that line of people back there just begging to get in?"

"I'm with the International Brotherhood of

Teamsters," Pete Connelly pleaded, "and I have a message for James R. Hoffa."

The guard continued to block his path. "You got some ID?" he asked in a bored tone.

"Of *course* I got some ID," Connelly said, pulling his wallet out of his jacket pocket.

Ignoring the incident, Hoffa continued with his tale.

"So there's Bobby," he said, laughing, "skinning the fucking deer with a nail file . . ."

Connelly rushed up to the group. "Jimmy," he said, "I got to talk to you."

Hoffa turned to look at him. "One moment," he said brusquely, holding up his hand.

Turning back to the guard, he said, "It occurred to me, heart in my mouth, that maybe I ought to ask him, 'Bobby, where did you learn—'"

"Jimmy," Connelly interrupted. "I have a very important message."

"I'm telling a story," Hoffa growled at Connelly, his eyes blazing. "You understand? I'm telling a story. You got a very important message to *you*. But it ain't so important to *me*. Just hang on one second, Petey. Okay?"

Abashed, Connelly nodded and stepped back, waiting for Hoffa to finish.

"It occurred to me to ask Bobby *where* he learned to skin. But . . . but . . . but," he stumbled, then gave up. "Aw, fuck it!" he said. "I lost my chain of thought."

"That's okay, Jimmy," the guard said, still smiling. "I get the picture. Reminds me of—"

A gavel rapped loudly and a deep male voice, like what Ciaro imagined the voice of God would sound like, interrupted. "Come to order," the voice ordered. "The room will now come to order."

As the voice pleaded for quiet, television cameramen who had been chatting on the side rushed to their equipment. Reporters ceased their conversation and straightened in their chairs.

"This is the Senate Select Committee on Improper Activities in the Labor or Management Field, meeting in general session on the twentieth day of August 1957," the voice intoned. "The meeting will now come to order."

Hoffa stood where he was, seemingly reluctant to take his seat and formally join battle. In reality, he was simply putting his game face on, adjusting his thoughts and focusing his energy for the upcoming ordeal.

The guard with whom he had been joking had quit laughing. Turning to Hoffa, he soberly whispered, "How do you think it's going to go, Jimmy?"

Hoffa, all thought of laughter and "stories" erased from his mind, looked sternly at the man. "How do I think it's going to go?" he repeated. "I'm going to win. You can put your money on it. Right—that's me—will prevail."

Gesturing with his head toward the front of the room, the union leader spoke, half to himself. "Look at him," he said, indicating a slim, dark-haired man in his early thirties, a dozen years younger than himself, who was sitting to the right of the voice. Hoffa knew he was not a member of the committee, yet he obviously was very much a part of the hearing. Sensing that Hoffa was staring at him, the man looked up from a sheaf of papers he had clutched in his hand and stared back, a tight smile on his thin lips.

"Look at the little fag," Hoffa said in a stage whisper to the guard, disgust evident in his tone. "He couldn't get laid in a whorehouse, but here he is trying to make a name for himself. Fuck him. Let him go get a job. If he wants a reputation, let him go rob a bank."

"Mr. Hoffa," the voice intoned. "Mr. Hoffa, will you please take your seat so these proceedings may begin."

"Someday," the guard confided in a tone of hero worship, ignoring the voice, "are you going to organize the cops?"

Hoffa turned to him and grinned. "The *cops*?" He laughed. "Shit, that would be easy. Someday we're going to organize the crooks."

Some months before, the Democrats had regained control of the Senate and, eager to show the party's dedication to reform, had created a bipartisan group to probe alleged racketeering in the labor movement. Commonly called the McClellan Committee after its chairman, John McClellan of Arkansas, the group began its series of investigations late in 1956 by looking at several unions, including that of the plumbers, steamfitters, retail clerks, and operating engineers. Not surprisingly, however, the committee soon shifted its focus to the Teamsters since the latter had long been reputed to be aligned with the mob.

Under the guise of scrutinizing possible abuse of the union's tax-exempt status, the committee began its inspection of the Teamsters in March 1957 by summoning IBT President Dave Beck. The committee was particularly interested in learning, McClellan explained to reporters, why Beck apparently took $370,000 from union funds for his own use, placed Teamster mortgages with a company in which he was part owner, bought a filling station in Seattle and ordered Teamsters to patronize it, and listed $35,582 as the cost of lunches for staff members in the Teamsters headquarters cafeteria despite the fact that everyone ate there for free.

Beck, who had no desire to go into these issues or

any others dealing with the Teamsters, delayed his appearance for more than two months, claiming that he had been advised by his doctor, not to travel. This in spite of the fact that he had just returned from a long trip to Europe and that three days later he had flown to Miami for a meeting of the Teamsters executive board.

In addition to being elusive, Beck proved that he had at least a few teeth. Since being elected Teamsters president, he had expanded his sphere of influence and worked hard at making himself appear respectable. He thought of himself as a "labor statesman" and ordered the Teamsters' public-relations staff to hammer away at that image, spending three quarters of a million dollars a year on a union magazine, the *International Teamster* to further that end.

His efforts had not been without success. Besides being president of the Teamsters, he was a member of the governing board of the University of Washington, a key participant at international labor meetings, and the chairman of an independent trucking-industry advisory committee. As a staunch supporter of President Dwight Eisenhower, he also commanded no little amount of influence in Washington.

However, he was no match for the committee. McClellan, the group's chairman, had a reputation as a diplomat and a gentleman from the Old South. While he tended to treat witnesses with courtesy and deference, the same did not apply to the group's chief inquisitor, a brash young man fresh out the University of Virginia Law School. Unlike McClellan, Robert F. Kennedy was abrasive, pugnacious, and frequently outspoken to the point of rudeness. His older brother, John, a senator from Massachusetts, was a member of the committee.

When Beck finally answered the summons in the

spring, he fell apart under Kennedy's relentless interrogation about his apparent use of union funds to pay for such items as a wardrobe full of expensive undershirts, two boats, a twenty-foot freezer, outboard motors, and the remodeling of his Seattle home. Beck centered his defense on his constitutional right against self-incrimination under the Fifth Amendment. During the month of May alone, Beck claimed that refuge 117 times, using it even when asked if he knew his own son, Dave Beck, Jr.

When it became apparent that he was doomed, Beck, in disgrace, announced that he would not be seeking reelection as Teamsters president. That left the door open for Hoffa, who, unlike Beck, was extremely popular with Teamsters around the country.

At first Hoffa was excited; his long-sought goal appeared within easy reach. But at the same time, his new prominence also brought him to the attention of the McClellan Committee, particularly to Kennedy, who was trying to lay the groundwork for a family regime in Washington and help pave the way for his brother John, to run for president in 1960. With Beck out of the way, Hoffa became Robert Kennedy's major target.

By the time Hoffa was summoned to testify, he was almost assured of being elected president at the Teamsters convention in Miami Beach six weeks hence. But Kennedy wanted to keep that from happening. After Beck's exit (he was later convicted of grand larceny), Kennedy instructed his handpicked investigative squad of former FBI men to dig into Hoffa's past, paying special attention to two Hoffa enterprises: the Test Fleet Corporation and a Florida land deal called Sun Valley.

On August 19, the night before he was scheduled to testify, Hoffa and Ciaro met with Blanchard to discuss strategy.

"Jimmy," Blanchard said with a sigh, "we've got a problem. A *big* problem."

"Oh, yeah," Hoffa replied nonchalantly. "You think these assholes are going to get me as easy as they got Dave? Beck was a cream puff. They got no idea how tough Hoffa is. No fucking idea."

"It's not a matter of how tough you are, Jimmy. It's how bad they want to get you. The federal government has a lot of resources. A lot of people. A lot of money."

"You mean Kennedy and those dickheads he's got working for him?"

"Don't write Kennedy off," Blanchard warned. "Just because you don't like him doesn't mean he doesn't know what he's doing."

"You're right about one thing," Hoffa said. "I don't like him. And he don't like me either. That little shit is out to get me. What he's doing is nothing but a fucking vendetta, plain and simple."

"Don't get paranoid on me, Jimmy," Blanchard remonstrated. "We're going to have enough trouble in that hearing room without you trying to slice up Kennedy every chance you get."

"Fuck him," Hoffa replied.

"Jesus," said Blanchard. "You're going to have to change that attitude."

"My ass! Kennedy's the one with the problem. He already told me he was going to get me. Said I was a corrupt little German and he was going to send me to jail."

"He *said* that?" Blanchard asked in surprise. "Just like that?"

"Exactly fucking like that."

"What did you say?"

"I told him I wasn't a fucking German. My family's Dutch."

"What else?"

"I told him if he thought he could send me to jail, he could fucking well try. But he'd better watch his ass, too."

"Why didn't you tell me this before?" Blanchard barked.

"It wasn't important. I've been threatened by guys a hell of a lot meaner than Bobby F-for-Fuckhead Kennedy. And none of them have got me yet."

"What did you do to make him say that? It couldn't have just come out of the blue."

Hoffa grinned. "The skinny little shit. He thinks he's so tough, jumping all over Beck's ass. Getting McClellan to toady up to him. Always telling reporters about how athletic he is. How he's such a whiz at sports like touch football. I'd like to play touch football with him."

"What's that have to do with this?" Blanchard urged.

"It ain't important." Hoffa shrugged. "Just take my word for it. He's a little prick."

"What happened?" Blanchard persisted.

"I told you, it ain't important."

"Aw, tell him, Jimmy," Ciaro interjected. "It's funny as shit."

Hoffa stared at his old friend. "You tell him then, Bobby. It makes my stomach hurt to think about that little fucker."

Blanchard looked at Ciaro and raised his eyebrows. "Well?"

"Wasn't much to it," Ciaro said. "One of Tobin's old friends, who's also a friend of the Kennedys, thought it might be good if Kennedy and Jimmy got a chance to meet. Sort of get to know each other before they got into the hearing room."

"So you went to his office?" Blanchard asked Hoffa.

"Nah," said Ciaro. "They met at this friend's house.

The friend threw a cocktail party for Jimmy, even though he don't drink, and invited Kennedy."

"So what happened?" Blanchard asked.

Ciaro chuckled. "So Kennedy shows up and right away he starts talking about how great a fucking athlete he is. How he keeps in shape and all. And then he turns to Jimmy and asks him what he does?"

"And?"

"And Jimmy says he don't do much. Lifts a few weights. Chops some wood up at Lake Orion. That kind of shit. Anyways, Kennedy looks at Jimmy's shoulders, which you got to admit are pretty fucking big, and he says, 'I'll bet I'm stronger than you are.'"

"It was all I could do to keep from laughing," Hoffa added. "That skinny little dipshit. Couldn't press his own weight, his life depended on it."

"So?" asked Blanchard.

"So Kennedy challenged him to an arm-wrestling contest. Lasted about two seconds. Jimmy slammed his hand so hard I thought his knuckles broke."

"That wasn't good enough for him." Hoffa snickered. "Said he wasn't ready. Wanted to do it again."

"So they done it again," Ciaro said. "Same thing. Jimmy slammed his ass before he even knew what was happening."

"He was so embarrassed that he left about ten minutes later," said Hoffa. "Claimed his wife was sick or something. But just before he left, he leaned over and whispered to me that he was going to get me. So I figure, what the fuck. He wants to get me, let him try. I'll slam his ass again."

Blanchard shook his head. "It isn't as simple as that, Jimmy. Robert Kennedy's a smart man. And a dangerous one. If he's really out to get you, as you say, you're going to have to be careful. Beck thought he could beat him, too, and look what happened."

"Beck was a chickenshit," Hoffa said. "Look at all

Jack Nicholson as James R. Hoffa.

Jack Nicholson as Jimmy Hoffa attempting to convince the workers to stand up for their rights.

On the picket line at Kreger's.

Jimmy Hoffa (Jack Nicholson) and Bobby Ciaro
(Danny DeVito) facing down some unexpected guests.

Jimmy Hoffa (Jack Nicholson) making his moves for the workingman.

The first of many confrontations between Jimmy Hoffa
and Robert F. Kennedy.

Jimmy Hoffa and Bobby Ciaro appear in front of the McClellan committee.

Jimmy Hoffa, the candidate for president of the
Teamsters Union.

Jimmy Hoffa addresses his loyal supporters as he
accepts the presidency.

Heading for prison, Jimmy Hoffa and Bobby Ciaro
maintain their innocence.

that crap he tried to pull about being sick so he could dodge testifying. Then he tried hiding behind the Fifth Amendment. I don't believe in that shit."

"From a legal point of view, that wasn't bad strategy," Blanchard said. "I might advise you to do the same."

"Then I'll get me another fucking lawyer," Hoffa said coldly. "I ain't going to run away from them. And I ain't going to hide."

Blanchard exhaled slowly, counting to ten before he answered. "Here's the facts of life, Jimmy. When you go in that hearing room, your butt's going to be on the line. The way I see it, you have three choices about answering Kennedy's questions. One, you can take the Fifth Amendment. Two, you can tell the complete, unvarnished, unexpurgated truth. Or three, you can try matching wits with Kennedy and the others."

"Fuck the first two," Hoffa said. "They ain't my style."

"Then you're going to try to outsmart them?"

"Fucking A. I'm as smart as Kennedy even if I never went to Harvard or to law school. I'm as good as he is. His old man wasn't nothing but a fucking bootlegger. The Teamsters got a lot of money in the treasury. We can fight for a long time. And that, by God, is what I intend to do."

16

·············

1 9 5 7

As soon as Hoffa took his seat at the witness table, the TV lights clicked on brightly, causing him to blink in surprise and discomfort. Since the hearings had started several months before, they had become a major media event, followed daily on television by an estimated thirty million viewers, and in newspapers and magazines by another fifty million.

Before McClellan's group began its public inquiry into the Teamsters, Hoffa was a virtual unknown outside the trucking industry. But once Kennedy announced that he would be a major witness in the committee's effort to clean up alleged corruption in the country's labor unions, his name and picture appeared on the front page of every newspaper in the country and on virtually every segment of television's evening news. His face was on the cover of *Time*, *Look* and *Life*, which had the largest circulation of any magazine in the country.

Hoffa, as Kennedy was ever willing to tell reporters, had been singled out for special attention

154

because he was a vile, corrupt, union goon who consorted and conspired with known mobsters, a megalomaniac who wanted to bring the entire country under his domination, and a petty thief who stole from his own people.

Hoffa did not categorically deny Kennedy's assertions. He freely admitted that he knew a number of men who had been labeled gangsters by public officials and the press. And he admitted that he had business dealings with them as well.

"If you was in the line of work I am, you would make it your business to know who could help you and who could hurt you," he told reporters on the eve of his appearance before the McClellan Committee. "I went to them for help because if I didn't, the others would have. Except I got there first. What I done was smart and necessary, not illegal."

He also admitted that one of his goals was to create a vast new union that would cover workers in all areas of transportation, including conductors on trains, airline pilots, dockworkers, and of course truckers. It would go far beyond anything that was in existence at the time and had the potential of being tremendously far reaching and powerful. That proposal set off a wave of angry editorial comment and prompted politicians to threaten legislation to prevent such an idea from ever becoming a reality. There was, in some influential circles, a considerable amount of fear that if Hoffa were successful in that endeavor, he could paralyze the country on a whim simply by announcing a national transportation strike.

"Look at my history," Hoffa had told reporters. "I ain't never called a strike that wasn't necessary. I've never ordered a general strike in my life, and I can't imagine why I ever would."

But it was on the issues of what Hoffa had already done, not what he proposed to do, that Kennedy planned to get him. It was the reason they were in this room today.

Before McClellan or Kennedy could speak, Hoffa was on his feet to apologize.

"I beg the committee's pardon for delaying these proceedings. I was en—"

Ignoring him Kennedy, started reading from his notes. "On the night of—"

Hoffa glared at him. "Excuse me," he said icily. "I'm sorry. Was I interrupting you?"

"I thought you had finished," Kennedy replied.

"No," Hoffa said. "I was in the middle of a thought. But it was of no consequence," he said, taking his seat. "You go on with what you were going to say."

Kennedy nodded. "Thank you," he said sarcastically. "I will. We refer now to the pension fund, to your stewardship, we could say to your *creation* of the same. In amassing these funds, this 'war chest,' this *unholy* war chest—"

Blanchard sprang up. "Mr. Kennedy," he said angrily, "you have used—no, you have *hammered*—us with the term 'war chest,' to which you have now added the adjective 'unholy.' Are we to understand that this is a *fact* or simply your *opinion*? If you intend to offer it as a fact to this committee, I'd like to point out that you have offered nothing to substantiate it."

"We—" Kennedy began, but Blanchard held up his hand.

"If I may finish—"

Kennedy cut him off. "You may finish in a *moment*, sir. In a *moment*. When *I* am done, then you may finish. As I was trying to say, the committee intends to pursue evidence of the movement of organized crime into the ranks of labor. We intend to investigate how this has corrupted some of the country's major labor organizations, specifically the Teamsters Union, which historically has been a refuge for mobsters and their ilk. Before we are done, we propose to *prove*, to make it fact, Mr. Blanchard," he said, nodding at Hoffa's scarlet-faced attorney, "that the Teamsters under David Beck and James R. Hoffa has been a breeding ground for depravity, dishonesty, and disingenuousness."

"Mr. Chairman," Blanchard yelled, popping to his feet. "I protest—"

"All in good time, Mr. Blanchard," McClellan interrupted. "You will have your chance to present your side of the argument. Right now Mr. Kennedy has the floor."

Blanchard slumped into his chair, fuming.

"I told you," Hoffa whispered. "This whole fucking thing is rigged. Kennedy wants to get me, but first he wants to get some headlines for himself and his jerk-off brother. This whole thing is just a show to promote the fucking Kennedys."

Blanchard, ignoring Hoffa's comments, whispered back, "I'm going to ask for a fifteen-minute recess. Then you and I are going into one of those back rooms and we're going to go over one more time this business about Test Fleet. And we're going to say a quick prayer that they don't have all the details. Okay?"

"Okay." Hoffa nodded solemnly.

They returned to find Kennedy nervously tapping his pencil against the tabletop, obviously anxious to begin his questioning. In front of him was a thick expanding file containing, Hoffa assumed, details about Test Fleet.

As soon as Hoffa was seated and the TV cameras were in place, Kennedy leaned forward. Without preamble, he began firing questions at the labor leader.

KENNEDY: Is it not true, Mr. Hoffa, that in 1948 the Teamsters were involved in a strike against a Michigan firm named Commercial Carriers?

HOFFA: That is correct.

KENNEDY: And is it also true that you intervened to help settle that strike?

HOFFA: Yes, I played a role in the negotiation that ended the work action.

KENNEDY: A major role.

HOFFA: A major role, yes.

KENNEDY: And is it not true that because of your intervention, the strike ended with terms favorable to Commercial Carriers.

HOFFA: I ain't sure what you mean by that.

KENNEDY: Very simply, did Commercial Carriers come out a winner?

HOFFA: That's an arguable point. What do you mean by "a winner"?

KENNEDY: Did Commercial Carriers profit by the terms of the settlement?

HOFFA: Profit how?

KENNEDY: With money? With terms more beneficial to its operation than to the union's.

HOFFA: That's called "negotiation," Mr. Kennedy. When one party sees things one way, and the other sees them another, then they sit down and talk about it and they come to an agreement.

KENNEDY: In this agreement, did Commercial Carriers come away with an unusual number of points in its favor?

HOFFA: I don't see how you can make a determination of such things. Both sides got something, both sides—

KENNEDY: Did Commercial Carriers get more than it gave?

HOFFA: I guess it depends on who's doing the assessing.

KENNEDY: Was Commercial Carriers *grateful* for your intervention in—

HOFFA: I should think so.

KENNEDY: —a strike that ended in their behalf?

HOFFA: I would say yes.

KENNEDY: Did they ever offer to "express their appreciation"?

HOFFA: They said thanks.

KENNEDY: Did they ever offer to express their appreciation in any way other than saying—

HOFFA: I don't—

KENNEDY: Did they ever—

HOFFA: I was trying to say—

KENNEDY: And I was trying—

HOFFA: Will you shut—

KENNEDY: I will not be—

BLANCHARD: Mr. Chairman! Mr. Chairman! Mr. Kennedy is harassing . . .

KENNEDY: I am not harassing . . .

HOFFA: The hell you're not !

MCCLELLAN: Gentlemen, gentlemen!

HOFFA: Kennedy ain't no gentleman . . .

BLANCHARD: If Mr. Kennedy will—

MCCLELLAN: Order! Order! We will have—

HOFFA: I'll abide by your rules when—

The news media had a field day. The next morning, on front pages across the country, readers learned of the latest twist to events in the Senate hearing room.

WASHINGTON (UPI)—The McClellan Committee hearing to investigate possible mob influence within the Teamsters Union opened in blatant disharmony on Tuesday with participants hurling physical threats at one another over allegations made by the committee counsel, Robert F. Kennedy, regarding alleged kickbacks to union Vice President James R. Hoffa, his wife, and associates.

Sen. John L. McClellan, the committee chairman, had to threaten to bring in federal marshals to restore order to the proceedings before the hearing could continue.

The raucous event marked the opening of what is expected to be an extended period of testimony from Hoffa, who appears to be next in line for the presidency of the International Brotherhood of Teamsters, a position that became vacant after David Beck announced last month that he would not seek re-election.

The verbal free-for-all began after Kennedy accused Hoffa of taking a kickback from a firm called Commercial Carriers following a strike against the Michigan firm almost a decade ago.

According to Kennedy, Hoffa intervened in the strike and helped settle on terms favorable to Commercial Carriers, in return for which Commercial Carriers created a corporation called Test Fleet, sold it to Hoffa and his associate Robert Ciaro at a giveaway price, then shuttled business their way.

Before Hoffa and Ciaro sold the business several years later at a fantastic profit, they allegedly made more than one million dollars.

"It was one of the most obvious attempts at extortion I've ever seen," Kennedy told reporters at the end of the day. "Hoffa set it all up so he could make a bundle, selling out his own union in the process."

Hoffa, while not denying that he and Ciaro operated a business transporting vehicles for manufacturers, claimed there was nothing illegal about the operation.

"There's nothing wrong with me starting an enterprise that has connections to the trucking industry," he said. "It is the only industry I know, and there's nothing about my job that would keep me from having a sideline business within that dealt with some members of the industry."

Blanchard slammed his copy of the *Washington Bulletin* on the table.

"You happy now?" he asked Hoffa angrily. "You satisfied? You couldn't just leave well enough alone. You had to go after Kennedy."

Hoffa threw his shoulders back. "I guess I lost my temper," he said. "So what?"

"You guess you lost your temper!" Blanchard mimicked. "Goddammit, Jimmy, why didn't you listen to me? What the hell are you paying me for if not my advice?"

"That little cocksucker . . ."

"No excuses!" Blanchard barked. "I don't *care* if you and Bobby Kennedy don't like each other. I don't *care* if you think he threatened to throw you in jail. I don't *care* if he's acting like a horse's ass. What I care about is getting you through this hearing intact. That's why you're paying me so much money. I want to get you *through* this so you don't end up like Dave Beck. I want to get you *beyond* this so you can go to Miami Beach and win the election for the union presidency."

"Okay," Hoffa said unhappily. "Okay. You've made your point. I shouldn't have lost my temper yesterday. I shouldn't have threatened to shove that law book up Kennedy's ass. Where do we go from here?"

"We *try* to recoup," Blanchard said, somewhat mollified. "We go back in there and try to pick up the pieces. We act nice and sweet. We say 'please' and 'thank you' and we *try* to answer Kennedy's questions as honestly and as straightforwardly as we can. If we don't, we're going to be spending a lot of time in that room. Do you want that?"

"No. But I—"

"Neither do I. So let's go back and try again."

Three days later Hoffa had finished his testimony before the group. But indications were that it was only a temporary respite, that the committee was not yet through with him. Before he was dismissed, Kennedy handed Hoffa an open-ended subpoena, meaning that he could be recalled for further questioning at any time. McClellan also released a document formally accusing the labor leader of forty-eight counts of illegal or immoral conduct ranging from granting union charters to men with long criminal records to keeping jailed Teamster officials on the payroll.

But the committee had been frustrated in its attempts to nail the labor leader conclusively. Despite Kennedy's eagerness to develop a substantial case against Hoffa based on the Test Fleet operation, the lawyer had never been able to come up with sufficient evidence. In the end, to Kennedy's bitter regret, there had been too many missing pieces.

Of the two, Hoffa was the more reluctant to see the confrontation end. If Kennedy was frustrated by his inability to find all the evidence he needed, Hoffa was just as frustrated by being required to limit his fight to a defensive battle. As chief inquisitor for the committee, Kennedy could direct the proceedings in whichever direction he chose, and Hoffa could only follow. But Hoffa, a veteran street fighter who knew the value of taking the offensive, never got the chance to do so.

Blanchard, breathing easier after it was all over, accurately characterized the experience as a "stalemate, an armed truce."

"Bullshit," Hoffa had replied. "That little fucker got away with every dirty trick in the book."

• • •

After the final gavel, the reporters, as if by prearrangement, broke neatly into two groups. One headed for Kennedy, the other for Hoffa.

Smooth and cool, Kennedy treated the reporters as equals, playing to their egos and enhancing his reputation as one of the guys.

"Are you satisfied with the outcome, Bobby?" one of them asked.

Kennedy made a face. "Of course not, Mike," he replied, addressing the *Times* man by his first name. "I won't be happy until Jimmy Hoffa is in jail, where he belongs."

"Do you think you've moved any closer in that direction?"

Kennedy pondered the questions. "Yes and no," he said finally. "I *know* that Hoffa has committed some indictable offenses, offenses which, if he's ever required to answer for in a court of law, are going to drag him down. The problem is, I can't prove them. Not yet. But I will."

"How sure are you of that, Bobby?" chirped a dowdy young woman clad in a wrinkled linen skirt and sandals. "How strongly do you feel that you're eventually going to get a conviction against Hoffa?"

Kennedy smiled. "I'm so sure, Barbara, that I can make you a promise. If I don't get a conviction against Jimmy Hoffa in the next six months, I'll jump off the Capitol Dome."

Hoffa, who had been eavesdropping, had to struggle to control himself. "That little prick," he growled at Blanchard. "He thinks he's so fucking smart. I'd love to get him into an alley. Just for five fucking minutes!"

"Calm down, Jimmy," Blanchard urged, nodding nervously toward the reporters hovering nearby. "The walls have ears."

TV newsmen surrounded Hoffa, Ciaro, and Blanchard in the front while the print reporters were elbowed not so gently into the background.

Hoffa, his back half-turned to the newsmen, was still arguing with Blanchard. "I took your advice in there and where did it get me?" he said hotly. "This time I'm going to ignore it and talk to these reporters. They got a job to do and I got something I want to say."

"Jimmy," Blanchard argued, "you can't win this fight through the media. You can't —"

"Quit telling me I fucking can't," Hoffa snapped. "I'm going to have my say whether you like it or not. Where does that piece of shit," he said, waving his arm toward Kennedy and the group of smiling newsmen, "where does he get off? He's fucking-A right I created the pension fund. For the benefit of who? That fucking rich kid couldn't find a workingman if you gave him a diagram," he said, his voice rising. "He doesn't have to worry about any goddamn pension. That little fuck was born with a silver dick in his mouth. And *he* tells me—"

"Jimmy, Jimmy, Jimmy," Blanchard said in a panic, "the reporters are listening to this."

"I hope the fuck they are," Hoffa said, turning to face the group.

Blanchard, looking pale and shaken, addressed the newsmen. "My client is going to be acquitted—" he began, only to be interrupted by a red-faced Hoffa.

"Mr. Kennedy," Hoffa snarled, "has an exaggerated notion of his entertainment value."

"Mr. Hoffa," interjected a blond reporter from the *Bulletin*, "Mr. Kennedy asserts that your only motive in inaugurating the Teamsters' Central States Pension Fund was the accumulation of personal power, and—"

"Mr. Kennedy's assertions lack only the merit of

being true," Hoffa rejoined. "As fiction, they are high drama, designed and intended to bring him to the public eye. What has this man done? What has he *done* with his little vendetta? What has he accomplished other than picking on the workingman? It's union busting, that's what it is. No more than that. As my lawyer says, I *will* be acquitted, because I'm innocent of the vicious charges brought against me. And then Mr. Kennedy can jump off the Capitol Dome, or whatever else he thinks at that time will bring him to the public eye."

Having made his speech, Hoffa waved off other questions. With Blanchard and Ciaro at his side, he bounded down the steps and across the sidewalk to where a car was waiting for him. Ciaro opened the door and stood back for Hoffa and Blanchard to enter. Blanchard climbed in and slid across the seat and Hoffa was ducking to follow him when an overweight man in a tweed sport coat and rumpled trousers appeared at his elbow.

"Mr. Hoffa," he said loudly. "Mr. Hoffa. Just a minute please."

Hoffa stopped and looked at the man, who was breathing heavily from his run after the labor leader.

"Jimmy," he panted, "thanks for waiting for me."

"Yeah," Hoffa said in a neutral tone. "What you want?"

"I'm Ed Harmon," the man said, "from the *Detroit News*."

"I know who you are," Hoffa grumbled, remembering the negative stories that had been written by Harmon and other *News* reporters about him and the Teamsters.

"How are these allegations going to affect your run for the presidency of the Teamsters?" Harmon asked.

"How are these allegations going to affect my bid to become president of the International Brotherhood of

Teamsters?" Hoffa mimicked. "Is that your question?"

Before Harmon could reply, Hoffa continued: "You know," he said slowly, "you'd think that the *News*, a hometown newspaper, one that makes its home in a city built on the automotive industry, you'd think I'd get a fairer shake from the *News*. You guys been printing quite a lot of detrimental stuff about me."

"What can I tell you, Jimmy?" Harmon shrugged. "We print it because it's true."

Hoffa stared at him. "Is that right?" he said. "Well," he added, turning to enter the car, "then you go on printing it."

Harmon, unwilling to be dismissed, stuck his head through the open window. "I wanted to talk to you about Test Fleet."

"Uh-huh," Hoffa said noncommittally.

"About your using Teamsters muscle to compel these certain companies to lease trucks from you. About your wife's involvement. And Bobby Ciaro's wife, too."

"Nothing could be further from the truth," Hoffa said.

"We have in our possession facts and figures which establish that it *is* true," Harmon said.

"Uh-huh," answered Hoffa. "Well, if you have those 'facts and figures,' why haven't you run them?"

"We plan to," Harmon responded. "Next week."

"Okay," Hoffa said softly. "But if I were you, I'd be careful. This is something of a volatile time, this time here. What with these hearings and the election coming up. If I was a reporter and I was going to print something, I'd want to be oh-so-sure that it was true."

"Oh, it's true enough," said Harmon. "And we're going to run it." Stepping back on the curb, he grinned tightly at Hoffa. "Thank you for your reaction," he said.

Hoffa, stone-faced, turned to his driver. "Let's go," he said.

As the car pulled away from the curb, the driver waiting for an opening in the rush-hour traffic, Ciaro turned to Hoffa from the front seat and handed him a box.

Hoffa looked at Ciaro questioningly, then opened the box. Inside was a sizable collection of campaign buttons in several sizes and colors, all bearing Hoffa's picture and the words *James R. Hoffa for President of the IBT*.

Hoffa stared absently at the buttons.

"Well," Ciaro prompted, "what do you think?"

Hoffa looked up and stared meaningfully at Ciaro. "I think I'm like Hitler," he said. "I'm fighting Russia and I'm fighting France." Jerking his head back toward Harmon, who was still standing on the curb, watching the car, he said, "Take care of that cocksucker."

17
. . . .
1957

Ciaro leaned back against the fender of the car, taking a deep drag on the Camel. In the dim light from the nearest street lamp fifty yards away, the cigarette glowed intensely.

"God, it's fucking hot," he said, wishing he were back on the banks of the Detroit River, where he might be able to catch a cooling breeze. August was a miserable time to be in Washington, what with the heat and the humidity.

"You can say that again," agreed Pete Connelly, who was leaning against the other fender. Standing back to back, the width of the car between them, they looked like estranged lovers. In reality, neither was overly fond of the other.

"What I was saying," Ciaro continued, "is you got to remember the basic principle: if it's got wheels, it's in Teamsters' jurisdiction."

"Uh-huh," mumbled Connelly, who had heard this lecture before.

"Well, if you want to organize, you got to know this

shit," Ciaro said impatiently, angered by Connelly's apparent lack of interest. "You got to be a fucking man. You don't go out there to bring back an excuse. You want to organize? Then listen to the Little Guy. He says *take names*. He says *do not take no for an answer* because if you will not take no for an answer, eventually the answer comes back yes. You got that?"

"Uh-huh," Connelly mumbled distractedly.

Turning to look at Connelly, Ciaro noted that he was watching the other end of the street, where a man and woman were arguing at the entrance to a disreputable-looking bar. They were too far away to hear the words, but they could tell by the tone that it was not a pleasant conversation.

Aw, fuck it, Ciaro said to himself, let the dipshit figure it out on his own. Impatiently he glanced at his watch, then at the storefront across the sidewalk. Lettering on the window read JOHNSON'S FUNERAL PARLOR.

The store was the last on a small block and to its left, where another store might have been, was the gaping entrance to an alley. As Ciaro watched, a man in baggy, wrinkled trousers and a yellow short-sleeved nylon shirt, tails dangling, scurried out of the darkness. Looking around quickly to make sure no one else was close, the man hurried over to Ciaro and Connelly.

"You the man who wants to see me?" he asked Connelly, who had walked around to Ciaro's side of the car when he heard footsteps approaching.

Connelly shook his head, jerking his thumb at Ciaro.

"It's me you're looking for," Ciaro said, stepping forward. As he approached the man he noted the tiny fragments of blood-spotted toilet paper stuck to his chin. Standing over him, Ciaro almost turned his head in disgust, repelled by the smell that emanated from the stranger, a mixture of dried sweat, stale beer, and embalming fluid.

"You got it?" Ciaro asked him.

The man nodded. "I got it if you got it."

Speaking to Connelly over his shoulder, Ciaro ordered, "Get the shit."

To the man, Ciaro said, "Let's see it."

Producing a small box that he must have been carrying under his loose shirt, the man smiled, revealing crooked, nicotine-stained teeth. "Here," he said, thrusting it forward.

Ciaro took the box and opened it. Inside, cushioned on old newspaper, was a stoppered glass beaker, the kind that one could easily find in a high-school chemistry lab. Holding it up to the light, Ciaro studied the contents.

Grunting in revulsion, he put the beaker back in the box and turned to the man. "Okay," he said. "I guess that's it."

Digging into his pockets, he extracted a handful of bills, which he handed to the stranger. The man smiled his thanks, revealing his stained teeth one more time, then disappeared back into the alley.

"Come on," Ciaro said brusquely to Connelly, who was backing out of the parked car with a shopping bag in his hand. Ciaro, taking the bag from Connelly, walked to the entrance of the alley, where he rested the bag on the top one garbage can and the box he had received from the stranger on another.

"Look in there," he told Connelly, nodding at the shopping bag, "and get me some tape."

Connelly rummaged through the bag, noting a roll of brightly colored wrapping paper, a length of dark red ribbon, a cheap pair of scissors, and a greeting card. On the bottom of the bag was a disposable dispenser of Scotch tape, which he removed and silently handed to Ciaro.

Taking the tape, Ciaro slowly and deliberately

began sealing the box. Accepting the roll of wrapping paper that Connelly handed him next, Ciaro unrolled a length sufficient to cover the package. Taking the scissors, he cut the paper and began wrapping the box. As he worked he talked, telling Connelly about a man who had been on his mind a lot lately, an old Irishman named Billy Flynn.

"Without a doubt," Ciaro said, "he was the most stand-up guy I ever met. This was twenty years ago," he explained. "Shit, that seems like a long time ago now. Anyways, in those days we was organizing the laundries and the owner of the Idle Hour was being a stubborn old bastard. So Jimmy decided that him and Billy—I was driving the truck— was going to light it up."

"Light it up?" Connelly asked.

"Yeah, light it up," Ciaro said. Glancing at Connelly he realized that the younger man had no idea what he was talking about. "Light it up," he said impatiently. "You know, firebomb it."

"Oh," Connelly said.

"That old bastard who owned the place, damned if I can remember *his* name, didn't want to sign up. So Jimmy tells Billy Flynn, 'Let's light it up.' So that's what they was going to do, except Billy fucked up. He used too much fuel and he spilled some on himself while he was spreading it around. So when he tossed a match on it, it went up—*whoooosh*—goddamnedest noise you ever heard. And it set him on fire, too."

"Aw, shit," Connelly commented. "That sounds fucking horrible."

"It was," Ciaro agreed. "Real fucking nasty. Burned him something fierce."

"So what happened?"

"So what you think, you dumb fuck? We took him to the goddamn hospital. Doctor said he was going to die. No doubt about it."

Ciaro stopped to admire his handiwork, lifting it and turning it this way and that in the weak light. That's pretty good, he thought, good as they would have wrapped it at Frank & Seder's. "Hand me the ribbon," he told Connelly.

"So what happened?" Connelly said, passing the ribbon. "What about Billy Flynn?"

"Oh, yeah," answered Ciaro. "Anyways, he's lying there dying and the doctor calls this priest. Put your finger there."

"So a priest shows up?" Connelly says, pressing down with his index finger.

"Sure he shows up. He's got to. It's his job. The priest, a real innocent-looking old man, probably been dipping into the sacramental wine that night, is standing there staring at Billy, who's all covered in bandages from head to toe, only his eyes and his mouth ain't covered, kind of blubbering to himself. And the priest starts trying to get Billy to make a confession."

"A confession?" said Connelly. "No shit."

"Sure," said Ciaro, snipping off the ends of the ribbon. "You know. Before he dies. Make a confession so he can go to heaven."

"Hey," said Connelly, "I ain't fucking stupid. I know what a last confession is. That and extreme unghon."

Ciaro laughed. "Unction!"

"Huh?"

"Unction. Extreme unction, not unghon, you dickhead."

"Unghon, unction, what fucking difference does it make? What happened?"

"So the priest is hovering over Billy and he's saying, 'Confess, my son. Admit what you did. Confess and meet God with a clean conscience.' And old Billy, he concentrates real hard and he looks the priest right in the eye—and now you got to remember that Billy was from the old school, his motto was never let *down*, never let *up*, never *forget*—and he utters his dying words."

Connelly, staring at the package, had lost interest in Billy Flynn. "What's in the present?" he asked.

Jerking himself back from his memories, Ciaro looked closely at Connelly. "A guy's dick and balls," he said matter-of-factly.

Connelly's eyes widened, his mouth fell open, and he stepped back two paces, staring at Ciaro. "Uhh, uhh, uhh," he stammered.

"Come on," Ciaro said, ignoring him. "Let's get the fuck out of here."

The Washington bureau of the *Detroit News* was located in two small rooms on the seventh floor of the National Press Building on Fifteenth and M, only a short walk from the White House. The front room, the one with a window, contained a single desk, which was occupied by the bureau's secretary/receptionist. The second room, larger but with the feel of a closet nonetheless, barely had space for three desks, a row of battered file cabinets, and two teletype machines, which clattered busily in a corner. One sported a sign reading UNITED PRESS INTERNATIONAL; the other said ASSOCIATED PRESS.

Ed Harmon sat slouched at one of the desks, his chair tilted back and his scuffed shoes with worn heels propped on the desktop, next to a stack of yellow copy paper. A battered typewriter had been pushed to the edge of the desk to give Harmon room to edit a story, which was being fed to him in takes by a second reporter, Harris.

"This is *good shit*," Harmon said, reading Harris's copy for the second time. "A great companion piece for my story on Test Fleet. It's really going to roast Hoffa's ass."

Harris, who was at least ten years younger than Harmon and dressed much more neatly, looked up from the piece of paper dangling from his typewriter and grinned. "Ain't it, though?" he said. "Wish I could be there to see him read it."

"Don't worry." Harmon laughed. "You'll know what his reaction is. I guaran-fucking-tee you, he'll let you know what he thinks."

"Listen to this," Harris said, lifting the paper that was still in the typewriter and reading from the page. "'. . . verifying on three occasions the charges against Hoffa. In the light of which, the attitude of the McClellan Committee—'"

"Ed?" said a young woman, appearing in the doorway from the outer office,.

"Yeah, Jenny," Harmon said, looking up. "What do you need?"

"This just came for you," she said, walking across the room and proffering a gift-wrapped package.

"What do you mean, 'just came for me'?"

"I mean a messenger just delivered it. Is it your birthday or something?"

"Not until November," Harmon said, accepting the package and looking at it curiously. "Was there a note or anything?"

"Just this," said Jenny, handing him a small envelope.

Harmon opened it. Inside was a card with a short message in nearly illegible script. It said, *Something to think about.*

Harmon turned it over. There was no signature.

"Did the messenger say who this was from?" he asked Jenny, who silently shook her head.

"Oh, well," Harmon said, grinning. "Guess it's a secret admirer. Hope it's a blonde with big tits.

Thanks, Jenny," he said, waving her away.

Turning to Harris, he said. "You were saying?"

Harris picked up where he left off, reading slowly as Harmon unwrapped the package.

"'. . . the attitude of the Senate committee, although combative, is both, it would seem, justified and necessary. The power to organize does not and must not coerce, either in—'"

Catching sudden movement out of the corner of his eye, Harris stopped and looked up. Harmon had opened the box and lifted out a glass container, which he was studying carefully, a frown on his face.

"What is it?" he asked. "What did your secret admirer send you?"

"Ummm," Harmon mumbled, "I don't know." As he turned the container to view the contents from another angle, recognition suddenly dawned. "Holy shit!" he exclaimed. "Jesus, Mary, and Joseph!" Hurriedly he stuffed the container back in the box.

"Well, what *is* it?" Harris asked again.

His face drained of color, Harmon stared at the other reporter. Harris thought he looked like he was about to be sick.

"What?" Harris began.

"Kill the story," Harmon said weakly.

"Huh?" Harris said, not comprehending.

"Kill the story," Harmon repeated more emphatically. "Kill the Hoffa story."

"Come on, Ed."

"Don't give me any shit, Harris," Harmon screamed. "I said kill the fucking story!"

On September 24, a month to the day after Hoffa's first appearance before the McClellan Committee, the group went back into session specifically to examine the possibility of leveling additional charges against the labor leader.

"New information has come to our attention that concerns Mr. Hoffa," Kennedy told reporters. "Not to mention the fact that his brothers in the labor movement are considering dire action against him and his union."

"You mean George Meany's threat to expel the Teamsters from the AFL-CIO if Hoffa is elected president?" asked one reporter.

"Exactly!" said Kennedy. "If even the AFL-CIO thinks he's crooked, then we can't be far wrong."

Working well past the normal hours usually kept by Senate committees, the McClellan group took testimony from an amazing forty witnesses in just four days. When asked by a reporter the reason for the frantic pace, Kennedy said, "It's pretty obvious isn't it? We want to prevent the election of James Hoffa as president of the Teamsters."

On September 28, the McClellan Committee issued a list of thirty-four more violations allegedly committed by Hoffa, bringing the total to eighty-two.

However, the committee's attempts to discredit Hoffa with the Teamsters and block his election failed miserably. On September 30, when the IBT opened its convention in Miami Beach, Hoffa was a heavy favorite even though there were four other candidates. One of them dropped out before the vote was taken and the other three polled fewer than five hundred votes among them. Hoffa received 1,208 votes.

"I knew you could do it, Jimmy," a supremely happy Jo Hoffa told her husband as they filed into the main hall at the plush hotel that was serving as the headquarters for the convention. "You've made me so proud."

"She's right, Jimmy," echoed Frank Fitzsimmons, who was walking one pace behind them. "You've been good to the Teamsters and the Teamsters have been good to you. They couldn't have elected a better, harder-working, more deserving man."

"Thanks, Fitz," Hoffa said, smiling tightly. "I appreciate your support."

They tried to slip in unobtrusively, but as soon as Hoffa set foot onto the stage, the delegates rose for a standing ovation. Followed by Jo, Fitzsimmons, Ciaro, and Connelly, Hoffa wended his way to a group of seats reserved for him and his entourage. With a wave to the delegates, he signaled to Joe Abrams, the emcee for the event, to continue reading the names of the newly elected officers.

"The Vice-President in charge of finance, Curt Dempsey," he read, then waited for the applause to cease. "Vice-president for planning, Gerry Laughlin. Our negotiating team: vice-president Dave Miller and John Bream. Head of the benevolent association, John Patrick Deeney. Head of the finance committee, Billy Flaherty. And finally, two men without whom the steering committee of the International would not be where it is today, Michael Burns and Rudy Hendera."

Abrams stopped while the house applauded. When it was quiet again, he looked over his shoulder at Hoffa, who was busily writing on a pad that Connelly had passed him soon after they entered.

"Thank you, thank you," Abrams said. "Thank you most humbly for recognizing these officers, for giving them your enthusiastic support. These men are the workhorses of the International. They are the ones who truly make the IBT run. Together they make a strong team, an *unbeatable* team. What really makes them unbeatable is the fact that they have such solid leadership from the top. They take their orders from the strongest, the most aggressive, the most admirable man ever elected president of this organization. Join with me now in welcoming the man all of you know as the Little Guy, the new president of the International Brotherhood of Teamsters, James . . . Riddle . . . Hoffa!"

Hoffa rose amid thunderous applause. Grinning broadly, he started for the lectern for his acceptance speech. Before leaving the group, however, he leaned over to Fitzsimmons and handed him the pad on which he had been writing. Looking down, Fitzsimmons saw that Hoffa had compiled a list of names—Dempsey, Bream, Burns, Hendera; roughly half of the newly elected officers.

Fitzsimmons looked up, puzzled. "What do you want—"

"Tomorrow morning," Hoffa whispered, cutting him off. "Go in and fire these cocksuckers."

Startled, Fitzsimmons stared at him. "But they was—"

"I know," Hoffa said, "but I want my own team."

"But all these guys?" Fitzsimmons whined.

"That's right!" Hoffa assured him. "One thing I learned, if you're going to whack a bunch of people out, do them all the first day. That way the ones who are left don't feel insecure. What they will feel, you see, is grateful. But you got to do it all at once and quick. Otherwise they'll turn against you."

"Jesus!" Fitzsimmons exclaimed. "I never looked at it that way." Turning to Connelly, he whispered, "You hear that, Petey? There's a fucking lesson there."

Connelly nodded slowly, gaping at Hoffa.

18
·············
1 9 7 5

While he was still thirty feet away, Ciaro could see that Hoffa was boiling. And it wasn't just from the late-afternoon temperature either. He sat as still as a stone, his jaw set in a rigid line, staring straight ahead. He did not even turn as Ciaro set the coffee cups down on the roof and opened the door.

Hoffa had changed his mind and turned the car's air conditioner all the way up. The fan was roaring so loudly it sounded like a rig traveling down the highway. In spite of that, the inside of the car was still warm, warm enough for Hoffa's shirt to be almost completely soaked with sweat.

Surreptitiously Ciaro glanced at the temperature gauge on the dashboard and saw that it was nearing the red line. If we don't get moving pretty soon, he said to himself, the engine's going to heat up and die. *Then* Jimmy will really be pissed.

"Any luck?" Hoffa asked as Ciaro settled into the seat, holding the coffees. He passed one to Hoffa and set the other on the floor so he could close the door.

"Did you catch him?"

"No," Ciaro admitted reluctantly. "Tried the club, the office, everywhere I could think of. But no Dally."

"Where the fuck is he?" Hoffa asked tightly. Lifting the coffee cup, he took a tentative sip. "That fucking cocksucker. That ungrateful son-of-a-bitch. When I think of all the money I made for him!"

"I know," commiserated Ciaro, hoping that Hoffa, in one of his famous tantrums, wouldn't take it out on him. "I know."

"Did you try the Gold Club?"

"Yeah," Ciaro replied, unwilling to remind him that he had already said that. "He wasn't there."

"Did you ask them to try the back room? The equipment shed? The place where they always play cards?"

"I tried, Jimmy. Every place I could think of." In an attempt to distract him, Ciaro pulled out his wallet and started digging through the compartments.

Hoffa looked at his watch. "It's getting late. I don't want to be here much longer."

"I understand," Ciaro mumbled, immersed in his search.

"I don't *want* to be here all night, Bobby," Hoffa repeated. Reaching under the seat, he removed the pistol from where he had stuck it earlier and placed it on the seat beside him. Ciaro glanced at him sideways, but said nothing.

Turning to Ciaro, Hoffa cracked a faint smile, the first sign that he was winning his struggle to control his emotions. "Guess I'm getting old, Bobby," he said quietly.

"Everybody gets old. Until they die."

Sighing in relief, Ciaro found what he had been looking for. "Ah, here that fucker is," he said, removing a small rectangle of cardboard from the wallet. Smiling, he turned to Hoffa. "This look familiar?"

Hoffa took it and held it up to the light, frowning because he didn't immediately recognize it. Then it hit him. "This is my old business card," he said with a grin.

"Fucking A," Ciaro said. "Surprised I still have it?"

"Shit, that was a long time ago," Hoffa said, examining the card. A piece of Scotch tape was holding it together where Ciaro had ripped it in half thirty-seven years previously. The area under the tape was still white; the rest of the card was an uneven brown, and the edges were worn. Hoffa read the lettering aloud: "James R. Hoffa, Organizer, Local 229, International Brotherhood of Teamsters." Still smiling, he turned it over and immediately recognized his own writing. *Give this man anything he wants,* he had scribbled.

"You remember when you gave me that?" Ciaro asked. "Just in case you don't," he said hurriedly, "it was the night I first met you. When you climbed in my cab and wouldn't fucking get out. You knew me better then than I knew myself. You *knew* I was going to join the fucking union in spite of everything I said. Didn't you?"

Hoffa smiled. "I had a feeling," he admitted.

"Feeling my ass. You always was good at reading people. At least most of the time. At least with me, you was."

"That was almost forty years ago," Hoffa said, staring into the distance. His voice softened. "You been with me a long time, Bobby."

"Don't get all teary about it," Ciaro said quickly. "After all, what the fuck else was I going to do?"

19
....
1 9 5 8

Ciaro gripped the wheel tightly, staring at the blinking red light in the rearview mirror. "Just my fucking luck," he mumbled to himself. One time in a fucking million I get a heavy foot and what happens? I fucking get caught."

He was still cursing himself when the state trooper sauntered up and stopped three feet away, his right hand on his pistol. It was impossible to read the man's face. His wide-brimmed hat created shade that stretched from his chin up, and his mirrored sunglasses made it impossible to see his eyes. "Keep your eyes straight ahead, your hands on the wheel, and stay in the car," the cop ordered, almost in a whisper.

Ciaro decided to ignore him. Reaching quickly for the latch, he opened the door of the new Impala and swung his feet to the ground.

"I *said*," the trooper snarled, his hand tightening on the pistol butt, "to stay in the goddamn car."

"Just hang on for a second, will you?" Ciaro said, raising his hands to eye level. "I ain't got a weapon. I ain't going to try nothing. I swear it."

"You aren't *listening* to me," the trooper hissed, lifting his pistol an inch out of the holster.

"Okay, okay," Ciaro said. "You win. I'm getting back in." Obediently he swung his legs back inside, put his hands together on top of the wheel, and turned his eyes forward. "What was I doing?" he asked.

The trooper, who had walked back toward the rear of the car to recheck the license plate, answered as if from a great distance. "Ninety in a sixty-five zone."

"Aw, fuck!" Ciaro groaned. "That much, huh?"

The trooper returned to the window, still standing carefully out of Ciaro's reach. Out of the corner of his eye, Ciaro could see the shiny Sam Browne belt, the dark gray of the trooper's uniform from crotch to shoulder, and a white on black name tag reading *O'Hara.*

"Officer O'Hara," Ciaro said, trying to sound conciliatory. "I'm sorry. I didn't realize I was pushing it that hard. It's just that I'm in a hurry."

"That's a hell of a hurry, pal," O'Hara replied coldly. "You got something particular you got to do? Someplace special you got to be to make you go that fast?"

Ciaro nodded. "I do," he said. "I honest-to-God do."

His hand still on his pistol butt, O'Hara ordered Ciaro to produce his license and registration. "But do it slowly," he cautioned. "Nice and slow or you're going to have a Magnum up your nostril."

Carefully Ciaro shifted his weight to his left buttock, reached into his back pocket, and removed his wallet. Still looking straight ahead, he offered it to O'Hara.

"Not like that, dumbshit," O'Hara barked. "Take your license and registration out and hand *them* to me. Not your whole fucking wallet."

As Ciaro reached into the wallet O'Hara spoke

again. "Now, tell me where it is you got to be? Explain to me in a believable fashion why you're in such a hurry you're exceeding the speed limit by twenty-five miles an hour."

"I work for Jimmy Hoffa," Ciaro replied.

For the first time O'Hara hesitated. "The hell you say?"

"I ain't shitting you," Ciaro said. "Here's my ID. You can see for yourself."

O'Hara took the proffered document and studied it closely. "Well, fuck me," he said quietly. "Why didn't you say so to begin with?"

"Didn't think it would make any difference."

"No difference?" O'Hara said. "Shit, if you work for Hoffa and you're in a hurry to get someplace, I sure as hell am not going to stand in your way. Personally I think that man's a great American, a—"

"Can I go now?" Ciaro asked. "I *really* am in a fucking hurry."

"You bet, Mr. Ciaro," O'Hara said, flipping a salute. "Just try to keep it under eighty and don't do anything reckless."

The rest of his sentence was lost in a squeal of rubber against pavement as Ciaro dropped the Chevrolet into gear and tore down the highway.

It wasn't easy finding a parking place on East Forty-eighth Street. In fact, Ciaro found it impossible. Giving up in disgust, he double-parked next to a dirt-streaked MG and walked back the twenty paces to the Copacabana Club.

Since it was barely midmorning, the club wasn't open yet. Undeterred, Ciaro banged on the door, pounding his fist against the frame so hard the glass rattled dangerously. "Come on," he yelled. "Come on. I know you're there. Open the fucking door."

He could hear someone stirring inside, which made him increase his efforts. "Goddammit, I hear you. Come on. Let me in."

A muffled voice replied, "I'm coming. I'm coming. Who the fuck you think you are? You can't read the sign that says closed? You fucking illiterate?"

Still grumbling, the man opened the door. He was in his late fifties, short and round with just a fringe of hair around the sides of his head, as neat as a monk's tonsure except, unlike a monk, Solly Stein had no hair in front. Plus he wasn't a Catholic. He was wearing dark blue pin-striped trousers, obviously the bottom half of a business suit, and a clean white shirt with the French cuffs turned up one fold. His collar was open, revealing a mat of gray at his chest. His red tie dangled loosely under the collar, the ends dipping below his bulging stomach.

"Who the fuck are you?" Stein asked pugnaciously. "What the fuck you want?"

"It ain't important *who* I am," Ciaro replied. "It's why I'm here."

"Okay, then why the fuck are you here beating at my door in the middle of the fucking night before I've even had a chance to digest my breakfast?"

"I'm here with a message for somebody who's inside. The message is from James R. Hoffa, who told me to deliver it face-to-face."

Stein studied him carefully, then made his decision. "Go away," he said, trying to close the door.

Ciaro got his foot into the opening just in time. "Maybe you didn't *hear* me."

"I heard you. But maybe you didn't fucking hear *me*. I said to go away. When I say you don't come in, you don't come in. Now move your fucking foot."

"Wait a minute," Ciaro said, fumbling for his wallet. "Just wait a fucking minute." Removing a business card held together by a piece of Scotch tape, he waved it under Stein's nose.

"You see this?" he said. "You see what it says? It says 'James R. Hoffa.'" Turning it over, he shoved it closer to Stein, only inches from his nose. "And you see what this says. It says, 'Give this man anything he wants.'"

Reluctantly Stein took the card and studied it closely. Thrusting it back at Ciaro, he said, "I don't care what it says. I don't care who you work for. I said go away."

Ciaro planted his foot deeper in the doorway. "I ain't going. Not until I do what I was sent to do."

Stein turned and called into the back of the club. "Joseph! Joseph, get your ass out here."

Straining to see inside, Ciaro heard heavy footsteps approaching. Seconds later a huge man loomed out of the darkness. "What you want, Sol?" he asked, towering over Ciaro, huge hairy arms dangling from the sleeves of a skintight T-shirt.

"Get this fucker out of here," Stein said. "I told him and I told him. This is my fucking club and I don't want him in it. I don't *care* who he says he works for. I told him to go away and he don't want to go. Why don't you help him." Standing back, he motioned to Joseph, who turned and took a step toward Ciaro.

Taking a deep breath, Ciaro lowered his shoulder and jammed it against the door, swinging it inward against Stein and his bodyguard. "You're going to fucking *care*," he mumbled, catching his balance and reaching inside his jacket.

"Are you goddamn insane?" Stein screeched. "Do you know who I am. Do you fucking know who I *am*?" Turning to his bodyguard, he ordered him again to eject Ciaro. Nodding, Joseph again turned toward Ciaro, but he pulled up short when he saw Ciaro's .45 pointed precisely between his eyes.

"Take it easy, Joseph," Ciaro warned. "Don't do anything stupid. I ain't going to be here long. Just long enough to do what I was told to do."

In the background, a half-dozen young women were practicing a dance routine on an elevated stage. They had been in the middle of a number when Ciaro burst through the door, but stopped when they heard the commotion. Now the women, the piano player, and the choreographer were all turned toward the men at the door, waiting expectantly to see what would happen.

"We're going in the back," Ciaro said soothingly to Joseph, tightening his finger on the trigger to prove he meant business. "I'm looking for a fellow and I was told he was here. He's about six feet tall with black hair. A guy from Detroit. I ain't going to shoot him or hurt him or nothing. I just got a message for him, but I got to deliver it to him personally. Now why don't we go in the back and see if we can find him," he added, gesturing with the pistol.

"You're the one with the gun." Joseph shrugged, turning to follow Ciaro's directions.

Slowly Joseph and Ciaro crossed the club and walked through a door behind the bar. Stein ran alongside them, still shrieking. "I'm going to have you killed. Tonight you're going to be sleeping with the fish in Sheepshead Bay. Do you know who my friends are? You dumbfuck, you're as good as dead. You fucking hear—"

"Shut up," Ciaro barked, swinging the pistol in Stein's direction. "You talk too fucking much."

Stein shut up.

Joseph stopped at a door at the end of a short hall and nodded.

Ciaro reached around him, turned the handle, and swung the door open. The interior looked like the main room of the social club in Little Italy where he and Hoffa had gone that night to met with Scialla and the others. There was a battered couch, several chairs, and a round, plain wooden table. Of the eight men in the room, three were lounging on the couch and four were sitting at the table, playing poker. One man was sitting back on a chair, kibbitzing during the card game. One of the men on the couch was D'Allesandro.

"Hey, Dally," Ciaro said companionably as D'Allesandro looked up.

Stein, who had rediscovered his voice, was shrieking again. "Do you know what this cocksucker did?" he hollered. "This fucking *goombah* comes in here and starts shoving me around. Cut him down! Cut him fucking down!" When nobody moved, he howled, "Okay, then give me a piece. I'll do it."

"Sorry to intrude," Ciaro said politely, ignoring Stein. "Someone sent me here," he said to D'Allesandro. "I don't like to mention any names. I don't think I need to. This 'somebody' said to give you a note." He reached into his pocket.

"It's okay," D'Allesandro said, holding up his palm. "You don't have to say anything else. I understand." Nodding at Stein and Joseph, he added, "I'm sorry you were put through this."

"Sorry!" blurted Stein. "Where do you get this 'sorry' shit? Sorry isn't enough. This is *my* club, and 'sorry'—"

"I'm not talking to *you*," D'Allesandro said coldly. Pointing at Ciaro, he spoke sharply. "This man is like a brother to me. You hear that? Like a brother. And I want you to treat him with the same respect with which you'd treat me."

He stared at Stein, who had again gone silent. "Do you understand? Can I say it any plainer?"

Stein's jaw dropped. "N-noooo, Dally," he stammered. "I understand."

"Did he say he was here from our friend in Detroit?" he asked Stein, who nodded. "And having said *that,* you told him to get out? To go away, that it was your club?"

"You don't understand, Dally. I just wasn't sure that he was who he said he was. I just—"

D'Allesandro waved to him to be quiet. "Thank you for making the trip," he said to Ciaro.

Ciaro nodded, handing him an envelope. D'Allesandro took it and made a small bow. Gesturing to one of the other men, he pointed to a suitcase in the corner. "Would you get that for Mr. Ciaro, please?"

The man retrieved the bag and delivered it to Ciaro. "Thank you," he said, taking it and hefting it for weight.

D'Allesandro addressed Stein. "I think you owe Mr. Ciaro an apology."

Stein, white-faced, swiveled frightened eyes on Ciaro. "I'm sorry, Mr. Ciaro," he said meekly. "I didn't know you was a friend of Dally's. I didn't know you were here to see him."

Turning to D'Allesandro, he said imploringly, "On my knees, Dally, if I had known this man was a friend . . ."

"Okay, okay," D'Allesandro said. "We get the point. You doing okay?" he asked Ciaro. "I'm sure that if you need anything while you're in New York, that Mr. Stein would be more than happy to help. Wouldn't you, Solly."

"I'd be *honored,* Mr. Ciaro. Anything you need. Anything at all, you just let me know."

New York City is always prettier after dark, Ciaro thought, looking northward over the vast expanse of Central Park, amazed as always at how such a large, comfortable green space could be maintained in the middle of an area as congested as midtown Manhattan. He was sitting on the terrace of a penthouse on Central Park South, a cool bourbon and water in one hand, a Camel in the other. At his feet, between his size twelves, was the suitcase he had taken earlier from D'Allesandro. He glanced at his watch and allowed himself to enjoy the view for another two minutes before grinding out his cigarette. Setting his drink on a nearby table, he reached for the phone. Silently he punched the digits. It barely rang once before a familiar voice greeted him from the other end.

"Hey, Jimmy," he said. "It's me. Ain't I always right on time? Everything went fine. Just like you said. Gave the note to the man. The message was understood and the reply was 'thank you.' He also sent a package . . . yeah, I got it right here. Don't worry, I won't let it out of my sight."

Listening, he reached for his drink, brought the glass to his lips, and took a small sip. "Yeah, I know what to do now . . . don't worry, it's as good as done. See you tomorrow, just before lunch. Okay . . . okay . . . and don't worry, it's safe. See you then. Good night."

Hanging up the phone, he reached for the pack of Camels sitting on the table, next to his drink. Tomorrow will take care of itself, he told himself. Tonight, I'm going to relax.

At eleven-ten the next morning, Ciaro walked into Hoffa's office at IBT headquarters in Washington. Proudly, he hoisted the suitcase. "Here it is." He grinned at Hoffa. "Just like I promised."

With Hoffa were Fitzsimmons, Connelly, and an architect named McNeeley. When Ciaro walked in, they had been clustered around a model of a housing community, which was sitting on a table near Hoffa's desk. The model depicted some three dozen tiny buildings, all laid out along miniature streets that formed a half circle around a large expanse of blue. Dotted among the tiny buildings were even tinier palm trees.

Hoffa left his place around the table and walked quickly to Ciaro, clapping him joyously on the shoulder. "It's good to see you," he said, "and it's good to see *that*," nodding at the suitcase.

"You have any problems?" Hoffa asked, taking the case. "Goddamn, it's heavy," he said in mock surprise. Looking at Ciaro, he asked, "You know what's in here?"

Ciaro nodded. "I got a good idea," he said.

Hoffa grinned at him. "A heart of fucking gold, that's what you got, Bobby Ciaro. I don't care if you're a dago. Give me a wop any day. You talk about *honor*, you talk about *loyalty*," Hoffa reached out and cuffed him lightly on the ear. "Give me *this* dago anytime," he said. "This calls for a celebration. I need some coffee." Turning to Connelly, he gestured with his head. "Petey, get me a cup of coffee, will you?"

Connelly sprang to do as he was told, returning with a china cup filled to the brim with steaming coffee he had drawn from an urn in the corner. He presented it ceremoniously to Hoffa. "Here you go, boss."

Hoffa nodded his thanks, turning his attention to the suitcase. Slowly he took a sip of coffee, replaced the cup in its saucer, and placed them both on a corner of his desk. Making a motion as though he were rolling up his sleeves, Hoffa grinned, lifted the suitcase, and placed it on his desk. Undoing the clasps, he flipped it open.

"Voilà!" he said loudly, gesturing at the contents. The suitcase, a regulation two-suiter, was jammed full of large-denomination bills, all of them in neat little packages of fifty, held together by brown paper bands. "Fits in nice, don't it?" he joked.

"Sure does," Ciaro agreed, smiling.

"You want this guy to continue?" Connelly said, jerking his thumb toward the architect.

Ignoring him, Hoffa swept his hand over the model. "Come look at this, Bobby. Ain't it fucking magnificent?"

"What is it?" Ciaro asked.

"What is it?" Hoffa asked in mock astonishment. "It's my fucking dream, that's what it is."

Ciaro leaned closer so he could read a small plaque on a corner of the model. It said, *Teamster Retirement Village, Sun Valley, Florida.*

"It's other people's dreams, too," Hoffa added. Turning to Fitzsimmons, he asked, "You know what that dream is, Fitz?"

"It's a dream of a community where working-men—"

Hoffa waved his hand. "It's a dream about a place where broken-up truckers can drink beer, fart, and lie about the waitresses they fucked."

Picking up the cue, Ciaro added, "It's a fucking truck stop with a patio."

Hoffa grinned. "That's right! You got it exactly." Turning on his heels, he started walking toward the door. "I got stuff to do."

"Just a second," Cairo said. Closing the suitcase and crossing the room, he handed it to Hoffa.

Stepping through the door, Hoffa was met by his secretary, who thrust a stack of papers at him. Hoffa sighed, took the papers, and handed her the suitcase. She staggered slightly under its weight.

Ciaro exhaled, slowly shaking his head. He stared at the model and mumbled, half aloud, "A retire-ment home for truckers. Fuck me. You want to make retired truckers feel at home, put a condom machine on the wall in the living room."

Hoffa popped his head back through the door. "If that's the way you think it should be, you talk to the architect."

Ciaro stared at McNeeley. "You think I *won't?*"

20
1958

In August, precisely a year after his first appearance before the McClellan Committee, Hoffa was summoned for a second time, ostensibly for questioning about his connections with racketeers and known gangsters.

"That is all bullshit, Al," he told Blanchard when he was served with the subpoena. "Bobby Kennedy is just pissed off because the jury failed to convict me on that drummed-up, chickenshit, wiretapping charge. Whatever possessed him to think he had a case against me on that is fucking beyond me."

"On paper it looked pretty good," Blanchard argued.

"On paper! Fuck paper," Hoffa said. "Once they got before a jury, there was no way in hell they was going to prove that I put taps on my own fucking telephones. I tell you, Al, that Bobby Kennedy is a sick man. He's got a one-track mind. He wants to see me in jail. He's so ambitious it's goddamn scary. Now that his brother's officially running for president, there ain't no fucking stopping him."

"He wants to be attorney general," Blanchard added. "He figures if his brother's elected, that's going to be his plum."

"God help us," Hoffa sighed. "That man has no conscience. No fucking conscience at all. I'll say one thing for him, though, he's a goddamn workhorse. He never knows when to quit."

"That's the pot calling the kettle black."

"Hey, no shit, Al, that guy is relentless. If it wasn't so fucking serious, it would be funny." Hoffa chuckled. "Let me tell you something. It'll make your day."

"Tell me," Blanchard urged. "I need some levity in my life."

"You see that gossip column in the *Bulletin* the other day?"

"Don't think so."

"Well, it said Kennedy was going home after his usual eighteen-hour day and he drives by my office here and he sees the light on. Must have been the cleaning service or something forgot to turn it off. Anyways, he sees the light, and according to the newspaper, he says to himself, 'If Jimmy Hoffa is still working this late, I need to be at the office, too.' So he turned around and went back and put in another three hours."

"That's interesting, but I don't think it's funny," Blanchard said.

"Yeah," Hoffa said. "Well, since I read that I make sure my office lights are on *every* night until two A.M. whether I'm here or not. Let him fucking figure that one out."

"Jimmy," Blanchard said earnestly, "we have to get serious about this. You've got to quit baiting Kennedy. Like sending him that parachute when the jury acquitted—"

"I thought that was great," Hoffa said. "After he made such a big deal about telling the press how he was going to jump."

"Well, I doubt if he saw the humor in it," Blanchard said. "The longer this goes on, the more I'm convinced that you're right, that Kennedy really *is* obsessed with you."

"I told you, it's a fucking vendetta."

"I know you told me. And now I'm beginning to believe it. This stuff about your association with gangsters and known hoodlums is just so much crap. It's just an excuse to get you back before the committee."

"What do you think he's really after?" Hoffa asked.

Blanchard considered the question. "If you ask me," he said carefully, "Kennedy's still bugged about Test Fleet."

"Test Fleet!" exclaimed Hoffa. "Shit, that's ancient history."

"No, it isn't, Jimmy, and I'll tell you why."

"Oh, yeah. Why?"

"Because I suspect there's more to Test Fleet than what came out in the hearings last August. You remember that guy from the *News*, what was his name?"

"Ed Harmon."

"Right. Harmon. Remember how he tried to pressure you that afternoon, saying he knew more about Test Fleet than Kennedy did? Said he was going to write a big story about it?"

"Well, that was bullshit, too. You never saw that fucking story, did you?"

"No, I didn't," Blanchard conceded. "Which is interesting in itself. I figure he never was able to put it all together. Either that or the *News*'s lawyers wouldn't let him go with what he had because they were afraid we'd sue them for libel."

"Which we sure as shit—"

"But that's immaterial. I suspect Harmon was onto something. And I suspect Kennedy may have that same material now. Except he isn't afraid of libel. He can drag you in and question you as much as he wants and there's nothing you can do about it."

Hoffa was silent for several minutes, pondering what Blanchard had said. "But why now, Al?" he asked. "If he thinks he's got something, it isn't likely to be something that developed last night or last week. Why did he wait until now?"

"I figure there are three reasons," Blanchard replied. "One, the election is just a little more than a year away and he figures his brother can cash in on the publicity. Two, he feels you're vulnerable right now, after what Meany and the AFL-CIO—"

"Those fuckers did me a favor," Hoffa interjected hotly. "Getting kicked out of the AFL-CIO may be the best thing that ever happened to the Teamsters."

Blanchard's eyebrows went up. "Oh," he asked curiously, "how do you figure that?"

"For one thing," Hoffa replied, "we don't have to pay them dues anymore. We was paying them almost a million dollars a year just to be under their umbrella. Now we can put that money to work for us. And for another, we don't have to work with their restrictions anymore. We don't have to walk that fine line about who we can sign up and who we can't, because as an independent union, we can sign up whoever we want. I've already told my people to go after every warm body they can find."

Blanchard shrugged. "That's all arguable. But you didn't let me finish."

"So go ahead and finish."

"My third point, the reason I think you're *really* being called back before the committee, is Kennedy figures he's got something strong against you. Either Test Fleet or something else. Maybe something you haven't even told me about."

Leaning across the desk, until he was only a foot away, Blanchard stared at Hoffa. "*Is* there something,

Jimmy? If there is, I need to know about it. *Is* he going to be able to nail your ass? "

Hoffa rolled his shoulders. "Guess we'll have to wait and see," he said. "But I'll tell you one thing. He ain't going to get me without a fight. He may not realize it, but it's going to be the fight of his fucking life."

John McClellan, the gentlemanly patriarch from Arkansas, opened the August 1958 series of hearings with a statement indicating the group was going to follow the agenda specified in the subpoena.

"As spelled out in the committee's interim report," McClellan said in his smooth Southern drawl, "the evidence has shown that in numerous instances Mr. Hoffa has aligned himself with certain underworld characters, who are a part and parcel of the criminal elements and compose the most sinister forces in this country."

"*Mister* Chairman!" Blanchard said loudly, springing to his feet. "I submit that the so-called evidence to which you refer has *not* shown—"

"Patience, Mr. Blanchard," McClellan said, unruffled. "You'll get a chance to talk. But right now you have to listen to me. As I was saying"—he cleared his throat—"it is unthinkable that the leaders of a powerful organization such as the Teamsters Union should have an alliance or understanding in any area of its activities with racketeers, gangsters, and hoodlums."

Blanchard was on his feet again. "Senator McClellan!"

"Enough!" McClellan said sternly. "You will please sit down and withhold your comments until I have finished. Otherwise I will charge you with contempt and have you locked up, or worse, gagged. Do I make myself clear?"

Blanchard nodded. "Yes, Mr. Chairman," he said, embarrassed.

"When Mr. Hoffa appeared before this committee last year," McClellan continued, "he was not president of this large and powerful union. Since then there has been an election and Mr. Hoffa is now the Teamsters' number-one man. For that reason, which is reason enough in itself, it is this group's duty to examine any possible ties between Mr. Hoffa and members of the organized-crime fraternity. That is why we have called you here today," he said, nodding at Hoffa, "and that is why Mr. Kennedy has a few questions for you."

"Mr. Chairman," Blanchard tried to interject.

McClellan held up his hand. "Later, Mr. Blanchard. Later." Then, turning to Kennedy, who was sitting on his right, his mouth in a tight grin: "You may proceed, Mr. Kennedy."

KENNEDY: Thank you, Senator McClellan. Now Mr. Hoffa, if you don't mind . . .

HOFFA: But I do mind.

KENNEDY: That's too bad, Mr. Hoffa, because I'm going to ask you some questions whether you mind or not.

BLANCHARD: Mr. Chairman, Mr. Kennedy is harassing—

MCCLELLAN: That is not harassment. Mr. Kennedy is simply stating a fact. Proceed, Mr. Kennedy.

KENNEDY: Mr. Hoffa, did you know a Billy Flynn?

HOFFA: Yes, I knew a Billy Flynn. He's dead.

KENNEDY: I'm well aware of that. But you did know him, did you not?

HOFFA: I already said I did.

KENNEDY: Did you know him well? Was he a close friend of yours?

HOFFA: I *knew* him. He wasn't any particular friend—

KENNEDY: He was a close friend of yours?

HOFFA: I knew him.

KENNEDY: He was a close friend of yours?

HOFFA: I knew him.

Kennedy paused to read his notes, giving Hoffa an opening. "Your turn, Bobby," he said with a grin.

"This is serious, Mr. Hoffa," Kennedy said. "We're talking about the vicious cooption of the field of labor, and you sit there, sir, smiling. *Smiling,* for God's sake. I want to know what you have to smile about? We're talking about gangsters here, vicious hoodlums who think nothing of committing incredible violence, people who have no consideration at all for other's rights, people who . . ."

Hoffa rolled his eyes. Leaning over to Blanchard, he whispered, "Listen to this little turd."

For the rest of that day and through the next morning, Kennedy hammered at Hoffa about his possible connections with underworld characters, not only in Detroit, but in New York, Boston, Chicago, New Orleans, and San Francisco.

"Jesus," Hoffa commented to Blanchard when they broke for lunch on the second day, "I didn't know I *knew* so many fucking people."

After lunch, however, Kennedy suddenly switched tactics.

"We've talked enough about gangsters and confirmed lawbreakers who you *might* know," he said. "Now let's talk about a couple of lawbreakers I *know* you know. Let's talk about Josephine Hoffa and Mary Margaret Ciaro."

"What the fuck!" Hoffa said loudly enough to be picked up by the TV microphones.

Blanchard protested, only to be ordered by McClellan to remain seated and silent. "This is a legitimate line of questioning for Mr. Kennedy to pursue," McClellan said. "He assured me during the lunch break that he has good reason to explore this subject. Go ahead, Mr. Kennedy."

KENNEDY: Let's go back for a moment, Mr. Hoffa. Do you remember the last time you were here and we talked about Commercial Carriers?

HOFFA: I remember.

KENNEDY: And you confessed—

HOFFA: I didn't *confess* anything.

KENNEDY: All right, you *conceded* that your relationship with Commercial Carriers exceeded that which normally exists between a union negotiator and management.

HOFFA: I don't like your use of the word "conceded."

KENNEDY: Very well, then. How would you characterize your relationship with Commercial Carriers?

HOFFA: It was a congenial one.

KENNEDY: "Congenial," eh? So "congenial" that Commercial Carriers set up your wife and Robert Ciaro's wife in a very profitable business?

BLANCHARD: Mr. Chairman!

Hoffa was furious. "That little motherfucker. That faggot. What right, what fucking *right* does he have to bring Jo and Mary Margaret into this?"

"Jimmy!"

"I wasn't fucking talking to you, Al. I was talking to myself. That no-good, fucking weasel. That skinny little shit who don't do nothing right but make babies, that—"

"Jimmy. . ."

"Don't fucking 'Jimmy' me. Did you see this morning's paper? Did you see what that shit-ass little mick has started?"

"Yeah, Jimmy. Of course I saw."

"Here," Hoffa said, thrusting a newspaper at Blanchard, "read what it says."

Blanchard sighed. Three columns across the top of the front page of the *Bulletin* was a devastating headline: KENNEDY ACCUSES HOFFA OF ENLISTING HIS WIFE IN MONEY-MAKING SCAM.

Under it was an unflattering story by Diane Mitchell, the *Bulletin*'s chief labor reporter.

> Robert F. Kennedy, the hard-charging head counsel for the McClellan Committee, dropped a bombshell Wednesday when he accused Teamsters President Jimmy Hoffa of using his wife and the wife of an associate, Robert Ciaro, as the principals in a questionable business set up as payment to him for his role in settling a strike.
>
> Kennedy, despite repeated screamed objections from Hoffa's lawyer, Alfred Blanchard, accused the labor leader of planning the escapade in 1949, long before he became a power in the national labor movement.
>
> "This is just one more instance of how Mr. Hoffa has repeatedly ignored the laws of this country in his role as a labor negotiator," Kennedy told reporters at the end of the day. "What he has done is illegal, immoral, and indefensible. He deserves to be in prison."
>
> Hoffa, most of whose comments were unprintable, said: "Kennedy is bent on a vendetta. He wants to knock me down and use my defeat as a springboard to get his . . . brother in the White House."
>
> According to Kennedy, Hoffa intervened in a strike involving the Teamsters and a Michigan firm called Commercial Carriers. After Hoffa negotiated a settlement which was highly favorable to the firm, Kennedy said, Commercial Carriers was so grateful it started a new business called the Test Fleet Corp.

Using its influence in the industry, Commercial Carriers then set up contracts between Test Fleet and some of the country's largest automobile manufacturers whereby Test Fleet, using equipment paid for by Commercial Carriers, would deliver new vehicles across the country.

Once Test Fleet was operational, Kennedy said, Commercial Carriers sold the business, which was valued at $100,000, to Hoffa's and Ciaro's wives, Josephine and Mary Margaret, for $4,000. In an attempt to mask the transaction, the women allegedly used their maiden names.

Several years later, Kennedy contended, the two women sold Test Fleet for $150,000, which they split . . .

"It isn't pretty," Blanchard admitted. "That's for sure."

"No shit!" Hoffa said. "What can we do about it?"

Blanchard gulped, knowing Hoffa was not going to be happy with what he had to say. "As far as the committee goes, nothing."

Hoffa exploded. "What do you *mean* 'nothing'? We can't let that little dickhead get away with this."

"Jimmy," Blanchard argued, keeping his voice low, his tone reasonable, "you *know* what the situation is. It's a stacked deck, just like you've been saying all along. There's nothing, absolutely *nothing*, we can say that's going to make any impression on that committee. Not with the two Kennedys and McClellan. There's just no way in hell we're going to be able to buck that."

As distasteful as it was, Hoffa grudgingly acknowledged that Blanchard was right. "So what *can* we do?" he asked.

"Wait," Blanchard replied.

"Wait? Wait for what?"

"The committee isn't a court," Blanchard said. "It can't convict you of anything. McClellan can't sentence you to prison. All it can do is make waves. Harass you. Generate publicity."

Hoffa plopped into his chair. Leaning back, he studied the ceiling. "So what happens next?"

"They're going to be finished with you in a couple of days. Then you can go back to being a labor leader."

Hoffa stared at his lawyer. "You mean *that's it*? Then we'll be free?"

Blanchard hedged. "Not exactly."

"Ah-hah!"

"The committee can send its material to a grand jury with a request to study the possibility of indicting you."

"You can bet your ass that's what Kennedy is going to do."

"I agree," said Blanchard. "I think it's a given. But what is not a given is we don't know what the grand jury is going to do."

Hoffa looked at him skeptically. "You don't believe that, do you? That a federal grand jury is not going to do whatever the brother-of-the-about-to-be-president asks. He could ask them to suck his dick at Dupont Circle with ten minutes to draw a crowd, and they'd fucking do it."

Blanchard grimaced. "I think you're right there, too," he said softly.

"So what chance do we have?"

"Our big chance is when it comes to trial. If it does. A trial jury is much more removed from the political process. We can work it so the jury is composed mainly of working people, people who are just as resentful of Kennedy's silver spoon as you are. We have a damn good chance of winning that battle, just like you did with the wiretapping charge."

"So in the meantime we just wait?"

"I think that's best."

"And you think the committee is through with me."

"I think so," said Blanchard. He paused, then added, "Unless, of course, there's something else. How about it, Jimmy? Is there something else?"

Hoffa picked up a stack of papers that had been sitting on his desk. Ignoring Blanchard, he focused on the documents. "Get out of here," he told Blanchard, not unkindly, "I've got work to do."

Two days later the committee dismissed Hoffa for the second time. After McClellan gaveled the session to a close, Hoffa approached Kennedy.

"Don't think it ain't been fun," he said.

Kennedy gave him a sly grin. "If I were you, I wouldn't get too buoyant," he warned. "I'm not through with you yet."

It was not an empty threat. The third summons came a bare two weeks later. Unfortunately for Blanchard, he was in Hoffa's office working on Test Fleet documents when the process server arrived.

"Look at this!" Hoffa raged. "Another fucking subpoena. Doesn't that asshole have anything better to do than keep hounding me?" He tossed the document at Blanchard. "Well, what is it they want this time? More on Test Fleet?"

Blanchard scanned the paper. "No," he said, "this time it's about loans from the Teamsters pension fund."

"Loans from the pension fund?" Hoffa asked in surprise. "All our loans are legit."

"Not according to this," Blanchard said, bracing himself for the explosion he knew was coming. "What is Sun Valley?"

"Let me see that again," Hoffa said, snatching the document back. "That motherfucker," he cursed after he had read it through thoroughly. "It's part of his fucking vendetta. He just wants to use me to get publicity for his brother."

"What's Sun Valley?" Blanchard repeated.

"It's my dream," he said absently. "Sun Valley is a retirement community in Florida. A place where old truckers can go to sit in the sun and play pinochle."

"A retirement community?" Blanchard asked, surprised. "For truckers?"

"What's wrong with that?" Hoffa snarled, leaning across his desk. For a second Blanchard feared that he was going to grab him by the throat. "Ain't truckers got the right to retire? Ain't they just as good as politicians and doctors and"—he let his lips curl—*"lawyers?"*

"Sure, Jimmy," Blanchard said hurriedly. "It just never occurred to me before. That the Teamsters had a retirement plan."

"They didn't until I started one," Hoffa said. "They didn't have shit. They worked twelve hours a day, seven days a week, for next to nothing, and when they got old or decrepit, the shipping companies tossed them aside like worn-out trucks. I went to work for them and negotiated a wage they could live on, a good mileage rate, paid vacations, health insurance, even a goddamn welfare plan. And now that fucking Kennedy wants to rip me apart because of a pension plan."

"He doesn't want to rip you apart *because* of the pension plan," Blanchard hesitantly pointed out. "He wants to ask you about some loans from the pension fund. According to him, they are loans you approved."

"He's just looking for a fucking excuse. He's going to keep hounding me until one of us dies. I fucking know it."

"Maybe," Blanchard said. "But right now both of you are pretty healthy, and when he beckons, you have to go."

"When do I have to be there?" Hoffa grumbled. "Next week?"

Blanchard looked at the subpoena. "Yeah, Tuesday. The sixteenth."

"That gives us a little time," Hoffa said.

"Maybe not enough," said Blanchard. "In the meantime I think you'd better tell me about Sun Valley."

Hoffa's September appearance before the committee was a virtual repeat of the one in August, except in this case the subject was Sun Valley rather than the Test Fleet Corp.

KENNEDY: Is it not true, Mr. Hoffa, that it was under your direction that a Teamsters pension fund was created?

HOFFA: Absolutely.

KENNEDY: And what is the purpose of this fund?

HOFFA: It's purpose, naturally, is to benefit retired truckers.

KENNEDY: To help them live out their golden years in some modicum of comfort?

HOFFA: If "modicum of comfort" means to help keep the wolf from the door when they're too old to work anymore, that's absolutely true.

KENNEDY: And this fund was created entirely for the benefit of the truckers?

HOFFA: Right.

KENNEDY: And not for union officials, like yourself and your associate Robert Ciaro?

HOFFA: Absolutely not. We ain't old enough to retire yet.

KENNEDY: Do you know a man named Henry

Lower?

HOFFA: Henry Lower? I ain't sure. What's he do?

KENNEDY: He used to be an organizer for the Teamsters. Now he has a development company in Florida.

HOFFA: A development company?

KENNEDY: That's right, a development company. He's building a community called Sun Valley, promoting it as a place for retired truckers.

HOFFA: Oh, yeah. Seems I've heard about that.

KENNEDY: I'm sure you have, Mr. Hoffa. I'm sure you have.

HOFFA: What does that mean?

KENNEDY: Did you ever borrow any money from Henry Lower?

HOFFA: Borrow money from this Lower guy? Why would I do that? I make a good salary. I don't live high on the hog.

KENNEDY: You aren't answering my question. Did you ever borrow twenty-five thousand dollars from Henry Lower?

HOFFA: I don't think—

KENNEDY: Did you ever loan money to Henry Lower?

HOFFA: *Loan?* I thought you said *borrow?*

KENNEDY: Just answer my question.

HOFFA: What *is* your question?

KENNEDY: I asked you if you ever *borrowed* money from Henry Lower or *loaned*—

HOFFA: Will you get off my fucking back?

MCCLELLAN (banging his gavel): Order! Order! Order!

For Hoffa, the result was still another splash of unfavorable publicity. The news media, especially papers like the *Detroit News,* the *Detroit Chronicle,* and the *Washington Bulletin,* devoted a large amount of space to Kennedy's accusations that Hoffa was a prime mover behind a complicated plot to line his and Ciaro's pockets at the expense of rank-and-file Teamsters.

According to Kennedy, Hoffa "borrowed" twenty-five thousand dollars from a former Teamster organizer named Henry Lower, possibly using an intermediary to collect the money surreptitiously. In return, Hoffa then "lent" Lower two hundred thousand from the Teamsters pension fund, money that Lower used to buy the land which was to be the future site of the Sun Valley community. Using the land as security, Lower then borrowed five hundred thousand in development money from the Florida National Bank of Orlando. But, Kennedy contended, the money did not come from the bank's coffers. Instead it came, as did the other two hundred thousand, from the Teamsters pension fund. The bank, allegedly, was simply the laundering agent. Once everything was in place, Kennedy said, Lower then made Hoffa and Ciaro partners in the venture, which meant they could profit from the sale of the lots, which were offered to Teamsters at inflated prices.

It was a devastating development, especially coming on the heels of the Test Fleet disclosures.

"Under this devious and self-serving plot," Kennedy told reporters at a news conference after Hoffa was again dismissed, "everyone profited—Lower, Hoffa, Ciaro, the Florida bank—everyone except the Teamsters, whose money was shamelessly used. Mr. Hoffa is going to have to account for his actions in this and other instances. As far as I'm concerned, I've only started to scratch the surface of Mr. Hoffa's illegal actions, especially concerning his administration of the pension-fund program and loans made by the fund. That is the area we're concentrating on right now. It's very likely that Mr. Hoffa will be back yet again before the committee."

Hoffa, grudgingly following Blanchard's advice, declined to comment.

21
1 9 6 0

Hoffa studied the two men carefully, and he did not like what he saw. They had come in off the street twenty minutes before, asking to see his secretary. Then they had told Katherine that they needed to meet with her boss on a matter of extreme urgency concerning Robert Kennedy. They refused to divulge more than that, other than to say it was personal and that they were sure that Hoffa would be extremely grateful to have the information they could provide.

The taller of the two, the one who called himself Bob, picked nervously at the cuff of his cheap brown suit and let his eyes rove around Hoffa's office. They came to light on the plaque on Hoffa's desk.

"What's that mean?" he asked, pointing at the inscription, trying to pronounce the Latin. "Illegitimate non carbon something."

Hoffa, who knew no more Latin than Bob, translated, "'Don't let the bastards grind you down.' It's my motto," he explained curtly. "Now, what do you want?"

Bob and the skinny one, who said his name was Jim, exchanged glances. Jim decided to be the spokesman.

"We understand you don't like Bobby Kennedy," he said.

Hoffa nodded. "That's no fucking secret."

"Would you like to know what he does in his spare time?" Bob asked with a malicious grin.

Hoffa stared at him. "Get to the point."

"Well," Jim said, "me and Bob have the privilege from time to time to make the acquaintance of some nice-looking young women—"

"*Beautiful* young women," Bob corrected.

"Yeah," Jim agreed, "*beautiful.* Better than just nice looking. Really classy broads."

Hoffa pointedly looked at his watch. "You got thirty seconds."

Jim looked at Bob and rolled his eyes. "What we're trying to say," he said to Hoffa, "is we know from first-hand knowledge that Bobby Kennedy also knows—"

"'Knows' in the biblical sense," Bob interjected, grinning slyly.

"—some of these young women." Glancing at Bob for confirmation, Jim added, "You might say he also knows them on a *professional* basis."

Bob vigorously nodded his assent. "*Their* profession, not his."

"Are you trying to tell me," Hoffa said angrily, "that you're here to try to *sell* me information alleging that Bobby Kennedy goes to *whores.*" At the word "whores" his mouth turned down in disgust.

"Yeah," Bob said eagerly, oblivious to the warning in Hoffa's voice, "that's what we're trying to say. Bobby Kennedy is a cocksman like you wouldn't fucking believe. And we can prove it."

Hoffa sprang to his feet and charged around the desk. Placing one huge hand around the back of

Bob's neck, the other around Jim's, he lifted the men out of their chairs and propelled them toward the door. "I'm going to let you walk out of here this time," he whispered menacingly, "but let me give you some advice. If I ever see your fucking faces around here again, or *anywhere* for that matter, I'm going to personally pound your butts so far in the ground you'll need a backhoe to get out."

Holding the men at arm's length, Hoffa shook them hard, hard enough to hear their teeth click together. "Do you understand me?" he hissed. "Am I making myself clear?"

Frightened into speechlessness, the two men bobbed their heads, signifying comprehension.

"Then get the fuck out," Hoffa said, shoving them toward the door. Neither man looked back.

As soon as the two men had gone, Hoffa pushed the button on his intercom. "Katherine," he said evenly, "get hold of Bobby and Blanchard and tell them I want to see them. Right now."

"No question about it," Blanchard said. "You did precisely the right thing. What I don't understand is why. I know for a fact that you don't much like—"

"I hate his fucking guts."

"That's what I mean. This Bob and Jim, whoever they are and however disreputable they may have been, may have truly been in possession of material that could have caused problems for Kennedy, especially now that his brother's in the White House and he's attorney general."

"You don't understand," Hoffa explained. "Me and Kennedy can't stand the sight of each other. If I could get him alone in an empty room, I'd break his arms and legs and twist his head around backward. But that's between me and him. What those two cocksuckers were trying to do was sell me information about his *personal* life. Even if it was *true*, it wouldn't hurt Kennedy so much as his wife and kids. I don't have any bitch with them. I don't want to hurt *them*."

Blanchard nodded slowly, telling himself that he would never understand this complicated man. His middle name isn't Riddle for nothing, he thought, suppressing the impulse to laugh.

"There's one other possibility, too," Hoffa said.

"That it was a setup!" Ciaro said, speaking for the first time.

Hoffa grinned. "Good ol' Bobby," he said. "He always knows exactly what I'm thinking. And he's right. I wouldn't put anything past that little prick."

"Not just him, either," Ciaro added. "You also got to consider that bunch of fucking goons he's put on your ass."

"The 'Terrible Twenty'?" Blanchard asked. "The team we hear has been detailed specifically to investigate you?"

"Terrible Twenty, my ass," Hoffa said. "I like what the *Tribune* calls them better."

Ciaro chuckled. "The 'Get Hoffa Squad.'"

Blanchard allowed himself a smile. "I have to admit it's appropriate."

"Whatever they're called, they're up to something," Hoffa said. "We haven't heard anything from them since McClellan's 'Playhouse 90' ended its run last summer. I want you to dig around, Al, see what you can find out. Bobby, I want you to see if you can find out who Bob and Jim were. If they were just a couple of sleazeballs trying to make a quick buck, forget them. But if they were working for the Get Hoffa Squad, I want to know about it. Okay?"

Both men nodded.

"I got a plane to catch," Hoffa said, checking the time. "I'll talk to you when I get back from Seattle."

• • •

Waiting on his desk when Hoffa returned from the northwest two days later was a subpoena from the Senate Permanent Subcommittee on Investigations, the successor to the Senate Select Committee on Improper Activities in the Labor or Management Field. It was no coincidence that it also was headed by McClellan.

Not surprisingly the subpoena threw Hoffa into a rage.

"What the fuck do they want *now*?" he asked Blanchard.

The lawyer shrugged, flipping through the document. "They're still interested in Test Fleet. Sun Valley, too, it appears."

"Jesus," Hoffa said in exasperation. "Ain't they ever fucking going to let it die?"

"Seems not."

"Well, fuck 'em. Forget the subpoena."

Blanchard paled. "You can't do that, Jimmy."

"Why the hell not? It's just another fucking Senate investigation. Tell them to stick it in their ear."

"No, Jimmy," Blanchard said carefully. "This subpoena may have come from McClellan, but he's only the surrogate."

"The what?"

"The substitute. He's only the stand-in for the Kennedys. No matter how badly you want to fight, the one thing you cannot do is square off with the White House. They—"

"*Square off with the White House?*" Hoffa screamed. "Then they shouldn't square off with me. You follow me? Don't tell me who I can't square off with. Don't *ever* try to pull that shit on me. Any man, *any* man, who fucks with me, I—"

Blanchard raised his hand, palm outward. "Hey,

Jimmy, it's not me. I'm not your enemy. They have a subpoena. A fucking subpoena!"

For several minutes Hoffa said nothing. "You're right," he grudgingly admitted. "I can't ignore a subpoena. But I sure as shit can find out what's behind it. It's time me and Bobby Kennedy had another talk. You set it up."

"I don't think that's wise," Blanchard replied.

"I didn't fucking ask you what you thought," Hoffa snapped. "*I said set it up.*"

Bobby Kennedy's office was a commodious corner suite, totally appropriate, or so bureaucrats thought, for the attorney general of the United States. Kennedy's desk was a huge slab of mahogany that dominated fully a fourth of the large room. The paneling on the wall was burled walnut, and the carpet, pure ivory-colored wool, was ankle-deep. Kennedy was slumped in a black leather judge's chair, his feet propped up on one of the drawers, which had been pulled partially open. Behind him was a group of husky, white-shirted, three-piece-suited men who looked like FBI agents, which is exactly what they were, FBI agents on detail to Kennedy to investigate Hoffa. Behind them, barely visible from where Hoffa was sitting, was the American flag, flanked by the banner of the Justice Department.

Hoffa, who had agreed to let Blanchard tag along only because he felt he needed a witness—*his* witness—to what might be said, turned the subpoena over and over in his hand, spinning it lengthwise and letting it slide through his fingers.

"You know what I say, *Mister* Attorney General?" he said evenly. Tossing the document nonchalantly on the desk, watching it slide across the polished surface until it stopped neatly in front of Kennedy. "I say fuck the subpoena. And fuck you, too."

Kennedy stared at him, keeping his silence.

"Any guy who needs his fucking brother to get elected president of the United States so he can get a job is a fucking joke. And that's what you are. You're a fucking joke. If it wasn't for your family, you'd be a fucking bond salesman somewhere. You'd be the brother-in-law that everybody made jokes about—"

"I don't know what you're trying to prove," Kennedy interrupted, "but you're proving it. Yes, indeed, Hoffa, you're *proving* it."

"I'm proving *what?*" Hoffa said pointedly, leaning forward in the captain's chair, one of a pair that sat in front of Kennedy's desk, separated by a small mahogany table on which rested a casserole dish-sized crystal ashtray and a silver lighter, both from Tiffany's and both inscribed with the Justice Department seal. "You have nothing on me. All you have is a TV show."

Kennedy dropped his feet to the floor and jumped up, seemingly ready to charge around the desk and strike Hoffa.

Hoffa smiled, not moving from his chair. "You don't impress me," he said. "And your office as attorney general doesn't impress me. Your *family* doesn't impress me, either. A bunch of rumrunners is all they are. I don't *need* three hundred million dollars and a brother who is president to whip your fucking ass, you little fag."

Blanchard, who had turned as white as the FBI agents' shirts, grabbed Hoffa's arm. "Jimmy," he began.

Hoffa threw his hand off, never letting his eyes waver from Kennedy's face. "You little shit, I'll beat your ass on those trumped-up charges. I'll beat your ass *again*. The Teamsters are clean and you—"

Kennedy, his face as red as Blanchard's was white, yelled, "I am going to see you in jail!"

Hoffa laughed mirthlessly. "For *what*? What did I fucking *do*?"

"Your loans . . ."

"The Teamsters pension fund has the best record in the country on loans," Blanchard interjected in a shaky voice.

Hoffa nodded. "He's right. The best record in the whole goddamn country. The plan benefits the *workingman*. Do you know what *work* is, you spoiled brat? To have to *work* to make a living? To feed your kids? To educate them? To—"

Kennedy turned to the men grouped behind him. "I want this man in jail. I am not going to stop until that happens."

Hoffa sprang to his feet, tired of the byplay. "Fuck you!" he roared. "And fuck your threats! And fuck your family! And fuck your goons! And fuck—"

Kennedy started around the desk, screaming. "What did you say? What did you fucking say?"

Before he could get around the vast surface, which looked as large as the heliport outside the White House, two of the FBI agents restrained him.

"Calm down, Bobby," one of them whispered. "Calm down. Don't do anything you'll regret."

Hoffa laughed. "Don't let him get hurt, boys," he said, turning on his heel and crossing the room. As he exited, Blanchard at his heels, he could hear Kennedy screaming, "I don't succumb to pressure. I don't succumb to threats."

Ciaro, who had been waiting in the outer office, looked up when the door opened suddenly and violently. Seeing the look on Hoffa's face, hearing Kennedy shrieking in the background, he could not help grinning.

"Did you have a good meeting, boss?" he asked.

Hoffa sat in his old chair, behind his old desk, in his old office in the Trumbull Avenue building that still housed Local 299. He liked being there whenever he could, even though his office in Washington was much fancier, what with its own shower and the mini-gym he had installed so he could continue working out with the weights. But for all its amenities, Washington was a place of convenience; Detroit was home. Jo and the kids were there and so was Lake Orion, with its rustic cabin practically hand-built by the Hoffas.

It was late afternoon, time for the early edition of the network news. Hoffa had switched on CBS because he had been tipped they were going to broadcast a segment of an interview with one of his favorite people.

While a man in a white smock tried to convince several million viewers that Bufferin was better than aspirin, Hoffa tuned in momentarily to Ciaro, who was in the next room lecturing a group of organizers.

"It goes without saying," Ciaro was saying, "that the Little Guy believes in you, otherwise you wouldn't be here. And he knows if you didn't believe in him, he wouldn't be where he is. But these are treacherous times. It's time to circle the wagons, to trust only brother Teamsters and not *nobody* else. If somebody comes up to you and starts asking questions, it don't make no difference what kind of badge he's got in his lapel, or what kind of ID he's got in his wallet. If you didn't go to high school with him, if you didn't fuck his sister, *don't trust him.* If anybody like that comes up to you, I want to know about it. Come to me or Petey and tell us. Or if you got any questions . . ."

Smiling, Hoffa returned his attention to the TV, just in time to see Bobby Kennedy's face light up the screen. As he watched, the interviewer, an empty-headed blonde, led Kennedy through a series of questions that had been written for her in advance by an assistant news director.

"Mr. Kennedy," the blonde was saying, "the word on the street is that Jimmy Hoffa has actually *threatened* you. Is that true?"

"Unfortunately, Peggy, it is," said Kennedy, arranging his face so he looked as somber as possible, "although I don't want to name names."

"Well, how do you feel about that?"

"How do I feel about it? To be candid, not real good. I have received both threats and vilification from certain members of the International Brotherhood of Teamsters, but I have made my decision. Nothing is going to stop me from doing what I think has to be done. Nothing and nobody. I swear to you that I will not stop until those certain corrupted individuals have been locked behind bars."

The blonde turned to the camera, smiling vacantly. "That's it from the Justice Department, Dave."

Angrily Hoffa strode across the room and snapped the TV off, cursing under his breath. He was returning to his desk, nodding at Ciaro who had entered his office, when Pam, one of the local's secretaries, knocked gently on the door.

"There's a man here, Mr. Hoffa," she said timidly. "He says he's from the Justice Department. And he's going through our files."

Hoffa and Ciaro exchanged quick looks, then both strode rapidly to the door and into the outer office.

A tall, slim man in an expensive suit and tight white collar had the top drawer open on the closest filing cabinet and was unloading folders, stacking them in a cardboard box.

"What are you doing?" challenged Ciaro.

The man turned, giving them a tight smile. He

had a shock of wheat-colored hair, a long straight nose, and startling blue eyes, which reminded Pam of a new leading man she had seen recently in a movie called *Picnic.*

"My name is Eliot Cookson," the visitor said softly and smoothly. "I work for the attorney general and I have a subpoena allowing me to confiscate some of your records."

"Get the fuck out of here," Ciaro growled, giving him a shove.

"Just a minute," Cookson protested. "Just a minute." Reaching into his jacket, he came out with a document neatly folded into thirds. "This is a subpoena," he said, waving it under Ciaro's nose. "It gives me the legitimate right—"

"You have the legitimate right to get the fuck out of here," Ciaro said. "Or I'll break your fucking neck."

Cookson looked around, seeing that other workers had gathered and were watching the show. "These people are witnesses."

Ciaro laughed loudly. "You're living on Mars, pal. These people *work* for the Teamsters. They didn't see a fucking thing. Now get gone," he added, pushing him toward the entranceway.

"You don't understand," Cookson argued. "I have a document signed by Robert Kennedy."

Ciaro bunched his fists. "Fuck Robert Kennedy," he grunted. "And fuck you, too. What do I have to do? Throw you out the window? Are you *deaf?*"

Pulling back his fist, he hit Cookson hard in the stomach. When the lawyer doubled over, Ciaro hit him again. And again. And again.

22

....
1 9 6 0

Despite the fact that the city was astoundingly popular with just about everyone he knew, Hoffa never had much of a taste for Las Vegas. It represented all the things he was not. It was artificial, ostentatious, frivolous, and money mad; adjectives that even Hoffa's worst enemies, and he had a lot of them, never attributed to the labor leader. Even though he was president of the largest independent labor union in the world, with almost two million workers formally in his care, men and women who trusted him with their welfare and that of their children, Hoffa was no Dave Beck. He cared little for the trappings of power and was, at heart, basically a Puritan who believed in the family, abstinence (from both women and wine), and the benefits of exercise and clean living.

Still, if the membership of the Teamsters overwhelmingly approved a proposal to hold the group's 1960 convention in the country's gambling capital, Hoffa did not feel it was his prerogative to veto the idea. But neither did he feel obligated to participate in the revelry beyond what was required of him officially. Tourists and fellow Teamsters hoping to catch a firsthand view of the man they had seen verbally slugging it out with Bobby Kennedy and John McClellan on TV for the last three years had no chance of spotting their quarry in the casinos or nightclubs. If they wanted a look at Jimmy Hoffa, they would have to go to the union's business sessions.

But even Hoffa made occasional concessions to the city's demand for pretentiousness by agreeing to appear at some social events. He was not a man to isolate himself from the membership. He *liked* to press the flesh as much as any politician; some said he was obsessed with making his presence felt among the rank-and-filers, a trait that stood him in good stead.

Hoffa knew the names of *everyone* who came to his meetings, as well as those of an astonishing number of members who never got involved in union politics. Ciaro was awed by the fact that his boss could walk into a large gathering of Teamsters, both activists and those who did little more than pay their dues, and greet virtually every one of them by name. *And* ask specific questions about their wives and children.

In Las Vegas, while he didn't frequent the blackjack tables or feed the slot machines, he was there every time the Teamsters gathered officially, even when Ciaro, sensitive to Hoffa's predilections, tried to talk him out of it.

"Honest, Jimmy, you ain't got to go to this thing tonight," Ciaro argued on one occasion. "It's just going to be a comedian warming up the crowd. Everybody has a few drinks and then they go into the main hall for your speech. You don't have to show up until you go on."

Hoffa looked at him incredulously. "What is this shit, Bobby? Have you forgotten Beck and Chicago?"

Ciaro looked abashed. "No, boss. It's just that—"

"Fuck that noise. You can bet your ass I'll be there as soon as the bartenders start pouring. Those are *my people,* Bobby. I have to be there to tell them how much I appreciate their support."

"Right."

"Besides, I might enjoy the show. Who's the comedian?"

"Johnny Jackson."

"No shit. Jokin' Johnny. He *is* funny. I want to meet him."

"No problem, Jimmy. We'll go a little early and go backstage."

Hoffa was never sure why they called it a green room. He had been in any number of TV stations and convention halls around the country, had been shuttled to those remarkably similar dreary cubicles where the celebrities were sequestered, like lions in a zoo, pending their call before the spotlights, and never had he been in one that was actually green.

Ciaro, operating with the efficiency of an arctic icebreaker, cut a path through the crowd to the area behind the stage and led Hoffa to an unmarked door. When the Teamster president entered, he was surprised to find not only the comedian, but Pete Connelly, Frank Fitzsimmons, and Alfred Blanchard as well.

Blanchard had a telephone receiver to his right ear, his finger in his left, and was huddled as far away from the others as the cord would allow, carrying on an earnest conversation with someone obviously back east, since Hoffa picked up a reference to "time differences."

Fitzsimmons had found—God knew whose it was—a bag of golf clubs and was practicing his putting on the worn carpet. Connelly was trying to talk to Jokin' Johnny, who was sitting in front of a mirror, a barber's towel over his shoulders, submitting to the ministrations of a makeup girl.

"Hey, Jimmy!" Jokin' Johnny called enthusiastically when Hoffa and Ciaro walked in. "Excuse me if I don't get up to shake your hand right away. Got to get this crap on my face first."

"Don't worry about it," Hoffa said. "Looks like you got enough to keep you busy right now, anyway."

"I'm really glad you stopped by, Jimmy," the comedian said. "Gives me a chance to go over my material with you."

"Well . . ." Hoffa began.

"Not really 'go over' it with you," the comedian added hurriedly, "just ask you if it's all right if I rib you a little. You know, kind of caricaturize you some. Exaggerate some of your features and mannerisms. I don't want to make *fun* of you or nothing."

"Better not," Hoffa said, pretending to issue a warning, "or I'll have to sic Bobby on you."

Glancing at Ciaro in the mirror, expertly sizing him up, the comedian responded, semiseriously, "Sure wouldn't want that."

"Me either," Hoffa shot back. "'Cause if Bobby couldn't handle it, then I'd have to step in myself."

Jokin' Johnny guffawed. "Shit, Jimmy, I think you ought to be up there instead of me. Anyway, what I plan to do . . ."

Out of the corner of his eye, Hoffa saw Blanchard waving at him, beckoning him to join him in the corner. "Excuse me," he told the comedian. "Business calls. You do whatever you want," he said, clapping him on the shoulder. "I know you don't mean no offense. It ain't like you're Bobby Kennedy or nothing."

The comedian laughed. "Goddamn, Jimmy, that's rich. You got a good sense of humor, which I'm terribly glad to learn."

"Let me go see what this call's about," Hoffa said, heading in Blanchard's direction. "As they say, break a leg."

"Hey," Jokin' Johnny said, "coming from the head Teamster himself, that is *funny*."

Hoffa's smile disappeared as he walked over to Blanchard. Even from ten feet away, he could see the lawyer was close to panic.

"What's up. What the fuck is it?"

"Two separate grand juries have handed up indictments."

"Uh-oh."

"Yeah," Blanchard said. "Big surprise. You've been charged with bribery and misapplication of funds. More or less what we figured was going to happen."

"Bribery?" Hoffa asked, raising his eyebrows.

"In connection with Test Fleet. They say you tried to buy a juror to vote in your favor."

"And the other charge? What did you say? Misapplication of funds?"

"Yeah. That one's a little more complicated. Kennedy was careful not to try imply that you *stole* any money. But his people got the grand jury to indict you for *misusing* funds under your control. Specifically the pension fund. Specifically in connection with Sun Valley."

Hoffa pondered this, staring at the wall behind Blanchard while he quickly weighed the implications. As he was doing so Blanchard spoke up again.

"There's more," he said quietly.

"More?" Hoffa asked, surprised. "I thought you said *two* indictments."

"That's right," Blanchard confirmed. "Two against you. But Bobby and Pete also have been indicted."

Hoffa's temper flared. "What the fuck they want with them? It's *me* they're after. Why the fuck they have to bring them into this? It's that fucking

Kennedy!"

"They're just trying to provoke a confrontation," Blanchard said, hoping to cool the flames.

"Well, they're fucking succeeding," Hoffa growled. "Those assholes. Don't they know I got things to do? I got a union to run? I got—"

"That's the point exactly," Blanchard said.

Hoffa paused. "That motherfucker. That no-good cocksucker. That—"

"You want me to tell them or you want to do it?" Blanchard asked, nodding toward Ciaro and Connelly.

"I'll tell them," Hoffa said quickly. "They're my people. I got them into this. If it wasn't for me, they wouldn't be in trouble."

Shaking his head, he approached the two men. "Boys," he said, "I got something to tell you."

Through the open door, Blanchard could hear Jokin' Johnny.

"This guy is up in heaven, watching as a big, black Cadillac pulls up," he was saying. "There's a Teamsters medallion on the side. The door opens and this *little guy* gets out. The guy who was watching all this turns to St. Peter. 'I thought you told me Jimmy Hoffa wasn't up here,' he said. St. Peter shakes his head. 'You got it wrong,' he said. 'That's *God*. He just *thinks* he's Jimmy Hoffa.'"

"What are we going to do?" Connelly whispered to Ciaro a few minutes later. They were sitting on stage in uncomfortable folding chairs, waiting for Hoffa to make his speech formally accepting the responsibilities of office for another term. Although Hoffa was supremely confident that he would win this latest round against his arch enemy, as he had won the others, Connelly was not as sure.

"What do you mean, 'What are we going to do?'" Ciaro whispered back, giving Connelly a look of disbelief.

"I mean what we are we going to *do*?"

"Don't worry about it," Ciaro said angrily. "We'll get some lawyers, the best the Teamsters can find, and they'll tell us what to say. Piece of cake."

Glancing at Connelly, he could see that he was not reassured, that his words had not performed any magic on the man's psyche. "Hey," he said more kindly. "I said don't worry about it. Everything is going to be copacetic. This ain't the fucking end of the world. It ain't like we're criminals or nothing. Not like we got to worry about going to prison. Cheer up, Petey. Everything's going to be okay. We're the fucking *Teamsters*. Ain't nobody going to hurt us."

"If you say so, Bobby," Connelly said, brightening somewhat.

"I say so! Now shut the fuck up and listen to Jimmy."

". . . the kings of old," Hoffa was saying—thundering—to an audience that was hanging on his every word.

He's come a long way, Ciaro thought, pride swelling in his chest. A long fucking way since the days when he didn't even begin to know how to make a speech.

"Those kings assembled retainers around them and they derived power from them. Just like I derive power from you. You are my retainers. You give me my strength. With you behind me, I will not be swayed. And neither will the Teamsters." He paused for applause, which he acknowledged with a slight bow, then continued.

"Our watchword is unity. We will stick together. We are a *brotherhood*. It's you and me. And we will not be swayed. Any man can make accusations. And any man can be a target. I am not immune. And neither are you. We can be subjected to all kinds of slander. We can be attacked by anyone, even those in government. *Especially* those in government. Sometimes, without even intending to, we can prompt these allegations. That's because we are powerful. Because we are united. And that makes others afraid. And jealous. And vengeful. And they want to tear us down. It is our very prominence itself that draws these attacks. We cannot stop the attacks, but we can be prepared for them. We have to be ever watchful for people who would try to take away the gains we have made in recent years. In my memory—in *your* memory—the Teamsters have become a power to be reckoned with. We represent the new middle class. We have proved that the workingman *is* somebody. And there are those who would damn us for that."

Hoffa paused again, waiting for the applause he knew was coming. When it subsided, he went on.

"We're at the top. We're number one. And we're going to stay there." Again he paused for the cheers.

"Management don't scare me," he said when stillness was restored. "And Bobby Kennedy don't scare me."

"That's the attitude, Jimmy," a man yelled from the rear of the hall.

"Don't let them get the upper hand," hollered another.

Hoffa held up his hand, signaling for an end to the comments. "You know what *does* scare me?" he asked, almost in a whisper.

"Nothing, Jimmy!" bellowed a man from the floor, lifting his beer glass high, splashing some on the man in front of him. "Nothing scares you."

Hoffa allowed himself a tight smile. "For fifty-five days they had me up there in Washington," he continued. "The members of the McClellan Committee.

They came up with a list, a list of a hundred and seven names. They claimed everyone on that list was a hoodlum. A hoodlum masquerading as a Teamster. Or vice versa. I forget exactly which. I sent questionnaires to every local in the country. I asked them to give me a legal history of every officer in that local. I asked them if they had any *hoodlums* among them. You know what the responses were."

"What was they, Jimmy?" a man in the third row yelled.

"We found," Hoffa said, ignoring the interruption, "four people. That's right *four*." Raising his hand, he ticked off the number with his fingers. "One . . . two . . . three . . . four. Four people among our officers that had a conviction of any kind. This is what the McClellan Committee wants to make a big deal out of. They say our membership, our brotherhood, is *riddled* with lawbreakers. With *gangsters*. Out of almost two million members and thousands of officers, we found *four* who had ever been convicted. Is that fair? Does that make us 'racketeer-influenced'? I say hell no, it don't."

Again applause shook the building. Hoffa waited. In the silence that followed, Ciaro heard an unfamiliar noise to his right. Glancing quickly in that direction, he saw that it was a waiter pushing a large dolly loaded with beer kegs. Empties, Ciaro figured. Dead soldiers. Go get some more, guy. Jimmy is really getting the men riled up. They'll want a *lot* of beer after he finishes.

"But that's what it's all about," Hoffa continued in a more subdued tone. "It's a boxing match, is what it is. You got to get in there and mix it up. If you want to dish it out, you have to get in close. There's a possibility that you're going to take a few punches yourself. Maybe get hurt a little. Maybe get hurt a lot. But that's what boxing's about. That's life, too, my friends. My brothers and sisters. It's give and take. It's mix it up. And that's what Jimmy Hoffa is not afraid of. That's why you've elected me your president. To mix it up. To fight for you. Because if you want to be number one, you have to fight for it. It's that willingness to fight that has made the Teamsters the best union in the world. It's what made the Teamsters what we are. Thank you for your faith in me."

The applause, the cheering, the whistling, the stomping of feet had not yet started. Hoffa had just finished the last vowel when one of the beer kegs being removed by the impatient waiter toppled off the dolly and hit the floor with a loud crash. The waiter and the kegs were out of Ciaro's line of vision but he *heard* the noise, which was almost immediately drowned out by the crowd's reaction. But he heard it and he thought it was a bomb. Quicker than a gunslinger in a western, Ciaro reached in his jacket and drew his .45. Spinning, he pointed the pistol at what he figured was the source of the explosion, hoping to find whoever was responsible in his sights. Instead he discovered he was pointing the weapon directly at Connelly's head.

Connelly, dumbfounded, only vaguely aware of the noise that had set Ciaro off, opened his eyes in horror, certain he was a dead man.

Embarrassed that he had been fooled, Ciaro grinned an apology and shoved the pistol back under his jacket. Of the thousands of people in the auditorium, all of whom were starting to cheer their president, only Connelly was aware of Ciaro's reaction.

"Sorry, Petey," Ciaro apologized, shouting over the clamor. "I thought we was being bombed."

"Bombed my ass," replied a shaky Connelly, convinced he had just stared death in the eye and had almost lost the blinking contest. "Don't you, of all people, know what a fucking *bomb* sounds like?"

23
......
1975

"**W**ell," Hoffa said, "it makes me glad to hear that you got nothing else to do."

"What I meant, Jimmy—"

"And since you got nothing else to do," he continued, angrily, "I suggest you hustle your ass back inside, get on the telephone, and find that prick d'Allessandro. Now hop fucking to it."

"Okay, Jimmy, okay," Ciaro grumbled. "Jesus, boss, you got to calm down. Otherwise you're going to have a stroke or something. It ain't worth—"

Hoffa cut him off with a glance, a hard-as-stone look that Ciaro knew well. It meant no more back talk; do as I say.

"I'm on my way," he said, sliding out of the Pontiac. "You want some more coffee when I come back?"

"Yeah," Hoffa said absentmindedly. "That would be nice."

Shrugging, Ciaro started back across the parking lot, checking his watch as he went. Almost five.

Where *is* that fucker? he wondered.

Looking up, he was surprised to see a face staring at him from inside the diner. It was the kid, watching him intently. There's something strange about that guy, Ciaro told himself, feeling the hair rise on the back of his neck. I don't like being stared at by someone who shouldn't be staring at me.

Entering the diner, Ciaro was hit by a blast of frigid air that almost stopped him in his tracks. Outside, the temperature was well above ninety. Inside, Fat Albert had the air conditioner cranked down to at least seventy. Almost instantly the sweat that covered Ciaro from head to toe turned ice cold, sending a chill through his body that made him flinch violently, as if a dentist had just drilled into a nerve.

"Goddamn," he complained to Albert in one long exhale, "you have that air conditioner set low enough to give a man pneumonia."

Albert, who was too busy to answer, simply grunted. Mumbling under his breath, he was clearing a booth recently vacated by a group of hungry truckers. He worked methodically, scraping the scraps of food left on the plates into one corner of a large black plastic pan. In the center of the tray, he piled the dirty plates, and around the edges, he wedged in the used glasses and coffee cups.

Ciaro looked around for the kid, anxious to ask him why he was so curious about what was going on in the parking lot. He spotted him standing near the window, watching him. Swinging onto a stool in his customary place at the counter, near the phone booth, Ciaro motioned to the young trucker to come over. Seemingly unresentful of the abrupt summons, the kid strode over, quickly and agilely, his blue-and-white running shoes making no noise on the worn linoleum.

"You didn't get any calls," he said, before Ciaro could ask him why he was watching him through the window. "Phone hasn't rung once."

Ciaro studied him. "Okay, Kid," he said guardedly, "thanks for keeping me covered."

"No problem. But if my dispatcher don't come through pretty soon, I might need your help, like you promised."

"Look, Kid." Ciaro paused. "Hey, I hate to keep calling you Kid. You got a name?"

"Sure I got a name," he replied. "It's Johnny. Johnny Longuro."

"Oh," said Ciaro, his eyes flicking to the tattoo on the kid's arm, the one with the initials *J.L.* "You're a wop, too, huh? Must be the biggest fucking fraternity in the world. My name's Bobby Ciaro," he added, holding out his hand.

"Good to know you, Bobby," Longuro said, taking Ciaro's hand and gripping it firmly.

For a skinny little shit, Ciaro thought, he's got a pretty good grip. "I been noticing your tattoos," he said. "The helicopter. I seen that kind before. On TV. Is that what they call a Huey?"

"That's right," Longuro said, mildly surprised. "Officially it's a UH-1. UH for utility helicopter. But nobody never called it nothing but the Huey."

"They used those in Vietnam, didn't they?"

"Fucking A," Longuro replied. "Used them for everything from carrying cold beer to the grunts in the boonies to ferrying dead bodies. The workhorse of the war."

"You worked with those helicopters, did you? Those Hueys?"

"Yeah," Longuro said cautiously, having run into too many people who were quick to berate him because he had had the misfortune to be drafted and sent to Indochina. "I was a door gunner. In the central highlands. Near Pleiku."

"A door gunner, huh? Sounds thrilling," Ciaro said. "Did you, uh . . ."

"Yeah," Longuro said softly. "It ain't something I'm really proud of. But it was my job."

"You mean—"

Longuro cut him off. "Don't say it," he warned.

Ciaro looked surprised. "Don't say what?"

"What everybody else says, soon as they find out I was a door gunner."

"Oh, yeah," Ciaro said, bewildered. "What's that?"

Longuro looked around to see who might be eavesdropping on their conversation, but there was no one within earshot.

"The fucking hippies," he spat. "The so-called love children. The ones who dodged the draft or ran to Canada so they wouldn't have to go. The ones who were so fucking keen to demonstrate against the war because they didn't have to fucking fight it."

"I don't follow you," Ciaro pointed out.

"Soon as they find out you were in 'Nam, *especially* a door gunner on a Huey, the first thing they ask is, 'Did you kill any women and kids?'"

"Oh," said Ciaro. "I didn't know that. Did you?"

Longuro glared at him. "The guys in my unit," he said coldly, "we had a stock answer for that. When someone asked if we killed women and kids, we always said, 'Sure. Ain't nothing to it. You just don't lead them as far.'"

Ciaro looked at him. "Is that a joke?"

"Yeah," Longuro said, straight-faced. "A little battlefield humor. You don't think it's funny?"

"Not particularly," Ciaro admitted. "Ain't nothing funny about killing people. Not even gooks."

Longuro looked at him. "You ever in the army?"

"Nah," Ciaro replied. "I was exempt because of my job with the union. Vital to the war effort and all that shit."

"Figures," Longuro said.

"What the fuck does that mean?" Ciaro asked sharply.

"A union official, huh? Big man in the Teamsters. Sounds like a rough job. What do you do, somebody crosses you? Let the air out of his tires? Disconnect his spark plugs?"

Ciaro stared at him. "Don't get wise with me, asshole. I ain't so old that I can't kick your ass and not even get out of breath."

"Back off," Longuro said, holding up his hands in a gesture of surrender. "I ain't looking for trouble. I'm just sensitive about 'Nam is all."

"While we're talking about being sensitive," Ciaro began. He never finished the sentence. Albert, who was on his way back to the kitchen with the pan of dirty dishes, stepped in a puddle of coffee on the floor. His foot slipped out from under him, forcing him to fling out his arm to grab the counter in an effort to keep from falling. The pan went flying, hitting the floor with a thunderclaplike crash and a roar of broken china.

In one smooth motion, Ciaro, who had heard the results of Albert's misstep but not seen what caused it, leaned over the counter, grabbed the shotgun he had secreted there, and lifted it smoothly from its resting place. Pivoting on the balls of his feet, he swung toward what he figured was the source of the explosion.

Albert, who had tumbled despite his efforts, was sitting on the floor staring at Ciaro. The room behind him was empty except for three truckers who also stopped to gape, hamburgers halfway to their mouths.

Shamefaced, Ciaro lowered the shotgun, pointing the barrel at the floor. Grinning nervously, he looked at Albert. "Sorry," he apologized. "Guess I'm a little jumpy today."

He replaced the weapon on its shelf and turned to Longuro, who had watched the performance in fascination, amazed at how quickly and gracefully the overweight, middle-aged man could move.

"Pretty fucking impressive," the kid said calmly. "But you mind telling me why you know there's a shotgun under the counter and why you're so quick to grab it?"

Ciaro stared at him. "That, my friend, is none of your fucking—"

Before he could finish, the telephone jangled loudly. Both he and Longuro leaped for it. Ciaro was quicker.

24

1 9 6 4

Bobby Ciaro often told himself that he would follow Hoffa to hell and back, ready to do whatever was asked of him under whatever circumstances. His loyalty was absolute, his bond to the labor leader stronger than that of many wives to their husbands. But one of Hoffa's precepts he was not prepared to accept was to give up drinking. He felt it was his birthright as an Italian, part of his national heritage, something passed on to him through his genes.

It wasn't as though he was a lush. Ciaro had a drink now and then, hardly ever before noon, and *never* when he was working. Occasionally, maybe once or twice a year, usually when he got depressed, he would hang one on. When he did so, his personality underwent a surprising metamorphosis, dulling rather than sharpening his tendency to be argumentative and combative. He tended to get nostalgic. To talk about the old days. To spin tales. To cry in his beer.

Maybe the fact that he was in Chicago had something to do with it tonight. Chicago had never been Ciaro's favorite city. His first love was Detroit, and to him, Chicago was always "that hellhole." The city depressed him.

Another contributing factor probably was the fact that he was on trial. He had been in jail more times than he could remember: for fighting, for picketing, for causing a disturbance. Even once, when the police could think of nothing else to charge him with, for loitering. But in the past, he or the Teamsters paid his fine and he walked away. This time things were more serious.

Under constant prodding from Washington— Bobby Kennedy should have been a Republican, Hoffa joked, because, like an elephant, he never forgot—federal prosecutors relentlessly continued their efforts to indict and actually bring him to trial. And where Hoffa went, Ciaro went as well. But how the two of them ended up being tried in Chicago was a complicated story.

Hoffa and Ciaro were originally scheduled to be tried in Tampa on charges stemming from their involvement in the Sun Valley escapade as well as on allegations that they misused the pension fund through illegal loans. Prosecutors, seeking *some* way to bring them to trial in federal court, zeroed in on the fact that the Sun Valley development had been promoted through fliers sent to prospective buyers. Therefore they were able to get a federal grand jury to indict Hoffa and Ciaro for mail fraud as well as the pension-fund irregularities.

At the same time, another set of prosecutors, also urged on by Bobby Kennedy, went after Hoffa and Ciaro on allegations having to do with Test Fleet. In that case, the two were indicted by a federal grand jury in Nashville, as Commercial Carriers had incorporated Test Fleet in Tennessee when they started the company. They faced two counts of illegally conspiring with Commercial Carriers to violate the Taft-Hartley Act, a law making it illegal for employee representatives, i.e., union officials, to take payments from employers.

Hoffa and Ciaro were scheduled to go on trial in Miami early in 1962 on the charges stemming from the Sun Valley case. Bobby Kennedy was delighted, bragging to reporters that Hoffa was not going to slip away from federal prosecutors this time. But as the trial date got closer Kennedy became worried about the testimony of the government witnesses, which upon close examination, seemed rather shaky. So when the Test Fleet indictments were handed up in Tennessee, the attorney general decided he had a better chance of convicting Hoffa there than he did in Florida. He turned his attention to Nashville.

Hoffa and Ciaro went on trial in the Tennessee capital in the fall of 1962. The jury, however, failed to find them guilty. The panel, in fact, made no finding at all. After three days of deliberation, the group said it was hopelessly deadlocked and unable to agree on a verdict. As a result, Judge Howard Thompson had no choice but to declare a mistrial.

Unfortunately for Hoffa and Ciaro, however, a much more serious issue arose. During the trial, there were repeated rumors that Hoffa was trying to bribe one or more jurors to vote against conviction. When he declared the mistrial, Judge Thompson also ordered another grand jury to investigate whether Hoffa and Cairo could be charged with jury tampering instead.

In the meantime, prosecutors were in a pickle. The more he studied the case in Florida, the more Kennedy was convinced that he would not be able to convict the Teamsters there on those specific charges. But rather than toss out all the work he and the Get Hoffa Squad had done, the attorney general began shopping for someplace else to have Hoffa indicted and tried. He chose Chicago. On June 4, 1963, a federal grand jury there indicted Hoffa, Ciaro, Pete Connelly and four other Teamsters for illegally obtaining twenty million dollars in loans from Teamster pension funds. Since it appeared that the Tennessee case would be some time developing, Kennedy decided to proceed with the trial in Chicago.

From the beginning, things seemed to go well for the defendants. Government witnesses, many of them the same ones that Kennedy was worried about in the Florida case, were proving to be unreliable in Chicago as well. Two weeks into the trial, federal prosecutors, with Kennedy looking over their shoulders, were making little progress in tying Hoffa and the others to the alleged crimes. Witness after witness took the stand and swore that they could no longer remember details they had shared with prosecutors some months before. From Kennedy's perspective, the case was going down the tube.

While the Teamsters should have been elated over these developments, Ciaro fell into a state of mild depression. The fact that he was in Chicago when he really wanted to be in Detroit was wearing on him. Also, he was secretly worried about the case in Tennessee, which was still hanging over their heads. If the earlier proceeding had not ended in a mistrial and he and Hoffa had been convicted of violating the Taft-Hartley Act, the most severe sentence they could have received would have been a year in prison. But jury-tampering charges were more serious. If they were convicted of those new charges, they could be sentenced to as many as ten years in prison.

With these things weighing on his mind, Ciaro decided to have a drink. Begging out of still another late-night meeting with the lawyers, he told Hoffa he was going to the Golden Goose to relax a little. Although his announcement caused Hoffa to raise his eyebrows, he made no comment.

"If you need me," Ciaro said, shrugging into his topcoat, "I'll just be across the street."

Sitting at the bar two hours later, his shotglass resting empty in a small puddle at his elbow, Ciaro was becoming loquacious. Having developed a first-name relationship with the bartender, he started relating the story about the night he, Hoffa, and Billy Flynn visited the Idle Hour Laundry.

". . . that stupid son-of-a-bitch," he said, not without affection. "That dumb mick, he couldn't stop smoking, not even ten goddamn minutes. Clumsy fucker, too. Spilled gasoline on himself, then when he went to light his cigarette, the fumes or some goddamn thing, *vaboom!* He went up like a Roman candle. Third-degree burns, all over his body."

The bartender, Frank, pretended not to notice that Ciaro was slurring his words. His job was to pour drinks, not be a temperance counselor. He listened to his customers' stories if he had to, but his duty, above all, was to keep them oiled and happy.

"Ready for another one, Bobby?" he asked, reaching for the bottle of house bourbon.

Ciaro nodded. "Ol' Billy Flynn. He's in the hospital, see, and this priest from the rectory across the street, a real grandfather type, comes in because the doctors know that Billy ain't got long to live."

"That a fact?" Frank interjected tactfully.

"It's a fact," Ciaro agreed. "This old priest comes to see Billy and tells him that he's dying, as if Billy couldn't have fucking figured that out on his own."

"Tough way to go."

"The priest asks Billy to confess. And ol' Billy looks him in the eye and he says," Ciaro paused, giving

Frank a serious look. "Do you know what he says?"

"I ain't got the faintest idea. What did he say?"

"Ol' Billy looks the priest right in the eye and he says, 'Fuck you!'" Ciaro downed the shot and pushed the glass forward for another.

"Just like that. That's exactly what he said to that poor old priest. Fuck you! And he knew he was dying. In my book, that took a lot of nerve."

"Sure did," agreed Frank, pouring.

"Just like Jimmy. The attorney general is after him. The whole Justice Department is after him. And you know what he says?"

"He says, 'Fuck you!'" Frank said, smiling.

"You're fucking A." Ciaro nodded. "That's exactly what he says. What a fucking guy. He built a union—a whole fucking *union*—with nothing more than a pair of balls and a billy club. Today, that union draws two million dollars a year in dues. And some bullshit fucking fag in Washington wants to tear it all down. You know what I say?"

"Let me guess," said Frank.

Ciaro grinned. "That's right. That's exactly what I say. Fuck him! The prosecutors ain't got shit. They ain't got *nothing*. Everybody is going to walk. Jimmy . . . me . . . even little Petey. Because the prosecutors ain't got nothing but talk."

"You really think so?" Frank asked.

"Fucking A," said Ciaro. "And as soon as I go take a piss I'll come back and tell you why." Rising unsteadily to his feet, he looked around for the men's room.

"Over there," Frank said helpfully, pointing to a door in the corner, beyond a small, worn dance floor.

"I'll be right back," Ciaro promised.

As he headed toward the rest room a man who had been sitting silently at the other end of the bar rose and followed.

Ciaro, fumbling with his zipper, hardly looked up

when the man walked up to the neighboring urinal. "Wish they'd go back to buttons," he mumbled. "At least you didn't have to worry about getting your dick caught in a fucking button."

"Is it true?" asked the man, unzipping his own fly. "What you were saying in there? About this trial? That they got nothing?"

Ciaro nodded. "Of course it's fucking true. They ain't got a thing. Nothing. Zip. *Nada.*"

Succeeding in getting his zipper undone, Ciaro looked both pleased and relieved. "You been watching the television?" he asked the man.

"Yeah. I seen it."

"Did you see those asshole prosecutors? Did you hear the bullshit questions they been asking. 'Where were you on this date?' And the guy answers, 'Man, I don't know. I was somewhere.' And the prosecutor asks, 'What were you doing?' And the guy answers, 'None of your business.' Ain't that a great answer? Ain't that how you have to talk to those cocksuckers. 'Ain't none of your fucking business. Ain't none of your *mother*fucking business.'"

Finished, Ciaro struggled with his zipper again.

"But what if they *did* have something?" the man asked.

Ciaro looked up and shook his head. "But they ain't," he said. "They ain't got *nothing.* That's because there ain't nothing to have."

The man began washing his hands. "I heard the government got to one of the guys," he said, watching Ciaro closely for his reaction.

"Where did you hear that kind of shit?" Ciaro asked, sticking his hands under the spigot.

"Don't matter where," the man replied. "I heard it. I heard that one of the guys, high up, was going to give Hoffa up."

Ciaro, who had been reaching for a towel, stopped

in midstretch. "Who *are* you?" he asked.

"I heard," the man said, ignoring Ciaro's question, "that the government had him."

"Had *Jimmy*?" Ciaro asked in disbelief. "Bullshit!"

"I heard," the man persisted, "that if anybody else agreed with that guy and corroborated the case against Hoffa, they'd get to walk."

Ciaro stared at the man as if he had just emerged from a flying saucer.

The man shrugged. "That's what I heard," he said, adding, "Take you, for example. If you'd cross over and testify for the government, they'd grant you immunity and let you walk."

Ciaro crumbled the towel angrily and slammed it into the trash receptacle. "You ain't got nothing!" he spat. "You ain't got nothing or you wouldn't be here."

The man smiled mirthlessly. "We got him all right," he said matter-of-factly. "And he's going away."

Ciaro began to chuckle. "Well, if he's going away, I'm going with him." Like a volcano spewing lava, he erupted in laughter. "You want *me* to give up Jimmy Hoffa?" he roared. "Goddamn, that's great. Best fucking joke I heard all week. *Me!* Give up Jimmy! You must be fucking crazy."

Looking around, he discovered that he was talking to himself. The man had disappeared.

Judge Thomas Shane peered over his half glasses at Daniel Jefferson, the chief prosecutor in the case against Jimmy Hoffa *et al.*

"Mr. Jefferson," he said, speaking through his nose in a style some eastern law schools viewed as patrician, "have you finished with your witnesses? I'm curious because I have before me a request from the defense to dismiss the charges on grounds that the government has not proved its case. And judging from what I've heard so far, I tend to agree with Mr. Blanchard."

"Your Honor," Jefferson pleaded, "may we approach?"

Shane stared at him, then slowly nodded. On cue, Jefferson and Blanchard strode to the bench and stood looking solemnly up at the judge.

"I assume you have a good reason for this," Shane said. "If you're just hoping that a personal appeal is going to sway me to rule in the government's favor on the defense motion . . ."

"No, Your Honor," Jefferson interjected. "This is about a witness, not the defense motion."

"Well," Shane said impatiently. "What is it?"

"We have one more witness, Judge. We would like to call one more man."

"You don't need a bench conference to announce that," Shane said.

"Well," said Jefferson, glancing sideways at Blanchard, "this is something of a special case. It involves immunity."

Blanchard opened his mouth to protest, but the judge cut him off. "In my chambers, gentlemen. We'll discuss it there."

When they returned to the courtroom twenty minutes later, Jefferson wore a smile and Blanchard was ashen. Hurrying to the defense table, he whispered desperately in Hoffa's ear.

The more he talked, the redder Hoffa's face became. Shane, who was watching carefully from the bench, noticed Hoffa's lips moving silently. The judge felt sure he made out the word "motherfucker."

"Call your witness," Shane instructed Jefferson after allowing what he felt was sufficient time for

Blanchard to explain the situation to his client.

"The government," Jefferson said, smirking, "calls Peter Connelly."

Painstakingly Jefferson led Connelly through his background with the Teamsters, letting him explain in his own words how and when he had first met Hoffa and how his uncle, Frank Fitzsimmons, had arranged for his job. From there he led him laboriously through his apprenticeship with the Teamsters and how he gradually worked his way, largely because of his uncle, into Hoffa's inner circle.

"And do you remember what happened in the fall of 1956? December sixth, to be specific," Jefferson asked

"Objection!" yelled Blanchard, rising to his feet.

"On what grounds?" asked Shane.

Blanchard looked confused. "Relevancy," he mumbled.

"Overruled!" Shane said.

JEFFERSON: Well. Do you remember?"

CONNELLY: I remember very well.

JEFFERSON: Please tell the court what happened.

CONNELLY: We went hunting. Up at Jimmy's cabin on Lake Orion.

JEFFERSON: Please explain who "we" is.

CONNELLY: Me and my uncle Fitz. Bobby Ciaro and Jimmy.

JEFFERSON: Anyone else?

CONNELLY: Yeah. Mr. D'Allesandro was there.

JEFFERSON: Who is Mr. D'Allesandro?

CONNELLY: Dally D'Allesandro. The guy what's connected.

JEFFERSON: You mean with the mob?

CONNELLY: Yeah.

BLANCHARD: Objection. Hearsay.

SHANE: Sustained. Rephrase that, Mr. Jefferson.

JEFFERSON: You mean the *reputed* mobster?

CONNELLY: Yeah. That's what I said.

JEFFERSON: And what did you do up at Lake Orion?

CONNELLY: Bobby shot him a deer.

BLANCHARD: Obj—

SHANE: Sustained.

JEFFERSON: *Besides* killing a deer.

CONNELLY: Jimmy and Mr. D'Allesandro, they had a discussion.

JEFFERSON: About what?

CONNELLY: About the pension fund that Jimmy had just created and . . . and . . .

JEFFERSON: And its use by organized crime?

BLANCHARD: Your Honor, I object to this entire line of questioning. The witness, obviously coopted by the government, has been testifying at length and we have heard nothing but hearsay, nothing to link my clients with Mr. D'Allesandro, nothing but—

SHANE: That's enough, Mr. Blanchard. Your objection is overruled. Please continue, Mr. Jefferson.

JEFFERSON: Thank you, your honor. Now, Mr. Connelly, can you please tell us a little more about this "discussion" between Mr. Hoffa and Mr. D'Allesandro?

CONNELLY: Sure. They laid out the scheme by which the pension fund would make loans.

JEFFERSON: To Mr. D'Allesandro?

CONNELLY: Yes, sir.

JEFFERSON: That's all, Your Honor. Mr. Blanchard may cross-examine.

BLANCHARD: Mr. Connelly, did anyone except you and the defendants hear the alleged conversation between Mr. Hoffa and and Mr. D'Allesandro?

CONNELLY: No, sir.

BLANCHARD: Then what, other than your so-called testimony, what *evidence* is there that such a discussion, such a fantastical discussion as you describe, took place?

CONNELLY: Well, sir, there's the hunting license.

BLANCHARD: The *hunting license?*

JEFFERSON: Excuse me, Your Honor, if I may, I'd like to offer into evidence a hunting license issued to Mr. Connelly in 1956, which was used as a sort of scratch pad by Mr. Hoffa and Mr. D'Allesandro to make notes on the scheme to—

BLANCHARD: I object, Your Honor. Most strenuously. We have not had a chance to examine this so-called evidence and we—

SHANE: Overruled.

Jefferson signaled to a man in the back of the room, who strode forward carrying a large package sealed with wrapping paper. Another associate was waiting inside the railing with an easel. When the man with the package put it on the easel, Jefferson stepped up and carefully removed the paper. Underneath was a blowup of a state of Michigan hunting license dated December 3, 1956.

JEFFERSON: As you can see, Your Honor, this license has Mr. Connelly's name and signature on it. On the back side—Mr. McConnell, will you please turn it over? Someone has scribbled the outline of a plan. These notations, we submit, are in the hand of James R. Hoffa and Carol "Dally" D'Allesandro.

BLANCHARD: Objection!

Hoffa, who had turned pale, leaned over and whispered to Ciaro. "Who the fuck keeps stuff that long?"

25
···········
1 9 6 7

After Connelly's devastating testimony, the road for Jimmy Hoffa and Bobby Ciaro ran abruptly downhill. Although the Chicago trial dragged on for another three months, Hoffa was never able to recover from the damage inflicted by his former aide. On July 26, 1964, the eight-man, four-woman jury picked to hear the charges convicted Hoffa on one count of conspiracy to defraud and three counts of mail fraud. Ciaro was convicted of one count of conspiracy and one of mail fraud. The others, except for Connelly, who went free because of his deal with the prosecutors, were each found guilty of one count of mail fraud. A month later Judge Shane sentenced Hoffa to five years on each of the counts on which he was convicted, which would normally have meant twenty years in prison. However, the judge also ordered the terms to run concurrently, which meant Hoffa's sentence was, in effect, five years. Ciaro drew three years and each of the others one year.

Unfortunately the Chicago sentence was only half

of Hoffa and Ciaro's troubles. Two months after the Chicago conviction, the two went on trial in Chattanooga on the jury-tampering charges. Although the government did not have another Pete Connelly to break the case against the Teamsters wide open, the accumulated power of the Justice Department proved overwhelming. In addition to the Get Hoffa Squad, which had been working full-time on Hoffa and nothing else for almost two years, Bobby Kennedy was able to demand the services of hundreds of other lawyers from U.S. attorney's offices across the country, uncounted Internal Revenue Service agents, and the vast resources of the FBI, with its state-of-the-art technology and its army of informers. Just before Christmas, less than six months after the conviction in Chicago, Hoffa and Ciaro, thanks to the vast accumulation of material against them, were found guilty by another jury. The panel deliberated only five hours and forty minutes before convicting each of them on two counts of trying to fix the jury in the 1962 Test Fleet case. Early in 1965, Judge William Defoe sentenced Hoffa to eight years in a federal prison, Ciaro to six.

As matters stood in 1965, Hoffa was facing thirteen years in prison, Ciaro nine. The good news was Hoffa would be eligible for parole after three years, Ciaro after two.

Naturally the two appealed, but they were fighting a losing battle. Even if a higher court overturned one of the convictions, there was still another pending against them. The chances of getting *two* convictions overturned were virtually nil.

Two and a half years after the appeals were filed, time ran out for the two. On March 7, 1967, a cold, rainy day, Ciaro and Hoffa met at Hoffa's Washington apartment for their final good-byes before surrendering to federal authorities. In retrospect, Hoffa pointed out, the time since the convictions had been relatively well spent.

On July 4, 1966, the Teamsters held its national convention in Miami Beach, and Hoffa, despite the two convictions, was treated as a hero. One speaker described him as the greatest American since George Washington. And secretary-treasurer John English drew foot-stomping applause when he asked for support for Hoffa. "He's not guilty," English proclaimed, "I say he's not guilty, and the *executive board* says he's not guilty. Come what may, we don't care. To hell with everybody else."

One of the more surprising demonstrations during the convention was the revolt against the reporters sent to cover the event. The Teamsters felt Hoffa had been ill treated by what they thought of as the "liberal press" and seemed determined to show their resentment. Hoffa set the tone himself in his keynote speech by urging the union's two million members to tell their "enemies" to go to hell. "Stupid reporters are writing filth, lies, and garbage about the union," Hoffa said to thunderous applause. Looking directly at the reporters crowded into the press section, he told them they were "overpaid" for the lies they wrote about the labor movement. "You shouldn't have the right to cover a labor convention," he said accusingly, prompting the delegates to begin chanting, "Throw them out! Throw them out! Throw them out." For the reporters, it was not a comfortable time to be sitting in the press gallery.

Although he was about to begin serving a long prison term because of crimes he committed as head of the IBT, including the violation of his trust as administrator of the pension fund, which was a crime against the union members themselves, Hoffa was greeted with affection and sympathy by the delegates. To show their regard, they voted him a twenty-five-thousand-dollar-a-year raise, giving him an annual salary of one hundred thousand dollars. And with only one dissenting vote they approved a proposal to set up a legal defense fund, of which he would be an immediate and major recipient. The IBT was flush with money and it did not want to skimp on its responsibility to the man who built the organization, even if a jury had determined that he had already taken more than he was entitled to.

The most important event of the convention, however, was Hoffa's disclosure of who he had selected to succeed him when he began serving his time in a federal penitentiary. It had not been an easy decision. It also was one that Ciaro strenuously opposed, one of the few times he questioned his boss's judgment.

When Hoffa told Ciaro that he had selected Frank Fitzsimmons to take his place as head of the Teamsters, Ciaro got so angry that he began stuttering.

"Jimmy, you c-can't fucking do that. That guy's an a-asshole. He's a fucking dummy. He can't even get your coffee without getting the cream and sugar wrong. It's because of his fucking nephew, who *he* brought into the organization—"

"Enough, Bobby!" Hoffa said sharply. "I'm the fucking president. I make the fucking decisions. And I say it's going to be Fitz."

Ciaro realized he was fighting a losing battle. "You're right, Jimmy, it's your fucking union."

"Have I been wrong before? Have I?"

"No, Jimmy, you ain't been wrong before. But I ain't so sure about this time. I think it's a big mistake."

"Then it's *my* mistake. I'm the one that's ultimately going to have to pay for it, ain't I?"

"You're right about that," Ciaro agreed, sulking. "But at least tell me why you picked Fitz."

Hoffa lowered his voice even though they were alone in his office. "It's simple, Bobby," he explained.

"Look at it this way. I agree with you about Fitz. He ain't too fucking bright. And he ain't exactly aggressive. The thing he does best in the whole world is he does what I tell him."

Ciaro grudgingly agreed. "Yeahhhh . . ."

"The thing is, Bobby, we ain't going to be in prison forever. When I come out, I want to be president of the Teamsters again. And my chances of doing that are much better if the man who *is* president is my man. Also, while we're away, Fitz will be doing what I tell him. It ain't going to be like we're really away, at least not as far as establishing policy and determining strategy goes. I'll still be calling the shots and Fitz will be my agent."

"I understand what you're saying, Jimmy, but I think you're taking a chance. What if Fitz decides he *likes* being the big cheese? What if he decides he's going to do what he *wants* to do and fuck you because you're behind bars and there ain't a thing you can do anyway?"

"Fitz?" Hoffa asked in disbelief. "Cross me?"

"Remember what you told me a long time ago, Jimmy? Never trust *nobody.*"

"I don't have any fucking choice, Bobby. This time I got to trust somebody."

"But Fitz?"

Hoffa shrugged. "Who else?"

When Hoffa told the convention delegates that he had picked Fitzsimmons as his successor, he was given another standing ovation. The next day, Fitz's appointment was formally ratified by a delegate vote, which was, really, a vote of confidence for Jimmy Hoffa.

Hoffa spent the next few months putting the union's house, as well as his own, in order. While he was gone, he would effectively be out of touch with the rest of the world. He could communicate by letter, but his personal contact would be limited to family members and one lawyer. For a hands-on administrator like Hoffa, this was the hardest thing to accept, harder than learning to live in a cell and having his life totally regulated, harder to adjust to than the loneliness, harder than saying good-bye to his family. Much to his relief, his wife Jo, his daughter Barbara, now married and living in St. Louis, and his son Jim, an attorney in Detroit specializing in labor law, were taking it better than he had worried they might.

Hoffa stared out his kitchen window, watching the sky turn from black to dishwater gray. Men and women on their way to work huddled in their overcoats and hid their faces under umbrellas. It's a nasty day, he told himself; a totally appropriate one to be going off to prison. He was fifty-four years and twenty-one days old, too young, he thought, to be dying, too old to be going to prison.

Looking down, he checked to make sure there was no lint on his dark suit and his somber tie was neatly anchored by the Teamster tie bar that Dan Tobin had given him more than twenty years before. This will be the last time I'll be wearing civilian clothes for quite a while, he thought, so I may as well look good. Behind him, he could hear Jo bustling about, opening and closing drawers.

"What are you doing?" he called out. "Packing a suitcase so you can come with me?"

Jo walked into the kitchen carrying an overnight bag. She forced a smile. "I was just putting together a few things I thought you'd need," she said softly.

Hoffa shook his head. "You don't take anything to prison," he said sadly.

Jo turned her back so he wouldn't see the tears that were forming in her eyes.

"It ain't the end of the road," he said gently, putting his huge hands on her shoulders.

"Everything's going to work out. We'll be back together finally."

Jo turned, not caring now if he saw the tears or not because they were tears of anger as well as sadness. "This is wrong, what they're doing to you," she said.

"You can't let good and bad interfere with each other," Hoffa said, trying again to explain his philosophy. "You just take it as it comes."

He wasn't fooling Jo and he knew it. Late one afternoon, at one of the darkest points in his effort to adjust to reality, Jo had come into their bedroom and found him sprawled across the carpet, beating his hands against the floor in anger, screaming, "I'm not going to go!" But by March 7, he had come to realize that he had no choice.

Before Jo could answer, their daughter Barbara entered with their four-year-old granddaughter.

"Hi, Dad," Barbara said, choking back her own tears. When she let go of her daughter's hand, the child ran to Hoffa and hugged his knees.

"Grandpa," she asked as Hoffa bent to pick her up, "could you bring me back a present from your trip?"

"Sure, honey," he said as lightly as he could. "I promise."

Setting her down, Hoffa put his arms around Jo's shoulders and guided her into the living room.

"You got nothing to be ashamed of," she said, as much for her benefit as his.

"Hey, honey, I know that. And neither do you."

Waiting for them in the living room were Ciaro, who had said good-bye to his family, and Fitzsimmons. Noting the strained look on Hoffa's face, Ciaro voiced his concern.

"You going to be okay?" he whispered.

"If I'm not," Hoffa replied, "no one's going to know but me."

Turning to Fitzsimmons, he forced himself to

smile. "Fitz," he said, trying to sound enthusiastic, "you're going to handle things just fine while I'm gone. I got confidence in you."

Fitzsimmons, pale and nervous, was not sure how to react. "I don't think there's anything more to be said on that," he said lamely.

"You're right, Fitz. We said enough already. But don't worry, you're going to do fine."

He was shaking Fitzsimmons's hand when the house phone rang.

"It's David," Jo said, covering the mouthpiece. "He wanted to warn you that there's a bunch of reporters waiting downstairs. He said he can take you out the back way if you don't want to talk to them."

Taking the phone from Jo, he thanked the doorman for his concern. "But I'll go out the front door," he said. "I ain't ducking nobody. Besides, the reporters, they got an assignment to complete just like me."

Taking his granddaughter's hand, his face set as rigidly as CiaD'Allesandroseen it, Hoffa walked to the elevator and pushed the down button.

"Jimmy," Fitzsimmons said nervously, "you know you ain't got to see those reporters. I can bring the car around back—"

"Forget it!" Hoffa said curtly. "I never ran away from nobody and I'll be damned if I'm going to start now. Drive the son-of-a-bitch right up to the front door."

Outside, he escorted Jo to the car and helped her inside. Then he kissed Barbara and her daughter good-bye, embraced his son, and turned, with all the joy of a man who might be amputating one of his own fingers, to face the newspeople.

"I know you all have a job to do, and I hope you're getting paid union wages for it, but I doubt if you are," he said, trying to add some levity to the occasion. Motioning to a couple of radio reporters, he waved them forward. "You guys with the mikes, get up here."

Standing hatless in the rain, he gave them a brief statement. "This is a very unhappy day in my life," he began. "I'm leaving my family and my professional responsibility for what looks like is going to be a long time. It ain't exactly my idea to do this. The attorney general's office, under that vindictive little weasel Bobby Kennedy, has wiretapped, room-bugged, surveilled, and done everything unconstitutional it could do to make sure I got convicted of something. For now it looks like Kennedy won. But I promise you one thing: I'll be back. Jimmy Hoffa was never a quitter and he ain't going to start now."

He also had a message for the Teamsters. "This will never be a weak union," he vowed. "Remember this. None of the courts, none of the legislators understand your problems. Only you, who work for a living, understand that. I hope and trust that those who have been a part of this conspiracy, this *vendetta*, will realize it's not just Jimmy Hoffa they are doing this to. If they can do this to Hoffa, they can do this to anybody. I urge everyone to beware of the constitutional rights they are losing."

Fighting to control his emotions, he continued: "That's all I have to say." Waving away attempts to question him, he climbed into the black Lincoln Continental that Fitzsimmons had provided for the short drive to the federal courthouse. When they arrived at 8:51 A.M., nine minutes early for his appointment—Hoffa was a fanatic about punctuality—he was not surprised to see still more reporters waiting. Studying this second group of newsmen, Hoffa sighed. "Where do all these people come from?" he mumbled.

On the courthouse steps, a few feet away, a TV

reporter was speaking into a microphone. ". . . waiting here for James R. Hoffa, the recently resigned
president of the International Brotherhood of
Teamsters. He is scheduled to surrender this morning to begin serving his thirteen-year term in the federal penitentiary in . . ." Looking up, he noted
Hoffa's arrival. "Wait a moment," he added for the
benefit of the rolling camera, "Mr. Hoffa just arrived.
Let's see if we can get his comments."

Hoffa turned to Jo. "Stay in the car," he ordered.

"You going to be okay?" she asked anxiously.

"When am I not okay?" he said, trying to sound
unworried.

Kissing Jo one more time, he turned to Ciaro.
"Let's do this thing," he said, climbing out of the
vehicle, his face rigid with resolve.

He and Ciaro had walked no more than two feet
when they were surrounded by reporters, most of
whom were screaming questions at him.

"Wait a second," Hoffa said. "Wait a second. Can't
we do this with order? Just hold on," he shouted, waving his arms. "Calm down."

The newsmen settled into an uneasy silence.

"That's better," Hoffa said. "Now, here's what I
want. I want the TV reporters up here," he said,
pointing to a spot on his left. "Okay. Now print people. You guys, I want you over here. That's good. Now
you photo guys can get in the middle."

Satisfied with his arrangement, Hoffa said gruffly,
"Okay, I'll take one question. Just one. Who's it going
to be?"

The *News*'s Ed Harmon spoke up hurriedly. "You
got any investment tips, Jimmy?"

Hoffa glared at him. "I understand the intent of
that question," he said between clenched teeth, "and
here's my answer. I didn't benefit by one dollar from
the loans made by the pension fund. Those were

legal loans which resulted in profits for the union members. And there's nothing wrong with that, is there? Is there anything wrong with that?"

From the back of the crowd, a reporter commented, sotto voce, "Not a fucking thing, Jimmy."

Hoffa grinned, showing his famous teeth. "You tell Bobby Kennedy that, okay?"

Five minutes later Hoffa and Ciaro chugged up the steps almost literally into the arms of a group of federal marshals, who had been waiting for them.

"You ready?" one of them asked.

"As ready as I'll ever be," Hoffa said.

He and Ciaro exchanged glances, then followed the men inside. Taken to a back room, they each were handed a gray prison uniform and a pair of cheap sneakers. "Put them on," a marshal ordered, handing them each a cardboard box, " and put your civie shit in here."

Fifteen minutes later they were escorted to a basement garage where a dark blue government van was waiting for them. Climbing into the vehicle, Hoffa noticed a pair of steel rings firmly anchored to the floor. Without comment, one of the marshals climbed in with two lengths of chain, which he ran through the rings and attached to manacles around Hoffa and Ciaro's ankles and wrists.

"Is this fucking necessary?" Ciaro asked hotly.

The marshal shrugged. "Regulations," he said indifferently. "You don't like it, write your congressman."

"You motherfucker . . ." Ciaro began.

"Shut up," the marshal said curtly. "You ain't working for a big union no more. Now you're just another prisoner, just another fucking con. I'm going to give you some advice . . ."

"If I want your fucking advice, I'll ask for it."

The marshal smiled maliciously. "Tough guy, huh? Well, let me tell you something that may be valuable to you in the next few years. If you want to survive, you'll keep your mouth shut; you'll do what you're told; you'll mind you own business; you'll sleep on your back, and if you drop the soap in the shower, don't try to pick it up."

"You cock—" Ciaro started to say.

"Hold it, Bobby!" Hoffa hissed, cutting him off. "We got a long time to be mad."

Ciaro clamped his jaws closed and glared at the marshal.

Moving his head, since he could barely move any other part of his body, Hoffa leaned close to the driver. "Well, asshole, what are you waiting for? Let's get this show on the road."

As they drove out the basement door and up a ramp to the street, they again passed through the crowd of reporters and photographers. Behind the newsmen, standing silently in the rain, was Jo. Spotting her, Hoffa tried to wave, forgetting his hands were manacled. Turning red with anger and embarrassment, he stared at the floor.

As they passed through the gauntlet of reporters Ciaro searched for a familiar face. He found it quickly enough. Just as the van reached street level, he spotted Harmon, who was standing a foot from where the van would pass, grinning broadly. Ciaro reared back, coughed up a wad of phlegm, and spat it at the reporter. It slid down the closed window in a long, white stream.

It was 192 miles from Washington to Lewisburg, a five-hour ride, given the marshal's reluctance to go over the speed limit by as much as a single mile per hour.

Once they got out of the city and were rolling down the highway, Ciaro leaned his head back and tried to sleep. Hoffa continued staring out the window, thinking ahead, making plans, already formulating his first set of instructions for Fitzsimmons.

He was shaken out of his reverie by one of the marshal's exclaiming to another. "Hey, what's this shit?" he asked in surprise.

Looking up, Hoffa could see a long line of rigs pulled over on the shoulder, stretching as far as he could see down the highway. "Hey, Bobby!" he said loudly. "Wake up! You got to see this."

By then, they were close to the first truck, an eighteen-wheeler with the name of a national trucking line emblazoned on its side and rear. The driver was sitting on top of the trailer, his legs dangling over the back. He was bundled warmly against the rain and cold and, clutched firmly in his gloved hands, was a placard that Hoffa read as the van sped by. WE'RE WITH YOU, JIMMY! it said. The next truck's driver had a different sign. And so did the next one. As they passed them one by one Hoffa grinned and bobbed his head in acknowledgment.

"Ain't that something?" he said to Ciaro. "Ain't that fucking something?"

26
....
1 9 7 5

"**Y**eah!" Ciaro said brusquely into the telephone. "This is Ciaro." As he listened the look of anticipation on his face changed slowly to one of dismay, and then impatience. "Hold on," he said. "I'll call him."

Longuro looked up expectantly.

"Ain't for you either," Ciaro said, glancing down the counter.

"Albert!" he called out loudly. "Albert. You got a phone call."

Albert, who had been busily cleaning up the broken china, put down his broom and waddled over. "Thanks," he said, taking the receiver from Ciaro.

"Yeah, this is Albert. Hiya, Droopy, yeah, same as usual. How I'm doing? Aw, shit . . . oh, well, can't win 'em all. See you."

He hung up the phone and backed out of the booth. Looking apologetically at Ciaro and Longuro, he shrugged. "My bookie," he said. "What can I tell you?" Dejectedly he shuffled back across the room and resumed his sweeping.

Ciaro looked out the window. The shadows were lengthening and he knew it would not be long before Albert turned on the outside lights and the neon sign lit up with the emblem of the grinning red fox.

"Jimmy ain't going to be fucking happy," he mumbled.

"What did you say?" asked Longuro.

"Nothing," Ciaro said quickly. "Just talking to myself."

Remembering there was something he wanted to discuss with the kid, Ciaro turned to face him. "Say, Longuro," he asked, "how come you was staring at me when I was out at the car a while back?"

Longuro worked his face into a puzzled frown. "Was I staring at you?" he asked. "If I was, I didn't mean anything by it. Guess I was just curious about who you was taking the coffee to. Wanted to see if you had a broad in the car or something. Thought maybe you might want to invite her inside." He smiled. "You know, introduce me."

Ciaro stared at him coldly. "For your information," he said evenly, "it ain't no broad."

"Then who is it? Why you so secretive about it?"

"That ain't none of your fucking business," Ciaro said. "Why you want to know anyway?"

Longuro shrugged. "Guess I'm just naturally curious."

Ciaro turned away, looking out the window again. "You know the old saying, don't you? How curiosity killed the cat?"

Longuro smiled tightly, fingering his Vietnamese cigarette lighter. "Yeah. Well, this cat's got nine lives."

27

1967

When Hoffa and Ciaro arrived at the Lewisburg prison, they were met by an assistant warden, who formally welcomed them to his facility.

"Prison is what you make of it," the man told them, speaking in a dull monotone, as if going through yet one more time a speech he had made hundreds of times before. "You're here to pay a debt to society. You can either make the best of the time you spend here and improve yourself in the process, or you can fight the system and make it tougher for both of us."

That's easy for him to say, Ciaro thought, already bored. He goes home to his wife and family; we stay here locked up like animals.

"Work duties will be assigned to you, hopefully somewhat commensurate with what you did before you got here, and you will be expected to perform those duties to the best of your ability, just as you would outside."

"Great!" Ciaro whispered to Hoffa. "We can organize the fucking lifers."

The official gave him a stony look. "Are you through, Ciaro?"

Cairo bit his tongue.

"You also will have a personal responsibility to maintain yourselves and your living area," the bureaucrat explained. "That means, keeping your cell clean, your bunk made, and your personal possessions in their designated place. You will, in short, conduct yourselves at all times as men who sincerely wish to resume their places in the free community as morally responsible people. Is that clear?"

Hoffa and Ciaro nodded.

"Very well," the assistant warden summed up. "Once the other preliminaries to your entry have been taken care of you will be escorted to your cells to await job assignments. I have assigned you to cells in separate sections of the prison. You," he said, turning to Hoffa, "will be in C Block, which, I might add, is a choice location since your row faces onto a corridor that empties into a courtyard. It is comparatively light and airy. And you," he said to Ciaro, "will be in A Block, which is the section nearest the infirmary. Jobs will be assigned to you later, based on your scores on the aptitude tests you will take tomorrow and what you did before you arrived here. If you have any questions later, you can make arrangements to see me through the chief guard on your block."

As soon as he left, the guard who had brought them in ordered them to remove the gray jumpsuits they had been issued for the trip to Lewisburg. "Those go back with the marshals," he said. "Here we all wear blue denim."

After they removed the jumpsuits, Hoffa and Ciaro were run through a delousing process, ordered to shower, and then taken to individual, adjoining cells where they were told they would be kept in isolation for twenty-four hours, which was normal for all newly arriving prisoners. Hoffa was given two sets of blue denim workclothes with the number 33-298 NE. Ciaro became number 33-822 NE.

The next day, when they were taken to their individual cells, Hoffa took one look at his new home and went immediately into a state of deep depression. The cell itself measured only seven and a half by ten feet. The furnishings consisted of a metal cot, a seatless toilet and stainless-steel washbasin, a rickety wooden chair and a footlocker the size of an overnight case, in which he could keep his clothes and the few personal items allowed—writing paper and pencils, razor, comb, and a few books. The walls were pitted cement, darkened with the graffiti of three decades of continuous use.

As he was marched to C-10, Hoffa counted the number of other cells on his row, noting there were a dozen in all. The bureaucrat had been right about one thing: a dozen feet away, tantalizingly out of reach, was a small courtyard that afforded a lot of sunlight. The man was also right about his cell being "airy," Hoffa cynically remarked to himself. The windows opening onto the courtyard, safe behind a wall of steel bars and a heavy wire-mesh fence, were always open, which meant he was only three steps away from camping out. That might be an advantage in the summer when the rest of the un-air-conditioned facility was a steambath, but it did not seem much to brag about in March when the outside temperature hovered in the thirties in the afternoons. Two days later, when a snowstorm swept through, Hoffa awoke to find his thin blanket liberally dusted with flakes.

Ciaro, who was probably expecting less than Hoffa, was not as disappointed as his boss when he got to his cell, A-7. Although its measurements were the same as Hoffa's and it was identically furnished, he did not have the dubious advantage of a nearby courtyard.

His only light came through a tiny window set high up on the outside wall, covered with bars and sealed with filthy glass that probably had not been cleaned since the prison opened in the early thirties.

Cursing softly under his breath, Ciaro sat on the steel springs on his bunk, not even bothering to unroll the lumpy mattress. Dispiritedly he worked a Camel out of the crumpled and almost empty pack in his pocket. Leaning back, he lit it, watching the smoke hang in the still air in a gray cloud.

Ciaro was wondering if he was going to survive Lewisburg or if he was going to die within those dull gray walls when a movement caught his eye. Looking up, he was surprised to see a guard standing outside his cell with a cardboard box in his hands.

As he watched, the guard fitted a key into the lock and opened the door, letting himself in. "They forgot to give you this extra blanket," he said, offering Ciaro the box.

Somewhat surprised, Ciaro accepted it, nodding his thanks. Without a word, the guard turned on his heels and was gone.

Wondering why they would bother to put a blanket in a box, Ciaro again plopped onto his bunk, holding the carton on his lap. It was awful heavy, he thought, to contain no more than a blanket. Curious, he lifted the cardboard lid and discovered that there was, indeed, a blanket inside. But there was more as well. Turning back one of the folds, he was delighted to see, neatly cushioned by the blanket, several cartons of cigarettes and what appeared to be a two-month supply of toiletries. Digging deeper, he found two relatively current Playboy magazines, a well-fashioned although obviously homemade knife of the type, he would learn, that prisoners called "shanks," and a handful of Hershey bars.

In the center of the packet was one of the most

highly treasured items that could be found in any penal institution, a pint bottle of store-bought bourbon. Even if it was one of the rougher brands, it was far and away smoother and better tasting than the homemade brew the cons called "crank."

At the very bottom of the box, tucked neatly away, was a crudely lettered note. Holding it up to the weak light, Ciaro puzzled it out. *From a friend of the Little Guy*, it said. *More when you need it.*

Ciaro smiled for the first time since entering the prison. Maybe this ain't going to be so bad after all, he thought. Influence helps, even when you're in the slammer.

Ciaro adapted to life in Lewisburg more quickly than Hoffa. Accustomed to being his own boss, going where he pleased, often flying twice across the country in a single workday, setting his own schedule, and having people come to see him on *his* terms, Hoffa was slow in conforming to the demands of prison.

Despite his previous experience and his score on the aptitude tests, the job that he was assigned was degrading and humiliating for a man of his capabilities. For forty hours a week, every week, he worked in a room filled with mattresses. On one side were the old mattresses, stained with feces, urine, and semen, and lumpy with age. On the other side was a huge container of cotton. It was Hoffa's job to rip open the old mattresses, remove the knotted cotton, and restuff them. The only good thing that could be said about it was that it helped pass the time.

Although he had never been much of a reader of anything but newspapers and magazines before he was sent to Lewisburg, in prison he became a book fanatic, voraciously devouring autobiographies, biographies, especially those of other labor leaders, and books dealing with labor and current affairs. Most of what he read was sent to him by his daughter, who was a teacher. In the growing library in C-10, Sward's *The Legend of Henry Ford*, Hardman's *American Labor Dynamics*, Mollenhoff's *Tentacles of Power*, de Toledano's *R.F.K., The Man Who Would Be President*, and Robert Kennedy's own *The Enemy Within* took their place alongside Toffler's *Future Shock* and Shirer's *The Rise and Fall of the Third Reich*. A pragmatist, Hoffa had little time for fiction.

Although he had spent a lifetime extolling the virtues of agnosticism, in prison Hoffa took to attending services at the Catholic chapel. He also developed an interest in his family's history and began cultivating a taste for classical music, thanks to recordings that his daughter also sent him.

He organized and headed a prisoner grievance committee and helped, through his considerable contacts in industry, arrange jobs for prisoners who were about to be released. Also, since he had become something of a self-taught lawyer thanks to his years of fighting the government in court, he offered his legal advice to prisoners. Perhaps more surprising than anything else, he became an avid letter writer, often spending hours composing lengthy missives to Jo, his children, his lawyer, and old friends. In one to Alfred Blanchard, he wrote:

> *I'll tell you, Al, I am pretty fucking disgusted. The humiliations never cease. Take today, for example. There was a group of legislators from Arifuckingzona or someplace visiting the prison so naturally they brought them by to see one of their star prisoners, namely me.*
>
> *It didn't matter that I was sitting on the throne, trying to rid myself of this bug-infested food they serve, but they brought them right up to my cell and pointed at me like I was a fucking lion in the zoo, saying "This is the powerful*

Jimmy Hoffa."
I wonder if I was expected to wave my dick at them or
something. . . .

But if there were bad days, there were good days,
too. When Hoffa was particularly depressed, Ciaro
usually managed to cheer him up. The fact that the
Teamsters never forgot him was a constant source of
inspiration. On his birthday, February 14, every year
that Hoffa was there, the Teamsters rented a private
plane and had the pilot make a half-dozen passes
over the prison, trailing a banner reading HAPPY
BIRTHDAY, JIMMY.

And then there were the incoming letters. At every
mail call, there were four or five from Teamsters
around the country telling him how much they
missed his leadership and how they were looking forward to him being released so he could return to the
IBT presidency.

His release became an increasingly touchy issue
with Hoffa. After less than three years, Ciaro was
promised parole. Although he was reluctant to leave
Hoffa behind, there was no way he could simply
refuse his freedom. Short of committing another
crime and hoping he would be returned to Lewisburg
as a parole violator, there was little he could do. And
there was little that Hoffa expected him to do.

"Don't be a fucking idiot," Hoffa told him when
Ciaro said that his case had been granted favorable
review by a parole board but he was looking for some
way to delay the action. "You done your time. You
deserve to be out of this place. Tell it good-bye and
good riddance."

"I hate to leave you, Jimmy," Ciaro had argued. "I
think you need me here."

"Need you here! Jesus Christ, you think I can't
take care of myself or something? You think I have to

have you here to wipe my ass or—"

"Nah, Jimmy. It ain't that and you know it."

"Well, what is it?"

"While everybody here respects you and you get a hell of a lot better treatment than a lot of other prisoners, part of the reason for that is because everybody knows I'm here to watch your back. We're a good team. Nobody is going to fuck with you because they know they'll have to fuck with me, too. And probably some others as well."

"You're talking like a man with a paper asshole," Hoffa admonished him. "I don't want to see you go because you're like a brother to me and I already miss my family bad enough. But I need you to get out of here so you can start laying some groundwork for when I get out. So far Fitz has been pretty good about following my orders, but in the last few months he's been trying to assert his independence. And I don't like that. That ain't why I named him to take my place."

"You worried?" Ciaro asked. "About Fitz, I mean."

Hoffa looked around to see who was near, but the two were alone near a corner of the exercise yard. "Yeah," he said, "I am. At least I think I am. Maybe you were right all along; maybe I shouldn't have trusted that dumb Irishman to begin with."

"What do you think we ought to do?"

Hoffa rubbed his chin. "I ain't sure yet, but we got time to plan. You ain't going nowhere for a couple of months and I figure I'm going to be here a hell of a lot longer than that. We'll figure something out. In the meantime, I got a hearing before the parole board in about six months. Maybe they're going to let me go, too. I been serving good time."

"I don't see why they wouldn't, Jimmy. They done it for a lot worse people than you."

28
·············
1 9 7 1

Despite Ciaro's optimism, the parole board was not forgiving. When Hoffa first became eligible in October 1969, he was fairly confident that his petition would get favorable attention. He had by then served one third of his eight-year sentence on the jury-tampering charge, which at the time was a standard criterion for release. He was shocked, therefore, when the board not only turned him down, but refused to tell him why. The group's only comment was to suggest that he reapply in March 1971, by which time he would have served four years, or almost one third of his thirteen-year combined sentence.

Hoffa was terribly confused about the board's decision, unable to attribute it to any known source. His arch enemy, Robert Kennedy, had been assassinated sixteen months previously, so he could not have had a hand in the proceedings. Besides, Hoffa had mellowed over the years, if only slightly, toward Kennedy.

As it turned out, the 1969 action by the parole board was only the first of several disappointments Hoffa would suffer at the group's hand. In March

1971, his request was denied a second time, again without formal explanation.

The second refusal struck him even harder than the first because, first of all, he could not determine *why* it was happening. Second, his personal situation was steadily worsening and he was becoming desperate to get out.

Hoffa had been able to endure life in Lewisburg only because he thought he could see an end to the experience. He believed, naively it turned out, that if he kept his nose clean and did what he was told, the system would treat him fairly. He was wrong. Twice he had been denied parole when others in similar circumstances had been granted it. And he had no idea how to get the board to look more favorably upon his requests.

In the meantime, things on the outside were changing. Beginning in 1970, Jo had suffered a series of minor strokes. To make it even worse, about the time the parole board was acting on his second request, she had a heart attack, which left her hospitalized in San Francisco.

After the parole board turned him down, Hoffa applied for a compassionate furlough, a rarely granted privilege to leave the prison for a limited time in order to be with a seriously ill or dying relative. Surprisingly, considering the parole board refusals, the request was granted. In April, he was allowed a five-day leave to visit his ailing wife. Although it was forbidden by the terms of his furlough, he also used the occasion to squeeze in two meetings on union business. On his second day in San Francisco, he huddled with Fitzsimmons about resuming the Teamsters presidency once he got out, whenever that might be.

The second meeting was with Blanchard and Ciaro.

"What the fuck is going on?" Hoffa asked angrily. "Why is Fitz suddenly treating me like I got leprosy and he's God's gift to the Teamsters. Even more important, why is the parole board fucking me around?"

"Regarding the parole board," Blanchard replied, "the best we can find out is that they're nervous about you wanting to take up where you left off with the union. They feel that it was because of the union that you went to prison in the first place and they don't want that temptation tossed at you again so quickly."

"What are you trying to say?" Hoffa demanded. "That I got to tell them that I don't really want to be president anymore?"

"Unfortunately that is *exactly* what I think," Blanchard replied.

"Those motherfuckers," Hoffa said. "They got me by the balls and they know it. And they ain't going to let go until I scream and beg for mercy."

"That's what it looks like," Ciaro agreed. "I know how much you hate to do it, but if it's that or stay in prison, I think you ought to tell them that you ain't interested in the union no more. Tell them whatever the fuck you think they want to hear, but get the fuck out of Lewisburg."

"Let me think about it," Hoffa said, dreading having to return to his cell.

On June 3, two months after his furlough, Hoffa sent his son Jim to a Teamsters executive board meeting in Washington with a letter from him affirming that he did not intend to seek the presidency at the forthcoming convention "because of my present legal difficulties." Again, because he thought he had no choice, he recommended Fitzsimmons for the job. He also formally resigned his other union positions, including the presidency of Local 299, a post he had held since 1937.

Two and a half weeks later Fitzsimmons was endorsed by the executive board at a preconvention meeting in Miami Beach. Appearing as a surprise guest at the meeting was President Richard Nixon, who was vacationing at his summer White House and said he just dropped in to congratulate the IBT president. It was not coincidental that Nixon was up for reelection the following year and was angling for Teamsters support.

At the union's convention a week later, Hoffa was hardly mentioned, except in discussion of some peripheral issues. Without fanfare, the executive board decided not to pay Hoffa the seventy-five-thousand-dollars-a-year pension to which he would have been entitled after his resignation, but to grant him a lump-sum award of $1.7 million. The group also voted to put Hoffa's son Jim on retainer in the legal department at thirty thousand dollars a year, and to continue to keep Jo on as the nominal head of the union's political action section for forty thousand dollars a year.

However, if Hoffa had hoped that resigning his union posts and denying interest in recapturing the presidency in the future would impress the parole board, he was mistaken.

In August, the group, again without explanation, denied Hoffa's parole request a third time. It was whispered to Blanchard that the denial came because Hoffa's son and wife remained on the union payroll.

The action sent Hoffa into the deepest depression he had suffered since arriving in Lewisburg. By then he had served four and a half years of his total sentence. No matter what he did to meet the unofficial "conditions" of the parole board, it seemed never to be enough. He began to suspect that there was more to his rejections than the petty whims of the parole board. Much more.

"Tell Bobby to find out what's going on," he angrily told his son on one of his visits. "Tell him to bust some balls if he has to, but find out what the fuck's happening."

Ciaro found Fitzsimmons on the sixteenth tee at the Glen Oaks Golf Club. The IBT president had just knocked a boomer 250 yards down the right side of the fairway. Since he was in a cart, Ciaro had no trouble catching up with the walkers.

"Bobby!" Fitzsimmons greeted him jovially. "I thought," he said, turning to one of the men in the foursome, "we were going downtown and meet him."

Ciaro replied before the man could answer. "Yeah. There's no point in that now. I'm here."

Fitzsimmons shrugged. "We were going out to meet you. How are you?"

Ciaro ignored the question. "I looked for you, over at the office. They told me you were here."

"How's Jimmy?" Fitzsimmons shuffled his feet nervously.

"Well, Fitz, you'd know if you took the time to communicate with him."

Fitzsimmons stared at the ground, seemingly suddenly interested in how much mud was on his spikes. "Aw, shit, Bobby, you know how that goes. Something always needs desperate attention, something comes up, somebody just *has* to see you. You know how that shit goes."

"Right, Fitz," Ciaro replied, taking him by the elbow and leading him away from the group. "Listen," he said once they were out of earshot. "Jimmy ain't good. You got to get him out. He's not well and he's not *doing* well. You got to get him out of there."

"I told you before, we're working on it. You got to

understand, it ain't that easy."

"I know that, Fitz, but I need to know how serious you are about it. I ain't kidding you. He's got to get out."

"I ain't shitting you, Bobby. We're working on it. I have a *plan*. But it's complicated and it involves some people I can't mention right now. As much as I'd like to share the details with you . . ."

"You got to get him out," Ciaro repeated stubbornly.

"We're *going* to get him out," Fitzsimmons replied.

"You have to believe what I'm telling you. He can't do the eight more years."

"You got to trust me, Bobby. Something's in the works. Something big."

Ciaro nodded solemnly. "Okay, Fitz," he said slowly. "Guess I don't have any choice. But listen to me carefully. You *got to get him out.*"

"Okay." Fitzsimmons grinned weakly. "I hear you. Now I got to get back to the group. We're holding up the next foursome."

Ciaro's next visit was to Dally D'Allesandro, who he tracked down at the Wayne County Airport just as he was preparing to board a private jet for Las Vegas.

"The plan is this," D'Allesandro confided when Ciaro told him about his conversation with Fitzsimmons. "The Teamsters endorse Nixon and kick in some money to his reelection campaign and . . ." His voice was drowned out by a taxiing plane.

"What was that?" Ciaro screamed, trying to make himself heard over the roar.

D'Allesandro held up his hand, waiting for the plane to put some distance between them.

"I said," he began again as the plane moved off, "they go to the president and they make him an offer."

"An offer?" Ciaro looked puzzled. "What kind of offer? How can they make a deal with the fucking president of the country?"

D'Allesandro sighed. "Look, Bobby," he said patiently. "I really do have to go. This plane's got to make another two stops before Vegas and there's going to be people waiting for it to show up. People I don't want to piss off and I know *you* don't want to piss off either. I'll be back on Thursday. Meet me at the club for lunch and I'll explain it all in detail."

"You ain't shitting me, are you? They're going to deal with that fucker Nixon to get Jimmy out of prison?"

D'Allesandro grinned. "I ain't shitting you, Bobby. I'll explain it to you on Thursday." Slapping Ciaro on the shoulder, he sprinted for the plane. As he got to the ladder he looked up at the cockpit and lifted his right arm, moving his hand in a circular motion over his head, the universal system for "start the engines." Turning to face Ciaro, he mouthed the word, "Thursday," then dashed up the steps.

Hoffa looked worried, very worried indeed.

"Jo," he said solicitously, "You shouldn't be here. You just got out of the hospital. You ought to be home taking care of yourself."

"Jimmy," she said patiently, "I got all the time in the world to take care of myself. It's you I'm sick over. You don't look too good."

Hoffa looked embarrassed. "I'm fine, Jo. All things considered, they take pretty good care of me here. I don't want for anything, except to get out and be back with you and the kids and the job. I been here almost five years now and it's beginning to wear on me. I'm ready to go home."

"Believe me, Jimmy, I'm ready for you to come

home, too."

"Why did you come all the way up here?" Hoffa said. "What's so important that you had to come here yourself when you should be home in bed? Jim could have told me, or Al could have left his precious practice and made the drive up here."

"Jimmy," Jo said, trying to suppress a grin, "you're going to get out. You're going to come home."

Hoffa stared at her. "What do you mean, Jo? Is something in the works? Is the parole board—"

"Not the parole board, Jimmy," Jo said anxiously. "The president. President Nixon."

Hoffa looked puzzled. "What do you mean the president? What's Nixon got to do with this?"

Jo smiled. "It's all politics, honey. Just like you always said. You scratch somebody's back, they scratch yours. This time the back being scratched is Nixon's."

Hoffa still did not understand. "Take it slow, Jo," he said, struggling to contain his excitement. "Tell me what's going on."

"It's really very simple. Nixon thinks he needs help in the election. He *knows* he needs money. And he knows Fitz because Fitz has been making contributions to Republican campaigns around the country."

"So?"

"So Fitz made a deal with Nixon."

"A deal?" Hoffa asked incredulously. "What kind of deal?"

"The Teamsters make a big contribution to Nixon's campaign," Jo said patiently. "And Fitz endorses Nixon for reelection. That makes Nixon obligated."

"And in return?"

"In return, Nixon gives you a pardon."

Hoffa rocked back. "A pardon. Damn! A *pardon*. I never thought of a pardon." He was silent for several minutes, contemplating the implications of the information that Jo had just imparted.

"Why didn't I think of that?" he scolded himself. "Of course, it would work. Nixon's the ultimate politician. He needs money; the Teamsters are flush. He needs votes; the Teamsters have two million members, not counting their families. *Of course* it makes sense."

Jo's eyes were shining and her cheeks, as pale as parchment when she arrived, were bright with color. "Yeah, Jimmy," she said. "I think it's about over."

"What's the timing?" Hoffa asked excitedly. "How soon?"

Jo shrugged. "We don't really know. We don't have any control over *when* Nixon will do it. But Thanksgiving is next week. Fitz figures you'll be home by Christmas."

Hoffa grinned broadly for the first time in months. "Christmas! God, Jo, wouldn't that be great? Christmas at home with you and the kids and the grandkids. God, it's going to be great to see them!"

"Don't get too excited, Jimmy," she warned. "It looks good now. Fitz says it's a sure thing. But you know how politicians are. Don't believe a thing they say until they actually do it."

Hoffa sobered. "You're right about that, Jo. Don't never trust nobody, not even the president of the United States. Still," he said, grinning, "Christmas! God almighty, home for Christmas."

On December 23, Warden Warren Hempstead summoned Hoffa to his office. With him was Alfred Blanchard and Jim Hoffa.

Seeing them, Hoffa's stomach did a flip. As soon as he walked through the door, he knew that the plan had worked.

"Good news for you, Hoffa," Hempstead said cheerfully. "Merry Christmas! You're going home!"

Hoffa looked around for a chair, not trusting his wobbly knees.

"Just like that?" he squeaked.

"Just like that!" Hempstead confirmed. A large man, a former all-state tackle at the University of Oklahoma, Hempstead's muscle had turned to flab. At almost three hundred pounds, he was at least seventy pounds overweight. His hairline had receded, and what was left was mainly gray, and he needed glasses even to sign his name. But he still had a body-builder's grip and twenty-seven years in the federal Bureau of Prisons had not made him so cynical that he was not excited to see a man who deserved it go free, a man he privately felt never should have been there in the first place. Hoffa had always gotten along with Hempstead, never blamed the warden for his continued incarceration or felt that the warden had any influence on the parole board's decisions not to give him his freedom.

Suddenly remembering that he had not greeted his visitors, Hoffa turned to his son. "Hey, Jim," he said, reaching out to embrace him. "God, it's good to see you. You too, Al," he added, taking the lawyer's hand. "Glad you're here to make this all legal."

"Sit down," Hempstead commanded, beaming. "Let's get these papers signed."

Hoffa sank gratefully into the chair. Accepting the pen that Hempstead proffered, he was surprised to see his hand shaking.

"Guess I'm a little nervous," he said, smiling in embarrassment. "It ain't every day a man gets to go home again."

"Just need you to sign this," Hempstead said companionably. "Then you can pack your stuff and get the hell out of here. Guess you won't be sorry, huh?"

Hoffa looked at him. "No offense, warden, but I won't be a bit sorry. Not one fucking bit." Lifting the pen, he was ready to sign where Hempstead indicated when Blanchard interrupted.

"Just a second, Jimmy," he said, reaching for the document. "Let me read it first."

Hoffa was chagrined. "Just like a lawyer," he said sheepishly. "That's why I pay him so much."

They all sat silently as Blanchard slowly scanned the document.

"Anything wrong?" Hoffa asked nervously when Blanchard seemed to be taking a long time.

"Oh!" Blanchard said in surprise, breaking his concentration. "No. Nothing unusual. Same stuff that's in every conditions-of-parole document I've ever seen."

"Such as?" Hoffa asked suspiciously.

"Such as, you have to agree not to use drugs. Is that okay?"

Hoffa nodded solemnly. "That's okay."

"Do you agree not to possess firearms?"

"Sure."

"Not to drink to excess?"

"I've never in my life drank to excess."

"I know that, Jimmy," Blanchard said in exasperation. "I'm just telling you what the conditions are."

"Okay. I agree."

"Do you agree not to commit any other crimes?"

"Yeah. Go on."

Blanchard looked at the paper, turning it over. "That's it."

"That's it?" Hoffa asked, eager to get finished. "That's all? You're sure?"

"That's all it says here," Blanchard repeated. Then, looking at Hempstead: "Is there anything else? Anything we don't know about?"

"If you don't know about it, I don't know about it,"

Hempstead said. "But if it will make you feel any better, I'll call Washington and double-check."

"I don't think—" Hoffa began, reaching for the paper.

"Wait a minute, Jimmy," Blanchard said, pulling it back. "Let's be safe. Just to be sure, let's let the warden make a phone call. Five minutes more isn't going to make any difference."

Hoffa sighed and sank back in the chair, impatiently drumming on the polished walnut arm while Hempstead spoke to his headquarters in D.C.

"That's it," Hempstead said, hanging up. "They tell me there aren't any other conditions. Everything's just as you see it."

"Great!" Hoffa said, lifting the pen. "Let me sign that fucker and get the hell out of here."

29
. . . .
1 9 7 1

Much to Hoffa's relief, Blanchard had chartered a small jet to take him and his son back to Detroit. As soon as the *Gulfstream II* was airborne, Hoffa sank back in his seat and closed his eyes. Thinking he was trying to sleep, his son dug in his briefcase and came up with a stack of documents, which he plopped on the aircraft's tiny table. With a groan, he picked up the top paper and began reading it.

"It's working out pretty good, ain't it?" Hoffa said, his eyes still closed.

Jim looked up in surprise. "You scared me, Dad. I thought you were sacked out."

"I got plenty of time to sleep, son. First of all I got to make some plans."

"You think you can just pick up where you left off, Dad? As if you haven't been gone for five years?"

Hoffa's eyes popped open. "Nobody said it was going to be easy. But give me a couple of weeks to get my feet back on the ground and we'll start laying the groundwork to get the presidency back. I figure if I start at the old local . . ."

"A lot of things have happened in five years."

"Damn right they have, and most of them because I made them happen."

The younger Hoffa studied his father before answering. "You don't think you know *all* that's been going on, do you? Just because you've been giving Fitz orders and he seems, for the most part, to have been carrying them out. That only scratches the surface."

"What the hell is that supposed to mean?" Hoffa said, bolting upright. "What the hell haven't you been telling me?"

"Calm down, Dad. I haven't been withholding any information from you. I've told you everything I know. But just about everything I know comes from Fitz. What if he wasn't shooting straight with me either?"

Hoffa pondered that. "Good point," he said. "Knowing Fitz, there probably is some shit that we don't know about. But it can't be too serious or I would have heard. Bobby would have heard. Shit, *somebody* would have heard and told me."

"Five years is a long time to be away, Dad. Even when you're trying to keep in close touch. People forget about you They develop other loyalties, make new alliances, marriages of convenience. If you aren't there to grant the favors, somebody else is. Loyalties shift. And Fitz has been the man on the ground, the dispenser of favors, the maker of thousands of tiny decisions which he didn't bother to share with you." He paused. "Or me. I can't give you any for-instances, but it is bound to have happened. It's just natural."

"Are you trying to tell me that Fitz has his own following? His own set of supporters?"

The younger Hoffa nodded. "He has to. We just don't know how many or how strong he is. He must be able to pull some pretty good strings. He finagled your pardon, didn't he? And my guess is Fitz has gotten to *like* this position of power, even if you thought he was only your surrogate. He isn't going to be too happy to see you come back."

"He set up the pardon."

"He had to do something. The pressure was on. He knew you still had enough friends to make it uncomfortable, maybe even dangerous, for him unless he made it look as though he were at least *trying* to help you."

"What are you saying, son? *Exactly?*"

"I'm saying that I think you ought to move slowly. Take it easy. You have plenty of time now. Get a good feel for the lay of the land. See who's still loyal to you and who isn't, and then act. But be cautious. Remember how you taught me never to trust anybody?"

"I've been waiting five years for this day."

"I know you have, Dad. But don't ruin it by acting precipitously."

Hoffa looked thoughtful. "It's not my style to be cautious, Jim. And I still got to do things my way. It's the only way I know how. I may have been in prison, but I wasn't totally removed from the scene.

"Dad . . ."

"The first thing I got to do is make a list."

"A list?"

"Yeah, a list. Who goes and who stays. Some of those guys were just like you said, disloyal. I know that and I know who they were. Some of them anyway. They thought that because they couldn't see me, I couldn't see them."

"Dad . . ."

"Well, we're going to find out who stuck by me and who sold me out."

"Please, Dad. Do me a favor?"

"What's that?"

"Don't go running in the door and start ordering people around. No matter how much control you think you've been exerting from Lewisburg, the fact is, it is *not* your union anymore. Not right now. Like it or not, it's Fitz's union."

"Because I put him there."

The younger Hoffa sighed. "Take it slow, Dad."

Hoffa grinned and leaned back in the seat. "We'll see," he said. "We'll see."

Four days later, two days after Christmas, Hoffa scheduled his formal reinstatement. Technically it was a welcome-home party planned by Fitzsimmons. But Hoffa had his own agenda. No doubt, he confided to Jo, Fitz had ideas about the celebration being a quiet little affair in which he would be toasted and given the opportunity to say a few words, all of which were anticipated to be in praise of Fitzsimmons. Then, Hoffa figured, according to Fitz's scenario, he was expected to fade into the background, maybe do a little repair work on the cabin at Lake Orion, and be happy with his pension payment. Except, Hoffa told his wife, things weren't going to be that way.

"I've always been a man of action," he said, "and I ain't going to quit now. Hell, just because I'm fifty-nine years old don't mean I'm ready for pasture. Look at those dummies on the Supreme Court, in their late sixties and seventies and still going strong. I ain't no different. I got a lot of kick left."

"What are you going to do, Jimmy?" Jo asked quietly.

"I'm going to go in there and tell Fitz how much I appreciate all he's done for me and for the Teamsters. Tell everybody there what a great interim leader he's been. The key word is 'interim.' I'm going to say that he's done good, but the old man has come back and its time to kick some fannies, get rid of the flab."

"Are you sure this is the right time for that?" Jo asked cautiously.

"Sure I'm sure. I've been doing nothing for five years except stuffing mattresses. Stuffing mattresses! Can you imagine how frustrating and degrading that's been?"

"I have an idea, but—"

"Now I'm ready to go back to work. Even before I went away, the three years before, I was only able to devote half my energy to the Teamsters because of all the legal problems, the threat of prison. Well, prison's behind me now. I've paid my debt to society. And I'm ready to go back to work."

"But are *they* ready for you?"

He did not answer immediately. Stopping in the middle of knotting a new tie, one of several that Jo had bought him for Christmas since all his old ones were outdated, Hoffa stared at his image in the mirror, noting the dark circles under his eyes and the lines that had crept into his forehead.

"That's what we're going to find out," he said softly.

With Ciaro behind the wheel and Jo at his side, it was like the old days. Cruising down Grand River Avenue and then left on West Grand, across Trumbull, to the graceful old St. Regis Hotel. Swinging under the portico, Ciaro brought the shiny new Pontiac to a screeching halt. Climbing out of the car, Hoffa offered Jo his hand, then together they walked through the door and into the lobby. Stretched across the far wall was a huge banner: WEL-COME HOME JIMMY!

"I told you it was going to be okay," Hoffa whispered to Jo, half dragging her down the hall to the banquet room that had been rented for the occasion.

Fitzsimmons was waiting for him outside the room, pacing nervously across the thick, blue carpet. "Jimmy!" he said loudly when he saw Hoffa approaching. Running up, he threw his arms around him and gripped him tightly. "Goddamn, it's good to see you," he said. Holding Hoffa by the shoulders, Fitzsimmons moved back a step and studied his old boss.

He had lost a lot of weight, Fitzsimmons saw, and his remaining hair was flecked with gray. But what surprised him most of all was how haggard Hoffa looked, as if he had not had a single good night's sleep during all the time he had been in Lewisburg.

"You look good," Fitzsimmons lied.

"Don't shit me, Fitz," Hoffa replied. "I look like death warmed over."

Fitzsimmons grinned nervously. "Nothing a little rest and some of Jo's good cooking won't fix, huh, Little Guy? A few weeks at Lake Orion, getting up with the chickens, chopping some wood, you'll be—"

"I know," Hoffa interrupted. "As good as new. Just being back makes me feel better. Seeing all the old guys, sleeping in my own bed, being with Jo, it's starting to work. I'm tired, but my energy is coming back."

Hoffa noted that Fitzsimmons had gained a considerable amount of weight. Always tending toward pudginess, he now had a big, round belly and three chins.

"The good life's starting to show on you, Fitz," he said, smiling wanly.

"Ain't that the truth," Fitzsimmons agreed, patting his stomach. "Listen, Jimmy," he said, his smile disappearing. "Before we go in there"—he jerked his thumb over his shoulder—"I want to talk to you for a minute."

Hoffa looked puzzled. "Talk to me? About what?"

Through the crack in the door he could hear the emcee talking to the crowd. "Ladies and gentlemen," he was saying. "May I have your attention, please. Jimmy will be out here in a minute. In just a couple of minutes. In the meantime . . ."

"In here," Fitzsimmons said, grabbing Hoffa's elbow and steering him toward a small room on the other side of the corridor. "Just for a minute."

Hoffa let himself be guided, followed by Ciaro and Jo. "Tell you the truth, Fitz," he said, "I'll be glad when this shindig is over. I'm still pretty tired."

"Well, you'll have time to rest up now, Jim," Fitzsimmons said, closing the door on the four of them.

Hoffa turned to him. "I want to thank you, Fitz. You done a good job. You kept it together. You did what you were supposed to do."

Fitzsimmons shrugged. "That's what you hired me for, Jimmy."

Nodding, Hoffa reached inside his jacket pocket and produced a sheet of paper folded in thirds. When Fitzsimmons looked at it, he could see that it was covered with Hoffa's notes.

"Tomorrow," Hoffa said, reading from the paper. "First thing. We call the press and tell them at the end of the week I'm going to make a speech. Got to get the TV there. They're important." Glancing at Ciaro, he continued: "Then we start work on the list."

Fitzsimmons looked puzzled. "What list?"

"Give it to him, Bobby," Hoffa said.

Ciaro produced another piece of paper and handed it to Fitzsimmons.

"These are names," Fitzsimmons said uncertainly, staring at the paper.

"That's right," Hoffa said. "These guys are out. Starting tomorrow."

"Out!" said Fitzsimmons. "You mean fired?"

"That's exactly what I mean," Hoffa said. "I don't like the way they behaved while I wasn't here to watch over them. I got no complaints with you, but they're different. They're as good as gone."

"Jimmy," Fitzsimmons began, paling.

"I got to get back in the swing," Hoffa said. "Indulge me. We got to get cracking."

Fitzsimmons shook his head. "Jimmy . . ."

Hoffa looked at him closely. "'Jimmy,' what?"

Fitzsimmons stared at him.

"Hey," Hoffa said. "Come on. You know what I always say: Tell me now because I'm going to find out anyway." Turning to his wife, he said, "Jo, why don't you go on out there? Tell them I'm coming. Soon as Fitz and I finish up."

Reluctantly Jo left the room.

"Now, Fitz. What you got to tell me?"

Jo was reaching for the handle to the door to the ballroom when she heard her husband shout, "You *what?* You fucking *what?*"

Turning abruptly to return to the small room, she heard Hoffa as clearly as if there had been no door there. "You half-dick piece of shit," he yelled. "You *what?* You fucking *what?*"

Two days later Hoffa met with Dally D'Allesandro in a private room at a downtown club.

"You sure it's safe in here?" Hoffa asked, looking around the tastefully appointed suite, taking in the still lifes on the wall, the highly polished antique settee, and the leather Queen Anne chairs.

"Of course it's safe in here." D'Allesandro smiled. "That's what this room is for. It's swept for bugs every three days. Behind the fancy wallpaper is more soundproofing material than you can find in a radio station's control booth. You'll notice there are no windows. That's another security feature. If I were to tell you the *deals* that have been cut in here . . ."

"Okay, okay," Hoffa said impatiently. "I get the picture."

Settling into one of the Queen Annes, D'Allesandro crossed his legs, careful to maintain the crease in the trousers of his twelve-hundred-dollar bespoke suit. With a wave that exposed a pair of diamond-studded, gold cuff links, he indicated that Hoffa should seat himself opposite him.

Ciaro, wearing a glum expression, stationed himself at the door. For all D'Allesandro's bragging about the security of the meeting room, Ciaro wanted to make sure no one burst in on them.

"Now," D'Allesandro said after Hoffa was seated. "Tell me again what you were starting to say earlier when I interrupted you."

"I said," Hoffa said slowly, "that I want you to kill the cocksucker. You understand? I want you to *kill* him."

"Fitzsimmons?" D'Allesandro asked.

Hoffa nodded.

"Okay," D'Allesandro said smoothly. "I got that. Now tell me why."

Hoffa grew red-faced. Just thinking about it threatened to set off another temper tantrum.

"He made a deal," Hoffa said angrily. "He got me out of prison—"

"I thought that was what you wanted," D'Allesandro interrupted.

"Let me finish!" Hoffa barked.

D'Allesandro raised his eyebrows but said nothing.

"He got me out of prison," Hoffa repeated, "but there was a condition nobody told me about. I mean *nobody* until that little cocksucker sprang it on me the other night."

"Which was?" D'Allesandro interjected.

"In return for getting out," Hoffa continued, "I am prohibited from participating in union business *in any way, in any form* for eight more years. Not until March sixth, 1980, which is when my prison sentence would have ended if I hadn't got the pardon."

"How ironclad is this so-called condition?" D'Allesandro asked.

Hoffa shrugged. "Right now, best we can tell, it's damn near unbreakable. Comes right from the fucking top, maybe even Nixon himself. I canned Blanchard's ass. He should have known about it, known how to fight it. What really makes me fucking mad is I would have been eligible for parole again in another six months anyway. And the parole board never turned anybody down *four* times without a damn good reason. I would have been free in another six months regardless of Fitzsimmons's fucking deals. That little fucking weasel . . ."

"What are you doing about it?" D'Allesandro asked.

"Doing? Shit, I'm doing whatever I can. Hiring the best fucking lawyers I can find to fight this thing. It's fucking illegal is what it is. So far the lawyers have not found another single case in which any such restriction was placed upon someone receiving a pardon. What that fucker Nixon did was violate my constitutional rights. He's the president; he ain't a fucking judge. There's a thing called the Separation of Power Doctrine that's supposed to prevent just this kind of shit from happening. Only a judge is supposed to be able to decide on punishment . . ."

"And in the meantime? While it's all tied up in court?"

"In the meantime," Hoffa said slowly, "I want some action. Fuck the lawyers. I want *justice.* I pulled that prick off a loading dock and he betrayed me. Are you telling me that you don't *understand* this?"

"I understand it," D'Allesandro said. "But I can't get *close* to it."

"You can't get close to it?" Hoffa said slowly. "What the fuck does that mean? Does that mean no? Because if that's what it means, Dally, I want you to know something. If you think I'm going to stand for being knifed in the back like that, you're out of your mind. If he doesn't get that condition removed, I'm going to do whatever I have to do, whatever it takes, to get the union back."

"What are you talking about, Jimmy?" D'Allesandro asked quietly.

Fitzsimmons's mannerisms were remarkably like those of Jimmy Hoffa, which was not surprising since Hoffa had been his role model. When he was making a speech, Fitzsimmons adopted the same arm-waving gestures, the same staccato manner of speaking, the same self-effacing recognition of thunderous applause. Walking off the platform, grinning and waving, he was the picture of self-satisfaction.

"That ought to hold those fuckers," he said cynically as soon as he was backstage. "Come on, Larry," he said brusquely to a husky blond-haired man standing in the background. "Let's get to the airport. I can't wait to get out of this fucking Michigan winter and into the California sunshine."

Larry bobbed his head in agreement. "You want this stuff to go, too, boss?" he asked, gesturing to a stack of documents Fitzsimmons had been given by the head of the organization to which he had been speaking, details about a home for wayward youth whose backers were seeking Teamsters support.

Fitzsimmons sighed. "Yeah, might as well bring it along. I'll try to go through it on the plane."

Walking out the backdoor of the hall, he was surprised to find a reporter from the local newspaper, Harold Brody, waiting for him.

"Hey, Frank," Brody said, walking up, notebook in hand.

"Hey, Harold, how are you?" Fitzsimmons said with what he hoped was enough warmth to appear friendly but not enough to encourage a long conversation.

"I didn't want to bring this up in there, Frank. I didn't want to piss on your parade . . ."

"But?" Fitzsimmons interrupted.

"You've known me a long time, Frank," Brody said, seemingly reluctant to broach the subject. "You know how I am about being careful not to spread rumors."

"Yeah. So what?"

Brody looked over Fitzsimmons's shoulder to see if their conversation was being overheard. The only person within possible earshot was Fitzsimmons's factotum, Larry. He had the trunk of the labor official's Cadillac open and was loading the stack of documents on the boys' home, putting them in with a golf bag and a new leather suitcase.

"Going to California, huh?" Brody smiled. "Going to get in a few rounds of golf? Leave us stuck in this January muck?"

"That's right," Fitzsimmons said tersely, trying to be patient. "What is it you wanted to know?"

Brody turned serious. "Well, Frank, you know what Jimmy's saying . . ."

Fitzsimmons looked exasperated. "Oh, shit. What now?"

Brody took a deep breath. "He's saying that you and some top guys in Nixon's office conspired to keep him out of the union."

Fitzsimmons struggled to hold his temper. "Nothing could be further from the truth," he said, watching in satisfaction as Brody began writing furiously in his notebook. "When Jimmy talks like that, he's lying in his teeth. And I got news for Jimmy Hoffa. I ain't that easy to get rid of. I didn't—"

Brody nodded vigorously, scribbling away. Out of the corner of his eye he saw Larry reach up and grab the lid of the trunk and bring it down. The next thing Brody knew there was a terrible roaring in his ears and he was lying on his back in a pile of dirty snow. Looking down, he saw that his overcoat was smoking slightly, little wisps of white were rising like tendrils into the heavy air. Fitzsimmons was on the ground next to him, spread on his face like a man preparing to do push-ups. As he watched, Fitzsimmons rolled on his side and looked at Brody with questioning eyes. His lips were moving, but Brody could not distinguish a word because of the ringing in his ears. Turning his head, he could see that the Cadillac was a heap of twisted metal with jets of flame shooting out from the ruin. There was no sign of Larry, no indication that he had ever existed.

Ciaro stood alone on the bridge, staring at the city lights and rubbing his hands together briskly, trying to bring some feeling back into his numb fingers.

Just when he was about ready to give it up and return to his car, a dark, late-model Cadillac glided to a stop, its tires making a soft hiss in the melting snow. Standing where he was, Ciaro waited while the driver pulled slowly forward until the rear passenger section was opposite him. With a barely audible whir, the tinted window slid down. Ciaro nodded silently to D'Allesandro.

"What is it that Jimmy wants?" D'Allesandro asked abruptly.

"He wants to talk with you," Ciaro replied, leaning over so he could look D'Allesandro in the eye.

D'Allesandro shook his head. "He's too hot," he said emphatically. "The whole thing's too hot. Tell him this shit isn't going to do him any good, Bobby.

You can reason with him. Tell him he's got to stop it. When it cools down, we'll talk."

"That ain't why he asked me to come here," Ciaro said. "He said to tell you he needs to talk to you."

D'Allesandro did not reply. With a wave to the driver, the Cadillac pulled away. As it departed Ciaro watched the window rise, unable to distinguish the noise of the electric motor from the noise of the tires humming through the slush.

30
....
1 9 7 5

After the bombing incident involving Fitzsimmons's Cadillac, the war between Hoffa and his successor settled into a verbal one. Although the conflict was no longer violent, it was nonetheless bitter. And as it progressed it became more and more public.

In 1972, when Fitzsimmons hired one of Nixon's top aides, Charles Colson, as the chief lawyer for the Teamsters, Hoffa eagerly pointed out to reporters that this was proof of a White House–based conspiracy to prevent him from challenging Fitzsimmons for the top job.

Fitzsimmons retaliated by warning high-ranking Teamsters that he would be "most displeased" if any of them attended a testimonial dinner arranged for Hoffa in celebration of his sixtieth birthday on February 14, 1973. A longtime Hoffa friend from St. Louis who shrugged off Fitzsimmons's threat and showed up at the dinner anyway, resigned from his three union posts two months later. He told reporters that Fitzsimmons forced him out.

Seven months after the testimonial, Fitzsimmons, in

a speech to the Western Conference of Teamsters, accused Hoffa of violating the terms of his furlough by discussing union business when he went to visit Jo in a San Francisco hospital two and a half years earlier.

In revenge, an angry Hoffa told an interviewer on a popular talk show, "A.M. Detroit," that Fitzsimmons was "crazy" and was seeing a psychiatrist twice a week for treatment.

To get even, Fitzsimmons fired Jo from her forty-eight-thousand-dollar-a-year job as nominal head of the Teamsters women's political action group, and canceled Jim Hoffa's thirty-thousand-dollar-a-year post as a Teamsters' lawyer. He also returned the war to the political front by arranging for U.S. Attorney General John N. Mitchell to issue an affidavit declaring that no one in the Justice Department had been responsible for the no-union-business restriction against Hoffa. Then, in appreciation for the show of support from the president's appointee, Fitzsimmons announced that the Teamsters were solidly behind Nixon in his fierce battle with Congress over Watergate, calling him "the most influential president this country has ever had."

Infuriated by the White House involvement, Hoffa turned the focus of his attack from Colson to Nixon's former lawyer, John Dean, who subsequently admitted authoring the restriction. Dean's confession, however, did little to help Hoffa in his fight to have it erased.

Although he was pouring considerable amounts of money into having the restriction removed by the courts, Hoffa was having no luck. His new lawyers first tried to get an appeals courts to overturn the Chattanooga conviction. If they could do that, they figured, the reversal would eradicate the eight-year prison sentence handed down by Judge William Defoe, thus freeing Hoffa of any parole restrictions.

However, that effort collapsed when the appeals court refused to give Hoffa a new hearing.

The next step was an attempt to have the restriction declared a violation of Hoffa's rights: (1) because the president had no authority to set punishment; (2) the restriction was an infringement of Hoffa's First Amendment right to freedom of association; (3) it violated Hoffa's Fifth Amendment right to earn a livelihood; and (4) it was illegal since it was the result of a conspiracy between Fitzsimmons, Nixon, Colson, and Dean. The court quickly sealed off this avenue by ruling that Nixon had acted within his authority. Because Hoffa's convictions stemmed from his activity as a union official, the court said, Nixon could justify putting restrictions on such activity.

The ruling was a major defeat for Hoffa, who had hoped to be able to run for president of Local 299, his old Detroit base, in August 1975. His plan was to use that as a stepping-stone in wresting the International presidency away from Fitzsimmons at the union's next national election scheduled for July 1976. When the court decision effectively ending his legal fight against the restriction came in early July, Hoffa pushed the panic button.

"Goddammit," he told Ciaro, "that clinches it. The judge has fucked me royally. If I just sit back and wait for that condition to expire, I'll be sixty-seven before I can even think about running for president again."

"Do you have any options left?" Ciaro asked.

"Yeah," Hoffa said slowly. "I can get rid of Fitzsimmons."

Ciaro blinked in surprise. "You tried that once, remember? And it didn't work out so well."

"Well," Hoffa replied, "I guess it's time to try again."

"You have anything special in mind?"

Hoffa smiled tightly. "As a matter of fact, I do. Here's what I want you to do. I want you to go see Dally . . ."

Ciaro was having a tough time making his point with D'Allesandro.

"I told you a long time ago," D'Allesandro said, "that wasn't the way to solve the problem. I still feel that way. You tell Jimmy."

"Look at it this way, Dally," Ciaro argued. "We tried it your way. We tried to put pressure on Fitz and that didn't work. Jimmy tried calling in some favors and getting Fitz voted out, and that didn't work either. We tried going through the courts and that failed. So we're back to square one, which is where you come in. All Jimmy wants you to do is meet with him, discuss the issue face-to-face."

"You think I'm fucking crazy?" D'Allesandro said, his temper rising. "Everybody knows that Hoffa and Fitzsimmons hate each other. If Fitz turns up dead, who in hell you think the cops are going to look at first?"

"They'll go to Jimmy, but he'll be clean. They won't be able to nail him for a thing."

"But if I meet with him, how fucking long do you think it will be before they find out? And then they start looking my way."

"You're smart, Dally. That's why you've survived so long. You'll figure out a way to do it so they can't prove it was you either."

"You're fucking insane. I can't meet with Jimmy. It's too dangerous. If Fitz gets bumped off even if I didn't have anything to do with it, they'll come to me. Make my life a fucking nightmare. And if I *did* have something to do with it . . ."

Ciaro looked at him steadily. "Does that mean you

won't do it? You won't meet with him?"

"You're fucking A that's what it means. I don't want to spend the rest of my life in prison. Not for Jimmy. Not for anybody."

Ciaro pulled a pack of Camels out of his shirt pocket and removed one of the cigarettes. Slowly he rolled it between his fingers, then tapped one end against his thumbnail, carefully packing the tobacco. Without saying a word, he reached in his trousers pocket and pulled out his lighter, pointedly flicking it to life. Exhaling a stream of smoke, he met D'Allesandro's eye and said coldly, "I didn't want to do this, Dally, but you don't give me any choice. I think you ought to meet with Jimmy."

D'Allesandro studied Ciaro. "Or what?" he asked calmly. "Is there an 'or what' with it?"

Ciaro nodded. "He says if you and him can't get together to reverse this thing, settle it satisfactorily, he's going to go to the press."

D'Allesandro laughed. "The press? What is he going to tell the fucking press? That I wouldn't kill Fitzsimmons for him?"

Ciaro shook his head. "He doesn't have to go into that at all, Dally, and you know it."

D'Allesandro did not respond, so Ciaro continued: "Remember how Petey brought you into Test Fleet and how Jimmy covered your ass? Remember that meeting at the Copacabana? Hell, you want me to keep going? I can list a lot of 'remembers.' I'm sure the guys down at the *Tribune* would be interested in what Jimmy has to 'remember,' not to mention the *Times,* the *Bulletin,* and all the networks. You want Jimmy to arrange a little news conference?"

D'Allesandro had gone white. His anger had been replaced with a coldness that made Ciaro wonder if the air conditioner had suddenly run out of control.

"Tell him," D'Allesandro said, enunciating his

words carefully, "that's not necessary. Tell him I know he doesn't mean it. Tell him I'll meet him. When and where?"

Ciaro allowed himself a tiny smile. "The truck stop, the Red Fox. Two tomorrow."

D'Allesandro nodded solemnly. "Tell him it's going to be all right."

Listening to the phone ring, Ciaro looked at his watch for the hundredth time. Five o'clock. He felt his blood pressure rising.

"Yeah," he said belligerently as soon as someone answered. "This is Ciaro again No, he ain't fucking here yet. Okay, right. Wait a—goddammit, I said wait a minute. I don't want any more fucking excuses. You find him and you tell him ten more minutes. It's five. We'll wait until ten after, then we're gone. You tell him we waited three hours and we're *gone*. He'll know what that means."

Slamming down the receiver, Ciaro kicked the door open. That motherfucker, he mumbled to himself, walking to the counter. Waving two fingers in the air, he caught Albert's eye. "Give me two more black coffees," he said.

Turning, he noticed Longuro sitting in the booth with the reserved sign on it, the one Albert always kept open for Hoffa.

"Jesus, kid," he said, walking over. "What the fuck are you doing still here?"

The young man shrugged. "Still waiting for that fucking part," he said.

"Oh, fuck," Ciaro said, pulling out his wallet. "Just because I'm going to be here all night doesn't mean you have to be here, too." He pulled out a business card and handed it to the kid.

"You're a Teamster, right. Let's see if we can't

roust some fucking brotherhood out of this thing. Call this number and use my name. Say *Bobby* said to call. Tell them what you need and tell them you need it right now. They'll take care of you."

Longuro nodded and started for the telephone.

"But don't take too fucking long on the phone," Ciaro called after him. "I want to keep it open for my call."

Reaching for his Camels, he was disgusted to find only one cigarette left. "Give me some smokes, too," he yelled at Albert, who was drawing coffee into two cardboard cups.

Longuro leaned over his shoulder. "It worked liked magic. He said he's coming right out."

Ciaro smiled. "You're fucking A he is. You remember that. The Teamsters take care of their own."

"How can I thank you?" Longuro asked.

Ciaro waved his arm. "You don't got to thank me. That's what brotherhood is all about."

Longuro seemed unsure about how to broach the subject. "You've, uh, you've got lots of pull, huh?"

"Yeah." Ciaro chuckled ironically. "I got a lot of pull. I'm the last fucking Mohican."

"Well," Longuro said softly. "Thanks anyway. I appreciate it."

As he handed back the card Ciaro had given him, they both noticed for the first time that there was another piece of cardboard stuck to it.

"What's this?" Longuro said, carefully peeling the two pieces apart.

Ciaro recognized it immediately. It was the Scotch-taped remnants of the business card Hoffa had given him many years before. Reaching out to take it, he was surprised when Longuro pulled it back.

"What's this say?" Holding it up to the light, he read, "'Give this man anything he wants, Jimmy Hoffa.'" Longuro looked at Ciaro in awe. "Is that really from Jimmy Hoffa?" he asked.

Ciaro was pleased. "You fucking A it is, son."

"Here's the coffees and a pack of Camels," Albert said, setting them down on the counter.

Ciaro pocketed the Camels and was reaching for the coffees when he stopped. Looking at Longuro, he smiled. "I'm going to show you something, kid," he said, motioning for Longuro to walk with him to the window.

"You want to thank somebody? I mean, thank somebody who really deserves your thanks?"

Longuro nodded.

Pointing toward the Pontiac where Hoffa was waiting, his silhouette outlined sharply, Ciaro said, "Go thank him. I want you to take this," he said, giving him one of the containers, "out to the car and thank that man."

Longuro hesitated.

"Go on," Ciaro urged, forcing him to accept the coffee. "Just do it. You want to thank someone, go thank him."

Longuro turned toward the door and Ciaro gave him a gentle push. "Go ahead. Just tell him thanks for everything."

As Longuro started slowly across the parking lot Ciaro sank into the booth, watching with a slight smile on his face as Longuro covered the distance to the car. Still smiling, he watched Longuro lean over and say something to Hoffa, then carefully put the container of coffee on the roof of the car, just as he himself had done earlier.

A bell rang in Ciaro's head. Why the fuck does he have to put *one* cup of coffee down, he thought. His eyes suddenly grew wide and his mouth dropped open as the answer came to him.

Even as he was sprinting toward the door he saw the kid reach under his sweatshirt and remove a long, black object. Ciaro got the door open just in time to hear two faint noises like air escaping suddenly from a punctured tire. That sound, he knew, was the noise made by bullets being fired through a silencer.

"Aw shit," he screamed as he burst out the door and ran across the parking lot. Longuro turned to look at him, his eyes as dead as hubcaps. "Hold on, Jimmy," Ciaro yelled, reaching in his waistband for his pistol, only to remember that he had given it to Hoffa hours earlier.

He was ready to attack Longuro with his bare hands, ready to face down the threat of the pistol, grab Longuro by the throat and rip out his Adam's apple, but he never got the chance. As he passed the shiny rig he had seen earlier, the one he had assumed was Longuro's inoperable one, the driver's-side door swung open and a man Ciaro had never seen before jumped to the ground. He had a sawed-off shotgun in his hand.

"What the—" Ciaro started to holler, but the blast from both barrels cut off the rest of the sentence.

Without a word, Longuro moved swiftly to the back of the trailer and swung open the door. Then he jogged to the front of the vehicle and grabbed Ciaro under one arm, motioning to his companion to grab the other. Together they dragged Ciaro's bleeding, lifeless body to the rear of the truck. Working as a team, as if they were lifting a sack of grain, they hoisted Ciaro up and threw him inside the trailer.

While they were taking care of Ciaro a vehicle with Deleware license plates glided to a stop beside Hoffa's car and a nondescript man climbed out of the passenger seat. He swiftly crossed in front of Hoffa's car, opened the door, and slid behind the wheel. Glancing swiftly around to see if he was being observed, he dropped it into gear. Then, as if he were in no particular hurry, he eased Hoffa's Pontiac out of its parking space and across the lot toward the interstate. As it pulled away, the cup of coffee Longuro had put on the roof when he reached for his pistol tumbled off and splattered across the blacktop.

The man driving Hoffa's car looked in the rearview mirror and saw the car he had arrived in fall into line behind him, with the kid at the wheel of the rig, bringing up the rear. He permitted himself a small smile; then, since he was a careful driver who had no interest at all in being stopped for a traffic violation, he turned his attention to the road.

AFTERWORD

Although this story is based on fact, the acute reader will notice several departures from reality. Most obviously some characters are composites, notably Bobby Ciaro and Carol "Dally" D'Allesandro. While they are drawn primarily from people who played major roles in Hoffa's life, their descriptions here include characteristics of several other persons as well. Also, this story was limited because of the demands of fiction and there are a number of other far-reaching events that could not be included in the novelization. Circumscribed by necessity, for example, were details about Hoffa's early life and the factors that shaped him; the labor movement in general and how he fit into it; particulars about the various legal struggles in which Hoffa was involved, battles that began in 1957 and lasted until the day he disappeared, July 30, 1975; and events surrounding his disappearance and most certain death. Although his body has never been found, there is little doubt that he was murdered, most likely by one of the reputed mobsters that he once befriended and trusted. Several possible motives have been suggested (as well as several rumored burial spots, most commonly the Meadowlands Stadium in New Jersey), but none presented so far seems to explain the circumstances as we know them. Unhappily for those who are obsessed with knowing why, the reason likely will never be known.